GYPSY NIGHTS

For Paul Andrew:
With best wishes
and love on
your journey!

Chrissy
8-23-13

GYPSY NIGHTS

Lives on Tour

Christine Fournier

4 square books

This book is dedicated to my late mother, Helen Winter Lacaze,
who saw raw talent, enthusiasm, passion, tenacity,
and determination in me as a young child.
Through her encouragement, praise,
and unselfish support she saw my dream
turn to reality when I danced on Broadway.

CHRISTINE FOURNIER
2011

Author's Notes

After fifty years in show business, it was time to share with others an insider's view of the work and lifestyle of 'gypsies,' dancers who go from show to show.

To craft a story that tells it 'like it is,' I went back to my roots as a young chorus dancer, cast in her first national tour. I asked myself, "Where do I begin?" Memories were strong, but to clarify and organize the story, I happened upon a route sheet of that first tour. There it was—the list of cities, dates and theatres. Time stood still as I slipped back to 1963–64.

To a twenty-two year old dancer, being cast in a major Equity show, a national company of a Broadway hit was a thrill beyond imagining!

I began to write down memories, city by city, people and places etched in my mind and heart. I saw faces of dancers, principals, and production team. The music, choreography, colorful sets and costumes, it was all there.

Gypsy Nights will take you on an adventure; first professional show, first love, emotional highs, lows, disappointments, discovery, intrigue and artistry. Names and situations have been changed, but the essence and spirit of characters and events are reality-based.

I hope in some way to entice you, excite you, and take you to a world that is truly unique and seldom experienced by the general public.

Gypsy Nights is dedicated to all chorus dancers who provide the backbone and heart of every musical. I am truly blessed to have shared the stage with them and now, you.

Tribute

There are so many performing artists, mentors, friends, and family I would like to acknowledge for inspiring and supporting me through out my career in the theatre.

If I had to choose one, who stands out as a beacon of inspiration in my career, I would choose the late director and choreographer, Bob Fosse.

His ingenious talent inspired me, and his mentorship shaped my talent. Through his unparalled artistry and example, I learned how to share his love of the process with others.

Thank you, Bob.

Acknowledgment

The following individuals were instrumental in bringing *Gypsy Nights* to you. It is with gratitude, love, and respect I wish to thank: Editors Dennis Rystad, Deborah Mink, and Bill Unumb; Cover artist John Lutz; Publicist Rachel Anderson; Publisher Chris Fayers; and my husband, Paul Fournier, whose belief, love, and support makes it all happen.

Gypsy/ jip-se/ noun: a member of a traditionally traveling people.

The Merriam-Webster Dictionary

Gypsy/ jip-se/ noun: a performer who travels from show to show.

A Show Business Term

Chapter 1

The Meeting

"Holy Crap!" Turning the corner of Broadway and 46th, Mally ran head long into a throng lined up under the marquee. "Damn that extra 5 minutes!" The huge clock in Times Square showed 9:30 am.

The stifling haze of the Manhattan morning engulfed her senses, invading every part of her body. Her hot, sticky hands plunged and fumbled anxiously through the cavernous dance bag. Perspiration clung, her forehead and neck taking the brunt of the unseasonable day.

Searching frantically, she found the small white card bearing her name, and the faint graphic of the masks, comedy and tragedy. This item was the necessary passport to audition admittance for a Broadway show. "Thank God, I joined Equity," she mumbled, as she got in line.

The audition, a necessary evil to gain employment, lay ahead. She would endure still another gut-wrenching experience in hopes of being cast. *Bravo Business,* a smash hit directed and choreographed by Owen Matthews, was being remounted for a national tour. Matthews was famous for setting the bar at the highest level possible! More than any other, this audition would be a race to the finish line, crossed by very few. But working for a Broadway legend was a prize worth the pain.

Mally inched her way along, eyeing the usual mix of competitors: Female dancers of every shape, size, and type: Tall, short, lean, voluptuous, demure, aggressive, hopeful, fitful, ambitious, and terrified. They were all here. She was no stranger to this company of dancers and their endless search for acceptance and employment.

It had been a year since she had tried to pass muster for Owen Matthews and failed. New to New York she arrived from Minnesota,

[handwritten margin note: Translate to line for MANNY JOHNSON]

with a head full of dreams, determined to set the commercial theatre on fire. Broadway's newest dance star! But in the year since the big fish from a small pond, reduced to a minnow in the ocean.

Owen had cut her from the first audition group, eliminating the future hope for Broadway. Imagine! A faint smile crossed her lips as she recalled that wake-up call, the supreme reality check. 'I'll be back, Mr. Matthews. You'll see,' she thought at the time, forcing herself to accept her dismissal. Indeed, she was back trying again. She'd take another crack at his demanding, unique choreography.

Moving closer to the front of the line, she felt butterflies fluttering in her gut with each step.

'All right, boys, I know you're there, but could you fly in formation?' She giggled at the thought.

"Next!" A brusque, but polished voice, cut through the air. Handing her Equity card to the stage manager, she waited while he examined it, handed it back, and gave her an audition card to fill out.

"Here you are, number 138. Please enter this door and take the first left to the backstage area. The changing area is in the basement, down the circular stairs." Mally started to go, but paused long enough to notice how attractive he was.

The sudden coolness of the theatre's interior was a welcome relief from the blistering wait of the past hour. Finding a corner in the change area, she filled out the audition card and set it aside. Mally changed with great effort, the fabric sticking to her sweaty body. Reaching in her bag, she found her dance clothes and jazz shoes in a scramble of layers. Slipping on her tights, she inched them along her moist skin. With her tights on straight, she added high cut trunks and a tank top. With a final tug, the top was in place. "Almost ready," she muttered, with a sigh. The last step, anklets and shoes, were added with relative ease. Stuffing street clothes into her bag, she put her wallet in an out-of-the-way pocket and zipped it shut. Card in hand she was now ready to meet the stage manager.

Taking a slow, deliberate in-take of air, she slowly let out her breath, rolling her shoulders as she ascended the winding stairs, the sounds of the audition beckoning her. Walking to the wings, she could barely see the top of Manny Johnson's head as he demonstrated the routine, calling out counts. Clumps of hopefuls watched with dread as others tried to ape Manny, Owen's right hand and the best assistant in the business.

Groups of six were called, in the order of their given numbers. As the combination was taught and tried, each dancer's moment of truth rushed by, as the process unfolded. Mally moved in to get a closer look at the required steps, marking the choreography as she absorbed what was coming.

"Next!" Several dancers stepped forward, Mally included. Having collected cards, the attractive stage manager entered the house, and walked to the production table. Mally's group took their places behind Manny. 'Keep breathing,' Mally thought.

The race began. A "5, 6, 7, 8" echoed in her ears as she took off. Copying Manny's moves, she committed the choreography to memory as she moved through space, aping him with determination.

The line glistened and heaved like a giant serpent bending, twisting, sliding and coiling. All around there was heavy breathing, moisture flying, muscles tensing, and adrenaline in high gear. Mally glanced into the darkened house trying to distinguish the small production staff gathered in muffled unison, as her group sweated and steamed, kicked and turned. Mally's energy on, her kicks high, her turns strong and balanced.

As the audition continued, Mally's memory took her back to the sound of her Russian Ballet teacher's voice, as he banged out a tempo with his cane. Music filled her as an ancient piano provided a perfect Chopin etude, a graceful counterpoint to the smell of rosin, reeking tights, and the ever-present aroma of fried onions from the diner across the parking lot. Her heart and breathing accelerated.

"I need 138. Please stay." Mally was jolted back to the present. She joined the newly formed line of sweaty dancers, the old memory of onions and rosin instantly fading away.

"Ladies, report back here at 1:00 p.m. for the singing call. Please wear dresses only, no slacks!" The single voice from the abyss was commanding and loud.

"God, isn't this great? We weren't cut!" A dancer standing near Mally embraced her with enthusiasm.

"Hi, I'm Pat."

"Mally." Smiling, she extended her hand. Pat returned the gesture, enthusiastically pumping her arm.

"God Mally, can you believe we're singing for Raymond Fletcher?"

Mally gasped, "You mean it? He'll be here?" Mally couldn't believe it. Fletcher was one of the giants of Broadway, a composer of brilliant shows. Suddenly she was back in the reality zone.

"Oh no, I came in jeans! I don't have a dress with me, or time to make it home to change before the call."

"Don't sweat the small stuff. I have an extra dress in my bag. I like choices." Mally took a good look at the beautiful young woman, deciding she must be one of the friendliest persons in the five boroughs.

"Come on, I know a place we can change and jazz ourselves up. Your face could use some fresh paint."

Mally followed Pat off the stage, down the circular back stairs and into the changing area. Once back in street clothes they exited through the stage door, walking into the daylight and crossing the congested street. Traffic was backed up from Eighth Avenue to Broadway. The sound of horns blasting intermittently announced disgruntled drivers, as they hung out of vehicle windows, yelling, desperate to get somewhere in the noon clog.

Pat and Mally walked to Howard Johnson's on the corner. They passed behind a row of occupied stools and headed toward the back. The Times Square eatery was jammed with hungry customers all demanding orders at once. The smells of burgers frying in greasy onions and fresh coffee brewing reminded Mally she'd skipped breakfast. Through the crowd and clatter the girls found the ladies' room.

Pat immediately piled the contents of her large canvas dance bag on the vanity. Mally was amazed. Pat's dance bag held dresses, shoes, dance clothes, jewelry, make-up, and sheet music.

I think you'll look good in this," said Pat, holding up a blue knit dress. "It picks up your amazing eyes. Go try it on!" Mally disappeared into the nearest stall and emerged moments later with bare feet.

"Oh well, we'll have to do something about that," Pat laughed, pointing. "I have sheer tights for you to wear. You don't happen to have a pair of heels in your bag?"

"Nope, I'm not very prepared."

"Now, for your eyes, they need definition," remarked Pat, as she began her meticulous task.

"Careful, I don't want to look like a hooker!"

"Relax, will you?" A minute passed as Mally faced the mirror. She couldn't believe the stunning, wide eyes that blinked back at her.

The two young women were definitely the antithesis of one another as they stood together. Pat, clearly had strong Irish looks: long, voluminous red hair, startling green eyes, and a statuesque carriage. Mally by contrast was pure Midwest, with bouncy brown locks, fresh peach complexion peppered with freckles, and big blue eyes, like puddles after a generous rain.

"Now a little blusher and you'll be as good as it gets," said Pat, proudly.

"Maybe I'll hit a solid B flat for Fletcher, who knows?"

"Yeah, who knows?"

A small group of tidy hopefuls remained. The sweating waifs had dolled up hoping to attract the attention of the power folks. The small spill of light mid house and constant murmur indicated where final decisions would be made. The group waited anxiously for further instructions.

Pat recognized her number, 85, and moved forward to begin her best 16 bars. When she finished, she heard "Thank you." Her heart sank.

"Let's hear 138, please." Mally walked toward the orchestra pit and handed her sheet music to the accompanist. In spite of her trepidation, her best 16 bars burst forth from somewhere deep.

"Wait!" An attractive middle-aged man had stopped on the other side of the orchestra pit. It was Raymond Fletcher! "Please sing full power, and give me a nice solid B flat." Mally repeated her 16 bars and ended by belting the requested note with every ounce of power she owned.

"Thank you!" Mally retreated upstage and joined Pat as they listened to the competition. The air was thick with anticipation and dread.

An authoritative voice began calling several numbers, adding numbers 85 and 138. Mally was suddenly lifted off the ground as a pair of arms wrapped around her in python fashion.

"We made it, oh God, we both made it," cried Pat. Mally suddenly snapped out of her fog and began to squeeze back as her eyes welled up. The voice continued.

"Ladies, be prepared to sign a standard, chorus contract for a national tour beginning October 1963 and ending August 1964. We will contact you when the contracts are ready. Thank you."

"Mally, come to dinner at my folk's place! I'll call you," suggested Pat. They exchanged phone numbers and hugs.

Mally changed and exited the theatre. At the corner she spotted several buses, but not hers. The press of rush hour in Times Square surrounded her. Suddenly she felt a wet drop splotch her nose as rain began to fall, spilling over midtown and her. Mally quickly found an ample awning under which to wait. As she stood exhausted and eyes closed, she began to drift back to the beginning.

Chapter 2

Mally

"Winthrop, not enough turn out! Stronger brushes through the ronde de jambe! There! Now keep your shoulders down, back arched! Better!" Victor's voice shouted with rigorous insistence toward Mally, as she moved across the humid studio floor.

It was Thursday at Victor Sobeloff's school. The Russian ballet master considered American girls hopeless when it came to commitment, élan, and stamina. Mally knew this and was determined to prove him wrong. She loved the discipline, and the Russian-based movements. How good the technique felt on her small frame! Her muscles ached, but her stamina remained strong as she worked through the floor combination today. Ballet school was where she was most at home.

Her parents divorced when she was born. Paula, her mother, worked full time as a secretary to provide for them. Mally's grandma, Martha, lived with them and took care of Mally while Paula worked. Both women took great pains to give her the attention she needed. Elementary school was difficult. "How come you haven't got a dad?" Some girls excluded her from play and birthday parties. Mally, undaunted, created a world of her own. She attended ballet school twice a week, never missing class even when a cold threatened. Paula took her daughter to see the film, *The Red Shoes*, a Hans Christian Anderson tale, in which a young woman falls in love with a pair of red shoes and dances in them to complete exhaustion and eventual death. Mally was intrigued with the story, but it was the brilliance of the beautiful Moira Shearer that captured her interest. She, too, was going to be as excellent a dancer, no matter what!

As class continued, she joined the line of twirling girls, moving precisely across the studio. Victor's shouts of correction, tinged with a tone of frustration, punctuated the music as well as his walking stick, banging on the floor.

"I want to see more point, Winthrop! Better! Now, double the pirouette," yelled Victor, apoplectic, but sincere. Mally felt in rare form. She felt perfectly placed, balanced, and unstoppable! When Victor added a sequence of jumps to end the class, Mally was airborne, with a final surge of energy lifting her to completion. As she finished the sequence, she noticed Suzy Johnson about to collide with her. Mally moved out of Suzy's path, instinct providing immediate safety.

Suzy was freckled, with waist-length braids, and a stocky build. She stood a foot taller than Mally, and was in the sixth grade. She would rather kick a soccer ball, climb a fence, or smack a boy around. But her mother had enrolled her in ballet class in the hopes that she would develop grace and poise. Suzy was just going through the motions like a prisoner serving out a short stretch.

"Class dismissed, girls!" The sound of Victor's commanding voice, and the double clap of his hands, brought the girls to an abrupt stop. They showed their admiration and respect by applauding Victor, and exited the studio quietly. The next class, the advance toe group, a little taller, a little older, stood waiting. Victor stepped into the room and motioned for them. "Come in ladies, please."

Mally's class slowly retreated to the dressing room. Towels whipped around cutting the air as conversations floated up and over the wet dancers. Mally slipped out of her soggy ballet attire and into her street clothes, putting her dance wear into her case.

As she glanced over to her left, she noticed Suzy had peeled off her dance clothes, and began to rifle through the jammed clothes rack searching for her street clothes. Oblivious to eyes watching her, she stood nude, and somewhat developed. Suzy looked different. She had noticeable breasts and hair between her legs. As Suzy slipped on a bra and panties, she noticed Mally watching.

"What are you staring at?"

"Nothing."

"My mom just got me matching underwear. I hate wearing a bra, it feels like a harness."

"How long have you been wearing one?"

"About six months. The worst part is I have my period!"

"What?"

"Why, my period! It's a drag. I hate bleeding."

"Bleeding? Why?"

"I'm twelve, so I bleed!"

Mally was stunned. Excusing herself, she left the dressing room and found her mother waiting downstairs inside the door. Paula met Mally up at Victor's studio every Monday and Thursday night following class. Mally was preoccupied and noticeably silent. Paula was puzzled by her daughter's mood as they hurried down the street toward the bus stop.

Rain had continued all afternoon into the early evening and it was heavier now. Finding a sheltered vestibule to wait in, Paula turned to her usually bubbly child, who was now stone-faced and pale.

"Mally, what is it?" Mally attempted to hold her head down, but Paula grabbed her chin and turned it up. One look revealed tears welling in Mally's eyes.

Suddenly, she let out a cry and grabbed Paula around her waist, holding on tightly and burying her face in her damp coat. The heaving of her small shoulders alarmed Paula. Holding her close she spoke softly. "There, there, Muffin, what is it? What's wrong?"

"You know Suzy Johnson? Paula nodded. "Well, she was standing naked in the dressing room, and she has bumps on her chest and hair between her legs and a thing called a period!" As the narrative went on, Paula tried to conceal her amusement.

"Mom, she bleeds!" Mally was a curious child and though her pubescence was a few years off, the time to explain had arrived along with the bus.

Pulling up to the curb, the bus splashed water onto the sidewalk. Stepping over the water, they boarded, and found a seat near the back. Gently, Paula began.

"Muffin, Suzy is at an age when her body is changing. Her breasts are growing and she has pubic hair. This happens to all young girls around the same age. You will start menstruating and this only means your body is preparing you for the time when you may choose to have a baby."

As she spoke she hoped her progeny would comprehend what she was saying. She needn't have worried. Mally was hanging on every word.

"For heavens sake, Muffin, ask me questions from now on!" Grasping hands they exited the bus and began to skip down the street toward home, jumping over puddles and laughing as the water splashed up.

Mally was jolted by the blare of a taxi horn. Back in Times Square, people were heading in all directions. Suddenly she spotted her bus, made her way to it through the mob and found a spot next to the rear exit where she was pinned by the crowd in a cloud of stale cologne and underarm sweat. Mally relived the events of the past few hours over and over, as the bus rocked through the crowded Manhattan streets. "Mally Winthrop," she smiled, "you're going on a national tour."

Chapter 3

Patricia

A potpourri of odors enveloped Pat Byrne, as she neared the family flat, tired and tense from the audition that day. A shifting mixture of flowers, pizza, fresh fish, and car emissions blended with the aroma of fresh baked goods. Home at last!

She fumbled for her key at the bottom of her dance bag. Unlocking the front door gained her passage into a cramped hallway lined with coats on a row of tidy hooks. The faint smell of grease, pipe smoke, and an orange peel, probably abandoned in a jacket pocket, hung in the air.

Passing through the narrow hall, she walked into familiar clutter. Daily newspapers piled on the ottoman next to her father's chair. The familiar scent of cooked onions, and fried potatoes lingered in the air, reminding her she had missed supper.

"Ma, where are you?" There was only silence. "Damn!" Pushing the back door open she stepped out into the tepid night air.

The sounds of the neighborhood intruded through the opening disturbing the quiet of the house. Over the back fence shouts of neighbors blended with the screams of delighted children. The ever-present rumble of the subway L above the street added to the Bronx symphony. It was a late summer evening. A light breeze stirred the hem of her skirt, the coolness dispelling the heat caught between her legs. At her feet, potted pink flowers lined the back stoop of the flat.

"Pat!" Maureen stepped from the kitchen through the screen door. Pat whirled around.

"Ma! You'll never guess! I got my first national tour!" Maureen let out a whoop as she hugged her daughter.

"Saints be praised! I've prayed for this day! Wait until Dad and the boys hear this!"

"We'll be hitting about twenty-two cities. Can you imagine?" Pat was a burst of energy, her excitement bubbling in all directions. "And Ma, I met Mally Winthrop at the audition. She's the nicest person! I think she's from the Midwest somewhere."

"Well, let's celebrate!"

"Oh, that's what I wanted to tell you. I've invited her to dinner with us on Sunday, OK?"

Maureen was already somewhere else as she nodded her approval. Before her was a tiny treasure of a toddler with big green eyes blinking in wonder at everything. Pat continued to talk, her voice trailing off as she retreated inside. Maureen fell away from the neighborhood sounds into the distant past.

It was 1952, and the long days of the Bronx summer were shortening. The few trees that lined the street were blazing gold in the fading light. Maureen was busily preparing dinner—Alan's favorite, corned beef and cabbage with boiled potatoes.

He was the light of her life. He came first, even before the children, Sean, Mickey, and the twins, Patrick and Patricia. Alan Byrne had been the neighborhood catch—the dream of many young women, but he only had eyes for Maureen Flynn. They were both Irish; he, born and raised in County Kildare, Ireland, and she in New York, the youngest of five Flynn daughters, living upstairs in the same building as the Byrne clan. Maureen smiled to herself as she added some pepper to the cabbage.

The door opened behind her. Seven-year old Patricia bounded into the room, frantically waving a paper.

"Mama, guess what? They're going to give ballet classes at school! They start in a week! Oh please, Mama!"

"Sweetheart, slow down. Let me see that paper." Taking the notice from Pat's firm grip, Maureen turned the knob to simmer, quieting the boiling cabbage. Unfolding the wad of paper, Maureen quickly read the announcement as Pat stood on her tiptoes, peeking around her mother.

"This looks promising, sweetheart. Your father and I have been looking for a class for you."

"Yes, please! It will be after school two afternoons a week. I'll be home before supper, I promise!"

Maureen looked at her excited daughter and smiled. Pat was a natural dancer with expressive, willowy arms and graceful lengthening legs. She had a natural strength and dexterity. Maureen knew Pat was ready for training.

"I'll discuss this with Dad, sweetheart. Now run along and wash up for supper. And tell the boys to come to the table."

Later, when the children were tucked in bed, Maureen entered the living room and sat on Alan's lap, curling up close to him. Sensing his fatigue, she kissed him gently on the forehead. Owning and running a bar seven days a week was tiring, so evenings with the family were precious.

Maureen reached into her pocket and handed him the announcement. When he had finished reading, he leaned back, lighting his pipe. His pipe was one of the true pleasures of life and when it came to making decisions, it was a welcome ally.

"Patricia wants to dance, Mo?"

"Oh, Alan, more than anything else in the world. You've seen the way she sits riveted to the TV every Saturday night watching those dancers on *Your Show of Shows*? She instinctively knows how to do it, Alan!" Maureen's voice was full of passion. Alan pulled Maureen to him, holding her for a moment.

"Mo, I want our kids to have what I didn't have growing up. My folks were dirt poor in Killcullen, but we have a chance to help Patricia and the boys succeed. Tell her to take the lessons."

"Oh thank you, dear. I love you." She brought her hands up to Alan's face and caressed his cheeks softly.

Pat began ballet lessons. Twice a week, after school, she would race to the school gymnasium.

Changing into her new dance clothes, she hurried out onto the varnished floor. As the afternoon light faded, Pat took her place in the line-up along a makeshift barre. Five other girls waited patiently.

Miss Grant, the ballet mistress, swept into the gym dressed in a long tunic that covered her thick torso. Her muscular legs were covered in black net tights. Large loops encrusted with cheap rhinestones hung from her ears giving her a well-traveled mystique. Her long black hair, braided into submission, hung down her back. Eyebrows painted black and tweezed into non-existence, gave a thirties' look to a tired face. Lips and fingernails, painted a fire engine red, mesmerized as she spoke and gestured. Sashaying about with the gait of a turned-out duck, to the educated eye, Miss Grant appeared to be holding a bit too tightly—and unsuccessfully—to her lost youth. The girls were much too in awe of her to pass judgment. They were there to dance.

Pat took to the technique easily. As she moved through space, she felt weightless. "Not so much arc in the back, Patricia. Bring your chest up, please, and shoulders down. Watch your relaxed feet, I need more point." Pat would react almost before Miss Grant got her words out. Two weeks later, Maureen received a call.

"Mrs. Byrne?"

"Yes, this is."

"This is Dorothy Grant, Patricia's ballet teacher."

"Oh yes, Miss Grant. What can I do for you?"

"I would like to meet with you for coffee as soon as possible. Would you have time this week?"

"Is anything wrong?"

"Oh, quite the contrary."

"OK. Thursday morning, 11:00 a.m. at Callahan's."

"I know it. I'll see you there."

On Thursday, the weather had turned cold. Maureen put on her fall coat with the large fake fur collar. Looking out the front door of the flat, she noted the hard rain and added a knit cloche. Grabbing an umbrella from the hall closet she hurried out to the street. Dodging passersby, she bent her umbrella out of the way, skirting puddles as she weaved through the deluge.

Heading toward Callahans's, three blocks from the flat, she stopped ⸺ited for the light. A spray of cold rain from pass- ⸺d chilled her feet. She reached the restaurant and

⸺udden warmth, Maureen removed her hat, shak- ⸺m herself. Closing her umbrella, she hung it on a ⸺he gazed over the restaurant and spotted a dark- ⸺ig. Maureen nodded, assuming it was Dorothy ⸺ward her. Dorothy rose and extended her hand

"Hello, Mrs. Byrne, I'm Dorothy."

"How did you know it was me?"

"Patricia looks just like you. I see where she gets her deportment and lean body." Maureen blushed as she removed her coat and slid into the booth opposite Dorothy.

"Please tell me what this is all about." A waitress arrived and Dorothy ordered coffee, while Maureen ordered hot tea with milk.

"I must tell you that your daughter has a gift. I have never seen one so young with the instinct for movement and the ability to execute everything given."

"You're saying that Patricia has potential?"

"I'm saying more than that! She's already beyond what I can offer her. I was a show dancer. You know, chorus work at the Copa, a short stint at Radio City. I was OK. I worked, but I never had a gift like your daughter." Maureen listened with fascination.

"Scholarships are available at some of the leading schools in Manhattan. Patricia would have to audition to gain admittance. I could recommend several." Maureen drank her tea.

"Thank you. I will have to discuss this with my husband."

"Don't wait too long, Mrs. Byrne. Your daughter has a gift and she should start now." Maureen paid the check. All the way back to the flat, her mind turned over everything Dorothy had said.

Later, when the kids had been bathed, read to, and tucked in bed, she sat down next to Alan on the settee. As was his habit, he was enjoying the peace of his pipe and the evening paper. When he saw Maureen he folded the paper, set it aside, and gazed with pleasure at her. Fifteen years hadn't dimmed her beautiful green eyes, creamy skin and wavy auburn hair. One look at her still intoxicated his senses.

"I had a meeting with Pat's ballet teacher."

"Yes?"

"It was interesting, very interesting."

"How is Patricia doing? Does she have promise, Mo?"

"More than you can imagine. Apparently our daughter has already excelled beyond what Miss Grant can offer. She strongly recommends that Pat study at a professional school of dance in Manhattan. She must audition to be accepted and there are scholarships available. Miss Grant is confident she could do it."

"What do you honestly think, Mo?"

"I'm apprehensive, but something in my soul is telling me this is right, Alan."

"It's not right to stand in the way of a gift that's God-given," replied Alan, firmly. "Let's do everything we can to make it happen." He noted a tear sliding down Maureen's cheek.

Alan took her in his arms and together they held each other as they talked of Patricia's future. Sometimes they lapsed into separate silences as the ticking grandfather clock punctuated thoughts.

Suddenly there was a swell of background noise. Maureen stirred and opened her eyes. The light from inside the apartment cast a soft glow as she sat alone on the back stoop. Gradually her focus returned to the present, and Pat's news. Dorothy Grant was right! Patricia was on her way.

Chapter 4

Contracts

"Miss Winthrop, this is Griff Edwards from the Lehrman production office. Would you come in this week to sign your contract for the national tour of *Bravo Business*? Rehearsals begin a week from Monday."

"Thank you, Mr. Edwards!"

"The pleasure is mine. Welcome."

Carefully hanging up, Mally sank down into the sofa and curled up with a pillow. She remembered Griff Edwards from the audition, when he collected audition cards from each dancer. It was Griff Edwards shouting instructions to those hired. "He is so commanding and attractive. I wonder if he's straight or if he's gay?"

Then there was Pat Byrne. They had exchanged phone numbers. Reaching for her dance bag and digging through the contents, she found the slip of paper on which Pat had scribbled her number. She dialed.

"This is the Byrne residence."

"May I speak to Pat? This is Mally Winthrop. I met Pat at the audition for *Bravo Business*."

"Yes, Patricia has told me about you."

"Is she at home?"

"No, she's off on some errands."

"Would you have her call me? I'm at Murray Hill 7-6735."

"Just a minute, let me write that down. What was the number again?"

"Murray Hill 7-6735. Thanks so much."

"Good bye, dear."

Suddenly, the door opened and Mally's roommate, Kathy Olson, walked in. Obviously agitated, she muttered four-letter expletives as she threw her dance bag in a corner. Collapsing into the nearest chair, she leaned back, closed her eyes and let out a long sigh.

"Kath, what's the matter?"

"You know the teacher of advanced jazz up at Carnegie?"

"Daniel Davis, right?"

"What a dick!"

"Oh? What happened?"

"I messed up in his precious combination, probably stolen from somebody else. He stopped class to berate me, if you can believe that. During his snit he said I was flat in every possible way!" Kathy had a colorful way of describing even the most minor occurrences.

"What did you do?"

"I stood there and took it! That asshole told me to repeat the combination alone. When I finished, he applauded! Can you figure that out? What a dick!" Then Kathy jumped to a new subject.

"Mal, let's grab a bite out. We haven't treated ourselves in a while. Frankly I could use a change of scene. What do you say?"

"Yes!"

Selecting an affordable restaurant across the street, Kathy ordered her favorite, a big, greasy cheeseburger with a large basket of fries. Mally chose a BLT and the soup of the day. Mally was facing the door when a familiar figure walked in. She recognized Owen Matthews, the director/choreographer of *Bravo Business*.

Owen Matthews was brilliant. He was thought to be the most innovative and successful choreographer of his generation. But others held him in somewhat less regard.

He was with a tall blonde, whose generous breasts and long legs were impressive. While they waited to be seated, she draped herself all over him. He did nothing to hide his delight as he fondled her ass. Mally felt a squeeze on her hand.

"Ah, Mal, close your mouth."

"That's Owen Matthews. He's the director/choreographer of the show I'm doing," she whispered.

"Yes, Mal, I know." Kathy leaned across the table, as close as she could get, shielding her face with her hand, while her voice became less audible than her normal range.

"If given half a chance, he'll screw every female dancer in his company!"

"Kath, don't exaggerate!"

"Hon, I know. A dancer friend of mine had an affair with him about two years ago. When he had enough, he dropped her! Bye, bye! Poor kid, he broke her heart. She ended up leaving the business."

"I'm sorry to hear that."

"He's a contemptible skirt-chaser, but a brilliant choreographer. Most everyone in this business would kill to work with him. You're going to have that chance!" She leaned forward, grinning. "But remember that some would skip the work and just kill him!"

The waitress arrived with the sandwiches and the girls dug in. Owen sat with one arm around his date's shoulder, while the other hand held a cigarette. He whispered all the right things in her ear, even occasionally taking a nibble. Mally frowned, and turned back toward Kathy, who had already devoured her cheeseburger. Kathy chuckled.

"Mal, wake up! Owen Matthews lives for the conquest. He adores women. Honestly, he's always sniffing like a dog on the prowl."

"I'll be working with him. Do I need all this information?"

"It's just a warning."

"Thanks, but I think I can handle myself."

"Good!" The girls headed back to the apartment. Mally could hear the phone ringing through the door. She picked up.

"Mally, it's Pat! How are you?"

"Great! Couldn't be better, and you?"

"I'm looking forward to signing. When are you planning to go?"

"Tomorrow morning. I want to get it on the dotted line!"

"Good! Let's meet at the Lehrman office and do lunch afterward. Is 11:00 OK?"

"It sounds great. You have directions and everything?"

"Yes! See you in the morning."

"Bye, Pat." Mally walked down the narrow hall and nearly collided with Kathy.

"Hey Mal, what I told you about Owen Matthews? Just dance and you'll have a great credit."

"Thanks, Kath."

"Good night, Mal. Congratulations!"

"Good night."

Mally suddenly felt exhausted. She got undressed but was too tired to bathe. She'd wait until morning. On the nightstand the clock ticked quietly as she fell into a deep sleep, cradled in the expectation of her first national tour.

The sound of hard rain against the window woke her. Jumping into a shower, she welcomed the warmth of the spray, easing the remaining sleep from her body and brain.

After she showered, practicality won over glamour. She threw on newly washed jeans, a periwinkle blue oxford shirt, and a blazer that was made for business decisions. Next came the necessary hit of caffeine. Reaching for a teakettle and filling it from the tap, she set it on the burner and turned the gas on. She heard the familiar whistle, turned off the burner and reached for the teakettle, carefully pouring over the teabag in her cup. As she sipped the warm brew, she polished off a cookie and browsed last week's *Backstage*.

Umbrella at the ready, she headed out and up the block toward the subway bound for Times Square. She allowed extra time for unexpected delays. She never knew if there might be a glitch somewhere in the New York subway system. But this day trains were running on time. She boarded the uptown local and her excitement built as the stops flew past: Thirty-fourth Street, Forty-second and at last, Fiftieth Street. She got off, crossed the long platform and climbed to the street above.

The rain was heavy. She put up her umbrella and started dodging pedestrians passing her on the street. Mally found she was one of many jammed around the elevator, waiting. She was pushed toward the back wall when the door opened.

"Twenty-three, please" she requested. It was difficult to see over the taller passengers. Finally her floor was announced. As she wiggled her way out, she wondered if the biggest New Yorkers spent their entire workdays just lugging up elevators. She located the Lehrman office and spotted Pat through the glass doors. Hugging Mally with bright enthusiasm, the girls sat down. A chunky receptionist with a dyed red pageboy spoke.

"May I help you?"

"Why yes. We're here to sign contracts for the *Bravo Business* tour."

"May I have your names?"

"I'm Patricia Byrne and this is Mally Winthrop."

"Let me check the list. Oh yes, I see. Well, have a seat. Mr. Edwards will be with you shortly."

Phones rang constantly. Delivery people came and went. More performers arrived for interviews or contracts. The office air was dry and over-heated in contrast to the cool rain pelting Manhattan, typical of the change in season.

Mally and Pat studied photos of Lehrman hits on the walls around them. "Well kiddo, this is it," Pat murmured. She was slightly nervous playing with her hair and pulling on the tops of her stunning boots. Her jeans accentuated her lean body. Her waist-length auburn hair was pulled back by a large barrette. 'She looks every bit the seasoned chorus gypsy,' Mally thought. Mally felt like she fit more on a college campus. Well, it had only been a year since she had.

"Miss Winthrop?"

"Yes."

"Please go through the double doors on my right. Follow the hall-way down to the end office on the left. Mr. Edwards is expecting you.

Miss Byrne, you will be next." Mally grabbed Pat's hands and gave them a squeeze.

Mally walked to the door marked G. Edwards. She had barely knocked when the door opened. Griff Edwards nodded and motioned for her to come in.

"Won't you have a seat, Miss Winthrop?" Griff Edwards walked around his massive desk. Reading glasses sat precariously on his nose. His professor-like appearance tickled her. She studied him quickly. He had the decorum of some of her instructors at the University of Minnesota.

"Miss Winthrop."

"Please call me Mally, Mr. Edwards."

"Ok, Mally. Please call me, Griff."

"Thank you!"

Griff studied the young woman sitting in front of him. Where did this sweet-faced delight come from? He liked her immediately.

"Here is your contract," he said, handing it to her across the desk. "Read it carefully and sign all three copies. Keep the pink copy for your records."

Mally took the contract from Griff and began carefully reading the formal document in her hands. She was unaccustomed to reading such staid text, but she understood all the written rules, regulations and expectations of the Lehrman organization.

Griff leaned across the desk studying her. She certainly was a welcome change from the jaded performers he had dealt with over the years. Freckles danced all over her cheeks and nose. He cleared his throat, trying to keep his business veneer intact. After devouring every word, including all the legal jargon, she signed all three copies of the contract, taking her pink copy and returning the others to Griff.

"Rehearsals begin on Monday, September 15th at 10:00 am. Come to the fourth floor of Dance Arts on 46th Street between Broadway and Eighth Avenue. Do you have any questions?" Griff's scrutinizing gaze totally mesmerized her, yet she held to her business-like decorum.

"No, I understand. You've been very thorough and kind. Thank you!"

Taking Griff's hand she shook it enthusiastically. He was surprised by her strength and energy. Passing Pat on her way down the hall, she returned to the reception area. She paged through a magazine without reading a word while she waited. Pat returned.

"Hey, Kiddo, I'm treating. What sounds good?

"Let's try Greek! There's a new restaurant on Eighth Avenue between 49th and 50th street." The girls walked out of the Lehrman office with a positive bounce in their stride. The sky over the city was now bright and clear. They walked down Broadway as if they owned it. Mally Winthrop and Patricia Byrne, young and gifted women, on their way at last.

Chapter 5

The Bronx

The steep subway stairs were still damp from the continual rain. Even after a year in the city, Mally was struck by the subway's unique smell. An odd blend of food, sweat, and a faint trace of urine, all hanging in the musty air, struck her nose. It was Sunday, and trains ran infrequently.

As she waited for the train she watched the water dripping down the dirty face of the opposite wall—tiny rivers in a slow race to the bottom. Colorful ads ran the length of the platform selling everything from hemorrhoid ointment and caskets to the latest hit musical.

After an eternity, the yellow-eyed creature with IRT/Bronx on its forehead arrived. Metal screeched against metal. With a whoosh, the door slid back, allowing her to enter. The cars jerked ahead and jolted and rocked down the long tunnel passage.

The car was full. Mally squeezed into the corner and took the tour route sheet from her bag. Immersed in the schedule she didn't notice the stranger leaning over her leering from the handrail.

"Hi, Honey." Mally's heart beat a little faster as she did her best to ignore him.

"Come on, be friendly," he insisted, his knees boldly nudging hers. Mally stole a glance at the subway map next to her, carefully avoiding the pest's eyes. Gratefully, she realized her stop was next.

The train lurched to a stop, as the door slid open. Mally bolted to the door and out, running along the platform until she reached the stairs to the street. The heavy air weighed on her. Her heart pounded as she heard someone catching up, getting closer. 'Just a few more steps and I'll be out of here,' she thought.

At street level, she felt a hand latch on. She was caught! The stranger was breathing hard, but his grip was strong.

"Leave me alone," Mally yelled, wrestling her arm as she tried to free herself. The more she fought the harder he held on, as though he was getting off on her fear. Passersby only glanced with ambivalence, assuming it was lovers' quarrel.

"Please, let me go," she begged, the authority leaving her voice.

"You heard her, let the lady go," the forceful voice interrupted, allowing for no argument.

The stranger released his grip, shrugged, and shuffled away. Mally relaxed noticeably, sagging with relief.

"Thanks so much," she said, rubbing her wrist.

"You're Mally, aren't you?"

"Yes. How did you know?"

"Pat described you to a T! I'm Patrick, her twin."

"Well, Patrick, if you hadn't shown up, I don't know what would have happened!"

"Nothing would have happened. That guy is all bluff and no stuff! Anyway, Ma and Sis insisted I meet you. If I'd come home empty-handed, I'd be sent to my room without supper," he laughed. Mally felt immediately at ease. She looked more closely at Patrick and saw that he was indeed a twin to Pat Byrne. He offered his arm as they set off down the street.

The apartment was lit for a holiday. A delightful mixture of aromas from food cooking in the kitchen filled the air. Crepe paper streamers hung everywhere, accented by bright balloons.

"Mally, welcome!"

Pat's mother, Maureen was slim, immaculate, auburn hair in an upsweep, and a sweet smile of welcome on her face. Pat came into the room and immediately embraced her.

"Mal, you look gorgeous!'

"Thanks, Pat."

"Mally."

A balding man with a reddish complexion approached from the kitchen, a twinkle in his eyes. With a hearty laugh, he seized her lifting her off her feet. His hug almost knocked the wind out of her.

"I'm Alan! Welcome," he chuckled, putting her down.

Mally stepped back and took a good look at the cheerful gentleman. Alan Byrne was certainly the personification of an Irishman. Outgoing, energetic, and sweet, he obviously adored his family and loved welcoming visitors. The apartment was modest, but it was filled with joyful people.

Mally, Pat and Patrick settled in the main room to visit with Alan while Maureen returned to the kitchen to put finishing touches on dinner. A loud buzzer announced others. Alan excused himself. Male voices filled the hallway as Alan returned.

"Mally, I would like you to meet my other sons, Mickey and Sean."

"Time to eat," announced Maureen. Taking her arm, Alan led her to the table. Candles flickered and the dishes shone on a bright yellow linen tablecloth. Everyone sat down, chattering in animated unison. At least three conversations and twelve hands were in motion at the same time.

Maureen served a soup steamy and loaded with potatoes and vegetables in a tasty broth.

Next, the main course was a large serving dish of roast pork and mashed potatoes. Mally noticed the potatoes had a distinct texture. With the first forkful she discovered, to her delight, chunks of flavorful cabbage had been folded in. Maureen noticed her reaction.

"Mally dear, is this your first colcannon? It's traditional for the Irish to blend cabbage into the potatoes. Those lumps give the dish character!" Everyone laughed and began telling stories of the Byrne kids' misadventures. Alan spoke of his homeland. The afternoon settled into early evening.

A drizzle began. Patrick and Mally strolled through the descending twilight. Wet streets reflected lights everywhere around them. Reaching the station and ascending to the platform, they waited.

"It's been lovely, Patrick. Thanks so much for the escort."

"You're welcome! I don't want anyone accosting you," said Patrick, with a wink.

"Well, you're terribly gallant and very tall," she added, with a giggle. A train approached. The blur of windows and closed doors slowed. They hugged.

"Thanks again. See you!" She turned and stepped into the car as the door swooshed open and quickly closed. From a seat near the window she looked toward Patrick and waved. As the train pulled out, she saw him wave again before he turned and walked away.

The car was empty, a definite change from her earlier trip. She watched the stations rush by and thought about her visit with the Byrne family. They had made her feel so welcome. She envied Pat having three tall, handsome, brothers.

Leaning back against the window of the rattling, rocking car, she dozed off. The train lurched and squealed along its route and came to a slowing stop. Mally awoke with a start. Looking out the window at the station, she realized hers was the next stop.

The roar and clatter of the departing train faded as she climbed out of the subway. A cool breeze was descending from the street. A downpour continued washing the sidewalk outside.

Mally stopped just before the exit and slipped on the jacket she had brought with her. Running quickly and skirting puddles, she passed an attractive man who nodded to her as he hurried along. Glancing back she realized it was Griff Edwards from the show, but he was already out of sight. Reaching the hallway of her building, she shivered and sighed with relief to be home. Soon, home would be the open road.

Falling into bed, Mally mentally prepped for the next day. Tomorrow it would all begin. The show would rehearse six weeks in town, and then depart for its first stop in Norfolk, VA. Now her desire to travel would become a reality. And, in the next nine months, the company would travel the length and breadth of the U. S. The adventure was starting.

Chapter 6

Rehearsals

It was one minute before ten. For the attractive and pleasingly fit men and women gathered outside the large studio on the fourth floor of Dance Arts, this would be home for the next six weeks. A minute later, Griff Edwards called the chorus into the room. Mally caught Pat's eye and the group entered. They smiled at the other with mixed expressions of dread and delight.

Director-choreographer Owen Matthews arrived, followed by his assistant, Manny Thompson. Standing next to the charismatic Owen, Manny appeared almost invisible.

"Good morning, ladies and gentleman. This is Manny Thompson. He knows my style complete. Please give him the attention and respect he has so richly earned from me. This entire show is in that notebook, known as the bible. Every detail of this show's staging, down to the last isolated head snap, is in there. As some of you know—and the rest will discover—chorus work is an exact science."

Mally had heard rumors that even the most experienced and well-rehearsed dancers would trip over their own feet when Owen appeared. He was tall, lean and solid. His hair was cropped short. A trim moustache accented a sensuous, serious mouth but the overall aspect of Owen Matthews was youthful . . . the boy next door. When he smiled, dimples popped out making him suddenly even more boyish.

Those for whom this was not a first meeting, knew more of the man. He was commonly composed, even solicitous. But when something or someone displeased him, his anger was astonishing.

But this day he was intent on the business at hand. Slouching slightly, he kept his hands in his pockets and smoked continuously.

Nodding to Manny and the ensemble, he moved slowly to the door, fluid and graceful as a Panther on the prowl. And then he was gone.

Manny took the dancers through a warm-up; making sure his charges were stretched and ready for a work out. He blocked the first dance, picking likely partners from the men and women who hung on his every word.

Mally was paired with Chad Chapman, an attractive blond with great timing. He had an affable personality, but it was his energy and masculinity that set him apart.

"Hi, I'm Chad," he said warmly, extending his hand.

"Mally," she responded, extending her hand in return. "Where are you from?"

"Born and raised in Detroit, Michigan." And you?"

"Minneapolis. In Minnesota," she added. A lifelong New Yorker had once asked her "So, what's the capital of Minneapolis?"

"I hear it gets pretty cold back there."

"Yes, cold enough!" Mally liked Chad's friendly, relaxed manner.

Manny set Pat up with Jonas Martin. He and Pat were suitably matched in height and build, but it was their incredible technique that made them perfect partners. Jonas sensed Pat's breath and timing. Manny placed them front and center.

There were seven couples in all, including one designated swing couple for each number. These dancers were assigned to cover any position at a moment's notice during the run of the show. They were expected to learn the entire number inside and out. Because a swing didn't perform a given number regularly, he or she had to be painstaking in accuracy, placement and precision. One wrong move could throw the other dancers off and injuries could result. Manny made sure the swings were well rehearsed. Mally and Chad were the assigned swings for a big dance number in the second act, *the Buccaneer.*

Manny worked the group all day. Actor's Equity required five-minute breaks on the hour. Lunches were an hour and half during a regular eight hour rehearsal day, but a company could be rehearsed ten out of twelve hours in one day, provided there were twelve-hour intervals between rehearsal calls. At six p.m., Manny called the first day quits. His spent and sweaty dancers filed slowly out of the studio.

Mally found a vacant chair and plopped into it, wiping the sweat from her face and hair. Closing her eyes for a minute, she leaned back. Someone cleared his throat next to her. Mally blinked open her eyes.

"So how was your day, Miss Winthrop?" She blushed at the sight of Griff Edwards.

"Good! And yours?"

"Busy. See you tomorrow."

"Good Night." A familiar voice followed.

"Hey, kiddo, you want to grab a sandwich?" Pat stood over her, shiny with sweat, her hair hanging down in long, wet strands. What a contrast to the way she had looked earlier in the day with her hair tied back for the rehearsal! She was already in street clothes.

"I'm starved," Mally declared heading to the dressing room to change. Her legs felt like anvils and her muscles ached everywhere. She peeled herself out of her soaked rehearsal clothes using a towel brought from the apartment. After slipping into her jeans and a sweat-shirt, she brushed her sweat-soaked hair, tucked it behind her ears, and put a bandana on. Returning to the hall she joined Pat.

Once in the elevator, Pat leaned against the wall and closed her eyes, as Mally slumped in a corner, dropping her dance bag on the floor. Chad hurried inside and rode to the lobby with them. They all stared at each other in tired silence.

By the close of the first week, Manny had blocked, rehearsed and cleaned four numbers for Owen to observe. Friday afternoon he saun-tered into the studio and up to the front of the room. A cigarette with a precariously hanging ash hung from the corner of his mouth.

"Ok, gang, let's see what you've got," he said, as the ash fell.

Owen put the dancers through their paces, one number after another. He stood, motionless, never shifting his gaze from them as they whirled and glided before him. Suddenly, a whistle blew. Everyone came to a quick stop and froze. Chests rose and fell, heavy breathing punctuating the silence.

Owen walked over and took Pat by the hand. Leading her to the front of the room, he turned and motioned to Jonas. Everyone else slumped, the heavy pressure abated for the moment.

"The following section is an example of my style in the truest sense. This is what it should look like. Pat, Jonas, take it four bars before the breakout and do it full out, please. A five, six, seven, eight!"

The rehearsal pianist beat out the pick up as Pat and Jonas broke into the routine. Their footwork was clean, inspired. They worked so closely they melded together. Turning and grabbing hands to face each other, they kicked in opposition, rounded backs, elbows tensed, smiling. After the breakout, they ended in a snap finish. The other gypsies went wild, clapping and whistling. Owen motioned for quiet. "Once again from the top, everybody."

The dancers took their opening positions and listened for the familiar count down. The accompanist banged away as the group took off in a whirl of gliding and turning, a mass of exuberant precision. Owen smiled and left the room. Manny took over.

"Good job. You're excused for the day." The ensemble applauded and grabbed dance bags and slipped out of the studio. Some went quietly, while others chattered enthusiastically, in anticipation of a two-day weekend. Pat was in a fog as she left the room, her mind whirling and filling with thoughts of Owen.

In addition to the dancers, the rest of the cast of *Bravo Business* was an exceptional one. Owen and his team had chosen the principals from other touring companies. The male lead had been standby to the star in New York, and was now a star in his own right on tour.

The entire ensemble sang and moved well, each member attuned to the unique style of the show. Owen's shows had a recognizable look and his ensembles had to support that. Most of the chorus, including seven singing couples, had come from seasons of stock and off-Broadway runs, so for them, a national tour was a new and exciting challenge.

The cast was getting acquainted. The gypsies, dancer-singers who move from show to show, were a mixed group. They were married and divorced, gay and straight. Some would have affairs. Friendships and rivalries could form. It would be a long, lonely road for some. Others would form bonds lasting the run of the contract or a lifetime.

Mally and Pat were in the glow of this brand new world. The first professional job is like no other. They would be immersed in it.

Rehearsals at Dance Arts intensified as the weeks wore on. While the ensemble rehearsed in the main studio, the principals worked down the hall in a smaller room. Once a number was blocked and worked, the two groups assembled for scenes and musical numbers. The management was painstaking as they prepared the company for the next nine months on the road.

Mally and Pat and the others repeated and endured precise fittings for everything from dresses to shoes. Every glance at a costume sketch or a swatch of fabric reminded them that this was a first class production.

The show was a take-off on corporate America. Bella Benson's costumes were designed to look like business attire, but had to have the flexibility to withstand the range of motion needed to perform the show. The clothing and set pieces had a cartoon-like style. Bright, cheery pastels were outlined in black to enhance the comic-strip feel.

One afternoon, as the female ensemble was rehearsing the second act opening number, the door at the end of the studio opened, and Vincent Lehrman, Broadway's biggest entrepreneur and producer of *Bravo Business*, walked in, accompanied by two assistants. He looked like a five star general with two privates clattering at his heels. They stopped in front of the mirror and turned in muffled conference. Occasionally they would glance at the women as they conversed in conspiratorial whispers. The women grew distracted as they were put through their paces, some fumbling their lines and blocking.

"Could we stop for a moment, please?" Manny clapped his hands and the number came to a halt.

"What do they want? This is unnerving," mumbled Pat, as she leaned against the ballet barre next to Mally, who stood wiping sweat off her face.

"Who knows? It must be important to stop rehearsal," Mally offered.

Lehman spoke loudly, in a pure New York voice. "There are no blondes in this chorus! We have redheads, brunettes, but no blondes!" Glancing in Mally's direction, he stopped.

"Ah, the little lady with the big, blue eyes. What's your name?"

"Mally Winthrop, Mr. Lehrman."

"Little lady, we're going to make you a blonde. Your hair will be maintained for the run of your contract. Do you have any questions?"

"No sir, thank you very much." Lehrman glanced around the room and noted one other chorine who would make the switch to a shade of blonde different from Mally. His business done, he exited in a grand sweep, his lackeys trailing in his wake.

"Hey, Mal, as a blonde you better watch it. You'll be jailbait for sure," snickered Pat.

"Well, at the very least, I'll find out if it is true."

"Oh yes! Blondes do have more fun!"

"Well, of course!" The two young women laughed. Manny's claps brought them both back to full attention as the rehearsal resumed.

He ran the girls through the scene they were working on prior to Lehrman's interruption. Working through the staging of the song, Manny carefully placed each woman in her position throughout the vocal portion of the number. By the end of the afternoon the number was complete.

Mally was sent a few days later by the Lehrman office to a chosen salon. Her hair would go from brown to champagne beige. After hours of painstaking bleaching, she emerged a stunning blonde. As she walked to the subway she passed a large picture window on Fifth Avenue. Her reflection stopped her. She scarcely recognized the sophisticated young woman blinking back. Several men passed by, giving her the once-over. "It's true," she chuckled to herself.

Chapter 7

Departure

The show was ready for an audience, their first, in Norfolk, Virginia. Cast members started arriving in front of the theatre where the Broadway production of *Bravo Business* was playing and where they had rehearsed during their final week in town. As the cast filed into two enormous buses for the trip to Idlewild International Airport, no one seemed to notice the new blonde in the group. Mally was disappointed as she took her seat. Suddenly, out of the general din came a familiar voice.

"Wow, who's the new girl? Blonde is great for your beautiful eyes." Mally caught sight of Griff Edwards, checking names on a clip board, as each gypsy boarded. "Thanks," she stammered, blushing lightly.

"Better watch that guy, Mal. He's after you," teased Jonas.

"Don't be ridiculous."

"We'll see," said Jonas, with a knowing smirk.

It was a tearful leave-taking for Maureen. Though she had rehearsed this scene many times in her mind, the reality set in as Pat was preparing to leave.

"Be sure you get enough to eat and watch your blood sugar! Did you pack your raincoat? Your heavy shoes?"

"Ma, will you relax?"

Alan chuckled to himself. Though Pat was his youngest, she was street smart, growing up with three brothers in the Bronx. He was confident she'd adjust to life on the road. But Pat was close to her family and he also knew she'd be a little homesick. That notion faded a bit as he saw her happy wave from the leaving cab.

"Thank God you made it," Mally cried, waving when she saw Pat get out of her cab and climb aboard. After stuffing her dance bag in the overhead rack, Pat made her way to the seat next to her new friend.

"I'm glad my folks didn't drive me all the way to the airport! Dad was pretty controlled and made jokes while we waited for the cab, but Ma, she was a mess!"

"My mom would do the same." She noticed Gil Fredericks, the company manager, taking a last minute head count. Cross-checking his list, he nodded at the driver and stepped off. With a gush of air, the door closed and the bus growled away from the curb.

The buses pushed slowly through the thicket of morning traffic. Mally slowly gave in to sleep in spite of the swarm of sound around her. Pat pulled out a paperback and began to read. Other chorus members sang and told jokes as the bus moved through Manhattan's concrete canyons and the Queens Midtown tunnel.

The bus suddenly jerked, waking her. They had arrived at the airport. The cast rose, crowding the aisles. Pat, who hadn't slept, got to the front exit several steps before Mally.

Mally miscalculated the steep steps and pitched forward, spilling the contents of her dance bag on the pavement. She felt large arms break her fall. Heads turned. Mally looked up at Griff.

"Not a good way to start your dancing career," said Griff, with mock seriousness, assisting her to her feet. He released her and bent down to pick up the scattered contents of her bag.

"Thanks." Mally felt her adrenalin rush subsiding. Griff smiled, "My pleasure. See you in Norfolk." He turned and slipped away in the crowd. Mally was shaken.

"Nice fall. You've got that guy eating out of your hands, Hon. I think what we have here is a potential affair."

"Oh, Jonas, please."

"Now, now, don't deny it, Sweet Pea. You're dealing with an older and quite possibly horny man. I'll have to big-brother you on this one," he said, as they entered the airport. Pat had stopped and was waiting patiently.

"What was that all about?"

"Just a little trip, I'll be fine." The cast was assembling in the waiting area and Gil was giving out information and instructions. Gil was a seasoned road manager and the best on the circuit.

"Ladies and gentlemen, since this is our charter, there will be open seating to Norfolk."

Mally and Pat caught up with the rest of the cast walking to the portable stairway on the tarmac. On the plane, Gil took another headcount. The Eastern DC6 was filled to capacity with the cast and orchestra. A strange quiet came over the group, performers being a superstitious lot. Finally the plane roared down the runway and lifted up over Queens, circled the city and turned south. The buildings receding below took on the look of miniatures, finally fading into a colorful picture map.

"Pat, look," Mally said excitedly. She had always imagined flying and marveled at the rush of take-off. She loved the weightlessness of flight, and wondered how that big hunk of tin and bolts seamlessly lifted into the sky. Looking around the cabin, she noted that several company members were already napping. Turning back she looked over and saw that Pat, too, was asleep. Mally put her seat back and enjoyed the steady hum of the engines.

Pat stirred. "Are we there yet?"

"Not yet. How can you sleep? This is so exciting."

"I miss my family already." Leaning closer she whispered, "I'm so glad you're on this tour, Mal. The other girls are so stuck-up." She closed her eyes. "You're the only real friend I have." The last trailed off into a mumble. Pat had dozed off once again.

Two hours later, the plane started its approach into Norfolk. Mally could feel the plane hesitate before descending. As the big bird touched down, a large group cheer from the cast acknowledged the safe landing. The excited applause continued as the plane taxied toward the terminal. Inside, the cast headed toward the local transport area where they were assigned buses to the hotel. They had arrived on their first leg of the unknown!

Chapter 8

Norfolk, Virginia

Griff Edwards handpicked his tour staff carefully: an assistant stage manager, prop, electric and grip technicians for the run of the contract. Additional techs, known as jobbers, were hired to fill in from town to town.

Dorcas Cavanaugh, the tour wardrobe mistress, was a bulldog of a woman. She wore her silver hair on top of her head in a huge bun, into which she stuck pins, pencils and other paraphernalia. She had a snappy voice like her Schnauzer, Puddles, who traveled with her. Her manner was intimidating, but over time the gypsies discovered an ally. She considered the chorus her children. Dressers and seamstresses hired for a local run came under her scrutiny. She insisted on excellence.

Sandy Irvin was musical director and conductor. He had been associate conductor of the Broadway production and knew every nuance of the score. He took a tour show every two years to break the monotony of working in New York. Sandy was a glib, but precise taskmaster. He kept the tempos brisk, helping the ensemble to keep numbers clean and fresh.

Sandy hired Alfred Moss, an incomparable harpist, who traveled with his wife, Marlee and Francie, their blind, sweet and docile Poodle, which instantly became the cast mascot. Francie stayed with Marlee at the hotel during performances.

Jimmy Swanks was the assistant conductor, and the finest keyboard man available. The other core musicians were Ben Phillips, trombonist, Teddy Lewis, string bassist, and Jack Henry, drummer. Sandy selected only the best he could find for the long haul, but had to rely on local union jobbers from city to city to fill out the sound required of the score.

Norbert Van was a favorite. Norry had been a top drag queen in the forties. When he retired from performing, he became a hairstylist, taking tours as well as working in New York between jobs. Flamboyant and demanding, he instinctively knew how to make each performer look his or her best. He understood gypsies. His long career and travels had taken him around the world. He understood this transient life. He was home.

Norry was catty to some and kind to others, dispensing advice, lending a shoulder and acting as a mother confessor when necessary. Styling wigs, giving haircuts and maintaining the look of the show were his main responsibilities. He would maintain Mally's hair each month, touching up the outgrowth as needed.

Company manager, Gil Fredericks, provided lists of accommodations for cast, crew and orchestra, addressed their concerns, and saw to their welfare. Company members chose where to stay based on their salaries and the length of time spent in a particular city.

In Norfolk the cast was housed within walking distance of the theatre. For the first few days, fittings continued. They rehearsed. Full run-throughs were about to take place, as the technical aspects of the production were being put in place.

During the first tech rehearsal on the set, a dialogue cross over was stopped as an elevator door was being adjusted to the track. Owen passed by, peering into the assemblage as he waited to continue. He stopped short as his gaze took in the pretty blonde.

"Hey, who's the new girl? Mally, is that you?"

"Yes! Do you like it?" Owen leaned in for a closer look.

"Blondes have more fun," he replied with a wink. Turning, he strolled to the footlights. "What a cliché," whispered Jonas, mockingly. Owen whirled around, glaring in the direction of the open door. He advanced.

"I hired dancers, not stand-up comedians, get it?" A hush fell over the group. It was the first time they had seen this kind of coldness come from Owen. As the tech resumed, the moment passed but some made mental notes to be more careful.

The final dress rehearsal ran late. At the end of the run-through Owen came up on stage to set bows. He backed up as he explained the sequence. Making a wide sweep with his arms, accidentally smacking Pat, he stopped abruptly.

"I beg your pardon, are you all right Miss Byrne?" Pat blushed.

Her attraction to Owen started in New York. When he sauntered into the studio each day, she noted his sensuality, his special élan. While the others took their required Equity 5-minute breaks, Pat stayed behind, studying his every move. His intensity, his body language and his soft voice made her weak with desire, his charisma stirring her. 'I'll bet he knows exactly what he's doing to me,' she thought.

As the cast, crew, and orchestra were excused, it was obvious that Mally's energy was at an all-time low.

"I'm going back to the room, Pat. I'm beat."

"Ok, Mal. I think I'll unwind with the boys. I could use a beer or two."

"You'll be okay?"

"I'm definitely safe with our boys," she winked.

"See you later, Pat." Mally grabbed her bag and headed to the hotel.

Hours later, she woke with a start. The room was stuffy and her nightgown clung to her soaked body. She padded her way to the bath-room. Running the water until it felt cool enough to drink, she stooped and allowed it to moisten her lips and run down her chin. It tasted of iron, but the wet was refreshing. She crossed the room and glanced at the window. Rain was streaking the glass.

"One forty-five," she muttered, looking over at Pat's empty bed. "The bars in Norfolk couldn't be open this late." The ticking clock became louder. The stale air engulfing her was a mix of old carpeting and bathroom disinfectant.

Climbing into bed, she turned on the small lamp. The glow was enough to illuminate her paperback and for a while it held her inter-est, but she kept wondering about Pat. Finally, she put the book down, turned off the light, and fell asleep.

In a dream she saw a face in front of hers. It was Griff Edwards. His hand stroked her hair and gently nudged her face. She startled, opening her eyes.

"Pat!" The clock read three-thirty. "Where have you been? I've been so worried!"

Pat smiled and drifted over to her bed. Lying down on her back, she kicked off her shoes. Sensuously sliding her jeans down her thighs, she wiggled her way out of them until she was able to reach down and pull them off. She appeared in a trance. Loosening the barrette at the back of her neck, her voluminous hair spilled out.

"You'll never believe this, Mal. I've found my soul mate." Pat stretched her lean body, her fingers reaching the headboard. As she extended her legs and arched her feet, she attempted to touch her toes to the foot rail. She relaxed and hugged herself.

"What are you talking about?"

"I spent the evening with Owen." She rolled onto her side. "Jonas and I went to a bar. You know the one across the street from the theatre? Anyway, we ordered beers and were having a chat when I spotted Owen. He was sitting by himself. Something came over me! I left Jonas sitting at the bar. I walked over to Owen's table and just sat down. Can you imagine?" Mally felt a strange pull in her stomach, remembering Kathy's warning about Owen and women.

"Mal, we talked and talked. He's so powerful, so famous, and I'm nobody. Truthfully, I am so terrified and attracted to him at the same time!"

"Pat, listen to me. Owen Matthews is a brilliant choreographer and mentor, but from what I've heard you don't want to get involved with him personally. He uses women."

Pat continued. "He said I could work a lot. He wants to help me."

"Pat, listen! What if he tries to get you in bed?"

"Please, Mal, stay out of my business. I'll be fine."

"But Pat!"

"Damn it, Mal, drop it!"

Mally felt the tears come, jumped to her feet and went into the bathroom. After locking the door, she reached for the tap, and splashed her face with the cool water. Minutes passed.

Calmer now, she quietly opened the door. In the spill of light she noticed that Pat was gone. Switching off the bathroom light, she crossed to her bed and noticed a note on her pillow. "Mal, I have gone down to the lobby to cool off. Pat."

Mally felt bruised as she got into bed, pulling the chenille bedspread up around her neck. Outside the rain was beating more strongly against the window. The sound soothed her as it had so often during childhood. She fell into a deep sleep.

The phone rang and rang. Mally pulled the receiver to her ear and listened.

"Mal, it's me. I'm calling from Jonas' room. I ran into him in the lobby and asked him if I could bunk in with him. Anyway, I apologize for the way I acted. My Irish got the best of me. I know you were just trying to protect me."

"Apology accepted. I'm glad you're ok. Did you get any sleep at all? It's already ten and we have a final brush-up at noon."

"Have you had breakfast?"

"Not yet!"

"Well, hurry up, start a shower. I'll meet you in fifteen!"

Mally thought about the day ahead, knowing that in just a few hours she would face an audience. She was dancing her dream. Minnesota was so distant. This was her life now.

Chapter 9

Opening Night

Like a low rumble of thunder before the storm, the night began with a charge in the atmosphere. The cavernous house filled with sounds of a sell-out. Griff had turned on the squawk box leading to each dressing room. Cast members heard announcements of 'half hour,' 'fifteen minutes,' and 'places.'

Backstage, the crew moved in practiced anticipation. On the floors above, dressing rooms buzzed with the company preparing for the show.

In the women's dressing room, gossip, shouts and stage paint, lent color to the scene. While some dancers stretched, others put finishing touches on hair and make-up.

Mally was exuberant. Her newly bleached locks had been set in a flip style. Soft, full bangs framed her face. Her eyes were standouts thanks to Pat's deft work.

Pat's long hair wasn't practical for the show, so Norry fashioned a traditional upsweep pulled tight atop her head, encircled by a small braid. Mally and Pat stood side-by-side at the mirror, transformed from tired, sweaty, chorines to dazzling women of the theatre. Griff's voice boomed through.

"Attention cast, report to the stage immediately." They hurried with the rest of the chorus down steps to stage level. Jonas caught up.

"Well, good evening you hussies," he chortled, brushing a lock of hair out of the way.

"Good grief, Jonas, you have on more eyeliner than I do," laughed Pat.

"You bitch!"

"You fruit!" Jonas grabbed Pat, hugging her. "Merde, Sweetie!"

Once assembled, the group fell silent. Owen stepped forward, surveying his cast. His gaze stopped at Pat for a brief moment, then back to the entire cast.

"Ladies and gentleman, I want to thank you for your skill and dedication. Remember to watch your numbers and keep your spacing accurate. You're one hell of a troupe. Break a leg!" He slipped out of the green room. Griff followed with his usual decorum of "Places, please."

The familiar goose bumps rose on Mally as the first notes of the overture came from the pit. Making her way to stage left, she stopped and stretched her arms over her head as she flattened her back and bounced gently, allowing her torso to loosen under the lining of her jacket. The house lights dimmed and a spill of stage light caught her eyes. She stepped into the whirl of dancers filling the stage.

The cast could do no wrong. Each scene and number brought enthusiastic laughs, punctuated by spontaneous and unexpected applause. As the show progressed, clothes scattered during the quick changes. Sweaty bodies hurried back into the next scene and number. Pat's tightly wound chignon was beginning to straggle. Mally's bouncy locks drooped.

At 10:30, the last big number of the night started. The dancers, gleaming in bright yellow costumes etched in beads, caught the stage light. Fourteen dancers worked full out, creating a massive, amoebic structure of interconnected parts with beating feet, quick turns, sharp kicks, and potent energy.

Both male and female dancers charged down center stage. A rising crescendo brought the audience to its feet in an orgy of screaming approval. The last note brought the dancers to a precise stop, leaving them frozen in their final pose.

Chests heaved and mouths gasped, desperately seeking air. Sweat on noses and soaked costumes remained of the four minute marathon. Never had the dancers had a reaction like the one echoing from the house. In the insular world of the studio, where dancers work hour after blistering hour, compliments are rare and reserved.

The performers bowed and smiled as group after group took a turn receiving the generous recognition. Some wept with relief. Mally was tired and happy. Pat chirped with delight. When the applause thinned out, the show curtain descended.

"Can you believe this, Mal?"

"Unbelievable!" Mally was last in line as she started up the stairs. A firm hand stopped her.

"Miss Winthrop, would you accompany me to the opening night party?" Mally, taken aback, was caught on the spot.

"Oh yes, I'd love to, Griff."

"I'll meet you in a half hour at my desk, stage right, ok?" She nodded, feeling heat rise up the back of her neck.

"You are quite beautiful you know," he said, staring intently. He winked and disappeared behind a set piece.

Mally could hardly contain her excitement as she floated up three flights of stairs to the women's dressing room. All around her women in various undress prepped for the party.

"Mal, are you all right?"

"Couldn't be better," Mally said, impishly. She pulled her arms through the sleeves of her finale dress, kicking off her matching pumps. Pulling off her trunks and tights was a challenge, as they clung to her like cellophane tape. She smiled as she plugged in her curling iron. While she waited for it to heat, she reached for a new pair of pantyhose.

Mally marveled at how good her new dress looked as she zipped herself in. She bought it for the opening. The fullness in the skirt twirled as she moved and the neckline was more revealing than her usual choice. Pat looked up and drew a breath.

"You look positively stunning, Mal! What a color!" Mally leaned in so the others couldn't hear and whispered, "Griff has invited me to the cast party!"

"Oh, Hon, he's had his eye on you since day one. Look at you! You'll melt the guy." Mally, half listening to Pat's chatter, was thinking about her date. Who was he?

Chapter 10

Griff

Griffen Zachary Edwards had worked his way from stage carpenter to stage manager, one of the most respected in the field. He worked for Vincent Lehrman. If Lehrman favored you, you had clout and job security for life.

Griff loved the work and was respected by everyone. He could be tough, not allowing for dishonesty or lack of discretion, and he wouldn't tolerate laziness.

The son of Casper Edwards, a stage technician, and Doris Canton Edwards, a seamstress, Griff grew up on the south side of Chicago, an only child.

Griff would go to work with his dad to watch and learn. Casper worked whenever a tour came through Chicago.

As Griff matured, he was hired to assist his dad, spending after-school hours and weekends backstage. He learned to run a light board, set rigging, track set pieces and call a show. He gained a superb working knowledge of technical theatre.

Casper continued to guide and inspire his son. They were now a tight team, hired to assist as show after show came to town. Griff was gaining the confidence of other stagehands; long time associates of his dad. Casper took immense pride in his son.

One afternoon, Griff was working a pre-set for a matinee when he saw Casper stagger and fall, clutching his chest. Rushing to his father he knelt and began blowing air into his father's mouth adding compressions. Frantically, he continued as Casper lay gasping. Others came.

"Somebody, call the medical technicians, now! Breathe, damn it, breathe," shouted Griff, as sweat flew. "Come on, Dad!" In the background he heard the squeal of a siren. What happened next was a blur. He felt himself being lifted up and aside as two uniformed medics took over, immediately applying CPR. No response. Again they tried. Again, and again there was no response. Casper's heart had given out.

In that moment, Griff lost his best friend, his mentor. Devastated, but cognizant of his responsibilities, he took care of details on behalf of his mother. Casper left him a wealth of technical skills and a true love of the theatre. Nothing in the world mattered more.

Griff continued to pick up work in Chicago. He was on a roster of jobbers, those local technicians hired to assist touring productions. Following graduation from high school, he joined the union and worked as a full time tech.

Working as a stage manager for a local theatre company, he heard that a Lehrman production was coming to Chicago and needed a replacement for their assistant stage manager. He gained an interview and was hired on the spot. Griff joined the tour for six months.

That world brought him to his first serious love relationship. By now, he was a seasoned professional in the theatre. However, in matters of the heart, he was green. He had dated a few women but sexually, he was relatively inexperienced. He had lost his virginity to a hooker on his eighteenth birthday.

Griff had only one steady girlfriend prior to his departure for New York. They had been promiscuous during their relationship. In time she put pressure on him to get married, begging him to get her pregnant. His dream was not hers. He broke off with her and left Chicago for the lure of New York, the heart of commercial theatre.

Griff stood watching people mixing in an orgy of self-aggrandizement at an opening night party early in his New York career. He noticed a stunning woman crossing the room. To his amazement, she was coming toward him. She stopped and smiled.

"You're Griff Edwards aren't you?"

"Yes."

"I'm Elise Mitchell." She had an easy manner and knowing eyes. Her full lips and her fair complexion were complimented by long, blonde hair that cascaded over pale shoulders. Her soft, rounded breasts peeked from her décolletage; her body was firm and graceful. Taking his hand in hers she looked into his eyes.

"Buy me a drink?" He nodded and allowed her to lead him to the bar. "Are you alone?" She was bold, sexy, unlike any woman he had been with. "My date split with someone else." Griff shifted. Elise's attention was turning him on.

They fell into a relationship. After a few months, they got married on a whim one weekend. He was held by his attraction to her independence, her almost coltish, maverick way of looking at life. They seemed to have nothing in common except a fierce desire to have sex. On more than one occasion, Griff suggested counseling with Elise. She refused.

Soon Griff was accepting more jobs on the road. He was in demand and the steady work kept him away forty weeks a year. He didn't really miss her except for the sex and he wasn't promiscuous.

Elise remained in New York trying to build a career as a singer. Occasionally she would join him for a week here and there, but it was painfully obvious that she was not happy with the arrangement. Unlike Griff, it was easy for Elise to fall into affairs while he was away. He heard rumors.

Closing a tour earlier than expected, he returned to New York to the apartment they shared. He looked forward to being at home. He slipped the key into the lock, opening the door. Hearing sounds, coming from the rear of the flat, he smiled, expecting Elise to appear at any moment. Moving toward the open bedroom door he looked into the room, surprised to see the strewn clothes. Then he saw what he could never have imagined.

Elise was there and so was a man. She was on top, her back to Griff. His mouth opened, but no sound came out. 'It's all true,' flashed through his mind. Shocked, he stepped back into the shadow of the hallway. Neither had seen him. He heard the sound of their sexual play continue. Quiet tears ran down his face. Leaving the apartment was easy. Six weeks later he divorced her, citing infidelity. She didn't contest it.

Following the divorce, Griff lived in a fog. He could not shake the hurt of Elise's deceit. As he withdrew he built a solid wall around himself and became intensely involved in his career. He trusted the work. He could control and count on it.

"Hello." Startled in his reverie, he saw Mally. Ah, yes, the girl with the fresh complexion and outlook. She was adorable. As he gazed at her she returned a warm smile. It had been a long time since he had felt an attraction like this, the first since Elise.

"You look very nice." He felt like a rusty sophomore with each word he spoke.

"Thank you. Is the party far?"

"Not at all, we can walk to the Commodore Hotel from here. Come on." They exited the theatre. A steady drizzle sent a shiver through her. Griff noticed immediately.

"Come here." Lifting his arm out of one sleeve of his coat, he tucked her inside, holding the coat out and around both of them. As they walked silently down the street, steering around puddles, she was aware of his warmth. She felt comfortable.

The opening night party was in full swing in the Commodore's ballroom, the clamor engulfing them as they entered. Cast, crew and press alike drifted around in tangled groups.

Griff raised his voice over the noise. "I'll check my coat and meet you at the bar, ok?" She nodded. Looking around the foyer area she spotted a restroom.

Inside, several women from the cast primped and dried their hair from the rain. Jackie Eldridge and Sonja Berger seemed often to be in shared conversation, and here they were again. Jackie was a veteran with a reputation for being a bitch. Sonja was a newcomer yet to be categorized.

'Well, touring certainly creates new and strange friendships,' Mally thought.

"Hey, how's Pat?" Jackie's question followed her into the stall. She didn't respond. Jackie continued.

"Mally, perhaps you didn't hear me?" Mally had heard all right, and chose to ignore her.

A moment later, she flushed the toilet, opened the stall door and stepped out. Walking past them to the sink, she ran the water, reaching for the soap. After washing her hands, she pulled down a lever to release a piece of clean towel to dry her hands on. Reaching into her handbag she pulled out a small brush and began to restyle her wet curls. Jackie and Sonja hadn't moved. They seemed to be studying her. For a few tense seconds no one spoke. Jackie broke the silence.

"I hear Pat has her sights on Owen." Mally ignored the remark and continued to work with her hair, eyeing Jackie in the mirror.

"Sorry, it's hard to hear in here."

"Yeah, sure," said Jackie abrasively. Mally slipped her brush back in her bag and turned.

"Pat's business is none of yours, Jackie," she snapped. Jackie fired back.

"Well, I'll be damned, Miss Minnesota. You've got balls after all!" Mally kept her cool and turned again to the mirror. She adjusted a bra strap that peeked out of her neckline, and exited the tight space. Griff was waiting at the bar. She was noticeably flushed and was beginning to perspire.

"What's wrong?" Mally explained the restroom encounter.

"Forget her. Jackie Eldridge is an old gypsy on the circuit. She's not happy unless she has a pot to stir. What would you like?"

"White wine, thanks." The barman nodded and placed napkins on the bar in front of them.

"And you, sir?"

"I'll have a vodka martini straight up with a twist." Waiting for their drinks, they turned to watch the crowd.

"We've got a really good group on this tour," said Griff. When the drinks were placed in front of them, Griff lifted his glass as did Mally, their glasses clinking.

"Happy opening, Mally!"

"Thank you! And the same to you, Griff." They sipped. Griff studied her. He felt as though he was admiring a rare painting.

"Would you care to sit somewhere a little more quiet?"

"I'd love to." He led her to a lounge off the main ballroom. Rich hanging tapestries, potted palms and overstuffed furniture added intimacy. Candelabras holding dozens of candles cast a warm glow throughout the room. Finding a comfortable sofa they both plopped down.

As Mally sipped, she noticed Griff watching her intently. 'He likes me,' she thought. 'I like him too.'

"This is the first time I have felt comfortable with a woman in a long time," he said.

"Really, I can't imagine you uncomfortable." Griff leaned back, observing this girl who was so endearing, so safe.

"You amaze me," said Griff, softly.

"Oh, why is that?"

"Because, you are completely without guile or an agenda," remarked Griff.

"From spending one evening with me?"

"I'm serious. So many women in this business are strictly out for themselves. A woman will act as though you're the one she wants, so you allow yourself to get involved with her, you fall in love and have what you think is a committed relationship. Then, she wipes you out. It's over. That's what happened with my wife."

"Do you want to talk about it?"

"Not really. It still pains me after all this time. Right now being with you is more important than spilling my history." Griff took a sip of his drink. He stirred and shifted his position.

Putting her glass down, Mally reached up and gently caressed Griff's face. He sighed under her touch. Then, glancing at his watch, he realized the hour. One stifled yawn from her confirmed it.

"Come on. I'll take you back to your hotel."

They stopped to pick up his coat and walked out of the hotel. Hailing a cab, Griff helped her into the backseat. Sliding in close to her and closing the door, he gave the driver instructions.

The cab pulled away, moving through the gray streets of Norfolk. Fog was beginning to settle in. They rode in silence. Sliding his arm around her shoulders, he gently stroked her hair, and kissed her, softly. He was gentle, sensuous. She was oblivious to the hour, the fog, and the autumn night. Being with him felt like being home.

Chapter 11

Seduction

Back at the Commodore, the party accelerated. A conga line had formed on the dance floor twisting like a wild, undulating snake. Owen led the pack with his nimble dancers following.

As the music peaked, Owen stepped out of line. Scanning the throng, he caught sight of her, as she was about to pass. Reaching for her, he twirled Pat to his body. Suddenly, the band changed tempos and the beat became a slow, languid tango.

The rest of the line pulled back to watch. Owen held Pat close, looking deep into her eyes. Though his gaze left her breathless, Pat carefully followed his lead. The tempo advanced faster and faster like an erotic Bolero. Sweat began to fly from Owen and Pat's entwined bodies as they turned and dipped. The crowd, caught in the moment, swayed in rhythm. Some yelled and whistled.

They spun and dipped. Their hot breath intertwined in a lush fore-play. Pins flew from Pat's upsweep, as flaming hair swung loose over her shoulders. Owen's cropped hair glistened. As the dance continued, he loosened his tie, shrugged off his jacket, tossing it aside.

Gliding slowly on a one, two, three, step, step, pause, he backed her across the floor. Changing tempo, their steps became quicker on a one, two, spin and hold. Oblivious to the crowd, Owen held right to Pat. Pat followed his command flawlessly, precisely.

They finished in a dip as the crowd burst into wild applause. Smiling and bowing, the two exited the floor. They were wringing wet as they moved out into the hallway. Someone from the crowd caught up to Owen and handed him his jacket. Slipping into it, he took Pat by the hand and led her out on canopy-covered terrace. A heavy rain was falling. Pat inhaled a large gulp of air.

"That was extraordinary," she purred. Owen moved closer.

Leaning down, he reached for her chin, caressing her softly. Slowly, he offered his mouth to her. He prolonged the moment moving from her mouth to neck, stopping briefly to taste her salt.

"Come on, let's get out of here." Taking Pat by the hand, they exited the hotel to a waiting cab. Their lovemaking had begun during their fiery tango, but was only the hors d'oeuvre before an exquisite meal.

Their lovemaking was ingenious, like Owen's choreography. Laughing, rolling, and twining themselves in and out of sheets, they climaxed repeatedly. He was daring, imaginative, and playful. Her perfect body complimented his passion. Owen took his time, tasting her, bringing her to near frenzy, and then allowed her to orgasm. Pat was encouraged to repeat her pleasure on him. After hours of love play they fell asleep, totally spent.

The night ticked by. As light started to filter through the drapes, Pat opened her eyes. For a moment she was lost. Where was she? Then she caught the cigarette smoke. Rolling over she saw Owen in the dim light. He was watching her intently.

"Baby, you're beautiful," murmured Owen. She smiled, as she thought about the previous night. She had been to ecstasy and back. Reaching for his waiting arms, she pulled herself onto his lap and reached for his cigarette. Owen watched as her lips wrapped around the tip, sucking in a deep drag.

"You're the greatest. I mean it." He took the cigarette from Pat and crushed it out in an ashtray by the bed.

Slowly, deliberately, he explored her with his tongue. Again and again he touched, tasted, and teased her incessantly as he helped himself. Pat moaned, unable to hold back, as she clung to him. Owen's insatiable appetite and Pat's need culminated in sexual fury, a mutual swoon of satisfaction and exhaustion. Following, Pat curled up in Owen's arms as he lit another cigarette.

Attempting to bridge the awkward silence, she spoke.

"When are you going back to New York?"

"I'm leaving in a couple of days, Baby," he said, casually. Pat tightened.

"I know. I just wish you weren't going," she whispered, the sting of parting already at hand.

"Look, no expectations or demands," he said firmly. Pat felt tears in her throat as she turned away.

"Come on, lighten up," he said, getting up. She watched him walk to the bathroom. His tight ass and muscular legs were fabulous. She could feel a twinge where he'd been before.

Owen returned, falling on the bed as he playfully grabbed Pat. She was turning on as he held her down. Straddling her, he tickled her into spasms of laughter. Their play turned to ferocious lovemaking, once again. Owen was insatiable, irresistible, and totally glamorous. Pat was his.

Chapter 12

Gossip

The whimsical humor and blatant sensuality in Owen's choreography captivated audiences everywhere. His movements mixed the ease of soft shoe, fluidity of jazz and grace of classical ballet. Owen's specialty was isolation and economical movements requiring clean execution and precise timing. He was tough.

One number featured the women as secretaries and the men as their bosses. They mimed flirtation. With ulterior and obvious motives, the men hit on their secretaries. The dancers leaped and glided across the stage, ending in a long, snake-like line with isolated head moves. The house rocked with laughter.

During the week's clean-up rehearsal, Owen's displeasure was obvious. He insisted that choreographic sections be repeated over and over again to his satisfaction. The dancers sagged. It became a long, grueling afternoon.

"All right, ladies, let's do the 'mix and mingle' section from the top, a 5, 6, 7, 8!"

The girls began the final section of the *Buccaneer* number, pounding out low kicks and crossing the stage to their next positions. Suddenly, a raucous howl rose from the upstage area just out of sight. The noise broke the women's concentration.

Owen stopped. As he blew his whistle, all movement and music came to a grinding halt. Nobody moved. Silence deadened the stage. Owen passed the pit and ascended the stage stairs.

"What the hell is going on here? Who has the balls to interrupt my rehearsal? This is not a fucking dog and pony show," he shouted caustically. Pulling back the teaser, he saw the small group of male dancers.

Owen approached, his cigarette ash hanging more precariously with each cat-like step. It was more than obvious the cause of disruption. Jonas was holding court. The group parted leaving Jonas front and center.

"Well Jonas, would you care to share your little story with the rest of us?"

Jonas tilted his head and gazed at his feet, nervously. His mouth twitched through a glob of cotton. Beads of sweat sprang from his forehead. Owen waited, staring intently at his best male dancer. Jonas shifted weight from one foot to the other, but remained silent.

"I see. Very well, everyone take ten. Jonas, follow me." The command was low-key, but compelling. Jonas followed Owen down the proscenium stairs and up the long aisle leading to an empty lobby. Owen stopped, looked around, and turned.

"Jonas, I think highly of your ability. Your dancing captures my style better than any other man in the business, but your attitude is shit. Your time is mine. One more interruption and you're out! Clear?"

Jonas nodded. "Yes, Owen, I apologize."

"Good. I'm glad we understand each other. Now let's go back to work."

Jonas was badly shaken by the scolding, keeping his mouth closed in Owen's presence. But around his cast mates he made his displeasure known, regaling his friends with an embroidered story of his near firing.

Pat changed and left the theatre. Owen was the only thing on her mind, as she stepped out into the warm afternoon sunshine. Horny at the thought of his bedding her, she failed to notice Jackie and Sonja as she passed. Jackie watched Pat disappear down the street.

"The bitch doesn't know the score," she hissed, taking a deep drag off her cigarette. Sonja perked up. "What do you mean?"

Jackie tossed her cigarette butt on the sidewalk. Pulling out another, she lit it inhaling deeply. The drag was soothing and she relished the smoke trailing out of her nose. Enjoying the moment, she set the stage.

"Ever hear of Vera Daniels?" Sonja shrugged sheepishly. Jackie, surprised, continued her juicy narrative.

"Vera Daniels was a major Broadway star. She shared many triumphs as well as her bed with Owen Matthews, who became her husband." The two women crossed toward a restaurant as Jackie continued.

"Mrs. Matthews developed a taste for booze and became a major alcoholic, dropping out of the business. After years of putting up with Owen's crap, his countless affairs, she was burned out. She got a legal separation, but refused a divorce. If you ask me, she's still wildly in love with that dick. Can you imagine?"

Jackie dropped the cigarette, grinding it out vigorously, as they reached the café. As they settled in a booth, Jackie lit still another cigarette and exhaled across the table toward Sonja, who leaned into the smoke expectantly.

"Owen's agreed to stay legally separated, probably because of their history. He made her a star."

"Does Pat know any of this stuff?"

"I can't imagine a woman like Pat being that big a pushover, but who knows? Vera Daniels had looks and talent too. I think Owen slips them some kind of voodoo drug!" Sonja hung on every word.

"Maybe he slips them a big dick."

"Big enough," Jackie muttered under her breath. A waitress showed up.

As Sonja gave her order she didn't see the angry spark that flashed in Jackie's eyes. As the din of the restaurant crowd rolled around her, Jackie thought of other times

Chapter 13

Winding Down

Griff removed the hot cloth and lathered his face. The razor slid smoothly over his skin. As he gazed into the mirror he thought of Mally. 'God, she's lovely.'

Completing his shave, he rinsed the remainder of cream off his face. Reaching for the shower he turned on the hot water, mixing and balancing it with water from the cold tap.

Stepping into the warm torrent, his thoughts returned to her, imagining her naked in his hands. Surprised, he felt a slight shift in his genitals. He hadn't been sexually aroused by anyone in years. Now he was thinking only of her.

He tried to resist the attraction. The hurt and agony from his marriage to Elise still gave him pause. Stepping from the shower he toweled himself off, and dressed. It was a short walk to the theatre.

It was Friday night in Norfolk with only three shows to go. The cast was on and totally focused, except for Pat. As the curtain came down, Mally fell into step with her.

"Are you all right?" Pat's large, green eyes welled with tears.

"Oh Mal, you were right. I got involved and I'm hooked. Owen's going back to New York tomorrow night. God knows when I'll see him again!"

"Pat, please. You'll get cast in another one of his shows," Mally assured. Pat smiled faintly.

Pat left the theatre. Arriving at Owen's hotel she summoned the courage and located the house phone. Dialing his extension, she waited expectantly, her heart pounding.

"Owen Matthews." Pat's breath caught.

"It's me. Can I come up?"

"I'm in suite 800, Baby. Remember? Don't keep me waiting a minute more."

Pat hurried to the elevator, entering the first open door. Pressing the button for eight, she waited impatiently for the door to close. Counting the seconds until she arrived on his floor, she felt her pulse quicken as the door slowly opened. Arriving at his door, she knocked softly.

The door opened. Owen stood there dressed only in a towel. The ever-present cigarette hung tidily from his lips. He held a bottle of champagne.

"Baby, I'm glad you're here." He motioned for Pat to enter.

Owen loved Pat's flaming hair and flawless skin. Closing the door behind her, he walked toward the bedroom. Pat followed. Setting the bottle down and placing his cigarette in an ashtray, he turned to her and began caressing her face.

"Oh Owen, I couldn't wait!" Owen smiled and slipped her jacket off, placing it on the back of a chair. Abruptly he turned and pulled her to him. Owen's ardor produced an immense erection that pressed against her, causing her stomach to tighten. She was already moist as he dropped his towel.

Owen was clever, intuitive. When he found a woman willing to play, he explored every inch, every erogenous nerve. Without a word he removed Pat's top, sliding it up and over her head. He quickly unfastened her skirt and let it fall. The snug fit of her sheer panties accelerated his desire as his fingers brushed the V of her crotch, now wet and throbbing. Once removed, he tossed them, and proceeded to play with delicacy.

Now free of any constraints, he pulled her to the bed. Pat waited expectantly for Owen to guide her into carnal exercise. He relished the taste of her, the way she quivered when he tongued her, moans begging for more. He continued to lick and suck as she lay open to him, one leg slightly raised. Holding himself above her with his arms supporting his weight, he slowly lowered himself, brushing her nipples. His hardness jabbed and poked along her thigh, sliding across her pubic hair. Finally, he slipped into her smoothly.

They clung and rocked and climaxed in perfect syncopation, basking in the richness of their lovemaking. Owen moved his weight off of Pat, leaned over and kissed her.

"Oh man, I'll miss this," whispered Owen. Pat reached his lips and gently ran her fingertips across his mustache.

"I love you, Owen."

Owen reached for a cigarette, lit it and inhaled deeply. Offering her a drag, she took it and snuggled into his arms. Playfully he caressed her hair and then began touching her breasts, tracing the nipples. The phone rang, jarring them both. Pat closed her eyes to keep the feeling.

"Hi." Owen's mood changed. Pat listened, trying to read the change.

"Yeah, I'll be in town on Sunday. Well, can it wait?" The more he spoke, the more annoyed he was.

"Yeah, the show looks great. Yes, I'll phone you. Bye." Owen set the receiver down, took a last drag and rose.

"Would you like a drink?" Pat nodded. Owen picked up two glasses from the bar, poured the champagne and handed her one. Pat tried to stifle her curiosity, but lost the fight.

"Who was that, Owen?"

"Shit, I guess you might as well hear it from me."

"What?" Pat was starting to feel a headache coming on.

"That was Vera, my wife." Pat sat back, astonished.

"Owen, you're married?" She couldn't keep the shock out of her voice. Owen set his glass down.

"Now Baby, let me explain. Vera and I aren't together anymore. It's been over for years, but she just won't accept it." Owen reached for her, tenderly kissing her lips, now salty with tears.

"Baby, please." Owen rocked her gently, caressing her face. He reached for a tissue, insisting she blow. Out popped a large honk, bringing them to laughter, followed by another ride on their erotic roller coaster. Soon the ride stopped and they curled up together. As they lay close, Owen gently stroked Pat's hair. She fell asleep.

Owen lit his last cigarette. As he watched Pat sleeping, he began to realize how much he cared, feelings that unsettled him. He hadn't planned on this.

Slowly crushing out his smoke, he turned off the light, allowing a dim glow from nearby buildings to guide him down to Pat. Holding her, he kissed her gently on the cheek. "I love you." Soon, he too was wrapped in sleep.

Chapter 14

The Last Of Norfolk

Turning off the annoying alarm churl, Mally worked her way out of bed. Padding across the room, she pulled back the drape. A bright, sunny day! The phone rang.

"Do you have time for breakfast?" Mally's breath seemed to leave her body.

"Griff! Yes!" A quick glance at the clock showed a morning half gone.

"How about in 30 minutes? I'll meet you at the diner across from the theatre."

"Great. See you." Mally set the receiver back.

As she stretched, she discovered her aching thighs and ass. Touring brought certain aspects: Late hours, heavy meals, sleeping in and a general lack of discipline, all playing havoc with her otherwise fit body. A quick hot shower helped the aches, and brushing her teeth completed her morning regimen. She swiftly pulled on her favorite jeans, a comfy long-sleeve shirt, and tied a bandana around her head.

The diner was full. Spotting Griff waving from the far end of a row, she smiled and started towards him.

"Miss Winthrop."

"Mr. Edwards." She glanced around, uneasily.

"It's ok. The coast is clear," said Griff, reassuringly.

It had been almost a week since they had shared a cab in the rain. Mally surveyed the menu, as Griff admired the view. It was obvious that even without make-up, she was stunning. Her flawless complexion, enhanced by a sprinkle of freckles over her nose, brought out her piquant features. A waitress approached. "What would you like?" Mally surveyed the menu and ordered an omelet and hot tea.

"I'll have a short stack and a side of bacon, and black coffee." Without losing a beat he reached across the table and took her hand. He was irresistibly strong and yet so gentle with her.

"I would like to take you to dinner some night," said Griff, grinning like a schoolboy.

"It's a date." They discussed the week in Norfolk to pass the time until breakfast arrived. They ate enthusiastically. When they finished, Griff took the check and paid up front.

Strolling together to the theatre felt so natural. Griff took her hand as they walked to the stage door. Stopping for a moment he held her firmly, staring deeply into her.

"Mally, you mean a lot to me. I feel comfortable with you," he murmured shyly. Pulling up on her tiptoes, she planted a gentle kiss on Griff's cheek.

They parted. Mally walked back to her hotel determined to stay in the reality zone. After all, Griff Edwards was the production stage manager and she was in the chorus. 'What does he see in me?' Not wishing to analyze further, she pushed the elevator button.

At her room, she slipped the key into the lock and opened the door. She heard the shower. Dropping her jacket on the bed, she headed to the bathroom door, slightly ajar. Pausing, she heard a strange sound over the torrent.

"Pat?" No response. "Pat, it's me."

Entering the bathroom she stood staring at the shower curtain. The sobs grew louder. Drawing back the curtain, she stepped back in surprise. Pat was curled up in a ball on the bottom of the tub. Her hair was soaked and hung down over her face, as the shower cascaded over her.

"Pat for God's sake, what is it?" Pat appeared to be in a trance, rocking back and forth, her arms hugging tightly to her chest.

Mally immediately reached for the faucet and turned off the spill. Grabbing a towel, she kicked off her loafers and stepped gingerly into the slippery tub. Sitting down on the edge and planting herself firmly, she began to lift Pat's mass of wet hair off her face, no easy task. Pat had volumes of hair. As she continued moving the towel over Pat's limp form, Pat's sobs subsided. After one long heave, she began to shiver.

"Come on, Pat." Mally braced to take most of Pat's weight as she eased her to her feet and struggled to keep the towel around her.

"Step over the tub. Now, sit down on the commode. I'll be right back." She scurried off to find Pat's bathrobe. Returning, she held it up and helped to guide Pat's arms into its terrycloth warmth. Pat's tears welled up again.

"Mal, he's married."

"What?"

"Her name is Vera Daniels, a former Broadway star! They've been separated forever. Owen says it's over, but for her apparently not enough to give him a divorce."

"Mal, what am I going to do? He's leaving tonight." Pat looked so small and vulnerable wrapped in her terry robe. They hugged.

"Look Pat, take it one step at a time. He obviously cares for you, so stop worrying."

"Mal, you're my only friend."

"Come on, let's dance. It's matinee time! Can you stand it?"

"I could stand a cup of coffee!"

"You got it. I'll be right back. By the time you're dressed I'll be back with it!"

"Great!" Pat got dressed and went to the bathroom mirror to brush out her hair. Looking closer she grimaced.

"It's going to take a lot of paint today, Irish!"

"Five minutes!" It was almost curtain. The ensemble began to gather backstage to take their places for the opening scene.

The production matched the original down to the smallest detail. The women looked perky and fresh in their bright pastels etched in black piping. The men wore colorful, well-tailored business attire designed to look street ready, but built to handle the constant wear over the next nine months. The fabrics used in the costumes had to stretch under the strain of a dancer's range of motion. The entire show looked like a comic strip coming to life.

Mally stood in the wings and did a few hasty stretches to warm up. From her position she could see Griff, calling cues. 'He's amazing,' she thought.

"House to half, slow fade, please. Five-four-three-two-one, Sandy, go!" The spotlights crossed enveloping Sandy Irvin as he walked to the podium, milking his entrance. He loved the sound of enthusiastic applause washing over him as turning to his musicians, he raised his baton.

The moment that all audiences wait for was here! Sandy swept his baton into the downbeat. The brass rang out and the orchestra was off on a jet stream of melody. The tempo was bright and snappy. The dancers waiting backstage started moving to the percussive beat as the curtain rose on the make believe world of *Bravo Business*.

During an afternoon performance, there was no allowance for slacking off. Matinees were more challenging as they were early in the day, drawing older, quieter patrons. During matinees, the tendency for some was to mark. They would save it for the evening show, but not in this show. Griff wouldn't tolerate it. Everyone worked full out.

Between shows the girls had a light snack and packed their wardrobe trunks, which had to be out for pickup by two in the morning. As they hit the dressing room, Griff's mellifluous voice rang out, "Half hour, please."

Mally's hair was straight and needed a bounce from the deft squeeze of a hot iron. She re-applied her eye make-up and gazed into the mirror, silently thanking Pat for teaching her to create great stage eyes. With a hair touch-up and a roll of deodorant, she was ready.

Pat reworked her hair and put on her tights. Extending one of her long legs into the fabric, she looked up and caught Jackie's cold stare in the mirror. She stared back for a moment, startled by the intensity of the look. 'What's gotten into her?'

Pat shook off the moment. She continued to pull on her tights, stretching past her mound and over her flat, muscular pelvis. Her long, well-shaped legs seemed to disappear into her shoulders.

"Fifteen minutes," Griff called. Mally threw on her kimono and headed down the hall to the restroom. Rounding the corner, she spotted Jonas.

With whispered urgency, Jonas spoke. "Can we talk?"

"What is it?"

"Just meet me," he insisted.

"OK, but I can't be out too late."

"Right, Miss Mal." Through the wall she could hear Griff's muffled announcement.

"Five minutes. Everyone report to the green room immediately." Hurrying back she threw on her costume and buckled her character shoes. She and Pat made their way downstairs, joining others in the actor's lounge. As the company assembled, Griff entered and made his way through the wash of pastels and hairspray.

"Company, tonight is our final performance in Norfolk. The management expects the same high caliber performance as always. As you finish each scene and musical number, please take your costumes to Dorcas. All hair items go to Norry and props to the prop boxes on stage right and left. Be sure to take all personal items with you. Check carefully around the dressing areas. The call time and location will be on the callboard posted near the stage door for tomorrow's travel. Your trunks must be locked and outside your rooms by 2:00 a.m. sharp. Are there questions?" The group stood silent, listening.

Owen arrived. He looked at his cast, making sure he had their attention. "Mr. Edwards is your commander-in-chief. His word is law. He has been entrusted with the authenticity and integrity of this show. Any discrepancies or questionable behavior will be reported to the New York office." Then, he softened.

"You're outstanding. It has been my privilege to work with you. Thanks." The cast applauded and Griff's voice rang out, "Places, please!"

Pat moved to a dark area upstage. As she started her stretch, she felt warm breath on her neck. Turning she came face to face with Owen. He kissed her gently.

"Dance well, Baby. I'll be watching." Pat felt flushed.

"Owen, this one's for you," she said softly.

"No, Baby, they're all for you from now on." Pat watched as he sauntered away in his typical fashion, hands in pockets, stooped shoulders. Placing the signature cigarette between his lips, he walked through the darkness like a knowing cat having snagged a bird.

Pat took a final stretch extending her leg and holding her position for a few seconds. Suddenly Jonas appeared.

"How's the chief?" Pat elbowed him playfully and continued to stretch. He joined her, rolling his shoulders just as a spill of light etched a path to the stage. The last show in Norfolk was about to begin.

The show sailed and with it, the audience, responding with energy and enthusiasm. The repetition of eight shows was a challenge. To keep the crisp quality of the show over a nine-month performance schedule, performers had to be disciplined. Now the show was fresh and the material new. It would take repeated performances to dull its finish.

After the bows ended, the cast dispersed. Stage effects were then placed in large crates for the move to Wilmington. Items that needed dry cleaning were sorted for the cleaning service in the next town. Dorcas handled the whole operation like a drill sergeant. No one messed with her.

Norry was in good form as well. He kept track of the specialty wigs and hairpieces. He would restyle each item at the next stop, and make sure that the pieces were well packed for the trip. They needed to last the entire nine months.

Griff's crew struck the set. Lights, light board, scenery tracks, set pieces of all sizes, drops and all furnishings were packed, stored and readied for travel. The scenery was built to withstand the abuse of set-up and load-out week after week.

Mally was the last to leave the dressing room. She changed into her favorite pair of faded jeans. She added a maroon and gold University of Minnesota sweatshirt for comfort and warmth. As she took a last look around she heard a knock on the door. Griff entered, looking about cautiously.

"It's ok, I'm alone," she smiled. He pulled up a chair and sat down.

"I'd like to take you to dinner tomorrow night in Wilmington if you're free. The crew is off and I could use some company." Mally felt a wave of excitement as he reached for her hand and kissed it. "I'd love to."

Griff stood. "Are you staying at the Allerton?"

"Yes, Pat and I are sharing."

"I'll call," he said, lifting her to her feet. Playfully, he leaned down and kissed her nose. "Don't miss the train." He slipped out quietly. Mally followed a few seconds later, finding Jonas waiting.

Chapter 15

So Long

For Pat, every second was precious. She hurried to Owen's hotel, feeling the last minutes with him closing in. As she waited anxiously for the elevator, she checked herself over, adding fresh lip color and running her hands through her flowing hair. 'Owen likes it this way,' she thought. Stepping into the elevator with haste, she reached his floor and walked quickly to his door. She knocked with more urgency this time.

"Pat, it's open."

Clothes, cigarette cartons, and scripts were scattered all over the suite. Pat heard humming. Curious, she followed the sound to an open closet door. As she approached a pair of hands reached out and wrapped around her waist. She backed up as Owen emerged.

"Hi, Baby." Picking her up, he moved to the bed, depositing her there. Kneeling down, he looked into her eyes.

"Baby, you did your best work tonight. Your timing is miraculous."

With the ingenuity of a magician, he began. Slowly, deliberately, he removed her boot. His fingers massaged her foot with exquisite pressure. She was mesmerized, fascinated with this new choreography. Leaning back, she waited.

Repeating his moves on her other foot, he pressed his mouth into her instep and began running his tongue in a weaving pattern across her arch, her heel, and toes. He slid her big toe in his mouth. Sucking firmly, he moved it around, sliding his tongue, over and under. As he tongued her, he watched.

Pat's eyes were closed, moans of pleasure filling the room. Moving her hips from side to side, she writhed in ecstasy to the rhythm of his sucking.

This was a first! No guy had ever produced this kind of foreplay! The more she vocalized, the more intense his moves became. He was urging her, daring her, preparing her.

Slowly he unzipped his fly and slipped out of his jeans. Naked and hard, he ran his hands up underneath the fabric of her panties. She was wet. Carefully his finger hooked the waistband.

She felt both the fabric and his fingers graze along her skin, across her pubic hair and along her thighs. Pat had reached a point of unbearable ecstasy. She could no longer wait as Owen braced himself over her. Pressing his pelvis against hers, he entered her slowly.

Her unbridled body exploded into ripples of pure erotic pleasure. She climaxed again and again as her pelvis produced a series of involuntary ripples. Finally released from the excruciating build-up of Owen's handiwork, she lay wet with perspiration, her hair tangled over the pillows. Owen switched gears, becoming more gentle now. He kissed her softly.

He lifted himself off and sat on the edge of the bed, lighting the familiar cigarette. He offered her a drag. Her eyes only half open, Pat took it and inhaled deeply.

"I'm looking for a lead dancer for my new show, and the producers will go with my decision. I want you only. Pat felt dizzy. Quickly she threw her arms around Owen's neck and kissed him. Owen returned her kiss adding, "This is strictly hush, hush, OK, Baby?" She nodded as if in a trance.

Time had grown short. They dressed, and he finished packing. Taking a last deep drag off his cigarette and squashing it out in the ashtray, he mumbled, "I'll miss you, Baby."

"Yes," she responded, still in a fog.

"Walk me out?" He picked up his bag and trench coat as Pat followed him to the elevator. Once inside, Owen held Pat close all the way to the lobby. As the door slid open, he abruptly pulled away. Pat fought back tears as Owen hailed a cab.

"Take care of yourself, Baby." Slipping into the cab, Owen closed the door behind him, never glancing back. Pat's chest tightened as she watched the yellow car disappear around the next corner. She was numb, spent, in need of sleep. Hailing another cab, she returned to her hotel, the ache in her chest distracting her reason.

Chapter 16

The Warning

The night air was heavy with humidity as Mally stepped out of the theatre. She spotted Jonas talking with his partner Gary. When he saw her he fell into step, as Gary took off.

"Let's get a drink," he said, grabbing her hand and guiding her across the busy intersection. They walked to a lounge on the next corner, a joint catering to a less elegant crowd.

Jukebox music underscored the atmosphere as they made their way through the fog of cigarette smoke, sweat, and cheap cologne. They found a booth at the back and sat down, just as a busty waitress, hair and make-up badly overdone, approached. Chewing a large wad of gum, she bent down over the table.

"So what are you two having?" She eyed Jonas up and down, giving him a flirtatious wink.

"I'll have whatever you have on tap. Mal?"

"Anything on tap is fine." The server left, her wide derriere swinging into motion, as dimples popped out through her tight pants. Jonas leaned back against the booth.

"Imagine waking up and finding that sitting on your face," he groaned.

"Jonas!"

"Just kidding, Mal. A silence began as they waited for their drinks. The last remnants of the candle on the table managed a faint flicker across their faces.

"All right, Jonas, let's have it." She suddenly wished she was back at her hotel.

"Mal, you ever hear of Vera Daniels?"

"I know she was a great Broadway star." Jonas leaned in on his elbows.

"Vera Daniels is someone to be reckoned with. She is still revered in the business and has a lot of powerful friends."

"So?"

"Gossip has a way of spreading, especially when someone has an axe to grind. It's common knowledge in the company that Owen and Pat are having an affair."

"Who would care?"

"I can think of one vicious bitch. Long story short, Jackie Eldridge and Owen had a thing years ago. He dumped her and she's been pissed ever since. Tell Pat to watch her back!"

The waitress returned with their order. As she placed the mugs on the table, she leaned toward Jonas with purpose, allowing her large, pendulous breasts to come close to his face. Pausing there she looked at him, a gleam in her eye. 'He's so damned cute. What a fun fuck,' she mused.

"Do you want anything else, Sugar?" Mally was now invisible. Jonas cautiously leaned back trying to keep some distance from the fleshy mounds. "No thanks. Just a check when you have a minute."

"For you, Sugar, anything." Smiling, she walked away. Jonas turned his attention back to Mally, who was deep in thought.

"What are you thinking, Mal?"

"I'm worried about Pat. She's so in love with Owen.

"That's a dangerous place to be," remarked Jonas, knowingly.

"I tried to warn her about his reputation, how he uses women," said Mally, sadly.

"A lot of women in our business have submitted and succumbed to Swengali Matthews! And the more gifted and beautiful they are, the more he takes them on. The list of his conquests is legend."

"So what happens now?"

"Try to listen, to support her. That's about all you can do."

Finishing their beers, Jonas found the waitress and paid the tab. The bar was unbearably loud at this point, the smoke-filled air was stifling, the music beyond conversation.

"Let's go, Mal."

They walked in silence. The night had turned chilly, prompting Jonas to remove his jacket and put it around Mally's shoulders as they continued toward the hotel.

The hotel lobby was quiet. Jonas paused and turned. "Night, Mal. See you at call. Remember what I told you, OK?"

"I will. Thanks!" Kissing his cheek gently, she turned and walked away. Entering the elevator she pushed the button for her floor. She was suddenly overcome with exhaustion as she leaned against the back wall. Arriving at her floor, she fished for her room key and opened the door.

She was a bit chilled. 'Ah-h-h,' she thought, 'A warm bath.' While the tub was filling, she undressed, her clothes sticking like pasta. She unfastened her bra with great difficulty, moisture twisting the fabric. While sitting on the commode, she poured jasmine-scented bubble bath into the filling tub and watched the bubbles rise. When there was depth enough to cover her, she stepped into the inviting mix.

Mally closed her eyes and thought about Griff. Through the bubbles she touched herself. She tensed with anticipation as she gently stroked and pushed her pelvis upward. As she imagined Griff's fingers there, she reached orgasm.

The sound of the door opening interrupted her pleasure. She quickly pulled the plug. Remnants of her bubble bath clung to her skin as she stood up. Slipping on her robe she entered the cool, dark room. Inching her way, she saw Pat in bed. She paused.

"Pat?"

"Yes," returned a sleepy voice.

"Are you OK?"

"Yes, is the alarm set?"

"Uh huh, for 5!"

"Yikes! Goodnight, Mal."

"Goodnight."

Mally was asleep almost at once, but Pat lay quietly replaying the torrid games she had created with Owen. She fell into a fitful sleep.

The alarm was jarring. Mally turned it off and reached for the inert body in the next bed. Pat was not easily awakened. Mally put on all the lights in the room.

"Pat, get up. It's time!"

Pat slowly kicked off the sheets and groaned as she stumbled her way into morning and a shower. Mally put on comfy clothes, pulling her messy hair under a cap. Her carry-on was packed with toiletries, a change of clothes, and some reading matter.

Pat's senses awakened from the rush of water, and stepping out of the tub reached for the closest towel. She wrapped her hair under a scarf and began dressing. The two barely spoke as they did a last minute check around the room.

"Ready?" Mally nodded and they made their way to the lobby to pay their bill. At the curb they noticed Jonas and Gary running toward them.

"Girls, can we share?" A cab pulled up and stopped, the driver waited.

"One of you up here with me, the others in the back," he growled. Jonas slid into the backseat, between Pat and Mally. Gary sat next to the driver.

"This hour is the shits," whined Jonas.

"Keep the volume down," ordered Pat.

"Oh, oh, the fabulous Patricia Byrne is craving sleep! Too much play, was it?"

"You're a flying fruitcake," edged Pat.

"You shameless hussy," parried Jonas hugging her.

Mally rested her head between the door and the seat and watched the trees against the night sky. The moon was still visible. Almost transparent, it seemed pasted to the blue wash. She liked how it looked through crater-like dimples and a tawny haze of pale yellow.

Gary was silent. He was the low-key half of the partnership, always thinking, observing everything and everyone.

The foursome arrived at the station and worked their way down to the platform for further instructions. Gil Fredericks, the company manager, noted each arrival like a mother hen counting chicks. As each cast member arrived, he passed out boarding passes with Pullman assignments.

On long trips, the members of the cast were given sleeping quarters. It was a nice perk and the weary performers welcomed the privacy and relative quiet of their compartments. Some of the gypsies would sleep the day away, waking in time for an evening meal. Others would chat, read, or play cards to pass the time.

Pat ruled in favor of a long sleep and tucked herself away in her compartment. Mally joined Jonas and Gary in the dining car for a quick breakfast, starting with several cups of coffee cut with cream and sugar. Soon the dining car filled with cast members in search of food. Breakfast orders were taken just as the train pulled out of the station en route to Wilmington.

After breakfast, Mally found her compartment. The gentle swaying of the train was soothing to her. She curled up with a collection of short stories by Truman Capote. After a few minutes she felt sleepy. Putting the book down, she dozed the rest of the way to Delaware.

Chapter 17

Wilmington, Delaware

The train stopped with a slight jerk and a hiss of steam. Mally and Pat stepped down to the platform. Through the crowd they spotted Gil Fredericks holding a sign, "To Bravo Business Buses." Picking up the pace they exited the station and boarded the bus with their comrades.

Droplets of rain ran down the bus windows, making meandering streaks on the glass. The wet streets of Wilmington reflected streetlights and windows of businesses from block to block during the short drive to the Allerton. The building was of uncertain vintage with an ornate edifice. A large awning extended out to the street from the lobby, allowing the girls to stay dry as they exited the bus.

The faded carpeting in the lobby was worn from years of guests. Leather couches, cracked with age, stood at tired attention. Here and there, several large potted plants looked in dire need of a drink. The desk clerk, a stout middle-aged man with a red bulbous nose, was slow-moving, but pleasant.

The girls found their trunks waiting at their assigned room. Pat walked to the window and looked out on the main drag. There was nothing there to indicate any nightlife. Only traffic lights and a few store signs showed any evidence of activity along banker's row. This would be home for the next week.

"I'm going to wash up," announced Pat, already out of her jeans. Running a bath, she returned to the bedroom and removed her scarf, allowing her hair to fall free. She undressed and disappeared into the bathroom, closing the door. Mally fell face forward on the bed. How good it was just to lie there. The phone rang, jarring her. Rolling over on her side she reached for the receiver.

"Beautiful! Say, I'm wondering if we could postpone dinner until tomorrow night? I'm beat." Mally felt a wave of gratitude through her fatigue.

"Sure. I'm beat too."

"Well, get a good night's sleep. I'll pick you up at seven tomorrow evening. Bye for now." Mally lay back and let out a long breath. Pat trotted across the room.

"Who was that?"

"It was Griff."

"You're a lucky girl!" Pat settled on the bed.

"Pat, are you OK?"

"Hell, yes! Who gives a shit if the great Owen Matthews calls," she said with new resolve. Then, she wavered.

"Mal, I'm so scared. What if Owen never calls again?"

"Stop it, Pat! Don't worry."

Mally took a good look at their room. It was old with peeling wallpaper and a musty odor, a combination of mildew, soiled carpeting and dust, reminiscent of all the old apartment buildings of her childhood.

"Want to watch the tube?" Pat nodded, pulling back the covers and sliding down into the sheets.

Mally, after much difficulty, found a clear channel on the bulky Philco in the corner. Retreating to the bathroom to run a fresh fill of water, it was time to soak. "I'll be out in a few minutes, Pat."

"Take your time." Pat propped up several pillows against the headboard. Even the Ed Sullivan Show, a favorite in the Byrne household, didn't hold her interest for long. Within minutes she was fast asleep. Only a dream of Owen would interrupt her rest.

Chapter 18

Owen and Vera

The plane touched down at LaGuardia. Owen sat fitfully during his cab ride to town. Arriving at his building on West Sixty-eighth, he took the elevator, arriving at his door to the sound of the phone ringing. Unlocking the door, he dropped his luggage and picked up.

"Matthews."

"Hi Darling, did you just get in?" Vera was tipsy. Owen shook out a cigarette, and lit the familiar smoke. Inhaling deeply he waited, knowing that it was useless to talk when she was tanked.

"I want to see you," she slurred, "tomorrow!"

"OK. Later!" Placing the receiver back, he lay back, watching the familiar curl of smoke circling over him. Closing his eyes he wandered through the past, as memories began to flood his mind.

As a kid he had been small for his age, almost delicate, possessing the face of an angel: blond curls, stunning blue eyes and dimples that accented his sensuous mouth and the cleft in his chin. His big brothers were athletes, but Owen had no aptitude for or interest in sports.

Instead, he studied dance. The undersized boy grew into a stunning man with a lean, muscular body and an eye for the ladies.

Arriving in Manhattan at eighteen, Owen was hired at his first open call. He was so impressive the director made him lead dancer. Vincent Lehrman spotted him. Lehrman, a young genius producer admired Owen's talent and obvious sex appeal. Instinct told him that Owen would be a sure winner. Following the show, the producer approached.

"Owen Matthews!"

"Yes sir."

"You can skip the 'sir.' We're probably the same age. Call me Vinny. It's more personal." He smiled as he scrutinized this dance wonder.

Lehrman liked Owen immediately. He offered him a part in his next show. Owen accepted the offer, and together they made theatrical history. Owen became an overnight sensation.

As Owen developed into an outstanding performer, his desire to choreograph became an obsession. Vinny could see the desire burning in him and looked for a project to back. Owen staged his first show for the Lehrman organization. The show was an instant hit.

Owen's distinctive choreographic style was the most innovative to ever hit Broadway. He became a major force, an unprecedented success. Vinny approached his wonder man.

"I think you're ready."

"Ready?"

"I want you to try your hand directing a star vehicle for a sensational new talent in town."

"Oh?"

"Her name's Daniels. Vera Daniels. She's been working nightclubs here and there. She's gorgeous, brassy, with legs that come to, well, you know."

"Come to where?" Owen smiled picturing Vinny on the other end.

"Don't be a smart ass, hoofer."

"Can she act and sing?"

"What do you take me for, a schlep? You know better," Vinny retorted, with mock indignation.

"When do I meet this paragon of talent?"

"Come to dinner tomorrow night. Say, seven?"

The next evening a uniformed doorman opened the cab door for Owen at Lehrman's Fifth Avenue digs. The polish of the doorman was equal to the polish on the floors of the lobby. Mirrors sparkled, reflecting wall sconces. An impressive chandelier gave luster to the pale, blue silk upholstered furniture done in a Louis XIV design. Owen felt like he was visiting a mini Versailles. As he entered the elevator, the uniformed attendant nodded.

"Vincent Lehrman's," said Owen, nonchalantly. He was unimpressed with Vinny's penchant for luxury. However, he admired his chutzpah, his drive. 'Hell, he's earned this,' he thought. Arriving at the penthouse, the attendant slid back the elevator door. Vinny's maid smiled when she saw him.

"Mr. Owen, sir. What a pleasure!"

"You're looking beautiful tonight, Esther," he whispered, planting a kiss on her cheek. She giggled as she took his coat.

Vinny's apartment was elegant, and decorated to perfection. The entire wall space from the front door to the drawing room was a parade of oil paintings, all masterpieces. Owen passed through the museum-like labyrinth and into the drawing room.

It wasn't hard to spot Vera Daniels. Her luminosity filled the room as though the surroundings were designed just to compliment her. Owen sensed immediately that she would complete any setting. Vinny approached.

"Vera, this is Owen Matthews. He will be directing you in your Broadway debut. Owen, Miss Daniels."

"Hello."

"Hi," said Owen, extending his hand.

"Cocktail, Owen?" Vinny moved to the bar. He lifted the lid on a crystal decanter.

"Scotch on the rocks," responded Owen absently, focusing on the vision of loveliness draped on Vinny's sofa. Vera returned a gaze that cooked his toes. Owen, attempting nonchalance, felt the burn of Scotch on his throat as he took a swallow. Vinny replenished his own drink and sat next to Vera. Owen chose a chair, opposite them.

She spoke softly. "Vinny tells me you're quite a pro." Owen's blush was obvious.

"You've seen my work?"

"No. I just heard about you from Vinny."

"He thinks you're star material," Owen said, nonchalantly.

"He's absolutely right," declared Vera with assurance. The throaty belly laugh that followed surprised him.

"The truth is I'm totally out of my depth. I've never been on a Broadway stage in my life. I'm depending on you to make it happen."

Owen's eyes never left her. Vera's raven hair outlined a flawless complexion of rich cream, a pair of Caribbean teal eyes, and full, red lips.

"You seem much too young to have accomplished all you have, Owen," said Vera, her husky voice belying a soft smile.

"How old do you think I am?"

"Old enough to know the score, and endowed enough to conduct the orchestra," she deadpanned, chuckling wickedly. 'God, she's hot,' Owen thought.

The attraction was mutual. Vera scrutinized Owen. His eyes twinkled with boyish innocence, yet they were worldly around the edges. She liked the graceful walk, the cat-like intensity in a pair of tight jeans, and his considerable package. He was irresistible.

Throughout dinner the conversation was professional. Owen explained the process of putting a production together. Vera sipped her wine slowly, hanging on every word. She glowed with anticipation. They were creating a vehicle just for her, an unknown from Nebraska.

As Owen spoke, Vera recalled how as a young teen, she had been so eager to leave the family farm and sing somewhere, anywhere.

Verna Wilson discovered her voice watching *The Hit Parade* every Saturday night in the front parlor of her parent's farmhouse. She would sing along, her melodious and powerful voice filling the rafters. Her parents were startled by their oldest daughter's natural ability and encouraged her to sing in the church choir. Sunday after Sunday, she sang. In time, Anna Fritz, the choral director, took her on as a private student.

Her strong alto became stronger. Her pitch was perfect, her range extraordinary. Anna encouraged her to read music. Verna developed enunciation and phrasing, and soon was singing more challenging pieces of music at practice. The country school offered no extra curricular activities, so she did the best she could, performing an occasional solo at church or singing in holiday events at the local Moose hall.

When she was seventeen, she applied for a voice scholarship at a music school in Omaha. She was accepted, and in the fall of her eighteenth birthday, she left the farm forever.

Arriving in Omaha full of hope and dreams, she lived in a dorm at the School of Performing Arts and attended all music-related classes. She worked diligently to improve. Not only did she develop musically, she developed physically as well. She became a stunning beauty.

Verna Wilson, the green young girl from North Platte, Nebraska chose the name Vera Daniels while walking past a local liquor store. It was the Jack Daniels label that caught her eye and imagination. She became aware of how she attracted men, men who wanted her. But, Vera wanted only one thing-a career in New York. This desire consumed her.

A year later, she left the School of Performing Arts and headed east on a Greyhound bus, counting the hours until she saw the Empire State Building looming ahead of her. She was gone forever from the family farm and the flat plains of Nebraska.

Vera's rumination faded. She refocused and joined in the Crème Brule, coffee and conversation. When the evening ended, Vinny said goodnight to his new team as they stepped into the elevator. It was obvious that they were heading to a more personal level. Owen helped Vera into a cab and paused to make sure she was comfortable. The scent of her drew him closer.

"Good night, Owen," she murmured.

"Good night." He closed the door and watched the cab as it pulled away from the curb. Turning, he walked down swank Fifth Avenue, passing building after building with uniformed doormen and manicured front entrances. An occasional limo or Rolls Royce stopped to expel or pick up well-heeled parties. At the corner of Seventy-ninth Street he hailed a cab and settled back for the brief cut through Central Park to his flat on the west side.

Owen's memory faded of the woman he once couldn't live and work without. He thought of his new inspiration. Pat was a fresh breath of excitement for him. Her beauty and talent brought back his passion and left him weak with yearning. He hadn't seen a dancer as extraordinary in years.

And, he longed for her sexually. Just the thought of her body, her smell and her touch turned him on. It had been only a few hours since he had held her, but his arms felt empty. To want someone so much was a new experience. He needed Pat. It was not yet a comfortable place to be for Owen Matthews.

Chapter 19

The First Time

Wilmington felt cooler than Norfolk. Mally decided slacks and a turtleneck sweater would be a good choice for the evening. Comfort was the key. The phone rang just as she was giving herself a final once over in the mirror.

"I'll be right down, Griff," she said eagerly. Pat stirred slightly. Mally found an extra blanket and put it over her. She checked her purse for her room key and closed the door behind her. Hurrying to the lobby she glanced around and spotted Griff by the front desk. He was in a great mood.

"You look beautiful! Come on, I know a terrific Italian restaurant not far from here. We can walk." Mally was suddenly starved.

"The air is pleasant tonight," she added, as Griff slipped his arm around her. The walk took only a few minutes and brought them to a quaint little café tucked in an old brownstone.

They were led to a table looking out on a courtyard at the back of the restaurant. Ropes of tangled dried flowers swung in the night breeze. A row of gas lamps bathed the entire patio in a soft glow. Tables and chairs were stacked and locked together by a thick chain that encircled the pile. The few trees and shrubs nearby were dry and leafless, ready for the coming winter.

"This patio is delightful for dining in the summer."

"How many tours have you done, Griff?"

"This is my fifteenth or sixteenth. I've lost count." Mally suddenly felt out of Griff's league. A waiter approached.

"The veal scaloppini is exceptional. Would you care to try it?"

"Yes." Griff handed the menus back to the waiter. "Bring us two orders of the veal scaloppini and a carafe of your finest Chianti."

"Yes, Mr. Edwards, right away," replied the waiter.

"Everyone knows you." Griff took Mally's hand and kissed it gently.

Manager, Ricco Donatelli, brought a bottle of Chianti, two glasses, and a breadbasket. He opened the bottle and poured. "Nice to see you Mr. Edwards," he said, extending his hand.

"And you, Ricco," Griff said, returning his handshake warmly. This is my friend, Mally Winthrop."

"Hello!" Griff continued.

"How's Antonia?"

"She's fine. We have a new bambino, definitely a mama's boy. We call him Dion." Griff smiled.

"Congratulations, Ricco, and my best to your wife and son."

"Grazie, Mr. Edwards." Ricco excused himself to greet others. Griff returned his attention to Mally, and pushed the basket of bread and butter toward her. She lifted the cloth napkin and selected a hunk of buttery garlic bread, and began to chew heartily. Griff chuckled.

"You dancers have such fantastic appetites, and yet, you're so slim. It must be the rate of burn off. You all have high metabolisms, I suppose." He lifted his glass, "To many more evenings like this."

Mally clinked his glass and sipped the wine, savoring the pleasant flavor. Griff broke off a piece of bread and began nibbling. He paused, wiping his buttery fingers on a napkin. He sipped his wine, slowly, never taking his eyes from her.

"Mally, I never thought I would fall in love again. You give me a reason to try." Mally took a generous sip of wine and set her glass down.

"Griff, I've never had a lover."

"I know."

Mally's eyes widened. "How do you know?"

"It's all in the eyes." Their order arrived.

Mally cut the tender veal with relish, enjoying the wonderful aroma of the sauce. At the first bite, she closed her eyes, and she sighed at her second. She suddenly realized that she was rushing and slowed down.

"Good, isn't it?" Griff offered her more wine. She sipped faster this time. The wine brought out the unique flavor of the meat. Mally savored each mouthful. Griff kept up with her, enjoying the texture of the veal, and the smooth and warm taste of the wine.

Griff poured more wine. They continued to bask in the ambience of the restaurant, taking occasional sips. Their dinner plates grew sticky from the sauce remnants. Griff noticed that Mally was feeling the effect of the wine and ordered espresso, which she gratefully accepted. Griff read the check and dropped some bills on the table. He suggested a walk. Ricco held the front door for them, smiling as they left.

Climbing the few steps to street, Mally shivered. A cool breeze ruffled her hair. Griff removed his sports coat and placed it on her tiny shoulders, putting his arm around her. Stopping short of his hotel, he pulled her close.

"Do you want to come up?" Mally's head had cleared a bit in the fresh air, and she was relaxed.

"Yes, I do."

The plush lobby was done in rich mahogany panels accented by furniture upholstered in exquisite brocades. In the center of the reception area was an enormous table on which an oversized floral arrangement dripped eucalyptus and other greens, enfolding Stargazer lilies, roses, and tulips. Lamps on low beam dotted the room and a large fireplace spilled warmth over the Persian carpet runners.

Griff's suite was grand. A fireplace beckoned and two enormous rooms, beautifully furnished in crème, soft beige and yellow, opened before them. Tall vaulted ceilings were covered by exquisite brocade fabric in tones of brown. Overstuffed furniture with large pillows filled the spaces here and there, and wall candelabras added an air of antiquity.

"This is one of my favorite hotels on tour. The furnishings and service are impeccable." Mally looked around and spotted a huge sofa, sat down and slipped off her flats. Griff joined her, putting his arm around her shoulder.

"I have thought about you from the first time you came into my office."

"Me, too," she whispered, softly. How many times she had imagined this moment!

Slowly, he covered her mouth with his. Sliding down with her on the sofa, he kissed her more fervently while his hands moved to her breasts, slowly pressing and massaging them. His mouth became her mouth, his breath her breath. Mally's breathing became deeper as she pushed into him, absorbed by new sensations.

Griff relished every moment. Day after day at Dance Arts he'd watched her. The Lycra fabric of her Leotard had accentuated her small, perfect breasts, the v-shape of her mound. When she was sweaty, her stretchy dancewear brought out every detail of her lean body, the sight leaving him horny.

Griff carefully removed her sweater and slacks. Finally, her flawless body was in his hands! The flat stomach, spare pelvis, and smooth skin were soft like a baby's. Her pubic hair was neatly trimmed into a small strip, adding to his hunger.

Mally noticed immediately the soft hair on Griff's chest. She gently ran her hands through it, stopping long enough to touch his nipples, which brought a sigh. She liked his reaction.

He was well built through his shoulders and arms, and his torso was muscular and lean. Her hands moved lower. She unbuttoned his pants and gently unzipped the fly. His abdomen was smooth and taut. Continuing her exploration, she carefully pulled his trousers open.

A large bulge beneath his white Jockeys, pressed against the fabric. Sliding his shorts down, she stopped and stared at Griff's penis. She'd seen them in art books, but his was far more enticing. He was fully hard and generous in size. His balls were nicely shaped. Mally took a deep breath, her excitement growing more intense.

Griff took over now, exploring, etching a smooth trail between her thighs. His hands traced the edge of her panties, teasing her as he moved across the damp fabric. They came off with a gentle tug.

Mally moaned through the new sensation. Griff's hands were gently exploring the inside of her thighs, his fingers brushing her softly as his mouth moved down her body, first sucking each nipple and then tracing down to her navel and lower.

She felt the warmth of his breath as he began to taste her. Quivering, the ecstatic sensations mounted in intensity as Griff's mouth changed rhythm, as he stroked her with the tip of his tongue. Mally let go, floating on a wave of exquisite surrender. Her body felt weightless. She was his.

"God, oh yes, yes," she murmured. "More Griff, oh please, more." She was wet and ready. Gently, he parted and partially raised her legs. Holding himself on his elbows, he began a slow pushing and probing. He planted himself more firmly. At first he moved slowly, easily sliding in and out, but as his longing intensified his moves became more aggressive.

"More!"

"Yes, oh yes!"

Griff began to come, heaving and thrusting until he burst. Mally could feel him pulsing inside of her. She felt herself open and let go, "Oh, oh," following him with her explosion. Panting for breath he stayed inside and began to relax. His reflexes pushed into her again, but the moment was passing. He relaxed, his weight merging with her.

For a few minutes they lay silently. Mally suddenly felt tears running down Griff's face. Reaching up, she gently wiped them away, kissing him over and over again.

"Griff, are you all right?"

"Oh Mally, I never thought that I could feel like this. You move me so." Smiling, she stroked his face.

"I love you Griff." Griff carried her to bed. He placed her under the comforter, lying next to her in spoon fashion. Snuggling closer, she thought she was in heaven. Outside, a heavy rain fell.

Mally didn't remember falling asleep. She awoke slowly. She could still feel traces of Griff from the night before. As she reached for him, she realized he was gone. On the pillow was a long stem red rose with a note attached.

"Darling, I'm off to the theatre. Last night was incredible."

For Mally, the night before felt like a dream, but here she was in his suite. She could taste and smell him. Pulling herself together she noted the time and reached for the phone.

"Hi Pat, it's me."

"Mal, sweetie, how are you?"

"Ecstatic! Meet me at the diner across from our hotel at 10:00, OK?"

"You got it!"

Mally wandered into the bathroom and peed. Standing, she reached for the handle and flushed the toilet. Turning on the shower she stood patiently testing the temperature of the spray. Climbing in, she drew the curtain. As the warm water caressed her body she thought of Griff's mouth on her, tasting, sucking, and her orgasm. Griff's experience and imaginative skill changed everything. Her hunger was intense, her experience was freeing, and she was in love for the first time in her life.

Turning off the shower, she stepped out and reached for a nearby towel. Looking in the mirror, she thought she looked different. She certainly felt different. Slipping into her clothes, she rummaged in her purse for a comb. As she tried to run it through her hair, she grimaced at the knots. Smiling, she gently removed the tangles made during their lovemaking. Then, as was her habit, she checked around the suite for any forgotten belongings and left.

The sun was already high in the sky as she stepped outside. Walking briskly, she thought of Griff. At the diner, she spotted Pat. Pat gave her a sly wink.

"Did you spend the night? Oh my God, it happened! You are different. I can see it!" Giving her a big hug, Pat eagerly asked, "Was he wonderful?"

"Yes! But, I'm not giving out details."

"I understand." A beleaguered waitress interrupted, "You two ordering?"

"Yes, black coffee and a tea with milk." Pat was eager. "Well?"

"It was unbelievable! Griff is incredible. The rest of the details are private, OK? I suppose we might want to look at the menu, Pat." Pat ordered pancakes and sausage, Mally an order of ham and eggs.

"Let's celebrate your de-flowering!" They laughed as they drank. "So what do you want to do today? We have until half hour. You want to check out stores or take in a movie?"

"Either!" Breakfast arrived and they ate heartily, their dancer's appetites in high gear.

At seven-thirty the theatre was a bustle. Chorus members selected spots in the dressing rooms. Once a gypsy had chosen a specific chair, it was his or hers for the engagement. Racks of costumes stood in changing areas. Dorcas bellowed her orders at jobbers, hired to assist. She was tough on them, expecting the costumes, accessories, and shoes to be kept in topnotch condition, and placed for easy access.

The clothing was marked with each person's name. All tights, trunks, and socks were laundered every other performance. Cast members were responsible for their own underwear, including bras and dance belts.

Norry kept tabs on all wigs worn in the show. He designed each performer's look and once set, it was Norry's job to maintain it. Cast members were not permitted to make changes without his permission. No one ever crossed him.

The week went by like a flash, the show stayed in solid performance shape and following the Saturday night performance, the load out commenced. Greensboro, North Carolina was next.

Chapter 20

Bus and Truck

Two Trailways bus coaches pulled up and parked. With a gush of air the large doors opened. It was Sunday, and the gypsies were on the move again.

"Did you pee, Mal? I'm not sure these crates have a potty." Pat dreaded having to hold it during a long trip.

Seasoned touring performers Dana and Dick Landry stood watching. Dana was a principal understudy, and Dick was training as Griff's assistant in addition to his ensemble role. They liked the double income and working together on the road.

"Don't worry, ladies, each bus has a restroom in the back. However, they do get a bit ripe," cautioned Dana.

"Dana, a bit ripe? Your never-ending southern gentility amazes me! They stink," announced Jonas.

"How gross," Pat groaned.

"Yup," he continued, playfully putting his index finger up a nostril.

Two tall, lanky bus drivers approached the group. "Folks, I'm Roy Grimms, your driver, and this here is your other, Will Eberle. If you have any questions be sure and ask. Please don't smoke or engage in lewd talk on the bus, OK? Thanks," he said cordially.

"Lewd? Hell, I'll have to wash my mouth out with soap," Jonas muttered. The cast began climbing aboard, placing their dance bags in overhead racks. Mally, Pat, and their pals found seats near the back. They began chatting as the buses pulled out.

The trip to Greensboro seemed endless. Several chorus members slept while others played games to pass the time. The Landrys began singing. Before long the entire group exploded into a mass chorale.

From his seat up front Roy took in the concert. These Yankee performers were interesting folks. The singing continued into the late afternoon.

The cast disembarked in Greensboro. As many sized up the place, it was obvious that the downtown area wasn't much. There were a few small retail stores, including a drugstore, cafe, bank, and the theatre. Their venue was an old movie house dating back to the 1920's. On the route sheet it was listed as 'auditorium.'

The hotel was old. The worn white octagon tile floor, with black tile patterns, suggested a bygone time of flappers and bootleggers. At one end of the small lobby was a coffee shop. Through the windows tied-back curtains revealed a counter and a few tables. It appeared to be closed for the day.

Next to the coffee shop, a small magazine stand displayed the local paper and a few outdated magazines, some snacks, and tobacco products in limited amounts. Next to it, a small two-chair barbershop stood empty of customers, save for the barber, who appeared to be napping.

The girls looked around and spotted a mahogany counter backed by a row of key slots. The desk clerk was trying his best to check-in the gypsies now crowding around him.

"Where can we find a restaurant?"

"The Mayflower is one block down on the opposite corner. It stays open until eight."

He handed Pat and Mally their room key.

"Yikes, we better get going," said Pat. The girls found their room up one flight of stairs and down a long, narrow hall. They noted the old-fashioned door with the glass transom at the top and the worn carpeting. The hall was dimly lit. Mally heard intense sounds.

"Someone's in the throes of passion."

"What an understatement," threw back Pat, opening the door. Jonas and Gary hurried down the hall toward them. Jonas stopped for a moment and listened to the moans emanating from the room next to the girls.

"They've been at it since we got in. It's pretty gross," said Gary, rolling his eyes.

"Say, you girls want to freshen up? We'll go on ahead and check out the smart Mayflower," suggested Jonas.

"I'm so starved I could eat the carpet," added Pat. The boys took off.

The next night the pre-show ritual was in full swing. As the overture began, the chorus lined up in their pre-set positions. The company performed well in spite of a lack of response. This audience was dead compared to others. Applause was scattered and the laughs seemed weak and unsure. At intermission, Chad Chapman caught up to Mally.

"Do you think they're dense or what?" Jonas happened by.

"Hey guys, they guaranteed you eight shows a week, a paycheck and free rides."

"Yeah, stop your bitching," said Gary. "This is Hicksville U.S.A., get it?"

"This audience is boring," Chad complained.

"Stop whining. How many tours have you done?"

"Just this," Chad said, defensively.

"Only nineteen more cities to go," said Jonas, backing Chad up to the wall. You could have me in the meantime, you sweet thing," he whispered. "Damn, you're cute and, unfortunately, straight. Shit!" Chad slipped away quickly.

"Cast report to the green room at five minutes," commanded Griff through the speakers.

Intermission passed and the cast gathered. It was obvious that Griff was loaded for bear.

"Ladies and gentlemen, we have a growing problem here. Not every audience is going to inspire you. Some will not react at all. You are paid to perform eight shows a week with the same energy and integrity. I suggest you nip this drag-ass attitude now. Places!" During act two the cast regained their spark. As the finale ended the audience gave a standing ovation. Griff's lecture worked.

The next night, following the performance, some of the girls complained of hunger. Performing on a full stomach was not a good idea, so most performers waited until after the show to eat. With the Mayflower restaurant closing at 8 p.m., the girls had nowhere to go. Willard suggested a diner on the main route to and from town. Roy decided to tag along and drove Mally, Pat, Marcy and Elaine, two singers from the show, to the neon world of long haul truckers.

The girls found a large booth in the diner, while Roy and Willard took stools at the counter up front. A young waitress appeared and stopped dead in her tracks when she saw the four young women in heavy make-up.

"We'd like menus and water." The girl stepped away for a moment. Pat perused the place adding, "I'll be glad to leave this burg! I've had it."

"Me too," added Marcy.

Elaine grimaced. "Well, what do expect? The waitress returned, passed out the water glasses and menus. She continued staring at the brightly brushed eyelids accented by false lashes.

"All right, what will it be?" Uncomfortable, and in no mood for levity, she shifted from foot to foot. Her shoulders slouched, her hair hung in strings, her skin was oily, and her lipstick had long faded. Cracked lips, tight with irritation, spoke with a thick drawl. The girls threw orders at her in rapid-fire succession. Collecting the menus, she stomped off.

"What a bitch," whispered Pat. "Can you imagine being stuck in a place like this?"

"That's probably why she has a burr up her ass," giggled Elaine, as she played with her fork.

Four rough-hewn locals at the table across the way stared through the greasy, cigarette-smoke atmosphere. The waitress returned with food, putting down plates unceremoniously. Slapping down the check, she retreated in a huff.

"Two-bit entertainers from that two-bit show," mumbled one. Unshaven, the men wore hunting gear, but the camouflage couldn't hide their disgust. "Bunch a whores," grunted another.

Conversation stopped. Pat, her Irish rising, put down her fork, slid out of the booth and stood before the group. One of the men pointed at her.

"If my sister looked like you, I'd string the bitch up and beat the living crap out of her."

"Nice, real nice," sneered Pat, standing her ground. One by one, the girls rose and carefully made their way toward the door. The men watched, but made no move.

"Boy, what a bunch of hick assholes!" Pat aimed her words over her shoulder, but within ear-shot of the men. "Bitch," one shouted. Pat hastened toward the door.

Roy stood, took the bill from Pat, and paid the cashier. Once out-side, the girls moved quickly to the bus. Willard, all six foot four of him, stood blocking the door. The restaurant became quiet. Willard towered over the leader of the group, who moved toward him. Willard was ready.

"Excuse me. Where do you think you're going?"

"Outside, after them bitches!"

"That's not going to happen! But, you can step outside with me to apologize."

"Mister, you can kiss my ass," he shouted, making a lunge at Willard.

Without missing a beat, Willard grabbed the redneck lifting him off the floor. There was a gasp from onlookers. The other hecklers stepped back. Willard held the leader, suspended by his jacket, eyeballing him nose to nose. Seconds passed before Willard let him down hard. As the guy fell with a thud, the others came to his rescue. Cursing, the leader of the pack pushed them away with a scowl and clamored to his feet.

"You'll pay for this," he hissed.

"I doubt it," said Willard, with an affable air. "Y'all have a good evening now, you hear?' He smiled as he made his exit, waving to the onlookers.

The bus was idling as Willard jumped on. Roy pulled out of the parking area as the redneck group ran out of the restaurant, shaking fists and shouting obscenities. There was silence and tension aboard. Willard moved along the aisle checking on the girls.

"I can't believe it," said a shaken Pat. What did we do?"

"You're a threat," explained Willard.

"What threat? We were trying to eat," said Pat, her voice rising.

"Local folks get pretty uptight if you look and act different."

"If we're not bloody hicks, you mean."

"Miss, you're different and, well, that scares people. It's over now." Mally was close to tears. The bus rolled to the hotel. As the others exited, Pat stopped.

"Thanks, guys."

"It's our pleasure. You ladies make life interesting." Approaching, Mally reached up and gave them both kisses on the cheek. "You were both wonderful back there. Thanks." Then, she walked briskly into the lobby, relieved to be back. Tonight, the world was not a friendly place.

Chapter 21

Points South

It was a relief to get out of Greensboro and on to Raleigh, a friendlier town. There was no need for a pep talk. Audiences were enthusiastic, bringing the cast up to their maximum performance level. On Sunday morning the show headed to Knoxville, Tennessee.

Set-ups on split weeks were demanding for Griff and his base crew. Even the most seasoned pros found the short time between load outs and set-ups arduous. Griff and Mally had no contact on the short engagements. Phone conversations had to do.

Pat went through moody periods. The silence from Owen intensified her insecurity. Wanting him as she did, she obsessed, which only increased her funk. Edgy, most of the time, she'd snap at Mally, then, moments later she'd apologize, the outburst forgotten.

"He'll call, you'll see," reassured Mally, placating the mercurial Pat. Sometimes it worked, but other times, Pat would retreat and sleep to escape her angst.

The show was well received in Knoxville. The company's stay was pleasant with the addition of unseasonably warm days and crisp nights, good for sleeping. On Thursday morning *Bravo Business* moved on to Chattanooga and an old movie house.

The Tivoli was not suitable to accommodate a large production and cast. There was no place for the chorus to change, forcing Dorcas and her crew to create a makeshift area in the basement. She strung a long rope across the area to divide the space, pinning large blankets together for a semblance of privacy.

The set-up was primitive at best. A space between the two hanging blankets allowed the men, who were dressing near the back wall, to exit on their way to the stage. Everyone moved quickly through the changes. There was no room for modesty. By the last show on Saturday, the blankets came down. Griff called a meeting at intermission.

"Ladies and gentlemen, your call is 7:00 am sharp. Your drivers will take you to the airport where you will board your flight departing for Jacksonville at 9:00 am. The hotel list is posted. I trust you all signed up two weeks ago. Your trunks must be outside your door by two am. Thank you." The cast took their places for the top of Act II.

The sun was not yet visible as a pink glow rose over the hills surrounding Chattanooga. The air was damp and fresh on the faces of the cast gathering at the curb. The familiar buses pulled up, as Jonas and Gary ran from the lobby.

"Sleep in, did you?" Jonas brought out the imp in Pat. The four climbed on board.

Willard remained at curbside, putting luggage in the compartment under the bus while Roy assisted with smaller pieces in the overhead. When he finished, he walked to the back of the bus.

"Miss Mally, Miss Pat, we want you to know how much we've enjoyed driving you. Good luck to you both." He quickly turned and left, waving to them from the curb where his bus was idling. Once all the gypsies were aboard, Willard climbed into his seat and closed the door. The buses pulled away. Downtown Chattanooga disappeared behind the mountains.

Chapter 22

Jacksonville, Florida

"Oh, my God, it's paradise." As the plane dipped lower through the clouds, the sun shone on the blue expanse of ocean beneath them. Upon landing, the gypsies stepped from the plane, the warmth of Florida enveloping them, as they shed their coats. Buses were waiting. After being driven through industrial areas to the downtown, the cast piled out at the Carlyle Hotel.

After checking in, the girls found their trunks waiting outside their room. Once they pushed the awkward pieces inside, they surveyed their digs for the next week, a spacious room, decorated in soft yellow, peach and lime green colors. The white rattan furniture had accent cushions matching the drapes in a leaf pattern. A small balcony, with a view of the pool and tennis court, was perfect for sunning and a sunken bathtub was inviting. It was perfect.

After unpacking, they washed up. Pat tucked the straggles of her hair back into a French twist. Mally brushed through the snarls in her flip and threw on a hat. The girls left in search of lunch. They found a charming Chinese restaurant minutes from the hotel. The interior was intimate and it wasn't busy. A pleasant waiter appeared.

"Good afternoon, ladies. Welcome to the Chrysanthemum." He offered water and menus and promised to return. Pat slid down into the fabric of the cushion. She was unusually quiet.

Reaching for a set of chopsticks, she tore open the wrapper and pried the two sticks apart.

"Thinking about Owen?"

"Mal, you know me pretty well. The man has me wrapped in knots. The truth is I'm a mess. I'm so in love with him."

"What do you think about when he's not with you?"

"Oh, come on, Mal. I think about what he looks like, what he's said to me, our lovemaking, things like that." Pat picked up her water and took a long swallow.

"Pat, if you could have him with you every day for the rest of your life, what then?"

"Wow! I'm not sure. It's so intense when we're together, I'm not certain we'd survive!" They both laughed.

"He'll call, Pat."

"Shit, I hate this waiting. I really didn't think I'd fall in love with the guy. But, Owen Matthews isn't just any guy, he's extraordinary," she murmured, as she folded and unfolded her napkin.

"Did he say when he'd see you again?"

"I suppose after Atlanta. It seems forever until then." The waiter returned with their orders and the girls ate heartily.

"Have you ever been here before?"

"No, though I have always wanted to. The audiences have to be a little more with it than those in North Carolina. You know, there's a naval base here. My oldest brother Sean spent a few months of his hitch here. He hated it though. He's a dyed in the wool New Yorker. After his discharge, he returned to the Bronx. Dad was disappointed."

"Why?"

"Dad couldn't see his oldest son in the bar business. He had some notion that Sean would go to college one day and become a lawyer or doctor. Sean's a bright guy."

"What's he doing now?"

"He works construction and loves it. He makes big bucks." The girls paid the check and returned to the hotel. Pat checked for messages, and found one waiting.

"Oh shit, Owen just called. Damn, I missed him!" Pat trembled during the short ride to their floor. Entering their room, Pat went straight to the phone and dialed New York. It rang twice.

"This is Gina, how may I help you?"

"I'm returning Mr. Matthews call. This is Pat Byrne."

"One moment please." Pat held.

"Hi Baby!" Pat's voice choked, her throat filling with emotion.

"Hey, what's this? Pat, we're not going to do this, remember?"

"I miss you."

"Miss you too."

"How's the new show coming?"

"Very slow, Baby. The money people are a pain in the ass. They've got the bread, but not the brains, if you get my drift."

"Yes, I understand. Do you still want me to come to New York over Thanksgiving?"

"Yes."

"OK." There was silence for a few seconds.

"I'm hard right now thinking about you."

"Owen, please! I can't take it."

"Sure you can, Baby. I'll see you and I'll show you. Bye."

"I love you, Owen." She heard a click. Her eyes welled up. Mally reached out, hugging Pat close.

"It's Ok. It's fine." The phone rang again.

"Griff, how's it going?"

"We've got a mess, but we'll have it straightened out. I've got to stay put."

"I understand."

"I love you," he said hurriedly, hanging up. Mally placed the phone on the receiver and glanced over at Pat, who had fallen asleep.

Deciding on a warm bath, Mally slipped into the bathroom. Running the tap, she sat on the edge of the tub. While sloshing her hand through the rise of water and bubbles, she thought about Pat, who was always first to show her bravura, her nonchalance. The truth was she was raw, vulnerable. A mere phone conversation had brought her to tears. Slipping into the bubbly brew, she rested her head on a folded towel. The warm water was a welcome relief. She thought of Griff.

Chapter 23

Beach Break

The new Civic Auditorium was a quality venue, superior to most with its spacious dressing rooms, changing areas, and a luxurious green room. An efficient and polite crew of dressers and other backstage personnel was a plus.

There was a charge in the air as the gypsies prepared for the show. Applause greeted Sandy Irwin as he entered the pit. On the downbeat, the show took off on an electrical charge. The Jacksonville audience responded to the show's humor and style with enthusiasm.

Following the performance, Griff handed Mally an envelope. "Someone left this for Pat. Would you mind giving it to her? I'll see you at the stage door." Mally found Pat changing and handed her the note. She perused the contents, a big smile growing across her face.

"Mal, I have an admirer," she whispered. "It appears that some gentleman saw me in the show, and wants me to join him for a drink."

"Gosh Pat, do you think that's wise?"

"Yes, I do," said Pat, setting the note aside.

"Well, I guess you know what you're doing."

"Don't wait up!" Pat was bright with excitement as she hurried out of the dressing room. Mally finished her post show routine and found Griff waiting. As they walked up the street, they noticed Pat conversing with an impeccably dressed man next to an impressive limo.

"Oh, Mal and Griff, I'd like to introduce Blaine Courtman."

"My pleasure," said Blaine, with an affable air. "This lovely lady has consented to have a drink with me. Would you care to join us?"

"Another time," said Griff. Blaine helped Pat into the backseat. She waved as the car pulled away. Mally was noticeably distracted.

"He's a total stranger."

"If I had the slightest doubt, we would have joined them. Come on, I have a surprise." Stopping at a car parked on the street, Griff unlocked the door.

"This is your chariot, mademoiselle," he announced with enthusiasm.

They drove in silence drinking in the star-filled night. Griff pulled up to an overlook and turned off the ignition. Ahead the moon carved a path of light through the sea. Griff and Mally carefully walked down to the sandy beach below.

Mally slipped off her tennis shoes and buried her feet in the sand. Griff joined her. The texture of the cool sand felt soft and grainy between his toes, reminding him of summers on Lake Michigan. Mally was mesmerized by the surf as it rolled in. They cuddled as the wind brushed them with salt air. The sound of the ocean breaking over the smooth, hard surface of beach held them in a hypnotic space.

"Oh, Griff, make love to me."

"Here?"

"Yes."

Mally removed his shirt and unzipped his pants. Her slacks came off quickly, and as he removed her panties, she writhed under his touch. He was hard as he slipped out of his shorts and into her with ease. Guiding her through the intensity of his thrusting, he pushed deeper and felt her tense and tighten around him as he shuddered inside her. Their mutual climax left them spent. Mally began to shiver. Griff stirred.

"Better start back. It's getting kind of late." Standing and shaking off the sand slowed them a bit as they dressed. A few grains irritated here and there, a reminder of their haste. The ocean air was chilly.

Shaking the last of the sand from their feet they slipped their shoes on. During the drive back to the hotel, she fell asleep against Griff's shoulder. He woke her when he had parked. Silently they walked back to the hotel.

"Goodnight, my darling!" Gently, they kissed. Mally closed the door and undressed quietly as Pat slept. Tiptoeing into the bathroom she ran a shower. Traces of sand gently slid off her legs and buttocks falling to the bottom of the tub. Her groin ached. Replaying every detail of their lovemaking, she reached down, stroking herself fervently. She was in love.

In the morning, the sounds of the shower woke Mally. She rolled over sleepily and sat up as Pat came into the room. Pat couldn't contain her excitement as she dried herself and then, tossed the towel aside, flinging herself on the bed. Her long, wet tresses sprinkled water.

"Mal, you won't believe this. Blaine Courtman is absolutely crazy about me. Isn't that wild?" Mally was awake now.

"Get this, he has homes in Vancouver, New York, and Miami Beach. He's thirty-five and has never been married."

"How did you find out all that over one drink?"

"Well, we had more than one. He asked me back to his yacht, but I thought I'd wait."

"What does he do for a living?"

"He manufactures shoes. Mal, he's filthy rich. He inherited the business from his grandfather."

"You're seeing a man who makes shoes? How appropriate for a dancer. And he has a yacht!"

"I plan to see him again," added Pat. Noting a frown on her room-mate's face she added, "Don't worry, my little mother hen, this chick can take care of herself. I have no intention of falling for this guy, but I will let him spoil me a little."

"Hussy!"

"You bet your ass! And, I might add, he has a nice one. He is really attractive." Then Pat noticed a look of disapproval.

"You're wondering about Owen," aren't you? Well, I'm in love with him, but he's in New York. I'm here and definitely in need of some attention."

"This is confusing, Pat. You're telling me you love Owen, and, yet, you're making yourself available to another man, a stranger at best. I just don't get it."

"Oh, Mal, lighten up. Nobody loses here. I get some laughs and a few nice dinners out of this."

The next evening Blaine Courtman and entourage were seated in one of the boxes. They were an attractive group. The women were trendy in the latest fashions and the men looked like models in *Gentleman's Quarterly*.

"Hey, Pat, if your admirer is the tall, dark and handsome job in house left box, can I take a crack at him?" Jonas was at full attention.

"His name is Blaine and he's taking me out to his yacht after the show."

"No shit? Hell, some girls have all the luck!" Pat caught Mally.

"Blaine enjoyed meeting you and Griff."

Mally walked into the dark room and reached for the light following the show. Dropping her bag, she lay across her bed and dialed Griff.

"Darling, how are you? Last night on the beach was incredible."

"Yes, it was," Mally said absently.

"What's wrong?"

"I am a little concerned. Blaine Courtman is smitten with Pat."

"Well, he'd better hurry. We leave on Sunday."

"No, you don't understand. He's after Pat. He's a millionaire many times over."

"What does he do?"

"He manufactures shoes. He's a very rich stage door Johnny."

Griff laughed. "I thought stage door Johnnies pursue only chorus boys these days. Let Pat sort this out, OK? I've got to make some changes for Memphis next week. Our equipment will be challenged. I'll call later. I love you."

"I love you too."

Chapter 24

The Suitor

The sea was bright glass under the full moon as Blaine, Pat, and entourage arrived at the marina. Pat couldn't help noticing all the yachts moored along the way.

"Which one is yours?"

"Guess!"

"Over there?" Pat picked the biggest boat she could find.

"Voila," shouted Blaine. While he led her up the gangway, Pat counted four decks. They entered an enormous salon.

It was evident that Blaine had impeccable taste and the money to indulge it. The room was appointed in dramatic colors and a select mix of fabrics done in detailed floral patterns. His choice of colors included merlot, mauve, navy blue and deep green shades. Fresh blooms in the finest candle-lit crystal vases were intoxicating to the senses. A sprawling Persian rug tied the whole scene together. Nearby, a pianist played softly. Blaine escorted Pat to a well-stocked bar.

"What would you like?"

"White wine," said Pat, still stunned by the elegance around her. The others in Blaine's party ordered cocktails. Blaine selected a gin martini and settled back to admire his date. His pals Johnny and Rod regarded Pat with great interest. Their dates, Madeline and Camille did not. Pat, aware of the other women's cold stares, made light of it.

Pat was high by the third glass of wine. Blaine suggested they dine as it was getting late. 'It's a good thing I can dance this off,' thought Pat, as she perused the lavish repast. A buffet table, the length of the room, was covered in white linen. An enormous ice sculpture of Neptune stood on display. Fresh flowers surrounded it, as long tapers held by silver candelabras flickered in the air conditioning. The presentation of food was stunning.

A chef stood by prepared to carve fresh ham, turkey and prime rib. Many varieties of potatoes, fresh vegetables, salads and a selection of breads added to the overflowing buffet. Flourless dark chocolate cake and petit fours were among the desserts.

Famished, Pat filled her plate, selecting a rare piece of prime rib to top it off. She was in desperate need of protein at this point. She selected a comfy chair and began eating. The others joined her.

"Pat, how can you eat like that?"

"I dance."

"There's another way to burn calories," intoned Camille, forking a bit of lobster into her mouth and moving her tongue deliberately over it.

"Oh, fucking? Well, that works, too."

Blaine took over immediately. "Let's dance after dinner," he remarked carefully.

The food had restored Pat's energy. "I'm ready for dessert! Got any-thing yummy?" She ignored Madeline and Camille as she walked by. A steward poured coffee. There was little conversation for the remainder of the meal.

"Say, let's take Pat's advice. The dance floor is down the deck," suggested Blaine. A few doors away a jazz trio sat ready. As the lights lowered and the music began, Blaine took Pat in his arms. The melody was languid and romantic. The others joined in.

Blaine held Pat close, his warm breath caressing her cheek. She caught traces of his exotic cologne as he glided and guided her to perfection.

"You're beautiful, Patricia, and you're fabulous on stage!"

"Thank you. Dancing's a lot of work. Some performances are easier than others, and some of the nights, too. Traveling gets lonely." Blaine moved closer.

"I can fix that." Leaning down, he kissed her softly. His tongue felt sensuous as it caressed her lips. Pat grew excited as Blaine moved down her neck, tracing a path with his mouth. Her audible sigh drew him closer. Pat felt a hand on her breast and froze. "Don't!" Blaine stopped briefly, resuming more fervently seconds later.

"I said, don't!" The others stopped dancing. Blaine, now visibly shaken, motioned his friends to step out. The musicians stopped play-ing and politely left the room. Blaine turned to Pat, holding his temper.

"I thought you expected this."

"Well, you thought wrong," said Pat, indignantly. "Do you think drinks and dinner aboard your luxury yacht requires sex in return?"

"I apologize."

"I want to go!"

"All right, if you insist." Blaine walked Pat to the deck and down the gangway. Signaling his limo driver, he turned to Pat and took her hands.

"Patricia, I assumed you were a swinger. I was wrong," he said softly. Pat pulled away.

"Good night Blaine," she said, stiffly. Blaine helped her into the back seat.

"Jack, please take Miss Byrne to the Carlyle. Please excuse me Patricia, I must return to my other guests. Goodnight." As the car pulled away, Pat watched Blaine ascend the gangway. En route she replayed each moment of her evening with him. She liked his attention until he got too familiar. Besides, she was in love with Owen. 'This is confusing,' she thought. Jack pulled up in front of the Carlyle and helped Pat out of the car. As the limousine pulled away, Jonas and Gary approached.

"Pat! What in hell?"

"Do you like the wheels?"

"His?"

"Yes." The three entered the hotel.

"What happened? You're back kind of early," goaded Jonas.

"He pounced."

"Yes! Details, please."

"Jonas, ease up!"

"You're going to see him again aren't you?"

"No."

"Patricia, you've flipped," chided Jonas. "I would take every inch of him and then some!"

"Well that's you kiddo." The discussion ended at the elevator.

Slipping into the dark room, Pat prepared for bed. Lying there, she thought about Blaine. A moment later, she thought about Owen. Was he really the reason for her hesitancy? The bluntness of her response to Blaine's overture now surprised even her. She felt needy, confused. She fell asleep fitfully.

Morning brought a ringing telephone. Fighting the daylight, Pat yawned as she picked up the receiver.

"Hello Patricia, this is Blaine." He paused. "I want to see you again."

"Well, Blaine, I . . ." He cut her off.

"Please, Pat. I would like another chance," he insisted. I understand you'll be in Miami starting the first of December."

"Yes."

"Great! I'll see you then. Take care of yourself." Pat hung up the phone and lay motionless as the door opened.

"Hi, Mal, where have you been?"

"I had breakfast with Griff. How did it go?"

"Mr. Courtman tried to seduce me, but I shook him off. He apologized. I left thinking that was the end of it. He just called as though nothing happened. He wants to see me again."

"I think we should head for the theatre, don't you? Want to grab breakfast?" Pat nodded. Once she showered and dressed, the girls were off for the day.

At the theatre the cast prepared for the matinee. The dressing rooms were buzzing. "Fifteen minutes, please," announced Griff, cutting over the chatter. A sudden rap at the door brought the women's voices down. A stagehand stood with a large package.

"Patricia Byrne?" Pat accepted the package and carried it to her spot. Puzzled, she peeled back the paper, revealing two-dozen yellow roses. Whispers crossed the room. She spotted a card and opened it carefully. 'Have a beautiful day, Miss Byrne. Yours, Blaine.' She showed the contents to Mally, resuming her make-up. Around them, chatter returned to full volume. Matinee time was fast approaching.

Chapter 25

Jackie

The dancers were dripping and spent as the matinee concluded. Two and a half hours of energized, focused, intense performing, left the gypsies ready for a much-needed break between shows.

Jackie returned to the dressing room and collapsed in her chair, sheer exhaustion overwhelming her. She removed her make-up in a trance as others came in. Minutes passed. Pat redid her chignon left straggled by the performance. As she looked up she noticed Jackie's cold, hard stare in the mirror.

"Well, well, aren't we the debutante," said Jackie, indicating the roses at Pat's make-up area.

Pat remained silent.

"God, don't you have enough men? How many does this make?"

"Lay off, Jackie," Dana said, firmly.

"Stay out of this Dana," warned Jackie.

"Come on, simmer down," Dana said, calmly standing up. Mally hurried out of the dressing room and spotted Griff locking a prop box.

"Griff, please follow me. I think there's a fight brewing!" As he entered the dressing room Dana was standing between Jackie and Pat.

"All right, what's going on in my theatre?"

"Griff, Jackie started it. She has it in for Pat. Ask anybody," declared Dana.

"Fuck off, Dana!"

"Here now, cut the language," said Griff. "Well, Jackie?"

"I have nothing to say, Edwards."

"Well, Miss Eldridge, there are rules in my company. The next time you cause any dissention whatsoever, you will receive a warning. If you continue, you will be fired and brought up on charges at Equity, end of story," he snapped.

There was tension in the silence that remained after Griff's exit. Jackie sat staring stonily in the mirror as the other women changed from costumes to street clothes. Mally, Pat, and Dana left the theatre together.

"Jackie's got a constant mad-on," said Pat, as they walked up the street. "Dana, you've worked with her. What's her story anyway?"

"Do you girls have time for a bite? Dick has to work with Griff between shows. He's going to call the show on Saturday afternoon." They spotted an Italian restaurant on the corner.

"I'm famished! Bring on the pasta," declared Pat.

"Can you believe that one's body? It's not fair," said Dana, winking.

Settling in a large booth, they looked over menus, promptly brought by a waiter. They decided to share a carafe of wine with their order and Pat poured. When their glasses were filled, Pat raised her glass.

"To peace," led Pat. "To peace," they chanted, taking sips. "Ok, Dana, spill about Jackie. What's her deal?"

"Well, I met Jackie years ago when I first came to New York. What a dancer! A young, brilliantly talented choreographer hired her. Guess who?" Dana sipped her wine slowly.

"Owen carried on with her, developed her and eventually dumped her. Jackie was totally humiliated and became bitter. She's still trying to survive in a business where youth, looks and talent are paramount."

"Well, this explains a lot," said Pat, turning her glass in place on the table. "I'm a painful reminder of the past." The food arrived and they ate enthusiastically, Jackie forgotten for the moment.

"I guess there's a lesson here, ladies. Stick with your principles and learn to type," cracked Dana.

The theatre was humming. The cast was still warmed up from the matinee. Mally ran into Jonas, his pout noticeable.

"What's wrong, Jonas?"

"Gary's pissed. He caught me coming on to a guy in the bar last night and now he's all bent out of shape. Together ten years and we still don't live on the same page."

"What do you mean?"

"We have different sexual needs."

"I find gay life confusing."

"Why?"

"I don't understand your open relationships."

"It's the beast, Mal. Our dicks are perpetually hard! We're impossible to satisfy! Say, how's your honey?"

"Satisfied, thanks."

"Touche', Sweetie. See you on stage." Mally came to a dead halt at the top of the stairs. Jackie and Sonja looked engaged in a conspiratorial chat. Ducking into the ladies' room and cracking the door, she listened.

"I'm going to get that bitch Patricia Byrne."

"You are? How?"

"When I decide how, you'll be the first to know, Sonja."

Mally felt a chill as she quietly slipped back into the dressing room. Changing into her first act costume, she gave her hair a final flip just as she heard Griff call places. On the way to the stage she fell in step with Chuck Mason.

"How's it going, Chuck?"

"I miss my girl in Philly."

"Can she visit?"

"Right now she's in her first year of college and pretty serious about her grades. I'm going to try and persuade her to come for Christmas."

Bravo Business was Chuck's first big show. His enthusiasm and boyish candor made him prey to sarcasm from the older, cynical gypsies. He was straight and a natural flirt. Well-built and cute, he was attractive to the company's women and men. Entering the dressing area at a dizzying pace, he crashed into Gary, who was bent over, tying a shoelace.

"Look where you're going, pup," snapped Gary.

"Sorry." Chuck changed out of his suit, handing his pants to a dresser. Wearing only his dance belt, he was unaware of being watched.

"Hey, Chuckles, care to hide the stick?" Chuck blushed.

"Guys, knock it off," said Chad, coming to Chuck's defense. Jim Sorenson, a bi-sexual, joined in.

"Leave the kid alone, OK?"

"Protecting the little straight lad, are we, Jim?" Jerry Thompson rounded out the gay men.

"Oh, fuck you, Jerry," Jim returned.

"Ok! And while we're at it, let's invite Chuckles!"

Dick Landry was the seventh male dancer and the only married man in the ensemble. He ignored the catty chorus boy talk, focusing instead on his goal of stage management. Griff saw Dick's potential and encouraged him to learn the technical side.

With a mix of relief and puzzlement Pat continued to wonder about Blaine. As she passed through the hotel lobby between shows, she heard her name.

"Pat, you won't believe this. Look," Mally said, pointing to a small TV set mounted on the bar. A newscaster repeatedly referred to Blaine in his report. A photo flashed on the screen as details were read.

"Blaine Courtman, the wealthy philanthropist and CEO of Courtman Enterprises, is on the move again. Four more industrial sites are being considered in Montreal, Seattle, Houston and Boston. A formal announcement will be made later this month."

"He has more money than Queen Elizabeth," mused Pat. "Imagine!" Mally could only wonder what Blaine Courtman's next move would be. "Yes, imagine!"

Chapter 26

Memphis, Tennessee

The train bound for Memphis lurched and wove through the Florida landscape leaving Jacksonville in the distance as it picked up speed. The moving landscape changed from palm trees to pine as the train rolled west.

Pat was preoccupied. Blaine was attractive, wildly rich and lived a lifestyle only found in novels. His attempt to seduce her had put her off at first, but now she toyed with the idea of giving him another chance.

Was an affair with Blaine worth the risk? What about Owen? He was currently focused on his new project in New York. How could she be that important to him? She tossed for hours, her old insecurities surfacing into a knot of mental confusion. Shortly before six pm she woke with a start.

"Pat, are you in there? Are you hungry?"

"I'm starved!"

"Well then, let's go!"

The glowing light of dusk was beginning to color the world outside as the girls made their way to the dining car. The sudden increase in noise was startling as they crossed between cars. The train bed below was a blur of dirt and pebbles, hitting the metal platform beneath their feet. Intermittent bursts of warm air rose from below. Weaving like two drunken sailors they passed through each car, grasping the backs of seats for support. Reaching the dining car, they were seated right away. It was still early and pleasantly quiet.

Tables were set with white linens, crystal glasses, silver setups and small arrangements of fresh flowers in tidy vases. Waiters in white coats moved down the aisle smoothly like sailors who'd found their sea legs. Pat spotted Jonas and Gary entering the far end of the car waving. Pat returned a wave. The boys joined them.

A tall, pleasant waiter approached. The menu was simple—a choice of two appetizers, two entrees, a beverage and dessert. The group ordered and settled into conversation.

"Tell us about Memphis," Mally insisted, with the tone of curiosity.

"Yes, please," urged Pat.

"The Peabody Hotel ducks are a sight," said Jonas. "They live on the roof of the hotel and every morning and every afternoon they are brought down on the elevator. A red carpet is rolled to a fountain in the bar lobby. The ducks waddle over to the pond and swim. People come from all over to see them."

"You're kidding!"

"No, no, it's true," added Gary, smiling. The arrival of dinner interrupted any further talk of ducks. The food was surprisingly good, and once they had eaten, the group broke up for the night.

Mally locked the sliding door of her compartment and pulled the shade. She undressed, washed her face, and brushed her teeth. When she was ready, she pulled her bed from the wall. As she sank into the welcome comfort of fresh sheets and the soft pillow cupping her head, she thought of Griff. She eased into a deep sleep.

"Memphis, Tennessee is next, half hour to Memphis." Pat woke with a start as she heard the voice of the conductor beyond her door. She was just finishing dressing when she heard a knock.

"Good morning, Miss Byrne!"

"Mal, bring it down. You're much too chirpy." The girls felt the train jerk as it came to an abrupt stop. Finding their way to the exit, they joined other company members on the platform.

Griff arranged for Mally to have her trunk brought to his hotel. Pat encouraged her to spend the week with Griff, feeling the need to be alone. The girls hugged and boarded separate buses.

Mally noticed trees laden with hanging moss creating a sense of calm and cleanliness on the drive to the hotel. The air was cool, dry, and pleasantly scented by flowers planted along the boulevards.

Mally arrived at Griff's hotel and introduced herself to the concierge, who discreetly handed her an envelope containing a key. The

Barleycorn was a well-appointed hotel overlooking the Mississippi. The gracious staff took care of every request down to the smallest detail.

Mally couldn't believe the large arrangement of roses, lilies, carnations and gladiolas in various shades of her favorite color, pink, as she walked into the suite. The mix of fragrances delighted her senses as she explored the two rooms, done in tones of mauve, purple, and rose to match the drapes and the flowers. Griff thought of everything, insisting on the best the hotel offered, down to the smallest detail.

Near the large canopy bed, a silver bucket held a bottle of champagne on ice, accompanied by a box of chocolate truffles. Large throw pillows lay piled at the head of the bed and a goose down comforter lay draped at the foot. A fireplace across from the bed was the topper.

Mally lay back and looked around. 'How did I ever attract a man like Griff Edwards?' While contemplating her miracle the phone rang.

"Welcome to Memphis, Darling!. Do you find everything to your satisfaction?"

"Gee, I don't know," she giggled. "It's perfect! How are you doing?"

"We're setting up and tight for time. I doubt that I'll get back before the show. I'll catch up with you tonight. Love you!"

The show was sold out all week. Memphis was a big convention town and management expected capacity audiences dominated by visitors. *Bravo Business* sprang into high throttle, bringing a high pitch of energy to delighted crowds.

Chapter 27

Tragedy

They were relaxed and looking forward to a day of sightseeing. It was Friday, November 22nd. As Griff took a swig of coffee, he glanced around the room. Putting his cup down, he looked over at Mally.

"There's something going on."

"What do you mean?"

"Take a closer look." Some customers appeared to be upset, some crying. At the cashier's counter a radio was blasting, an audible undercurrent of distress, but indistinguishable to them. A waiter approached wiping tears from his eyes.

"What's happened?"

"Someone just shot the president in Dallas." Griff grabbed the check and headed to the cashier, with Mally at his heels. From the radio above the checkout, an announcer blasted details.

"John Fitzgerald Kennedy was shot moments ago, as he rode in his motorcade with first lady Jacqueline Kennedy. He is being rushed to Parkland Hospital in Dallas with Mrs. Kennedy at his side. No further details are available at this time."

Mally and Griff stepped outside into a gray wash of mist and drizzle. Friday, November 22, 1963, was suddenly horrific and incomprehensible.

Together they walked through an open door of a bank, minimally staffed. Those on hand stood riveted watching a small TV in a corner. It was unsettling to see a replay of JFK stepping off Air Force One with Jackie at his side. Jackie was impeccably dressed in a stunning pink suit and hat, carrying a bouquet of roses, the perfect picture of grace and style. Her handsome husband stilled the world with a mere wave of his hand. The news repeated over and over.

Walter Cronkite, fighting tears, announced, "From Dallas, Texas, the flash, apparently official; President Kennedy died at one p.m. central standard time, two o'clock eastern standard time, some thirty-eight minutes ago."

"Oh my God," cried Mally, unable to control her sobs as she clung to Griff.

"Come on, let's get out of here." The rain was heavy now as they ran down the street looking for shelter. Minutes passed as they paused under an awning.

"Let's get to a dry room and a TV," Griff said. "I must phone New York."

Following arrival at the hotel, Griff turned on the TV. The networks repeated footage of the president and first lady's arrival in Dallas. Newscasters Cronkite, Huntley and Brinkley, and Severeid continually updated viewers.

Now a darker vision took over. A color guard appeared carrying the flag-draped coffin of JFK, placing it on Air Force One. Jackie followed close behind.

Tireless announcers asked the same questions over and over, "Who is the shooter? Is there more than one?" The F.B.I. claimed responsibility fell on "a single assailant, acting alone." Griff dialed New York.

"This is Griff Edwards. Please put me through to Mr. Lehrman." Griff waited, watching the news images. A voice broke through.

"Hello, Griff."

"Vinny, I'm calling from Memphis."

"Yes, I know. How are your numbers for tonight?"

"We're sold out."

"Good. I want the show to go on as usual. Clear?"

"I'll inform the company, Vinny. Thanks." Griff returned to the sofa and sank into it.

"Griff, they found a suspect who may have shot the president. They are questioning him now. His name is Lee Harvey Oswald. They picked him up in a movie theatre in Dallas. What did Mr. Lehrman say?"

"I'm calling a show tonight."

"You're kidding!"

Vinny is practical. He has four hits running simultaneously. Broadway is dark tonight. He'll take a bath."

"But Griff, we're just one of many national companies out on the road!"

"We're the largest single grossing tour in the country. He's trying to save his ass."

Mally decided to go to the theatre early to collect her thoughts and do a long warm-up. As she walked she noticed several storefronts draped in black fabric displaying photos of JFK. At the courthouse the flag hung at half-staff.

The mood at the theatre was solemn as crew and cast began preparing for a performance. Mally found Pat silent and distraught. The other women sat quietly. Only Jackie could be heard.

"Oh, for the love of whatever, lighten up. The audience needs distraction tonight," said Jackie.

"Cast, report to the green room at five minutes," announced Griff. They gathered looking like condemned prisoners.

"Company, I'm reminding you that tonight's audience deserves the same high energy and precision you have given all week. We're paid professionals. Let's behave accordingly. Thank you."

During the opening number, the chorus was choreographed to surround a coffee urn and beat on it, showing collected agony for the lack of caffeine. The more the ensemble shook fists, the more emotion released. The response out front was deafening.

Following two shows on Saturday Bravo Business packed up and loaded out. There had been no time for the famed Peabody ducks or some good blues music. The assassination was too large and too personal even for Beale Street to deal with.

Chapter 28

Atlanta, Georgia

"Hey, Dick. Getting settled?" Mally and Pat spotted Dick Landry as they sought their Pullmans.

"I'm trying to distract Dana, so I've sent her to order breakfast. Atlanta's her hometown and she's excited. As a matter-of-fact, I'm kind of excited too. Dana's clan is great. They love the fact that she married a Yankee boy."

The girls met for lunch after a relaxing morning. Chad entered the car at the far end and spotting the girls, approached.

"Hey, kids. You know that Oswald guy who supposedly killed JFK? He was shot dead by a guy named Jack Ruby, kind of a hood they say."

"Good God," exclaimed Pat. The noise level changed as Chad opened the door and exited the car.

"Maybe we should eat." After ordering lunch, the girls stared out the window in silence. Pat played with the cutlery.

"Is the world going mad?"

"Yes," said Mally, sadly. When their orders arrived they ate without enthusiasm.

"I'm going back to my compartment. I'm sick and tired of all this news. I'll see you later, said Pat, wearily.

The train traveled across Tennessee and on into Georgia, heading to Atlanta. Through the raindrops meandering down the windows, one could see tree trunks imprisoned by heavy vines. As the miles clicked by, the rural landscape changed to urban sights. The train swayed and tooted at each crossing as Atlanta came into view. Porters announced the arrival up and down aisles as cast members gathered and waited. After boarding chartered buses, the gypsies opened windows, allowing the humid air in.

Atlanta was surprising. In addition to stately mansions, manicured lawns and moss-covered trees, reminiscent of *Gone With The Wind*, a more poignant scene was evident. Care-worn people disenfranchised by immense poverty sat on stoops in front of dilapidated buildings. Young children played in trash-filled gutters, while the homeless picked for food in garbage receptacles as they wandered aimlessly.

The bus pulled up in a section of town untouched by the marginal survival witnessed minutes before. Griff had recommended a charming hotel. Flower-covered vines wound around pillars on the veranda. Antique rockers stood in a row by the front entrance. The lobby was furnished with green velvet upholstered settees. A small, glistening fountain stood prominently at the center of a courtyard. Pat smiled at the obvious ambience. "The only thing missing is Rhett Butler."

Pat was oblivious to everything as she let the soothing stream flow over her tired, stiff limbs.

When she finished, she turned off the faucet and stepped out. As she dried herself she looked in the mirror and ran her hands over the parts of her body Owen explored. The memory excited her. Peering out the bathroom door she heard little snoring sounds erupting from her roommate. Pat's wet hair dripped on the carpet as she crossed the room and reached for a ringing phone.

"Hi, Pat."

"Griff, hang on, she's right here." Pat nudged Mally.

"Hi Darling, how about a nice, romantic dinner tonight?"

"Oh yes!"

"I'll pick you up at seven."

Pat changed into jeans and a turtleneck. Even in casual clothes she was a stunner. "You look refreshed. I like your hair in a ponytail."

"Well, I'm exploring tonight. Dana gave me a list of some of the better clubs in town. I've persuaded Jonas and Gary to be my dates."

"Please, be careful."

"Mal, don't mother me, OK?" She dialed Jonas.

"Hey tart, you ready?"

"Yes, Patricia. Did you wash your privates?"

"I'm not going to dignify your question, you fruitcake! I'll meet you by the fountain." Then a new thought occurred. "Jonas?"

"Yes?"

"No Esther Williams stuff, Ok?"

"You bitch!"

"It's Owen. Is Pat in?"

"You just missed her, Owen. Can I give her a message?"

"I'm coming to Atlanta this coming weekend. Don't say a word, OK? I want to surprise her."

"OK, Owen. Thanks for calling." Mally sat lost in thought. She imagined Pat's delight at seeing Owen. 'Maybe he really cares,' she thought. 'One can hope.'

Stepping into the shower, the warm rush of water enveloped her. Washing hair felt terrific under the warm stream. Her skin felt slippery and soft to the touch. She thought about Griff. As the soap and water ran to the drain, she breathed quickly, producing her orgasm. When the ache had subsided she stepped from the tub.

Selecting a wool jersey dress with a soft collar and flared skirt was perfect. After doing her make-up and hair, she added a touch of cologne, looked in the mirror once more and turned out the room light.

Occasional murmurs from the front desk help were barely heard over the fountain in the courtyard.

"May I have this evening?" Griff was the picture of Madison Avenue sophistication in a dark blue suit. He lifted her up. Pressing his lips softly on hers he lingered, admiring the view.

"You look absolutely stunning."

"You look pretty snazzy yourself." The air was sultry as they got into the backseat of a waiting cab.

André's four-star restaurant perched on top of Atlanta's tallest building. Patrons traveled by private elevator on the outside of the building.

"Good evening, Mr. Edwards. Your table is ready sir."

"Karl, this is my guest, Miss Winthrop. This is her first visit to André's."

"How do you do? Please follow me." Their intimate corner table had an expansive view of the city. Atlanta was thrilling at night. Griff ordered a bottle of champagne. Choosing the house specialty—Chilean

Sea Bass and André's signature Caesar salad followed. A waiter opened the champagne and filled their glasses. Griff raised his.

"I love you, my darling Mally."

"I love you too, Griff!"

Following dinner a small combo set up near the dance floor. As the music drifted across the room, Griff lead Mally to the floor, enfolding her in his arms.

"You're dancing beautifully, Griff."

"And you're leading," he whispered.

"Oops," she giggled. After a romantic spin around the floor Griff picked up the check and suggested a cab ride back to the hotel. As they rode through the humid evening, Griff held Mally close, grateful to have her near.

Across town, business was picking up. Pat, Jonas and Gary and two other gypsies from the cast, Marcy White and Elaine Langston, partied at Daddy's Digs. They already had tossed off a couple of rounds and Gary was feeling no pain.

"I'm going to boogie," he announced, weaving as he stood.

"I'll dance with you, big boy," shouted Elaine, pulling Gary out to the dance floor. Through the noise and smoke they found a spot on the dance floor and started moving to the beat. Pat and Jonas joined in. Before long they were attracting a crowd, who egged them on.

Marcy sat alone. The throbbing in her ears and the beat of the music only intensified her longing to join in. Through the smoke she saw a stunner of a man approaching. He was dark and lean, wearing a cut off tee shirt that revealed a washboard of muscle above his belt. His skin-tight jeans looked painted on his beautifully sculpted legs, but it was his enormous package that taunted and teased. Marcy liked the view.

"Hi, and you are?"

"Marcy."

"Phillipe. Come with me."

Boldly taking her by the hand, he walked her to the dance floor and pulled her close. 'Oh my God, he's sexy," Marcy thought. His moves were erotic and encouraging. Marcy did little to resist. She felt herself turning on with each grinding move.

"You're quite the dancer," she sighed, pressing closer.

"Thanks. I'm a stripper."

"Ah, come on!"

"No kidding," flipped the handsome stranger. "I work at the best strip bar in town."

"Sounds intriguing," added Marcy.

"You're here with friends, right? I'd like to meet them." A wave of disappointment came over Marcy. She had hoped for a private party, but it was more than obvious that she was not in Phillipe's game plan. 'He must be gay and very naughty,' she thought.

Jonas, Gary and the other women trouped back to the table, hot, sweaty, and exhilarated. Marcy quickly made introductions. The group sat down to cool off.

"My club has a late show. Would you care to join me?" It was unanimous except for Gary, who was quietly slipping into the background.

"Oh my God, Gary, be careful," Pat shouted, over the din. Gary tried to stand, but fell back into the chair.

"Come on, Hon, let's take a walk," coaxed Jonas. Gently lifting Gary to his feet he enlisted Phillipe's help to the men's room.

Entering the nearest stall, Gary fell to his knees and threw up, gagging. Jonas held him firm. Reaching for some toilet tissue he wiped Gary's face and shirt. Gary clung to him, whimpering.

"Sweetheart, let's get you a cab." Ordering the driver to take Gary to the Allerton, he bent down and gently kissed him on the cheek. "Have the concierge assist you to the room, OK?" Gary nodded weakly. The cab pulled away.

Meanwhile, Pat, Elaine and Marcy caught up to Jonas and Phillipe. A walk to the club would feel good. The night air engulfed them with fragrant humidity.

Hot Crossed Buns, was packed. The large room had a platform at the center with a huge cage hanging overhead. All around the perimeter of the stage customers drank and laughed. A large bar at the end of the room had a full-length mirror reflecting the room's mass of bodies moving through thickets of smoke. Phillipe and his new acquaintances were shown to a front table. A young, well-built waiter approached.

"Slumming tonight, Phillipe?"

"Larry, these are my guests. We'll have champagne all around." Phillipe noticed his new companions' interest in the surroundings. "You are going to see things here you don't see in other clubs," he remarked casually. He caught Jonas looking him over. The champagne arrived and Phillipe filled their glasses. "Welcome to Atlanta," he toasted.

A spotlight appeared on a tuxedoed announcer. Welcoming the crowd, he disappeared through the darkness as music began. Six men entered dressed in suits. Jonas giggled watching each man remove his clothing, a piece at a time. Pants were the last to come off revealing firm and fit bodies in thongs. Jonas stared at all the eye candy as the men undulated.

"Jonas, you're drooling," giggled Pat, returning her attention to the stage.

At that moment, Phillipe leaned in and whispered, "Do you like the show, Cheri?" Jonas felt a hand on his leg, and fingers moving along his inner thigh felt fabulous. The action stopped short of his crotch. 'Damn, I've got a hard-on,' he thought. Distracting himself from his growing horniness he turned his attention back to the stage just as the number had finished.

"I think we should have that number in the show," he said, casually. The applause died down as the announcer returned.

"Ladies and gentlemen, Hot Crossed Buns is proud to present the one and only Jeanine Taylor!" A single spot hit center stage, revealing a statuesque blonde wrapped in a full-length mink cape.

"She's extraordinary," sighed Pat.

"Wait," Phillipe whispered.

Jeanine Taylor's rich voice cut a swath through the crowd holding them with her sultry moves and throaty renditions of standards. She descended the stairs, interacting with the crowd along the stage. At the end of her number the audience went wild. When the clamor wore thin a drum riff began.

The six dancing men returned clad in g-strings, their well-toned bodies oiled. One held Jeanine's mic as the others removed her cape, revealing her exquisite body. Scantily clad in the briefest bikini, her exquisitely long legs brought gasps.

Moving across the stage, she sang *Old Devil Moon*, the men following. From above, the cage slowly descended. Inside, a well-built man in a thong knelt, his hands bound. He was brought out and placed at Jeanine's feet.

A mating dance of sorts began as Jeanine undulated, swayed, and moved explicitly to the percussive beat. The audience sat mesmerized as she teased and caressed her captive. Building to an erotic finish and final pose, there was silence, then wild applause. Jeanine, her partner, and the chorus men all graciously accepted the ovation. Left to take a solo bow, she blew kisses to the crowd. Slowly she reached up and pulled off her wig. A mature, dark-haired man stood before them. The crowd gasped collectively. A baritone voice boomed over the throng.

"Thank you all for coming. You've been a fabulous audience. Come back and see us soon," he said, waving on his exit.

"He is one of the top drag queens in the world," said Phillipe, proudly. Would you care to meet him?" Everyone nodded. Jonas watched Phillipe as he left the table. 'This guy is so sexy, so gorgeous. I just have to have sex with him,' he thought. Minutes passed. Phillipe returned with Jeanine Taylor.

"This is Johnny La Mont," announced Phillipe. "Johnny insists on buying a final round." As the gypsies enjoyed their drinks, Johnny held them captive with stories of his unique career. Later, the girls excused themselves, thanking Phillipe for a great evening. Jonas remained, quietly listening to Phillipe and Johnny's conversation. Would he see Phillipe again?

"It's been fabulous. Thanks for a great show, Johnny," he said, rising. He turned to Phillipe.

"If you're interested in catching our show I can arrange house seats. You can reach me at the Allerton, room 415."

"I'll keep it in mind," Phillipe said, adding a wink. Jonas hailed a cab. As he rode back to the hotel he thought about Phillipe. He just had to have him.

At the Danby, Mally and Griff settled in, enjoying the comforts of a cozy fire. He offered her a brandy and she took it, allowing the warmth of its texture to permeate her mouth. The phone rang.

"My God, who is that?" Puzzled, Griff took the call, returning his attention to her.

"That was Vinny. We'll be dark tomorrow night in deference to JFK. I'll notify the company, crew, and orchestra. The audience will be refunded."

Griff needed a break from business and the media bombardment of the past few days. He thought about the late president. How he wished he could turn back the clock.

Chapter 29

Fateful Morning

Mally woke up and noticed Griff about to leave. "Where are you going? There's no show tonight."

"I know, but ironically, it's a break for us. The Viscount is a complex old theatre with a small backstage area. I want to get over there to assess any possible problems," he said, tucking his shirt into his jeans.

"You love it," declared Mally as Griff reached for her playfully, planting a kiss on her nose.

"Yes, but I love you more. Say, why not order room service? The funeral starts at 10:00 on all three networks."

Mally moved slowly to the bathroom and turned on the tap. The cold water felt refreshing as she rinsed away traces of sleep. Back in the bedroom she picked up the phone. 'Hot oatmeal, raisins, brown sugar and cream with a hot tea chaser sounds good,' she thought to herself. "This is Room 518. I'd like to order breakfast."

Coverage of the president's funeral had started. The endless image of the rider-less horse, boot backward in the stirrup, was seen. Jackie, her children, Bobby and Ted Kennedy stood by, as the flag-draped coffin of the late president passed on caisson. Little John-John, the president's young son, saluted his father. There was a knock. A bellman arrived with breakfast. He handed her a bill. "Thank you so much."

Returning to TV she was struck by the funeral procession entering Arlington National Cemetery.

"How odd," she thought. "I'm watching the first performance of a scene that will play for lifetimes. And I'm eating oatmeal!" Taking the last few bites she watched the closing coverage and turned off the set. Glancing at the clock she realized that it was close to noon.

Mally moved quickly through her shower and dressing. She'd surprise Griff by bringing lunch, knowing his tendency to skip meals while working. Throwing on a pair of jeans and a sweatshirt, she pulled her hair back into a bandana and slipped on loafers.

In no time she was walking in the direction to the Viscount Theatre. While waiting at the light, she spotted Jonas entering a diner with a man she didn't recognize. Quickening her pace, she crossed the street and stepped inside. Jonas waved from a corner booth when he saw her.

Mally leaned down and kissed Jonas before turning her attention to his friend.

"Mal, I'd like you to meet Phillipe Danier."

"Hello. May I?" He moved over to allow her to sit down. "How do you like Atlanta?"

"Very much from all I've seen. You should see our show."

"I'd love to. I have always admired Broadway dancing," said Phillipe.

"Phillipe and I met at a dance club. He's quite the dancer," added Jonas. "He showed me some amazing moves." Mally saw a smile pass between Jonas and Phillipe. Deciding she had intruded enough, she rose.

"I better get going. I have to order take-out. It's nice to meet you. Stop back when you come to the show, OK? See you, Jonas."

"What an attractive woman," Phillipe mused, watching Mally walk away.

"Isn't she adorable?" Jonas reached across the table, touching Phillipe.

"I had a great time."

"Yes. Let's order. You'll need even more energy tonight."

Jonas blushed remembering their hot sex. Phillipe had called early, inviting Jonas to his apartment. They carried on all morning. Something about Phillipe compelled Jonas. He was commanding, stunning to look at, and sensual. He was perfect.

In the past—before Gary—Jonas had always sought the quick fix to his on-going horniness. He favored intense sex, no romance, and no repeats. Once he had his fill he moved on quickly and without regret. He maintained this attitude and insisted on it from his tricks.

"Cheri, meet me at the club tonight about eleven. I have a late show. I'll reserve a table for you." Phillipe walked to the register, paid the bill, and left. Jonas remained to finish his coffee and think.

Gary had been his partner for the past ten years. His ability to tolerate Jonas' liaisons had kept them together. He was deeply in love with Jonas. Lost in the past, Jonas remembered their first encounter.

Chapter 30

Gary

It was a trying audition. Typing the men would have saved time, and narrowed the field of dancers vying for a job. Management had not extended that courtesy. Jonas' energy was waning.

"Damn it," he hissed. Stubbing his toe, while going over the combination, didn't add to his mood. Sitting down, and removing his jazz shoe, he examined his toe for evidence of his fumble. Satisfied that nothing was permanently damaged, he rearranged his sock and put his shoe back on.

"Are you all right?" Jonas glanced up into a sweet face.

"Yeah, I'll survive," he muttered, without enthusiasm.

"Long audition. I was cut earlier."

"Oh? Well, I'm probably next."

"Good luck."

"Thanks."

Jonas heard his number and bolted for the stage. Dozens of men stood watching the competition going through a difficult ballet combination. The complicated leaps and turns would have challenged Nijinsky, the greatest male ballet dancer in history.

Jonas assumed his position, took a deep breath and took off whirling and jumping, his energy returning. When the music stopped his toe throbbed furiously as he stood gasping for air.

"Thank you. That will be all." Jonas left the stage, relieved that the torture had ended. He found his belongings and began dressing. Pulling his jeans up over his sweaty tights, he slipped a long sleeve tee shirt over his head. His chain was woven through the wet hair of his chest, rising and falling with every breath. Jazz shoes were replaced with loafers.

"That was quick. I'm Gary."

"Jonas."

"Yes, I know. I asked about you."

"Oh?"

"Do you want to go for coffee? It's a little early for beer."

"Sure."

It was a hot, muggy day, the air engulfing Manhattan in a thick, deadening fog. Jonas was refining an audition piece, dripping, as he moved through the rented space of the rehearsal studio. Sweat seeped through his tank top, tights and dance belt. He felt clammy and tired as he tried again and again to fit a combination together. Rewinding the music tape, he continued repeatedly, stubbornly. Stopping before the large mirror he looked past his reflection, and noticed Gary watching him intently.

"You're early."

"Yeah, my voice coach wasn't feeling well, so he cut the lesson short."

Gary was relaxed and able to take life as it unfolded. Jonas found his calm attractive, a quality he wished for. High strung and short on patience, being around Gary held his mercurial moods in check.

"I'm stuck. Nothing is going together," he complained.

"You want to have lunch?"

"Sure. I'll just be a few minutes. I'll meet you in the hall by the soda machine."

Showers were installed as a courtesy for those renting studios. Jonas slipped out of his workout clothes and stepped into the beckoning spray. As the water enveloped him, he reached for his shampoo, feeling instead a hand on his arm. Startled, he quickly turned to see Gary, nude.

"What the hell?"

"I was hot and sticky too, so I thought I'd join you." Before Jonas could respond Gary backed him into a corner and held him firm. He began stroking Jonas' buttocks as he kissed him. As his caresses became intense Jonas felt his arousal building. Mild-mannered Gary had disappeared for the moment, and a new man took over, one strong and dominating. Gary knelt and began stroking Jonas. As the water cascaded over them, he performed oral sex. 'God, he can do what ever he wants,' Jonas thought, feeling his climax close. His explosion was sudden, intense.

When Gary had finished he stood.

"Jonas, please do me!" He was breathless with want. Returning pleasure to Gary, Jonas stroked and played. Feeling Jonas' mouth around him, Gary writhed, begging for more, and soon climaxed. The shower had turned cool just as Jonas' daydream ended. Instead, Phillipe Danier replaced the image of Gary in Jonas' mind. Phillipe was all he could think about.

Chapter 31

Stripper Man

The Viscount was originally a vaudeville house, restored with attention to every detail of its gaudy, glorious past. Mally heard the shouts and clattering as she entered. From the wings she saw stagehands working, stage light fluctuating from full light to black and the sound of Griff's commanding voice. Boldly she stepped into the flood, squinting into the gloom of the house.

"Griff, is that you? I've brought lunch."

"Guys take a half hour." In moments Griff was hugging her.

"How's your day?"

"It's challenging. Some of the equipment is out of date, but I think we've taken care of it," said Griff, with assurance. Though he was obviously tired he ate with enthusiasm. Rolling his shoulders he settled into a slump.

"I have a remedy for that."

"Oh?"

"When you finish here come back to the hotel. I'll run you a hot bath and add a full body massage."

"You've sold me, Sweetheart!"

Jonas found the noise level deafening at Phillipe's club. A host led Jonas to a ringside table. Ordering a beer he had barely settled when the lights went to black. A searing trumpet blasted through the din.

At center stage a lone figure stood motionless. "Phillipe, Phillipe, Phillipe," the crowd chanted, as he began moving to a drum riff. The crowd clapped slowly to the sultry, suggestive moves. Phillipe was enticing, and explicit, calculated to please.

Dressed in a skin-tight jumpsuit, Phillipe reached down and slowly pulled the zipper, revealing a finely developed chest and stomach. Continuing, he showed just enough body to tease and hold the crowd. Unzipping much lower, he stopped. The crowd was suddenly silent. In one move, the rest of the costume tore away revealing his stunning body clad in a brief bikini.

The music suddenly changed, and Phillipe danced full out, no holds barred. His technique and style surprised Jonas. Phillipe wasn't just a stripper working for a few bucks in a cheap club. He was a finely tuned dance machine, as good as any. Phillipe's turns were strong, his adagio moves were fully extended, and he didn't hold back on the sell.

Keeping the best for last, Phillipe waited for the stage to darken save for a small spotlight on his face. Reaching each side of the bikini, he tugged, the piece falling a way. Playfully throwing the discarded item into the crowd, he disappeared during the blackout.

The crowd was frenzied. Phillipe reappeared as the lights came up, carefully robed to receive his fans. Bowing repeatedly, he thanked the audience. Spotting Jonas down front, he blew a kiss before exiting.

Jonas thought, 'a stripper who is an accomplished dancer!' He suddenly felt a hand on his shoulder.

"Cheri."

"You were incredible. I didn't know you could dance like that!"

"You never asked. Come on, let's get out of here." They walked in silence. "I'm taking you to the Hotel Danville. It's impressively old and infamous."

"Why?"

"I came out here," he said, softly. They entered the hotel and found a small bar. Phillipe ordered brandy and a beer for Jonas. Phillipe lifted his snifter. Jonas followed suit.

"I'd like to know more about you." Phillipe settled back, his eyes never leaving Jonas.

"Well, since you've asked, I have a colorful history, Cheri. I was born in the French Quarter of New Orleans. My mother was a prostitute and my father, a city official. When she got pregnant she wanted an abortion. He talked her out of it. He couldn't marry her or claim me as he was already married to the crème of society, but he did provide my mother with enough money, and so it went. Mother continued to turn tricks. When I was thirteen I ran away. I never saw her again. I heard she was murdered, possibly by one of her johns. The authorities never found her body." Jonas let out an audible gasp.

"So is the life of a hooker. Anyway, I ended up in Atlanta. I was waiting tables at the time. George Mathis spotted me. He was cultured, wealthy and liked pretty, young men. He was a very attractive older man. I guess I was curious, and very naive." Jonas was rapt.

"One night I agreed to meet him at this hotel. He ordered champagne, and when I was suitably pliable, he seduced me. I cooperated. I guess I always knew I was gay. George took me completely in hand after that night. He taught and gave me everything, and, in exchange, I gave myself totally to him. He kept me for five years before he ended it. I owe him a great deal." Jonas sat noticeably quiet as Phillipe continued.

"I have a current partner, André Glessier. We've been together a few years, but I suspect he wants out. So, I need to plan my future, alone. Would you recommend me to your management if a spot opens up?"

"It's a long shot that anyone will give notice, but yes, of course," Jonas said, encouraged by the notion.

"Thank you. I reserved a room. Let's go."

Chapter 32

Changes

On Friday night, talk circulated backstage that Chuck Mason had put in his two-week. 'Maybe Owen will hire Phillipe.' The thought gave Jonas additional energy. He had left a pair of house seats at the box office for Phillipe.

"Hey Chuckles, are you jumpin' ship?" Chad was the first to inquire.

"Yes. I miss my girl back in Philly."

"Lord, what a bimbo," murmured Gary under his breath as he spread his pan stick on. "Imagine quitting weeks into a national tour! What kind of nincompoop does that?"

"Half hour," announced Griff through the intercom. "Cast, please meet in the green room at intermission. Thank you."

"Oh, God, I'm running late," exclaimed Pat, who hastily applied skill to her hair. "I'm such a mess!" Mally put down her comb and stared at Pat.

"If you broke out in hives and gained fifteen pounds, you'd still be acceptable!"

"Thanks, Mal. I love that you're my friend."

Griff's "Places, please," was loud through the squawk box." The cast began their preset in the wings as they waited for the downbeat. Mally and Pat took their positions. Jonas stretched to ensure his form this evening. He had to be at his best for Phillipe.

Owen Matthews arrived at the theatre and was promptly showed to the back of the house. He immediately looked for Pat on stage. He missed her more than he imagined. She opened his senses, she made him feel alive, and she distracted him from his unresolved issues with Vera.

He was pleased with his work. This was a consistent ensemble, skilled and greatly talented gypsies, every last one! At intermission he headed backstage.

"Ladies and Gentleman, we have an unexpected surprise tonight," announced Griff. As Owen walked in, Pat let out a gasp.

"Cast, you look great," enthused Owen. "I had a gut level feeling when I hired you, and you have proven me right. Let's see how you've held up after four months. I'll stop in from time to time."

The cast moved immediately to make their second act change. Pat stopped when she heard Owen's voice.

"See you following the show, Miss Byrne?" Pat nodded and hurried up the stairs.

"Owen? "We've lost Chuck Mason. He put in his two week," said Griff.

"You're kidding! Why?"

"He's more homesick than ambitious. The good news is that Jonas knows someone here in Atlanta, a possible replacement. Do you want to give the local guy a shot? You could audition him while you're in town." Owen brightened at the suggestion.

"I can stay over until mid week. Who's the guy?"

"His name is Phillipe Danier. Jonas thinks he can cut it in short order."

"Well fine. I trust Jonas' eye even when his dick is in overdrive! Let's set up the audition for Monday at noon. Would you arrange an accompanist, Griff? It'd be nice if this guy can sing too. I want Pat and Jonas to come in. We'll try the guy on some couple choreography." Griff used the intercom.

"Jonas Martin, please report to Griff immediately." Jonas dashed down four flights of stairs.

"Well, it looks like Owen will audition your friend, personally. Tell him noon sharp on Monday."

"Griff, you're a keeper," Jonas shouted, as he dashed back to the dressing room.

Meanwhile Pat hurried through her prep for the second act. Her hands were shaking as she gave her hair a last-minute inspection.

"Hey Pat, slow down, you've got the job," observed Mally.

"I have waited for this evening for weeks, and now that it's here, I am so nervous."

"Why?"

"I'm afraid to expect too much from Owen."

Jonas hurried to clean up and change. He felt good. He had danced well and was anxious to hear Phillipe's opinion and get a look at André. Knowing they were lovers made him curious.

Checking his appearance and taking a few deep breaths helped. Arriving at the stage door he looked around. At that moment the doorman handed him a phone message. He quickly read, "Mon Cher ami, I am unable to attend tonight." It was signed 'Phillipe.'

Crest-fallen, Jonas left the theatre and walked to the hotel. As he put his key in the door he could hear the phone and rushed in. He immediately recognized the soft voice.

"Jonas, Phillipe."

"What happened?"

"Cheri, I'm so sorry. André got back from Europe and refused to leave the flat. He wanted to catch up and insisted I stay in."

"Do you do whatever he wants?"

"Yes, pretty much."

"Well, someone in the company has given notice. You have an audition set for Monday at noon with the director, Owen Matthews."

"Cheri, that's wonderful. I'll be there. Tell me what to expect."

"Be at the theatre, warmed up, and ready to go by noon. Owen is a stickler for punctuality. If you like I could teach you some of the material beforehand."

"Thank you! No matter what happens, I appreciate this!"

"Why don't you come Saturday night? You could see the staging first hand. It might help your audition," suggested Jonas.

"Good idea. Why don't you set aside two tickets?"

"Great! Pick up your house seats by seven-thirty. The show starts at eight."

"See you after the show, Cheri?"

"Yes, of course." Jonas' mind was racing. He had oiled the gears, and now it was up to Phillipe to nail the job.

Owen and Pat arrived at his hotel following dinner. He had barely closed the door when he began his customary ritual, teasing her with his tongue as he undressed her. There was urgency in his maneuvering as he kissed her deeply. Removing combs from Pat's hair produced a wave of red brilliance. Then, with deliberate force, he picked her up and carried her to the bed.

By now she was close to an orgasm, but she held back. Pushing her on her back, Owen was eager to give her pleasure as his tongue took over. He was already hard and seeing him naked was intoxicating. She now lay fully ready for him. Their lust reached a feverish pitch that peaked, sending them on an excruciating wave of satisfaction. It was a while before Owen pulled out. He reached for the familiar cigarette, lit it and offered Pat a drag.

"I couldn't wait until Thanksgiving," Owen whispered, gently smoothing her hair.

"Oh, Owen, I'm so in love with you," said Pat, touching his face.

"I'm holding a special audition for you a week from Monday in

New York. Your fare will be arranged. Take the red eye out of Atlanta at midnight. You can take a cab from La Guardia to my coop. Do you want an expense check or would you prefer cash?"

"I'd prefer you weren't so business-like," Pat snapped, stifling the emotion welling up.

"Hey, what is this? Baby, I just want to get the details out of the way so I can concentrate on you."

"Sorry," she sniffed, changing the subject. "What's the new show about?"

"It's a compilation of material I never used in my other shows. It will be heavy, heavy dancing, strictly presentational. I will feature you. You can handle it now." Pat was aglow as Owen detailed the project.

"You will be sensational, Baby. Now let's get some sleep." Owen turned off the light and tucked Pat in next to him. Moments later, they were asleep.

Chapter 33

André

During the Saturday matinee, the cast's collective energy took off. By half hour Saturday evening the company was revved for the sellout crowd.

Dana's entire family was out front. She was psyched and ready to go. Jonas was ready to go as well, ready to show off for Phillipe, ready to show the demands of Owen's work, and what Phillipe could expect at Monday's audition. He wondered about André. What sort of man held a free spirit like Phillipe?

Sandy swung into the downbeat. The opening office tableau brought a giant hand. Solid reaction to the first scene was a good indication that tonight's audience was clearly there to have a good time. Pat and Mally met in the wings.

"What's new with Owen?"

"Can you keep a secret? Owen is holding a private audition for me for his next show. He's flying me up on the red eye next weekend."

"Pat, that's fabulous! I'm so happy for you!"

"Thanks, Mal. I appreciate your support." The first act finished to lengthy applause. Jonas ran into the girls as he took the stairs, two at a time.

"Jonas, slow down," Pat cautioned. Have you spotted lover boy?"

"Cool it," snapped Jonas. "He's fifth row center on the aisle and the guy with him is gorgeous. He's coming back after the show. Can either of you join us for a drink?"

"I'm game."

"Pat?"

"Not on your life, thanks!"

"Oh that's right. You'll be engaging in some pre-dawn exercise!" Pat ignored the comment.

At intermission the crowd milled around outside as André Glessier stood under the marquee enjoying a smoke. Motioning for Phillipe to step closer, he put out his cigarette.

"Dear one, I think you're ready."

"Ready?"

"You're ready to leave. It's time."

"Who is he?"

"Pierre Dermonde. We've been involved for the past year. I must be with him."

"Pierre Dermonde? He's a brilliant designer!"

"Yes, I know," said André, his obvious pleasure showing.

Phillipe stopped listening. He was thinking back to the day he first met André. He was posing nude for a local art class. He noticed an attractive gentleman pointing in his direction, as he conversed with the class instructor.

"Class, take a fifteen minute break. Phillipe, please come to my office." Phillipe complied, slipping on a robe.

The stranger was devastatingly handsome with a smile of perfect teeth. His features were classic, his hair, prematurely gray and wavy, his body, muscular and tan. Phillipe guessed he was in his mid-forties.

"This is André Glessier."

"Hello." Phillipe whiffed exquisite cologne. He could feel André's eyes scrutinizing him. He welcomed it.

"I would like to use you in a fashion layout. I would like you to pose nude to show simplicity and natural lines of the body. I will pay $200.00 an hour. Interested?"

"Yes."

"Good. We shoot tomorrow."

The next morning Phillipe rushed to André's loft. Phillipe noticed it was decorated with attention to every exquisite detail. The staff moved about with impeccable efficiency.

"Welcome, Phillipe." André was more handsome than he remembered. They shook hands.

"May I offer you a glass of wine?" Phillipe nodded.

"I prefer red." André nodded to his personal assistant, Mavis, who was off in a gallop, her horn-rimmed glasses sliding easily down her nose. André showed Phillipe to the set.

"My line for this coming summer is sleek, stark, but sensual. I want to photograph your well-defined body. You'll stand there," said André, pointing to the spot. Our models will pose around you. Will this be a problem?"

"Not in the least."

The door opened suddenly, and three models entered, their stylists fussing about. They were tall women, all over six feet, with short, cropped hair, anorexic-thin bodies and pouty mouths. Mavis reappeared carrying a glass of wine and a bottle of baby oil.

"Here you drink this, and I will do this," she offered, removing Phillipe's robe. Standing nude while Mavis applied oil, Phillipe now drew attention from the models, watching with interest.

Phillipe was muscular and lean. His dark, wavy hair accented deep brown eyes, eyes that looked like deep chocolate pools. His beautifully shaped buttocks, flat abdomen and long legs fascinated Mavis as she carried out her assignment, her horn rims slipping further down her nose. She was now eye level with Phillipe's crotch.

"It won't be necessary to oil anything else," said André, tactfully.

The shoot began. Phillipe posed on command. The models worked in perfect sync, creating compositions that were sensuous and exotic. Satisfied, André wrapped the session in one day.

"You work very well. You should consider a career in modeling."

"I prefer dancing. I supplement my living by posing."

"Come and join us for dinner. I insist you come along." André, his staff, and Phillipe enjoyed a hearty meal and stimulating conversation. Later, he approached Phillipe.

"Would you care for a lift?"

"Sure." André signaled the valet, who drove up in André's exquisite Rolls Royce. As they drove away, André spoke first.

"Tell me about yourself."

"There's not much to tell. I live alone, I'm unattached, and I like it that way."

"I see."

"I want sex with you, just sex and nothing more. Agreed?" André smiled at Phillipe's direct approach.

"Well, of course." Phillipe felt a tap on his shoulder. Startled, the flashback abruptly faded as he realized he was still standing under the marquee with André.

Phillipe was notably impressed as he watched the show carefully. 'The style and line of each piece of choreography is brilliant,' he thought to himself. At times he tapped his feet, absorbed in the wonder of it all, unaware of André's eyes on him.

From his view at the back of the house, Owen was pleased. Pat performed with her usual brilliance. She was star material as he envisioned her featured in his next show. He had singled her out at the audition last fall, knowing full well that she had what it took to make it on Broadway. Being his lover was a bonus.

Following the show, he found Jonas and Pat. "I'd like you both at the audition for Chuck Mason's replacement on Monday at noon. Pat, I want you to work the 'Buccaneer' ride out with him. Jonas, you will demonstrate any of the men's combinations and work with him on my style. Agreed?" They nodded with enthusiasm.

Phillipe and André waited at the stage door, as Mally approached first.

"Mally, may I present André Glessier?" There was small talk before Jonas arrived. As he joined them, he was noticeably calm, unlike his demeanor at the theater earlier.

"Jonas, this is André. André, Jonas. He provided the house seats."

"Thank you very much. Would you care to join us for a drink?"

"We'd love to," said Jonas, eagerly.

"Come, we'll take my car." Jonas sat up front with André, while Phillipe visited in the backseat with Mally. When they arrived, the doorman extended his hand.

"Monsieur Glessier, so good to see you."

"And you, Richard."

Mally and Jonas were impressed by the lavish interior. Ascending an elaborate curved staircase, they were escorted into a private salon.

"What a beautiful room, the colors are exceptional together," said Mally, looking around.

"You like my place? I bought a forgotten warehouse a few years ago and had it converted into this club."

Conversation centered on the show. André was lavish in his praise, complimenting them both, repeatedly. Phillipe sat quietly and listened.

"How difficult is the choreography to execute?"

"It's very difficult without solid training in classic ballet and jazz. Tap helps too," Mally explained.

"Owen is incredible. You can learn a lot doing his style," Jonas added.

André ordered appetizers and champagne. They toasted their way through several refills. Mally noticed that Jonas was growing conspicuously quiet.

"You've hardly said a word, Cheri," observed Phillipe.

"I'm fucking tired if you must know," Jonas mumbled, caustically.

"Cheri, I meant no offense." Mally had enough. Standing, she nudged Jonas, helping him out of the chair.

"Please, excuse us. It's been a rather long day."

"May we call you a cab?"

"No, we'll find our way. Thank you for your hospitality," said Mally, as she steered Jonas out of the room. When they were gone, André turned his attention to Phillipe.

"Does your friend have a drinking problem?"

"No, but he drank on an empty stomach. He was nervous," remarked Phillipe.

"Why, Phillipe?"

"He knows we're lovers."

"Yes, of course."

"We're having sex."

"Does he know we have an open relationship?"

"I've told him very little about us."

"Phillipe, how do you feel about this man?"

"I like the sex, but I think he is falling for me."

"Ah yes, complication." André knew Phillipe was headstrong, opportunistic and not easy to bridle. From the beginning, André had called the shots. His maturity, money, and position held Phillipe. But, what could Jonas offer? And once Phillipe was cut free, what would he offer, when the challenge was gone? André left it at that.

Chapter 34

The Accident

Mally and Jonas rode in silence. "Jonas, what happened back there? Why so sullen?"

"Because I'm in love for the first time in my life, and he belongs to someone else," he slurred.

Arriving at their hotel, they noticed a crowd of people and a police squad car at the main entrance. Mally managed to get Jonas out of the taxi and walked him carefully to the entrance. A flustered Chad stopped them.

"Gary's been in an accident. Witnesses say a speeding car ran him down and took off!" Jonas jolted, pushing Mally aside as he tried to walk steadily. Mally approached an officer standing by.

"Please, sir, tell us what happened!"

"Do you know the injured party?"

"Yes, he's a friend of ours." The officer took out a note pad.

"According to the report, Gary Hanson was crossing the street and was hit by a speeding car. On impact he rolled to the curb, here," he recited, pointing. "Those who witnessed it said the driver never stopped."

"God! Where is he? I want to see him," Jonas screamed, as the officer tried to restrain him.

"I think we'd better take him inside," he insisted. Mally followed as the officer took Jonas in hand, walking him into the lobby and helping him into a chair.

"Son, your friend is on his way to Atlanta General where everything possible will be done." Jonas put his face in his hands and sobbed.

"I don't fucking believe it," Jonas spat out. The officer handed a card to Mally.

"This is the number for Atlanta General E. R. Call in about an hour and you'll be updated. I'm very sorry about this. Good night." Mally nodded weakly at the officer and then turned her attention to Jonas, who was staring into space as he rocked back and forth.

"Stay put, Jonas. I'll be right back." Locating a row of phones and keeping a watchful eye on Jonas, she dialed Griff.

"Griff, Gary Hanson's been hit by a car. He's at Atlanta General. What should I do?"

"I will notify Owen. Does anyone else know about this?"

"Chad told us. I didn't see anyone else from the cast."

"I'll talk to Chad. Where are you right now?"

"We're at our hotel."

"How bad is Gary?"

"I don't know, but the officer at the scene told me to call Atlanta General E.R. for an update."

"I'll call. Can you stay with Jonas tonight? I imagine he is pretty distraught."

"Yes, of course."

"I'll inform Owen and we'll take this a step at a time. Good night, Darling."

The phone rang stirring the sleepers. Owen sat up slowly and grabbed for a cigarette as he struggled to focus. He was irritated as he juggled the phone with one hand and his lighter with the other.

"Yes?"

"Owen, this is Griff."

"Well?"

"Gary Hanson's been in an accident. He's been taken to the E.R." Owen, now fully awake, took a deep drag. Pat slept soundly nearby.

"Call a company meeting on Monday before the show. In the meantime, we'll audition Jonas' friend. If he can cut it, he will fill Chuck's spot. Call New York in the morning and find someone who knows the show well enough to cover Gary on such short notice."

"I'll check. In the meantime I suggest we withhold any news of this from the company."

"Thanks, Griff. You're on top of it as always. Goodnight."

Owen put down the phone, crushed out his cigarette, and slipped beneath the sheet. But, could he fall back to sleep? It wasn't going to be easy to replace two solid dancers on such short notice. As was his habit he mentally began charting his course.

"Stay with me," wailed Jonas. Mally fished in Jonas' pockets and found his room key. It was difficult to handle his dead weight as she managed to get him into the room. The forceful, sarcastic gypsy looked so vulnerable and helpless. Slowly, she helped him undress. Sleep claimed Jonas almost immediately. The stillness of the room engulfed and stifled her. Glancing at Gary's empty bed, Mally felt numb. Picking up Jonas' key she quietly slipped out.

Her room felt cool. She undressed and turned on the shower, checking the temperature. It felt just right. The spray felt soothing, distracting her for the moment. When she had finished showering she dried herself. Mally chose a pajama set, slipping on the loose fitting top and buttoning it. Stepping into the bottoms she felt the comfort of soft flannel against her skin. Her scuffs warmed her feet. Completing her nighttime ritual she grabbed Jonas' key and headed back to his room. She could hear his labored breathing as he slept.

Griff frowned as he got a glimpse of himself in the mirror. He noted his bed hair and the bad taste in his mouth. The running tap was appealing as the cold water forced open his sleep-crusted eyes. He was grateful for the ability to sleep through irresolution and uncertainty. This was going to be a rough week. Slipping into his jeans he added a tee shirt. Requesting directory assistance, he dialed the number and waited.

"Atlanta General Emergency."

"I need an update on Gary Hanson. He was brought in last night around midnight."

As Griff waited he contemplated the need for black coffee and got out a list of male dancers who had been under contract to the Lehrman office. He looked for those associated with *Bravo Business*. A voice interrupted his thoughts.

"I have an update on Gary Hanson. However, hospital policy forbids me to give out details unless you are family." Griff immediately went into his business mode.

"This is Griffen Edwards, production stage manager of *Bravo Business*. We are currently at the Municipal Auditorium. Mr. Hanson is a dancer in the company. As his representative professionally, I need an update on his condition. If he cannot return and resume his responsibilities as stated in his contract, I need to know immediately. The management will have to make other arrangements. He has no family to speak of."

"Of course Mr. Edwards, I understand. Mr. Hanson is in the recovery room in guarded condition. He sustained fractures of the pelvis, femur, and rib cage, and he has a slight concussion." Griff sighed.

"How long is the recovery for such extensive injuries?"

"Given the nature of his condition he will probably be here for two to three weeks, followed by a six-month rehabilitation period. So much depends on the patient."

"Thank you for your help. You have been most kind. When can Mr. Hanson receive visitors?"

"He will probably sleep off and on for the next twenty-four hours. Visits should remain short. He is being monitored carefully. Our staff will be happy to assist you as much as possible."

Griff returned to his notes and spotted a familiar name. Joe Pinto had been in the Broadway cast for over two years and was presently on hiatus. Noting a number on Long Island, he dialed. A casual voice answered.

"Joe, forgive the intrusion on Sunday. This is Griff Edward's calling from Atlanta."

"Hey, Griff, how are things?"

"Not so good. One of our male dancers was severely injured last night by a hit and run driver. We are in a bind. One of our regulars has just given notice, leaving us with two spots uncovered. The existing swings will be on overload."

"No shit?"

"Are you available?"

"I don't know. When do you need me?"

"Yesterday," said Griff, with a chuckle.

"Wait a sec!" There was a short pause. "Oh balls, give me a minute to pack," he laughed.

"Does that mean yes?"

"Hell, Griff, of course."

"Be here Monday night before the show. We'll arrange your flight to Atlanta and transportation to the theatre. You will have five days to learn the spot."

"You got it! Oh, by the way, who got hit?"

"Gary Hanson. He's pretty banged up."

"No shit? Gary? We go back ages. Well, count me in."

"You can watch the show as you rehearse, OK?"

"I kind of know the piece. I'll just need placements."

"Done," said Griff.

"Griff, you're the best. They're damned lucky to have you."

"Thanks, Joe. It's a scramble at the moment. We look forward to having you. See you soon." Just as he put down the phone it rang.

"Griff, it's me!"

"Yes, Darling!"

"Have you heard anything about Gary?"

"Gary's in intensive care and will probably remain in the hospital two to three weeks. The rehab is about six months for the kind of injuries he sustained."

"Oh, that's horrible! Do you have a replacement?"

"We've picked up Joe Pinto. He was in the Broadway cast for two years. He'll arrive tomorrow night."

"That's a relief."

Jonas awakened from sleep. It took him a few seconds to grasp the previous evening. Then he remembered. Gary had been in an accident! The realization sent him into gear. He showered, dressed and stopped at the front desk for directions to Atlanta General. Taking a bus gave him time to psych himself for the visit.

Jonas ruminated on the long ride to the hospital. How could this have happened? Jonas shuddered as he stepped from the bus and walked into the hospital. Getting off at ICU he found a nurse who directed him. He found Gary awake.

"Oh my God, Gary," he cried, reaching for him.

"I'm so screwed! You can tell that, right?"

"Don't talk like that," Jonas said, gently patting Gary's hand.

"No, it's OK. It was time to stop dancing. I'm burned out."

"Quit dancing? I can't relate to that," said Jonas sadly.

"I guess you'll have to leave me in Atlanta. I overheard the doc say that it will be at least three weeks before I'm released, then another six months before I am rehabilitated. I guess I'll have to see if my Aunt Fran will take me in. She's the one person who can tolerate a gimp gay man," he added, dryly. They reminisced for a while until the attending nurse suggested Gary rest.

"Bye, Hon, I love you," Jonas murmured, as he bent down and kissed Gary. Tears blurred his vision as he set down the hall and on to the elevator.

Jonas felt an overwhelming sense of loss as he left the hospital. It was Gary who loved him unconditionally. It was Gary who had put up with his infidelities. It was Gary who encouraged him through career challenges. As he climbed aboard a bus and sat down he began to examine his life.

Chapter 35

Jonas

Jonas was different. He was curious about boys, starting at age ten. This discovery and interest grew following an incident during school recess. He happened upon two classmates fondling each other in an isolated spot on the playground. He was curious as he watched their activity, his excitement growing. However, asking him to join them sent him running.

Jonas developed into the class clown, smarting off frequently, much to the chagrin of his teacher. One day he was rewarded by having to stay after school to clean blackboards. It was late afternoon and he was anxious to finish. As he worked at a feverish pace, he realized he wasn't alone. Turning, he saw Tommy Erickson watching him with interest.

"Hey Jonas, what are you doing?"

"Helping Mrs. Schultz," he said absently.

"Where is she?"

"She left. I have to hurry. The doors are locked at five."

"I've got something to show you. Want to see?"

Jonas was naturally curious and followed Tommy into the small cloakroom. The winter sun was fading as they stood together in the darkening space. Tommy pulled Jonas closer. Never taking his eyes from Jonas, Tommy unzipped his trousers and pulled his penis out.

"Want to touch?" He reached for Jonas' hand and placed it on the smooth, soft surface. Jonas felt it stiffen. He liked how it felt, liked Tommy's moans of delight, and ached for the same. Unzipping his fly he allowed Tommy to do the same. The feeling of dread mixed with urgency only served to turn him on more. Jonas shook as Tommy's hands explored his shaft. It was a strange feeling, but he liked it. He liked it a lot. Tommy's warm lips found his. How long they stood in the darkness that afternoon he couldn't say, but their secret meetings lasted through the rest of the school year until Tommy and his family moved away.

In high school, Jonas excelled in sports. He preferred soccer and soon became captain of the squad. One night, following a game, he and teammate Jim Farraday were invited to join some of the opposing team guys for pizza. Jonas was reluctant at first, but agreed that it was good sportsmanship, so he and Jim caught a ride.

As they noshed on pizza the group rehashed the game and eventually talk turned to girls. Simple banter turned into crude remarks. Jonas was noticeably quiet.

"Hey, Jonas, why are you so quiet?"

"Not much to say," he said, passively.

"Oh? Maybe you like it better with guys," said one.

"Don't," said Jonas, trying to change the subject.

"That's it! You're a fag!" Jonas got up and walked outside. Moments later Jim joined him.

"Those guys are saying stuff like, 'That queer needs a lesson.' Is it true?"

"Let's get out of here." They grabbed their gear and headed down the main drag and out onto a dirt road. Jonas looked back, spotting headlights. The headlights appeared to be following them.

"Come on, step on it," Jonas shouted, entering a field at full clip. In the background the mountains stood out against the large expanse of earth and grass. The headlights left the road.

Trying to outrun their pursuers was futile. The truck caught up to them and spun around, the headlights blinding them, blocking any escape. As Jonas' eyes adjusted to the bright beams he saw opposing team members bolt from the back. He and Jim were surrounded quickly. The largest of the boys approached Jonas.

"Hey queer boy, want to sample my hardware?" Two boys grabbed Jim pulling him aside while the remainder of the group took Jonas from behind.

"Now, you're gonna get what you like, faggot!"

In an instant Jonas was forced to the ground. As the jeering grew he felt his hands being tied behind his back. He screamed, but it was no use. He struggled more forcefully as his jeans and under shorts came off.

"Ok, pansy ass, you asked for this," yelled the biggest boy unzipping his fly. Jonas felt his legs being forcefully held open.

As he tried to mentally prepare he felt the first piercing hardness and repeated thrusts in and out. He tried to scream, but no sound issued. As he lay face down in the dirt, grit filled his eyes and nose. His body wrenched in pain and hot tears stung his eyes as he was repeatedly violated. Somewhere in the background he could hear Jim's cries mixed with laughter from the others. 'Jim is being forced to watch,' he thought desperately. When the boys were done, they kicked him repeatedly.

"Faggot, damn faggot," the boys chanted. Jonas heard squeals and pleading behind him and repeated taunts and jeering piercing the night air. Jim's cries continued and then abruptly were silenced. Laughter and grunts followed.

Next, Jonas heard a truck start. Doors slammed and tires spun, tearing up the ground. The noise of engine and laughter grew faint until at last silence took over. 'Thank God, they're gone,' he thought.

Somehow, he found the strength to roll over on his back. Slowly he worked his hands free. His wrenching sobs of anger and frustration were absorbed by the star-washed night. Though he was weak he managed to stand and pull up his jeans, wincing as he felt the raw skin sting in protest. He stepped tentatively toward Jim, who was lying inert a few feet away.

"Jim?" No response. He shook Jim more vigorously. "Come on, Jim!" Jim finally opened his eyes. His face was badly bruised and swelling.

"Jonas? Don't leave me!"

"I'm right here." After calming him he found Jim's clothes and helped him dress.

"Can you stand?"

"Oh God, I don't know." Jonas helped Jim to his feet with great effort.

"We'll lay low for a couple of days. You can stay with me," suggested Jonas. Neither he nor Jim ever mentioned the rape again. The following week they both quit the team on the pretense that their grades were suffering because of soccer. The administration bought it.

During the summer Jonas attended movie musicals. He would return home and mimic the dancers he admired. Working in front of a mirror in the privacy of his room, he honed his movement and sense of style. He was agile, well developed and had an instinctive sense of timing, developed playing soccer. Tired of hiding his true identity, he instinctively knew that dancing was the journey to take.

His mother, Elizabeth, recognized his natural ability and located an excellent school in L.A. Jonas commuted four times a week where he studied ballet, jazz, tap, and modern dance. He quickly grew proficient and confident.

Charles Martin, Jonas' father, had little interest in his children. Jonas was the middle child of three. He had an older and younger sister. His older sister Roxanne was a social climber with big plans to find a rich husband. His younger sister, Jami was his ally. She knew he was gay and kept his secret. She, too, was sexually aware early on.

Jami was tall and lean with exquisite features. Sexually active at fifteen, she often dated two or three boys at once. Jonas teased her about her fickle ways and she would tease back, cruising attractive boys with him. They adored each other. She, like her mother, encouraged Jonas to pursue dancing.

Then the unthinkable happened. Jami went to a party one evening and in the ensuing social whirl spotted a stranger, who immediately attracted her. Brad Donnelly was tall, muscular, and tan. The visible parts of his body were tattooed and enticing. Jami wasted no time in egging him on. The attraction was mutual and throughout the course of the evening they drank, smoked grass and had sex. Later, he offered her a lift on his Harley. Already euphoric and anticipating further action, Jami accepted.

Revving his machine as Jami climbed on the back, Brad drove off heading down Pacific Coast Highway. It was a perfect evening as the moon etched a path across the ocean far below. But rounding a tight switchback he lost control of his bike. In a brief shriek of steel and cries and sparks the bike flew off the road and into the night and silence and death.

Back at the Martin estate, a continual ringing of the phone brought attention. It was three in the morning. Elizabeth Martin reached for her bedroom light and picked up.

"Is this the Charles Martin residence?" Elizabeth felt a chill as she heard the stranger's voice.

"Yes it is. This is Elizabeth Martin. To whom am I speaking?" Then it was swift, shocking, a stab to the heart.

"This is the California Highway Patrol, Mrs. Martin. I regret to inform you that your daughter, Jami Martin has been killed. I'm very sorry for your loss." Little was heard beyond that moment.

Jonas was devastated. Jami had accepted him and loved him unconditionally. As time wore on he immersed himself deeper into training, knowing that Jami would have insisted. Then, one day, he left home for good. L.A. was where he would find acceptance, living life on his terms, attending classes.

Jonas matured into a fine dancer. He was boyishly handsome with hazel eyes that twinkled with humor. His well-developed torso, powerful legs and tight, round buns attracted both men and women in class. But it was his smile that exuded a quality hard to resist.

Ken Sutton was attracted to Jonas. He, too, was a dedicated, forceful personality. His jazz style was erotically fluid and visceral, but it was his ballet technique that singled him out. Ken could leap higher and turn faster than anyone. Outside the studio he was without pretense, pleasant and attentive.

After a long, grueling rehearsal one evening, Ken suggested Jonas spend the weekend at his family's estate. Ken, an only child, had free run of the place. His parents were on an extended holiday in Europe. Jonas jumped at the chance. After changing, they drove up into the hills overlooking L.A.

Ken turned into a gated area and slowed down. Reaching the guardhouse he nodded at the attendant who opened the gate. Riding through the property Jonas noticed a lavish panorama of gardens and well-groomed trees. A large Tudor-style mansion included a swimming pool, tennis court, and carriage house. Ken parked and turned to Jonas. "We're alone."

Inside the house, Ken began to ascend an impressive winding staircase. As Jonas followed, he observed exquisite antique trappings. He felt like he was in an F. Scott Fitzgerald novel. He was excited to be with Ken. Entering a large bedroom he saw a magnificent view of L.A. sprawling in every direction, through the large windows.

"It's yours. I'll be across the hall. How about a swim?"

Jonas found the bathroom, undressed and found a large fluffy towel to wrap himself in. The house was quiet as he walked along the hall. Strolling past an open door he stopped. Ken stood naked. Stunned, Jonas stood riveted waiting breathlessly. Without a word Ken took Jonas by the hand, leading him to the bed. Removing Jonas' towel he covered Jonas' mouth with his, kissing him passionately.

Falling on the bed, they made love like kindred souls. Their love play was gentle, soft, and slow with Ken leading and Jonas following. Then they switched roles. As their mutual passion swelled, their lovemaking grew intense, hard, throbbing. The hours went by as they continued their insatiable consummation. Exhausted, they fell asleep coiled around each other.

Over the next two years they were lovers. Ken found an apartment and Jonas moved in. They spent their class time working feverishly, and free time exclusively with each other. Though close, they both knew that it was just a matter of time before each would go his separate way. It was the nature of their chosen profession. Dancing came first.

Jonas was hired for a weekly television variety series, becoming the featured dancer. It was a steady paycheck and he loved working in front of the camera. He was a fantastic technician with a powerful persona.

Ken sought his place in the ballet world. By joining an established company, he would have an opportunity to work with both classic and modern choreographers. Jonas understood Ken's desire for a ballet career so when the San Francisco Ballet hired Ken, Jonas knew it was time to leave California. He would seek work in the New York theatre, a place known to bring heartbreak, uncertainty, and brutal politics. But, he was ready.

Owen Matthews spotted Jonas at an open call and hired him. Jonas gained the respect of his mentor with his exceptional technique and vivacious personality. Owen developed him into an accomplished performer. Every moment spent off stage was preparation to get back on. This was his life, and he relished every second of it.

Chapter 36

The Audition

Owen faced a challenging week replacing two dancers. One dancer was a seasoned performer, the other, an unknown. He was relieved that Joe Pinto was on board. Phillipe Danier had yet to prove himself. He had Jonas' endorsement, but Owen reminded himself that Jonas could be thinking with his dick.

At 11:00 Jonas walked into the theatre and out on stage. The work light cast eerie shadows on the flats upstage. As he put down his bag he heard footsteps.

"Good morning, Cheri. Am I too early?" Phillipe emerged from the shadows.

"No," Jonas said, tonelessly, trying to keep the strain out of his voice as he slipped on his jazz shoes.

"Are you all right, Cheri? You seem off today," said Phillipe, sensing something.

"My partner Gary was critically injured Saturday night. He has to drop out of the show. Your timing is impeccable." Philippe caught the edge in Jonas' voice.

"I'm so sorry, Cheri." What happened?"

"He was hit by a driver, who took off. He's in I.C.U. at Atlanta General," explained Jonas, his eyes misting. Suddenly changing the subject, Jonas stood and walked to center stage. He stretched and then turned to Phillipe.

"Owen has a specific style that you'll have to mimic. Let me count out the last thirty-two bars of the buccaneer number. It falls later in the second act, remember?" Phillipe nodded.

"You warmed up enough?"

"Yes, Cheri."

"All right, let's begin. We don't have a lot of time."

He counted out the first combination. Executing a jazz slide on each foot, he made a wide circle, and moved quickly into the starting position for the grueling portion of the choreography. Shooting his legs out one side at a time from a bent knee position, the repetitious movement challenged his thigh muscles as he felt the burn, his heels taking the brunt of his weight. The movement was pure Owen beginning with a series of kicks, developed from the knee and punctuated with a pointed foot, the stooped shoulders, locked elbows and relaxed wrists.

Phillipe watched as Jonas demonstrated flawlessly. When Jonas stopped the only visible movement was his chest rising and falling as his lungs gasped for air. Then he motioned Phillipe to stand behind him. Beginning the combination again, he purposely danced under tempo, allowing Phillipe to follow.

"That's good, but a little more shoulder here. You need more force in your kicks in this section. Watch your line, cleaner there, keep your head directly over the downstage shoulder with your chin up, back hunched. Good, that's it. Please repeat this." After a few tries Phillipe had it.

"Let's go over the soft shoe section of the 'Secretary' number. Ready?"

Jonas' footwork was stylish and precise. Phillipe was quick and focused as he repeated the combination again for Jonas, who scrutinized every move.

"Remember, Owen is meticulous to the point of being obsessive, but it's that precision and attention to detail that makes his work so fabulous. If you perform it with that in mind, you'll look great." Jonas glanced at his watch and noticed it was close to noon.

Owen entered backstage with Pat at his side, followed by Griff and an accompanist. When everyone had assembled, Jonas introduced Phillipe.

"Phillipe, I'd like you to meet Owen Matthews, our director. And this is Griff Edwards, our production stage manager. Pat, I believe you two are acquainted?"

"It's a privilege to be here," said Phillipe, his stomach churning. Griff brought the stage lights to full as Owen beckoned Phillipe, Pat, and Jonas center.

"I'm going to try you on two combinations from the show. They are diametrically opposed in style. Jonas will demonstrate the secretary combination and Pat, standby for the buccaneer ride out. Ready? Please begin."

Jonas took off in a whirl of exuberance. He felt good, confident, as he glided, and jumped, his earlier funk now history. Finishing, he stood dripping wet and waited for Owen's instruction.

In an instant Phillipe was standing behind and to the side of Jonas. Owen shouted the countdown and the music began again.

At first, Phillipe was tentative as he tried to execute the demanding choreography. He began to feel more at ease as each minute passed. His mind whirled as his body moved through space accelerating his heart rate. With all the gusto he could muster he went the mile, aping Jonas and enjoying the moment.

Owen came forward. Phillipe stood riveted, a trickle of sweat running down his back. His hair was soaked and matted against his forehead. His chest rose up and down rapidly as he gulped air through his nose and mouth.

"Take a moment to catch your breath. Pat?"

Jonas and Pat began. Their execution was flawless. Every turn, every kick, every nuance of Owen's style was perfect. They appeared to share a heartbeat. When they finished Jonas stepped aside, allowing Phillipe to take his place. The accompanist played at full tempo as Owen watched every move.

Phillipe was superb. In a show of amazing dexterity and finesse, he mimicked the combination to perfection. Grasping her hands, Phillipe took charge as though he had done the combination for months. When they finished, Pat stepped to the side to catch her breath. She was spent and exhilarated.

"Good, very good," Owen shouted, walking back on stage. Griff followed.

"Do you sing?" Phillipe nodded as he pulled out sheet music from his satchel, handing it to the pianist. "Good," said Owen, glancing at Griff.

Phillipe's rich baritone was smooth and polished, as good as any chorus singer Jonas had heard. Pat was agog at the show of training. Phillipe's enunciation was clean, his control, flawless.

"Well, I have everything I need," said Owen. "Would you wait for a moment, please?" As Owen and Griff conferred near the orchestra pit, Phillipe's heart rate quickened. After a moment they returned.

"We start rehearsals tomorrow at ten a.m.," said Owen, smiling.

"I'm hired?"

"You go into the show a week from tonight. Griff, please take care of the particulars. Thank you." Owen sauntered toward the exit, beckoning Pat to follow. Griff retreated to the office to complete the paper work.

Jonas and Phillipe now stood in the work light, the stage shrouded in shadows. Phillipe reached for Jonas and kissed him. It was deep and sensual, arousing Jonas.

"How about getting together tonight?" Jonas drew away.

"I can't tonight," he said, fighting his growing libido.

"See you at rehearsal." The two left the theatre and without words, walked in opposite directions.

Backstage was abuzz as half hour was called. There was speculation about Chuck's replacement. During the fifteen-minute call, Griff requested a meeting five minutes before overture. Mally's hair was trussed in rollers and begging for a comb out. Pat was dressed and ready early. The two headed for the greenroom.

Owen made his way through the throng. Griff followed wearing his headset. The group settled down as they readied themselves for an announcement.

"Ladies and gentlemen, we have some good news and bad," said Griff, his professional posture in place.

"Gary Hanson was critically injured in a hit and run accident Saturday night." There was a collective gasp. Noting the reaction, Griff continued carefully.

"Under the circumstances, Gary will not be able to continue the tour. However, we are lucky to have a Broadway veteran, Joe Pinto. He joins us and will begin rehearsing tomorrow. We also found a replacement for Chuck here. Both replacements will go into the show a week from tonight. Owen?"

"Folks, we have a lot to do this next week. Naturally I expect your cooperation. For the time being, I want Chad to serve as swing for Gary's entire show. Chuck you will finish out the week doing your usual. I want you at rehearsal on Friday when we put the new guys in. Since Chuck's notice and Gary's accident, I'm appointing a new dance captain. He has no idea about this. Jonas, step up here." Jonas was stunned.

"Jonas, you will put Joe and the new guy into the show. I expect everyone to work at his or her level best, and then some, got it? Good show!" Griff, with his usual decorum, excused the company.

Chapter 37

Joe

Joe Pinto checked in at La Guardia Airport. On his way to the gate he stopped to pick up a new paperback and some smokes. He had a few minutes to kill, so stopping at the lounge for a drink seemed a good idea. There he could view men. No one caught his eye so he proceeded to the gate. Aboard the plane he ordered his customary scotch and soda. The motion of the aircraft lulled him to a place left behind.

At sixteen Joe was a champion swimmer. He preferred the after meets, hanging around locker rooms so that he could observe other young men naked as they showered and dressed. He fantasized sex with them, especially with the most attractive.

He reluctantly dated girls in his sophomore year for show. With his handsome features and fit body, girls were an easy mark. The deception worked for a while. He was considered the most desirable boy in school.

All that changed with the arrival of Jordan Hendrix. Jordan was tough competition with his good looks and engaging personality. For that reason Joe planned for weeks to snag Donna Whittier as his date for senior prom. She was a prize, the homecoming queen and prettiest senior girl. Spotting her one morning, he cornered her at her locker.

"The prom's coming up." He felt in charge, ready to bag her.

"Sorry Joe, I already have a date."

"Oh? Who?"

"Jordan Hendrix," she purred, delighting in her admission. Without another word, she closed her locker and left Joe standing as crowds of students passed by.

Joe, undaunted, went to the prom stag. Donna's rejection only made him more determined to attend. The little bitch wasn't going to cow him! As he roamed the gymnasium he saw Jordan enjoying attention from Donna and others. Later, he noticed Donna alone. Jordan had disappeared.

Feeling a need to relieve himself, Joe walked to the men's room at the far end of the hall. Stepping to the urinal he unzipped his fly. When he finished, he was about to repair himself when Jordan walked in and stood next to him. Joe glanced over and saw what he would not have imagined. Jordan was caressing his penis, glancing over as he moved his hand up and down his hardened shaft.

Joe felt the familiar stirring and longing. "God, I want him," he thought, as he stood calculating his next move. With the full understanding of what he was about to do, he nodded, indicating the row of stalls.

Jordan followed Joe into the furthest from the entrance and locked it. The close space created an tight intimacy. With sudden urgency, Joe pulled Jordan to him. Aggressively tonguing him, he made a playful pattern across Jordan's lips. Jordan, horny and eager, allowed him full access as he opened his pants, letting them fall to the tile floor. Joe plunged his tongue deeper as he aggressively stroked Jordan. Jordan could feel Joe's hot breath as his mouth explored his shaft, his moans becoming louder and more urgent as Joe increased his fervent sucking.

The pressure was excruciating. Jordan finally let go, his climax exploding. His entire body shook as Joe held him tightly around the legs. Joe was hard and ready.

Eagerly, Jordan kneeled in front of Joe, returning the same pleasure he relished moments before. The more Joe moaned the more Jordan intensified his action until Joe twisted and rocked through his release. Their hearts beat wildly as they stood holding each other in their secret space. For the moment, their lust had been quelled.

At last their straight act was over, but they would have to be cautious. They continued to unleash their perpetual horniness on each other all summer. Their secret meetings ended when college took them to different coasts.

By the end of his first year at college, Joe discovered his true passion. With intense fervor he pursued dance, studying with the best in New York. Though he was a late bloomer, he was an instinctively strong dancer with a powerful presence. Soon he was a flawless technician. At his first open call audition he caught the attention of Owen Matthews, who hired him immediately. Now, a seasoned gypsy, he was on his way to Atlanta, to replace an old colleague.

Chapter 38

Replacements

Joe arrived sipping coffee and dragging on a cigarette. He introduced himself to Jonas, taking a good look at the new landscape. 'The dance captain is cute, and probably a good lay,' he thought. Jonas didn't notice. He only considered the work ahead.

At ten Owen strolled in accompanied by Griff, who was on hand to give assistance wherever needed. A local jobber would serve as pianist for rehearsals.

Phillipe arrived greeting everyone with enthusiasm. He was introduced to Joe, the only one he hadn't met. The landscape was improving as Joe considered Phillipe. He might pursue him later, but at the moment he was there to put out as a dancer. Griff brought over the contracts for both men to sign. They were given scripts and vocal books.

The rehearsal began. Jonas placed Joe and Phillipe in each number in the first act, as Owen looked on. Jonas went through each movement pattern with counts, demonstrating Owen's style to perfection. Joe and Phillipe followed as Owen reviewed each dancer. Joe had little trouble following because he knew the choreography. Phillipe was a quick study and before long was up to speed. As they worked Jonas made notations and periodically conferred with Owen privately.

Joe was assigned Chuck's spot, a position more challenging of the two, while Phillipe learned Gary's show. They were given a vocal rehearsal and assigned lines throughout the show in addition to the large amount of choreography the show required.

As rehearsals intensified, Phillipe and Joe felt increasingly comfortable in their assignments due to Jonas' attention to detail and Owen's guidance. Owen was not only pleased with his two new dancers, he was impressed with Jonas' meticulous work and dedication.

Owen began formulating a plan. Manny Thompson, his right-hand, was leaving to venture into television production. He would be a serious loss to Owen's creative infrastructure. Jonas was the obvious choice to replace Manny. He was the quintessential Owen Matthews dancer. There wasn't a movement, a line, or subtext in his choreography that Jonas lacked. He emulated Owen's high standard.

On Friday, the entire ensemble and principal understudies arrived for a run-through. Joe and Phillipe worked in their assigned positions throughout the show. By afternoon's end, Owen was pleased.

Mally, Pat and Jonas visited Gary between shows on Saturday. It was difficult. Mally and Pat had become close to him and he was sorely missed. They reminisced fondly about their shared adventures and could have chattered on at length but they could see Gary tiring and knew they should let him rest. The girls kissed Gary and left Jonas alone. Jonas took Gary's hand.

"How are you feeling?"

"Better. I don't feel as shitty as I did when I first woke up after the accident. These are good people."

"That's a relief."

"However, I have fired the Jell-O and rutabagas," he said, with a twinkle.

"Hon, you haven't lost your wit!" Then Jonas paused, his voice choking. "Gary, I don't know what to say. I've been a real jerk to you lately. I hope you can forgive me."

"I love you Jonas, always have," said Gary, quietly. "Be careful. Don't add too many notches to your suitcase, OK?" Jonas bent down and kissed Gary. Then, executing a shuffle-ball-change, he ended with an elaborate pose.

"I love you too, Hon."

Phillipe was tired but elated as he returned home to prepare for his departure on Sunday. He was legit at last and only too happy to leave stripping. Leaving André was another story. He was everything to him. André had legitimized his life. Who could replace him? As he pondered he packed and waited for André's return. He wanted to say goodbye his way. He wanted to make it good.

With the addition of Joe and Phillipe to the company, Owen decided to travel to Miami to oversee Monday night's show. Under the circumstances, Pat's audition in New York would have to wait. There was plenty of time to expose her to the production team. At the same time he could bring Jonas into the picture comfortably. Everything was shaping up.

Griff made arrangements for Gary at Atlanta General. Gary's surgery would be covered by his Actor's Equity insurance and the Lehrman organization would cover the rest. Once he could be moved, he would return to New York to live with his aunt and continue his physical therapy. It had been an eventful two weeks in Georgia but not, he thought wryly, in ways he had expected.

Griff left Atlanta early on Sunday morning in order to arrive ahead of the trucks. His routine involved setting up his production office, checking out the theatre for potential problems, and getting settled at his hotel.

Owen had phoned New York on Friday, persuading the producers to postpone Pat's audition. There was no hurry now. He knew she was ready and ripe for a career boost. And, he had every intention of continuing their relationship. If she was working with him, the chances of their staying together was almost assured. The business had a way of estranging lovers when separated and he would make no allowance for losing Pat. He needed her now. And he would have his way.

Chapter 39

Miami Beach

Miami's eighty-five degree weather was intense. Coats came off as the gypsies allowed the glorious warmth of the air and ocean breezes to caress them. Chartered buses were waiting to take them to Collins Avenue on Miami Beach. Gil Fredericks had secured special hotel rates for the company at select hotels along the ocean. The troupe would commute from Miami Beach to Dade County Auditorium in Miami.

Mally and Pat chose the Di Lido, a sprawling luxury complex with an Olympic size pool and rows of cabana huts dotting the beach. Their gigantic room had an ocean view from the balcony.

As if the temperate weather wouldn't wait, they pulled a selection of warm weather clothes from their trunks and changed quickly. Soon they would be walking Collins Avenue, fueling first at Wolfie's, a nearby delicatessen. Following lunch, they began their exploration of boutiques and tourist shops along the avenue. Pat noticed an impressive limo parked at the curb.

"Get a load of the stretch. Miami Beach must be loaded with millionaires." Suddenly, the toe of her sandal caught an edge of uneven pavement, pitching her forward. Two arms reached for her, breaking the fall. Dazed and more than slightly irritated, she pulled away, trying to steady herself. 'Boy, what a klutz,' she thought.

"Hello, Patricia."

"Blaine! Where did you come from?"

"A few miles down the road. I'm visiting my Aunt Yvonne on Fisher Island."

"Do you remember Mally? Jacksonville?"

"Yes, of course. How are you?"

"Fine, thanks," Mally responded, stiffly.

"Where are you staying?

"At the Di Lido," said Pat, still flustered.

"Nice choice. They have great amenities. Our clients stay there on occasion. Well, I'd best be going," said Blaine, signaling his driver. Waving to Pat, he closed the window as the car pulled away. 'Talk about a brush-off,' Pat thought, as they continued down Collins Avenue, the afternoon heat and sun invading their senses.

There was always excitement when the production hit a new town, and tonight was no exception with the addition of Joe and Phillipe. They were ready to carve out a place in the company with their dancing and stage presence.

Spirits were high. Jonas brought a large bottle of champagne to share following the performance, filling the sink with ice to chill it nicely. Joe chose a spot to mingle and get acquainted. Phillipe took a seat at the far end of the dressing table. He liked to take his time getting acquainted.

This theatre experience was new to him. He had been a headliner, an elite strip tease star. Now he was an integral part of a greater whole. It wasn't just about him. Looking over at Jonas, he caught his glance in the mirror.

"Places, please." Some cast members took their opening positions, while others marked time warming up in the wings. Phillipe caught up to Jonas.

"Thank you, Cheri," he whispered.

"You're welcome. See you after the show."

"You certainly will," said Phillipe. The opening scene began.

Joe felt right at home. He was doing Owen's choreography, steps that he had done many times in New York, brilliantly. Phillipe was nervous at first, but as each number passed he felt relief as his confidence grew. Following bows, a cheer went up as the cast surrounded Joe and Phillipe. Owen appeared, obviously pleased.

"Good show guys! You made everyone look great!" As the congratulating subsided, cast members dispersed. Jonas and a few others went to the men's dressing room to enjoy the chilled bubbly.

Mally and Pat returned to clean up and prepare to take off for their evening destinations. The warmth of the tropical air had made sauce of their face paint. Pat's hair was straggling as she took it down. The clatter in the women's dressing room slowly subsided as each woman departed for the night.

Mally hadn't spent time with Griff in a while. He had been so preoccupied with getting the replacements ready, handling Gary's situation and setting up in Miami that he hadn't noticed when she passed by his desk. She looked forward to seeing him tonight. As she primped she replaced the smudged mess on her face with a fresh coat of makeup, a little rouge and a touch of lipstick. Examining herself in the mirror she decided she looked presentable.

Chapter 40

Mixing and Mingling

Pat readied herself for Owen. Everything had to be perfect! She redid her make-up, re-styled her hair and changed into her sexiest panties. As she sat looking at her image in the mirror, thoughts of the past emerged. She was back at Performing Arts High School during her senior year. She had been accepted into the most advanced jazz class in the curriculum. It was there she met Tim Bartel.

Tim was fabulous looking, probably the best dancer in the school. Pat was instantly smitten. His blonde, closely cropped hair suited him. His flirtatious brown eyes fascinated and teased. His sensuous mouth beckoned seductively when he smiled, accentuating his irresistible dimples. His large tool was packaged and positioned purposely in his tights. Watching him incessantly, Pat felt the pleasure of wetness between her legs.

Weeks passed and flirtation turned to dating. Pat was mad about Tim. When he turned his attention on her he was such a turn-on. Pat became totally besotted, going along with what suited him sexually. He was intensely imaginative, demanding, and dominated her completely.

Pat constantly brooded about other girls snatching Tim away, and stopped eating, becoming alarmingly thin. Pat convinced Alan and Maureen that her weight loss was due to the grueling demands of the dance department.

Tim tired of Pat in time. She was far too clingy and malleable. And her emaciated body was a turn-off during sex. For him, it was over.

With the arrival of spring break, Tim told Pat he was going out of town. Reluctantly Pat accepted his plans. At the close of school he walked her to the subway and kissed her as they parted. The kiss was not a lingering, passionate one, and left her uneasy.

The following week Pat decided to go shopping for a new Easter outfit. She enjoyed the unseasonably warm weather, and the Fifth Avenue shops all decorated for spring. Feeling thirsty, she stopped for a soda. The ice cold Coke tasted good.

Glancing across the street, she saw someone familiar. Suddenly, her breath caught. Standing at a traffic light was Tim with a stunning girl! Pat thought she must be mistaken. Then the unimaginable happened. Tim kissed the girl passionately, oblivious to the traffic and pedestrians around them.

'No, it couldn't be! Not Tim,' she thought, feeling a wave of nausea. Pat was numb as she sat wondering what to do. Should she rush over and confront him? Should she try to forget what she saw? Or should she convince herself she was mistaken? Gathering her belongings she went out on the street. From her vantage point she saw Tim and the girl get into a cab.

Pat called Tim's apartment. 'No answer! But of course, he's out of town. No, it must have been someone else. I'm Tim's, I'm the one he wants,' she thought over and over. But no matter how hard Pat tried to convince herself, she was sick with doubt.

All through Easter she brooded, sequestering herself away from family and friends. Maureen became deeply concerned about the changes in Pat's behavior and appearance. When she and Alan tried to broach the subject, Pat lashed out at them.

Classes resumed on Monday. Pat took great pains with her make-up, wearing her hair the way Tim liked it, adding a sprig of flowers to her ponytail. She chose a lavender leotard, his favorite. With nervous anticipation she waited, scanning the hall as students passed. Suddenly, he approached.

"Tim!" She kissed him fervently.

"Pat, stop it," he said, abruptly pulling away.

"Tim, I missed you so much."

"Oh? I never missed you." The remark stung.

"I don't understand," she responded weakly, fighting back tears.

"Well, understand this. I don't want to fuck you anymore!"

"Oh please, Tim. Don't do this! I love you."

"Fuck off!" He brushed past her, slamming the door.

Shaky and weak, Pat ran to the restroom, sobbing. Then, she felt the wrench in her gut, the flush running up her body. Quickly she kneeled over the commode as she gagged and heaved. Reduced to sweats she repeatedly threw up bile. She crumpled to the floor.

Hearing voices, she quietly closed the stall door and locked it. Pulling herself up on the toilet seat was a challenge, but she knew she had to regain her equilibrium. Reaching for the roller, she slowly unwound toilet paper and wiped her mouth. The voices were close.

"How's Tim?"

"He's incredible! We practically spent the entire break fucking. He's the best fuck, no doubt about it."

"Details, I want details," insisted the other. Pat could scarcely breathe.

"Well, he fucked Pat Byrne for weeks until she got too clingy. She was lovesick and all he wanted was to poke. He knows that's all I want, so he's tailor made!" They laughed as they exited to the restroom.

Pat remained motionless. It hurt so much she was weak. 'Tim dropped me, just like that,' was all she could think about. 'I'm worthless!' She had given herself entirely to him and he repaid her like this! As that reality hovered, she rose, unlocked the door and walked to the sink.

The cold water felt good on her face. Her head was throbbing. Reaching for a paper towel she glanced at herself in the mirror. She was shocked! Gaunt and pale, her natural beauty frayed-around-the-edges. Her spirit was broken.

Pleading sudden illness at the office, she was excused for the day. She remained out of school for a week, claiming the flu. When she returned she transferred to another jazz class. 'It'll be a cold day in hell before I trust another guy,' she thought.

Now, as Pat sat before the dressing room mirror, the memory of Tim Bartel's betrayal faded. 'Had that happened only five years ago?' Pushing it from her memory, she concentrated on tonight. She would soon be with Owen.

After numerous toasts to Phillipe and Joe, the gypsies finished the champagne and left for the night, leaving Jonas and Phillipe alone.

"You were great tonight, Phillipe, a real quick study."

"I owe you, Cheri. May I show my appreciation?" Jonas was already hard. As if in a trance he rose, walked to the wall switch, and turned off the lights. The room was plunged in darkness. The thought of sex on theatre property heightened Jonas' excitement. Slowly, he found his way to Phillipe, who immediately reached down and peeled off Jonas' dance belt. His hands explored Jonas as he considered the safest place to play.

Jonas was weak with longing. His heart beat wildly as Phillipe locked the door to the restroom. Teasing Jonas into willing submission was easy as Phillipe's deft hands took over, leaving Jonas writhing with expectation. With each move Phillipe brought him closer to eruption. He had been taken beyond any place he had been before. Phillipe was the best.

They entered the shower. Turning on the spray, Phillipe pulled Jonas under the cascade, kissing and fondling him continuously. Following their shower, they dried off and dressed, departing for the hotel to try and satisfy their rampant lust.

Mally and Griff met following the show. After a light supper, the two walked along the beach, holding hands and enjoying the night air. The gentle tropical breeze was a welcome relief from the emotional two weeks in Atlanta.

"Darling, come back with me tonight." Returning to Griff's hotel, they made love for hours, falling asleep entangled in each other's arms. It was delightful sleeping with the balcony door open, the sound of the surf beneath them, as the ocean breeze wafted over them.

Further down the beach, Pat arrived at Owen's hotel to find him on the phone. Patiently she waited, while Owen continued, failing to keep the annoyance out of his voice. 'It must be Vera,' she thought, grudgingly.

"I'll call you when I get in. Bye." Owen reached for Pat, enfolding her in his arms. His mood became softer.

"Baby, I've missed you," he whispered, stroking her hair. "With your audition put off until fall, would you consider coming into the New York production of this show?"

"I don't understand."

"I thought maybe you might come back to New York."

"I love this company, Owen. Why would I leave?"

"I just thought if you were in New York it would be easier to be together, that's all."

"Easier for whom?"

"What?"

"I want to know," said Pat, tears welling. "Am I just a convenient fuck?"

"For crying out loud, you've got me half crazy wanting you. Pat, please don't start this shit."

"It's not shit, Owen. I've been hurt, been hurt badly in the past. I was a sexual convenience for a guy I was deeply in love with. He betrayed me, threw me away like garbage. I won't let it happen again."

"I'm not going to throw you away, Pat. I love you. And you're going to have to trust me. Do you understand? You're going to have to trust me. You're the woman I want, just you." Owen could see that Pat still wasn't convinced.

"Pat, what is it? What's wrong?"

"Why haven't you and Vera gotten a divorce? Why does she hang on? Why is it that when she calls while I'm here, you constantly placate her?" Owen reached for Pat and held her. Stroking her hair, he spoke softly.

"Vera made it clear she will never give me a divorce, not without a major war. We have joint assets, investments accrued through years of hit shows together. I must be careful, Pat. I made earlier choices that screwed things up, indiscretions she will never forgive me for. Vera's capable of inflicting pain and humiliation, and itching to take me down if I don't play her game. She could create a lot of damage."

"Do you think she has any idea about us?" Owen pulled away and reached for a cigarette. Lighting it, he took a deep drag.

"She must never know, Baby. It could be dangerous for you, for your future career. She's twisted, wildly possessive. In her mind, I will be back, that we'll reconcile, so of course she is constantly checking up. That's why I placate, play her game. It's sheer survival of the fittest, Baby. One thing she doesn't know is how much I'm in love with you.

"Oh Owen, I love you so much," Pat cried, as she reached for him, holding him as if her life depended on it. In doing so she set her future course, a course with a man who would challenge her heart and her craft.

The week in Miami played out. Joe and Phillipe got comfortable in the show, Owen left for New York promising to call Pat, and the company got sun and rave notices. On Saturday night the company prepared for the move to New Orleans. The show would perform a three-week run at the Civic Theatre. Load out proceeded uneventfully. On Sunday, the company boarded a train bound for Louisiana.

Jonas and Phillipe were in full blown lust. They were now inseparable, but had to behave discreetly for professional reasons. Each waited for the train to pull out. As the miles flew by Jonas went to Phillipe's compartment. The clicking of the train's wheels against the tracks, the intermittent whistles at crossings, and the constant motion of the swaying cars drowned out their rowdy play.

Chapter 41

New Orleans

Gil was waiting as the cast exited the train, holding a list of hotels for quick reference. Company members were advised to make their selections for New Orleans the previous week. The weather had turned cool.

Mally selected a rooming house recommended by Dana and Dick. Before her stood a pillared two-story mansion surrounded by a high iron fence. Sculptured cornstalks were carved into the ironwork every few feet. As she walked through the imposing gate a winding walk led her through a thicket of flowering bushes to an enormous veranda. A tidy row of colorful rattan furniture had a welcoming appeal.

Mally checked in and was directed to her room, an old fashioned affair heavy with the charm of an era long gone. A huge gas jet fireplace stood at the center wall. Her eyes noted every detail of the room. The big brass bed, with a sagging mattress. Two floor-to-ceiling windows. Their federal pane glass. And their heavy, ball-fringed drapes hanging in scallops. A ringing phone abruptly interrupted her Tara musings.

"Mal, it's me."

"Pat, hi! How are you?"

"Better now! I cancelled my sign-up place, a gloomy, dust-catching pit. It had a funny smell, Mal. I just couldn't do three weeks in that firetrap.

"So where are you now?"

"I got a decent rate at a really neat place on Canal Street."

"Good! Are you hungry for lunch?"

"Yes! Phillipe mentioned a place called Tu Jacques. It's on Decatur Street, across from Cafe Du Monde at the French Market. It's open late for lunch."

"Great. I'll grab a cab and meet you there about one."

The Civic Theatre carried the flavor of days when theatre patrons, in their finest attire, traveled by carriage. The walk was lined with shrubbery as stately as the large fountains on either side of the portico. The lobby was graciously carpeted in a rich oriental pattern. Fully stocked bars were strategically located at both ends of the lobby. Pygmy palms in large ceramic pots added elegance to the theatre's reception area.

The house seats and massive drapes were done in royal blue upholstery accented with gold trim. Gilded horse-drawn Roman chariots marched around the plaster proscenium arch.

Griff had worked the Civic before. The technical equipment had been updated in recent years and there was ample space to store sets and props. Special tracks had to be put in over the existing stage floor and fly space had to accommodate several large scene drops. Several set pieces were bulky and would need to be struck during musical numbers. The massive show scrim was handled with care. It was an integral part of the production used to mask the upstage area needed for crossovers during scenes.

The locals were excellent. Griff looked forward to working with these old-timers, seasoned pros who'd seen it all. With his hand-picked capable staff, he could relax and enjoy his time in New Orleans with Mally.

Jonas and Phillipe checked into a quaint inn in the heart of the Quarter. The establishment had been in operation since the 1800's and had been refurbished several times. Though Jonas had played New Orleans before, Phillipe agreed to be his guide, showing him new points of interest. Numerous gay establishments lined Bourbon Street, places they planned to check out.

Jonas was madly in love. He never felt this way before. His first lover, Ken Sutton, had been his first real romance. Gary had proven a faithful friend and companion, though Jonas had never been in love with him or satisfied by him in bed. He had turned to tricking to satisfy his rampant sexual needs.

Phillipe was another matter. He was aggressive, demanding, imaginative, controlling, the dominant partner in bed. With Phillipe, Jonas became daring, outrageous, his insatiable lust satisfied. How soon their passion would burn out, he did not know. How long Phillipe would stick around, he could not guess. For the time being he was in heaven.

The opening night crowd lined the plaza in anticipation of this much-touted musical, winner of several Tony Awards and a Pulitzer Prize. The sell-out audience couldn't miss the obvious satiric flavor of the material and responded with overwhelming enthusiasm. At the end of the performance, Mally and Pat decided to share a cab. Walking unescorted at night was not recommended.

As they left the theatre they walked under the lengthy canopy, grateful for cover as the misty night air turned into a drizzle of cool rain. The dampness chilled their bodies, still cooling down from the performance. Mally buttoned her winter-weight coat and raised her collar closer to her neck. Pat's waterproof trench coat staved off the moisture, but she wished she'd worn a heavier sweater.

Through the rain, the top of a cab was visible. Hailing the driver, Pat opened the passenger door and got in, Mally close behind. The driver, an older gentleman, glanced back at the girls, his facial expression suddenly changing.

"No ladies, I can't," he blurted.

"What's the problem, sir?"

"Miss, colored cabs must take colored fares. I could lose my license. I'm sorry," he said, shaking his head. Mally exited the cab, pulling Pat along.

"I don't get it Mal."

"Pat, we're in the heart of Dixie. There are separate racial cabs here." Just then, another pair of headlights could be seen through the thick mist. The driver was white.

"Can you take us to Canal Street and the French Quarter?" The cabbie nodded and the girls got in. Sliding with difficulty across the back seat in their wet clothes, they attempted to get comfortable.

Bourbon Street was jammed as Jonas and Phillipe made their way through the throng. They heard music coming from an establishment on the corner. Peering in, the all male crowd looked worth investigating.

The place was packed to the rafters. Thick clouds of smoke hung in the air over the raucous clientele like gray smog. In the corner, a three-piece combo blasted Dixieland music, while men gyrated to the beat. Men cruised the vicinity with a single purpose, to get laid. There was an eclectic assortment of possibilities. Some patrons were young and pretty, some old and paunchy. Well-dressed business types, bikers, hustlers and leather boys crowded the small space.

Jonas and Phillipe found convenient stools allowing them ample visibility. Jonas ordered a beer for himself and a cognac for Phillipe. They toasted and returned to scope the trade. Phillipe spotted Joe Pinto, who just arrived out of the rain.

"What's up?" Joe glanced quickly over the scene and mused, "Obviously, not mine!" Phillipe excused himself to look for a restroom.

"Seriously, anything looking good here? I need some relief."

"Yeah, that's obvious," said Jonas, an edge creeping into his voice.

"So, you snagged the French hunk, Jonas!" Looking beyond them, Joe spotted a potential.

"Ciao. I see some serious flesh." Joe walked toward the dance floor.

Through the clamor Jonas noticed Joe already moving in on a pretty one.

As Jonas finished his beer, he felt an arm sliding around his shoulder. Phillipe's warm breath invaded his ear. Feeling the familiar tightening in his stomach, the rush of desire in his limbs, he was more than ready. The gray wash of rain chilled them as the night air closed in making their return to bed all the more inviting.

Mally and Griff enjoyed the city together, discovering a treasure trove of unexpected delights. Their favorite haunt was the Café Du Monde in the French Market. Whether stopping for a recharge after exploring all day or a treat following a performance, they indulged in cups of Chicory coffee and the Quarter's traditional, puffy beignet, deep-fried pastry pillows rolled in powdered sugar.

Griff introduced Mally to noted eateries such as Brennan's, The Court of The Two Sisters, and Galatroix's. They browsed antique and curio stores, and galleries, occasionally peeking in voo-doo shops designed to entice visitors with lurid stories of black magic and haunting in the infamous Quarter.

Mally loved the bookshops, coffee houses, street musicians and peddlers around Jackson Square and the popular carriage rides with Griff. They walked for hours, staring in shop windows, enjoying the chill of the drizzle that fell almost daily and ending an evening together at Griff's luxury hotel suite. The special ambience that was New Orleans lent itself to the growing love between them.

Christmas was fast approaching. Mally and Pat enjoyed shopping in the Quarter, gathering tiny treasures to send home. Stores and restaurants trimmed for the holidays reminded them of Dickens' *Christmas Carol*. Christmas lights twinkled everywhere, entwined in massive green garlands carefully looped over storefronts. The constant drizzle enveloping the city, made palatable by the mild temperatures, was a reminder that the show would soon be leaving the south, moving to colder climes.

Chapter 42

Christmas Aboard

The mood was festive as cast, crew, and orchestra gathered for a party aboard the train-a party thrown by the producer, and supervised by Griff.

After a special buffet dinner and drinks, the group assembled to sing Christmas carols and exchange gifts, arranged through a name drawing. Norry Van volunteered to play Santa, causing pandemonium. He made a jolly, swishy St. Nick as he carried out his duties, his ample belly made possible with packing material.

Each cast member was given a sterling key ring and pendant on which the show's logo was embossed—a gift from producer Vincent Lehrman. Norry called out each person's name, coyly interjecting playful remarks, as he handed out gifts ranging from blatant and tacky to thoughtful. As a final note, Norry whipped off his beard and gave a toast to the assemblage.

Griff followed. "I want to wish you all a Merry Christmas! You are an exceptional company!" A massive cheer arose punctuating the festive affair. Some began to leave. But the rest remained, drinking, singing, and becoming even rowdier.

Pat returned to her Pullman. She thought about her family in the Bronx. The smell and taste of Aunt Kerry's traditional Irish Christmas meal was unforgettable as she imagined herself with the entire Byrne clan. There would be eight courses of traditional dishes and the family toast led by her dad. Following dinner the family gathered around the beautifully decorated fir. Presents were opened to shouts of enthusiasm, everyone guessing what treasures were hidden under the colorful wrappings and shiny bows reflecting the light. An offering of cognac and the singing of traditional carols topped the evening. After the guests departed, the immediate family attended midnight mass.

As Pat lay on her makeshift bed, she tasted her tears. Thinking of Owen only intensified her angst. Where was he tonight? Did he celebrate Christmas or was he oblivious to the holidays? Was he with Vera? Maybe he was on the make! She immediately pushed that thought away.

She longed for him. The soft warmth of her genitals accepted her fingers as she rubbed repeatedly feeling her orgasm building. All the while she imagined that it was Owen bringing her satisfaction until she succumbed. When the ripple effect passed she fell asleep.

Mally had enough rabble, returning to her Pullman. As she undressed she heard a knock on the door. Griff slipped into her compartment and took her in his arms, kissing fervently. Slipping into bed, they felt the sway of the train as it rocked them to sleep. The state of Louisiana had passed. They were in Texas.

Jonas and Phillipe made their way to the club car. Ordering nightcaps they sprawled in a booth, allowing the growing buzz to take hold. Joe Pinto approached. Without invitation, he slid in next to Phillipe.

"Well, if it isn't the two lovebirds," he slurred, a bit loaded. Jonas was noticeably annoyed.

"What do you want?" Joe smiled slyly. "I want him," pointing to Phillipe. "We could be hot together!"

"You're pissed, Joe," said Jonas, his ire rising.

"And you're selfish, selfish, selfish," Joe chanted as he tried to stand. He fell in a heap.

"He's passed out, Cheri. Let's get him back to his compartment. Do you know which one?"

"He's next to Jim Sorenson." With the tilt of a couple of tipsy sailors, Jonas and Phillipe carried Joe to his Pullman, pulled down the bed, and placed him on top of the covers.

"I hope he has a major hangover tomorrow, the asshole," Jonas said, removing Joe's shoes.

"Cheri, forget him. Let's get to bed. It's late." Settling in Jonas' compartment, they fell asleep wrapped in each other's arms to the clicking of the tracks beneath the train's wheels. Houston was hours away. And how would Texans react to a sophisticated show like *Bravo Business*? Tuesday's audience would tell.

Chapter 43

Holiday Cheer

Fifty-seven degrees on Christmas morning! It was obvious that the lack of snow and cold made this holiday different for those raised in the northern half of the U.S.

Mally and Pat checked into the Rice Hotel. A desk clerk, dripping with Texas charm, greeted them. They were given a generous discount for the week.

The fragrance of flowers greeted their noses as they opened the door. Pat noticed a card with her name tucked into an enormous floral arrangement and opened it immediately. Noting the contents she sighed, "Is it any wonder I love him?"

As far as Mally was concerned the reviews were still out on Owen. She saw what his long silence did to Pat. He definitely had a Swengali effect on her.

"Do you want to take a walk? Maybe find a church nearby?"

"It doesn't feel like Christmas. I'm staying put," Pat murmured. The phone rang.

"Merry Christmas, Darling. How would you two like to join me for dinner later?"

"Griff! Where are you staying?"

"I'm at my usual in Houston, the Viceroy. How's the Rice?"

"We got a terrific deal on a lovely room."

"Good. I'll take care of everything. See you at seven." Carefully, she turned to Pat. "Griff has invited us out for dinner tonight."

"OK. I could use the company. Spending Christmas alone is a drag."

Later, the girls showered and dressed for dinner. Pat wore a striking black velveteen sheath with simple pearls at her throat and ears. Mally dug out a bright red wool dress with a matching jacket. It was pleasant to dress up after constantly living in jeans.

Griff arrived at seven. Mally and Pat looked beautiful as they headed downstairs. Griff brightened when he saw them. The threesome set out for a dinner under a starry night in Texas. As was Griff's style, he selected a top-notch restaurant-this one with a panoramic view of downtown Houston. The Delmont Grill specialized in Texas steaks and seafood. When they arrived, the manager greeted them enthusiastically.

"Mr. Edwards, how good to see you!"

"Good evening, Rudy. May I present Mally Winthrop and Patricia Byrne?"

"You are a lucky man, Mr. Edwards." Signaling the hostess, they were shown to a table on the perimeter of the bar and flush with a large window overlooking the city.

"This restaurant makes one revolution an hour. That way you see the whole skyline of Houston."

"What a view," Pat observed. Mally loved the ambience of the restaurant brightly decorated for Christmas. Once drinks were ordered they settled into pleasant conversation. After ordering dinner, Pat excused herself to find a restroom. As she passed the bar a hand reached out.

"Patricia!"

"Blaine! How are you?"

He looked at her with delight. "We're destined to meet again. I think about you a lot. You're here at the auditorium, right?"

"Yes, we're here for the rest of the week. And you?"

"I'm involved in business and some pleasure. I have a brother in town. I spend the holidays with him and my sister-in-law. They're expecting their first child and have promised me the role of godfather."

"That's wonderful, Blaine."

"Say, what are you doing tomorrow evening?" Pat felt an instant flush across her cheeks.

"We open. Why?"

"One of the big money men in Houston is a theatre buff. He's bringing an entourage to opening night, a tradition. Would you care to attend a post-theatre party? I'd be honored if you would accompany me."

"I would love to," she said without hesitation. Weary of the waiting game and craving some male attention, Pat was ready for some fun.

"Wonderful! I'll meet you at the stage door following the show."

"Is it dressy?"

"Oh yes, very. But you needn't worry," he said, coyly. "You'll be the most stunning woman there, I promise you." Pat excused herself, and returned to the table. Her absence had been noted.

"I know, you thought I fell in. Isn't this wild? I bumped into Blaine Courtman. He's asked me to some millionaire's party tomorrow night after the show."

"I think that's great," remarked Griff.

"Better than great," Pat enthused, raising her glass. The three toasted, chatted, and dined away the remaining hours of Christmas.

Chapter 44

Houston

The huge audience was unusually boisterous. Big laughs repeated continuously throughout the evening. Owen's choreography brought down the house. It was a great beginning to this phase of the tour.

Pat received two-dozen long stem yellow roses from Blaine. The women's dressing room was abuzz. "My Lord, what incredible roses," Dana exclaimed. 'Who's the sender?"

"It's a secret," teased Pat, adding a wink.

Jackie had another log to fuel her fire. 'That damn Byrne bitch,' she thought to herself. 'Who does she think she is?' She vowed to get even with Pat, who seemed to have it all.

Pat dressed in one of her sexiest dresses, the one that best showed her phenomenal figure. The satin fabric in forest green brought out her eyes and contrasted with her flaming auburn tresses. A plunging neckline was shameless and purposely so. Her sheath was tea length with a tantalizing slit that ran from the hem to her upper thigh. A pair of her highest heels served to give her shapely legs the added height and allure.

Stepping into the mild night, she spotted Blaine, who greeted her warmly. Once they were comfortably seated in his stretch limo, the driver pulled away from the curb.

"You look fantastic. I'm bewitched completely."

"Thank you. You're sweet," purred Pat, savoring Blaine's attention.

As they drove, Blaine opened a bottle of champagne and poured two glassfuls, handing her the first. Lifting his, he made a toast, looking like a lovesick kid.

"To you, Patricia."

As she sipped, Pat felt the tiny bubbles tickling the back of her throat. She relaxed. "How could I have misjudged this honey,' she thought. 'He's attentive, sincere and wildly attracted to me.' She could tell he would be hers with little effort. She liked that.

The car pulled up to an impressive building. The chauffeur opened the door and helped her out, followed by Blaine. She gazed up the tower.

"We're guests of Gregory Morgan the third. He is a third generation oilman, filthy rich and a great lover of theatre. He brought fifty of his closest friends to your show this evening. Come on, he's anxious to meet you."

"I'm kind of nervous," Pat offered, momentarily dropping her façade.

"Don't be. He'll be putty in your hands."

The thirty-story ride to the top penthouse took only seconds. When they reached the Morgan floor, the doors opened into an exquisite penthouse. Guests wandered back and forth as Blaine led Pat through the throng of well-heeled guests.

Gregory Morgan was surrounded by a bevy of beautiful women all animated in their quest to impress him. He spotted Blaine and Pat.

"Blaine, please," he insisted, nodding at Pat.

"Gregory, may I present Patricia Byrne from the cast of *"Bravo Business."*

"I'm delighted to meet you! The show was fabulous, just fabulous," he gushed.

"Thank you, Mr. Morgan."

"Please call me Gregory." The other women stared at Pat. She was much too attractive and had the audacity to steal their thunder.

"Blaine, please show Patricia to the bar. The buffet is nearby as well."

"Thank you, Gregory," said Pat, as Blaine led her away.

"The pleasure is mine, Patricia." All eyes focused on Pat as she walked through the throng. Her deportment and stunning looks could not be ignored.

"Are you hungry?"

"Yes, I'm always hungry!" Blaine took two champagne cocktails from the bartender and escorted Pat to a lavish buffet, complete with a grandiose ice sculpture typical of Texas cowboy astride a reeling horse. Blaine suggested moving to the terrace where there was less noise and fresh air.

Pat was relieved she brought a jacket. Blaine took the cue, placing it on her shoulders. As he did so, his fingers brushed her neck. Pat shivered slightly. The champagne had suddenly gone to her head, and she needed to eat. Blaine picked at his food, as he watched Pat scarf hers. He was obviously more interested in her than prime rib. Pat felt sated as she finished the last morsels on her plate. Blaine set her dish aside and taking her hands in his, moved closer. Without resistance Pat allowed him to kiss her. His lips were soft and sensuous. When she did not pull away, he kissed her more aggressively.

Pat's resolve to play it cool dissolved. Blaine stood and took her by the hand. Looking around the terrace, he spotted a perfect set-up. Leading her to a corner obscured from sight by thick shrubbery and overgrowth, he made his play. 'I have to have her,' he thought.

Blaine caressed Pat as his tongue ran along her neck. As he continued, she was becoming wet. Exploring, he reached down the front of her décolletage and squeezed her nipples. They tightened and shriveled under his touch. She was panting now, moaning with anticipation.

Blaine explored as he found his way to the slit in Pat's dress. Opening the fabric, he moved upward. His warm hands exposed her panties, his fingers slid under the lacey fabric with ease. There, he gently caressed her genitals.

"Do you want me to stop?"

"No, don't stop!" The excitement of being barely out of public view turned her on even more. Blaine knelt, sliding her panties down her legs as she waited breathless. Holding her dress out of the way he put his mouth on her, his warm breath increasing her desire. Flinching slightly, she allowed him to continue. There was no resistance, no outrage this time. She wanted sex, only sex. She was starved and craving it any way she could get it.

Blaine moved his tongue in and out, accelerating the tempo as he pried her open with his hands. She felt her orgasm coming as she moaned her delight. Blaine's heart beat wildly as he stroked her more fervently, Pat's moans guiding his moves. When he felt her ready, he covered her mouth with his and tongued her while she peaked. Holding her while she shook he waited patiently for the ripples to subside.

"Oh Pat, be mine. Please do me," he whispered.

Without hesitation, Pat knelt before Blaine. His fly was bulging as she unzipped him. He gasped at the touch of her hands on his engorged shaft. Placing her mouth around him she heightened his craving, building the intensity and rhythm as she moved up and down. Moments later, he exploded through his intense pleasure. Weak in the knees, he held her shoulders to steady himself.

The sounds of others near by brought them to full attention. Hurriedly Pat smoothed out her dress, allowing it to fall to her ankles. Blaine zipped his fly, and produced a handkerchief to wipe the smear of lipstick from his mouth and Pat's. When they were repaired, they left their hiding place and walked back into the penthouse. Thanking their host, Blaine and Pat excused themselves and returned to the waiting limo.

Now they were connected. Blaine experienced his fantasy woman, Patricia Byrne. Pat felt a marvelous release as well as an undertow of emotions. She was no longer exclusive to Owen. Without realizing it she had set complications in motion.

Chapter 45

Oklahoma City

Load out was underway as Griff and his crew prepared to move the show to Oklahoma City, where the company would celebrate New Year's. The trek between cities would be shorter this time.

In the meantime, Pat thought about Blaine. He was good. He turned her on, provided necessary relief, and didn't take her for granted. She was aware that the slightest encouragement on her part would keep him interested. She was also aware that it might be some time before Owen showed up. She had no illusions. They were separated by distance. For the present she would not allow her feelings for him to cloud her logic. As much as she loved Owen she would simply have to do without him and take advantage of Blaine's attention.

She liked Blaine's flexibility. His tremendous wealth afforded him the opportunity to be wherever it suited him and that suited her. That night at Gregory's had proven their sexual compatibility. She was shameless in her desire to have it her way, noting how perfect an arrangement it was. This time she was calling the shots.

Pat was handling a double-edged sword. Caution was paramount if Owen was never to find out. Even the length she would have to go, to keep her business from Mally, would be difficult because she cherished Mally's friendship. Sharing her involvement with Blaine would only complicate matters. No, it would be her secret.

New Year's Eve arrived and the Municipal Auditorium management along with the local chamber of commerce threw a party. Unlimited drinks were offered as well as a lavish midnight buffet. A band was hired for the cast's enjoyment.

Everyone attended. It was a pleasant diversion for the company to participate in a traditional evening. Mally and Griff were joined by Pat, Jonas and Phillipe at one table while some of the others including Dana and Dick Landry mingled with the locals.

Jackie and Sonja were noticeably quiet during the party. It was obvious they isolated themselves to gossip freely, a favorite pastime for Jackie, given her hatred of Pat, the enemy. Jackie lit a cigarette and took a deep drag, allowing smoke to slip out her nostrils, enjoying the comfort. Glancing briefly at Pat and her comrades her ire surfaced.

Pat's beauty and dance ability, and Owen's obvious favoritism galled her beyond measure. Owen was now bedding Pat, and that was unforgivable, justification for her getting even, and she would. But, first she would wait until the moment she chose to strike. "That bitch won't know what hit her and it will serve that bastard Owen right," she snorted triumphantly.

Sonja listened with fascination and misplaced admiration. Her dislike for Pat was based on Jackie's point of view. Sonja was young and impressionable, without a clue about whom she was dealing with.

Chapter 46

Tulsa

The cast's recent foray through the south had dulled their memory of cold but winter was now well and truly upon them.

The drastic change would require longer warm-ups. Tulsa's weather was blustery and cold. Snow flurries were a daily constant.

Cast members scurried to the theatre through heavy winds, with collars up, hats in place, and cranky moods.

Jim Sorenson and Joe Pinto developed colds. Rumors circulated that they were sharing a bed as well as germs. Jonas and Phillipe kept to themselves, spending free time in the throes of passion. Mally and Griff met for breakfast on matinee days and talked every night after the show.

Dana and Dick were living their lives status quo on tour. Dick was running the show for Griff on matinee days. The management was pleased with his work. His aim was to develop into a full time stage manager. This opportunity to hone his skills was building a future that hopefully included a baby with Dana. She had been dancing professionally for ten years and more than ready to start a family soon. She wanted the white house in Jersey, the fenced-in backyard, and three kids to play in it.

Friday night, company manager Gil Fredericks suffered a major heart attack and was hospitalized. The following morning Griff was informed by doctors that Gil must be left behind until he was well enough to return to New York.

The setback was upsetting. Griff had worked with Gil a number of times and knew him to be the best road manager in the business. Now he would be replaced with a lesser known from New York. Griff needed to act quickly, and made a call to Lehrman's residence.

"Vinny? Griff Edwards. Sorry to call you at home. We have an emergency here in Tulsa."

"Yes, Griff, I've already been informed about Gil Fredericks. His wife, Bernice, is on her way to Tulsa now."

"Do you have someone?"

"Yes, as a matter-of-fact. Cal Friedkin will join you in Kansas City next week. If you can't have Gil, Cal's your man. He will be fine for your company."

"Thanks, Vinny. I appreciate your quick work on this one."

"Don't mention it. Say, I understand you've replaced a couple of dancers recently. It's a shame about Gary Hanson. I've known him for years. He was a consistent performer."

"Yes. Well, thanks for your help."

"Don't mention it Griff. I like to keep you happy."

Meanwhile, Jackie Eldridge was making her own arrangements as she busied herself composing a letter to Vera Daniels. It would be sent as though written by Pat. 'This is just too good,' she thought. 'Of course if anyone finds out about this, I'll be nailed to the wall!' Jackie knew that extreme caution was crucial.

The Tulsa run ended. The production prepared to move up the central portion of the U.S., where winter was even more intense. Blizzard conditions blanketed the corridor north from Oklahoma to Minnesota with twelve inches of snow in some parts. The company was scheduled to depart by 10 a.m. on Sunday morning for an early evening arrival in Kansas City, barring any complications.

The cast was advised to keep warm clothes handy. Mally found her red car coat amongst her clothes and chose a long, hand-knitted muffler, mittens, cap and her fur-lined boots. She was a true native Minnesotan.

Pat preferred glamour to warmth and had decided to wear her new fedora. Her suede boots would serve her feet and her stylish trench coat would have to do, with a turtleneck sweater for layering. The coat was waterproof, but not made to keep out the wind and cold. She managed to find her leather gloves in the bottom drawer of her trunk and grudgingly stuffed them into her pockets. Mally and Pat spotted Jonas and Phillipe on their way to the bus.

"Hey, Strangers, how are you?"

"Hi, Doll. I'm OK, but my beau has a terrible cold." Phillipe tried a forced smile, his nose noticeably red and irritated from repeated blowing. The gypsies filled the bus. Soon, they were on their way to the station.

When they arrived at the platform area, they spotted Griff giving out Pullman assignments in Gil's absence. When he completed his chore, he left the station and grabbed a cab to the airport, where he would meet his crew.

After boarding the train, everyone settled for the trip ahead. Mally felt rested and joined Dana and Dick in the club car for coffee and a light breakfast. Pat excused herself and retreated to her Pullman. Jonas ordered coffee for himself and tea for Phillipe, returning to act as nurse.

Jackie and Sonja found a quiet part of the lounge car. Jackie ordered a Bloody Mary with a beer chaser. Reaching for a Chesterfield, she lighted it and took a deep drag. As she exhaled she smiled at Sonja, who sat sipping a ginger ale, the smoke from Jackie's cigarette framing her face. 'How sweet it will be,' she thought. 'I'll have my revenge. The bitch will fall, the prick will suffer and I will win.' She smiled with peculiar detachment at her clever plan.

Chapter 47

Kansas City

The downtown skyline was a winter wonderland rising through clouds heavy with snow. Kansas City plows pressed and pushed through drifts. Ice crystals danced in the air as a wind chill reminded the gypsies Florida was a pleasant memory.

Mally checked into the Muehlebach Hotel and ordered room service. Then she dialed home to Minneapolis. Mally's step dad, Frank Herman answered.

"Mally, baby, where are you?"

"We just arrived in Kansas City, Frank. We'll be in Minneapolis next week."

"I know. Your mom is waiting. Here she is."

"Hi Mom, can't wait to see you! Oh, before I forget, I'll need a ride to and from the theatre if I stay at the house. Is it too much trouble?"

"Are you kidding? Frank's thrilled. His lodge brothers are getting glassy-eyed hearing about the show."

"Great! Well, I'll see you two in a week. I love you!"

"Love you too, Muffin. Hurry home and safe trip."

Mally hung up and stretched across the bed. She was ravenous. The cold always increased her appetite. Ordering room service was quick. In minutes there was a knock at the door. Mally paid the bell-man and rolled the cart to the bed. She watched the news as she ate, enjoying staying put after the long ride that day.

The cast was lodging at the Muehlebach. It was centrally located downtown, within walking distance to the theatre. The hotel offered every possible amenity including a variety of shops and restaurants. The more seasoned gypsies helped the newcomers make their selections. If a place was a dud the word spread.

Jonas ordered chicken soup, hot tea with a brandy chaser for Phillipe and a hamburger deluxe with fries for himself, adding a beer to wash it down. After eating, they took a hot shower then burrowed under the covers to cuddle, watch TV and sleep off their weariness.

Pat couldn't help but notice the telegram shoved under the door to her room. Quickly, she sat on the bed and opened the contents. 'I'm thinking of you as I meet with the new show brass. I love and miss you. Owen.'

Pat missed him more than she cared to admit. He was the man she really wanted. His message made her longing more intense as she brushed away tears. 'I have to be patient,' she thought. 'He's worth the wait.' Patience was something foreign to her.

Mally finished her bath, and slipped into her robe. Before she had a chance to settle with her new paperback, the phone rang. Griff's voice on the other end warmed her immediately.

"Griff, where are you?"

"Here at the Muehlebach. How's your room?"

"Cozy. And yours?"

"The usual, but it's convenient and the service is great."

"I'm glad you're safe, Griff."

"The airport just closed due to a major blizzard out there. Air traffic is backed up all the way to New York. I got a call from Gil's replacement. He's stuck at La Guardia. God, all this weather reminds me of winters in Chicago when I was a kid. They were pretty nasty."

"Minneapolis winters are too! Say, will the show go on?"

"You bet! We're sold out. Well, I'm off to finish tech. The Music Hall is a good old girl. Not many problems to speak of. See you later." As she hung up, she felt a chill. Moving off the bed she walked to the window and gazed out. 'Good old winter,' she mused.

Chapter 48

The Bitch

Jackie carefully penned her poison. As she wrote, she sipped a coke and sucked on a cigarette.

'Dear Miss Daniels: This isn't an easy letter to write, but it's necessary for all concerned. I'm asking you to let Owen go. You see, I'm in love with him and he loves me. We've been seeing each other for months and plan to live together. He doesn't love you anymore. Please give him up. He needs me. Sincerely, Patricia Byrne.'

Jackie laughed as she sealed the hotel envelope and addressed it to Vera. She remembered the address of their coop on Central Park West, having attended a party there years before. As she rode down to the lobby she looked at herself in the elevator mirror.

'Jackie, you're the best! You'll ruin Patricia Byrne and it couldn't happen to a nicer bitch!' As she exited the elevator, she spotted the concierge.

"Sir, where can I buy a postage stamp?"

"Right over there, Miss," the bellman said, pointing to a gift shop across the lobby. You'll make the six p.m. pick-up if you hurry. There's a mail slot next to the elevator."

"Thanks." Reaching the stamp machine, Jackie was feeling more powerful with each passing minute. She put change in the dispenser, waited, and took the small cardboard container as the machine coughed it out. Affixing the stamp to the envelope, she hurried to the mail slot. 'This is the last step,' she thought, relieved.

"May I take that for you, Miss?" Turning, she spotted a mail carrier coming toward the box.

"Yes, thank you," she oozed. "How long will it take my letter to reach New York City?" The man glanced up as he unlocked the box, placing the contents into his sack. He smiled. 'Wow, get a load of the hot bitch! Man, those tits,' he thought as he continued to look Jackie over.

"Well, given the weather right now, my guess, about five to seven days."

"Oh? Well, thank you for the information," she said, smiling.

"Glad to help. Say, you staying here?" Jackie stiffened, her smile suddenly gone.

"Yes. Leaving shortly though."

"Hey, that's a real shame. I get off soon. I'd buy you a drink, get to know you better."

"I'm meeting my husband," Jackie said, briskly. Turning she hurried to the elevator. As the door closed she thought, 'These fucking rubes always want into my pants.'

The gypsies trudged to the theatre. The heavy snow had been shoveled into piles at the stage door, making the entrance accessible to the company. Shaking clothing and stomping feet was necessary before the company could proceed to the dressing rooms.

Out front, the full house was clamoring for the show. The muffled swell of voices in the audience came through the intercom as Griff announced 'places.' The cast took their positions as the overture began.

Sonja stood in her spot, stretching to get her muscles supple. Jackie approached, pulling her into the darkness upstage.

"Guess what? The bitch's days are numbered," whispered Jackie.

"You mean you actually sent that letter?"

"Yeah, and in a few days all hell will break loose! I can't wait."

"I didn't think you'd go through with it."

"You didn't think I'd go through with it? Do you know who you're dealing with?" Sonja, shocked, stepped back. Gaining her equilibrium she stammered, "I mean, is it worth all the trouble it might cause?" Jackie grabbed Sonja's arm with a vise-like grip.

"You listen to me, you little shit. If you ever breathe a word of this to anyone, you'll be sorry! Got it?" Sonja nodded weakly as she pulled herself from Jackie and hurried away.

Audience after audience, undaunted by blizzard conditions, applauded enthusiastically through each performance. Frequent snowfalls and high-spirits continued until closing night.

Chapter 49

The Letter

The phone rang repeatedly. For Owen it had been a grueling week with his backers, trying to work out a proposed budget for the fall production. He was tired and preoccupied as he lit a cigarette.

"Matthews."

The voice on the other end was all too familiar, and out of control. "Owen, you son-of-a-bitch!"

"Vera, slow down. What's going on?"

"So you have someone stashed on tour, do you?"

"What the hell! What are you raving about?"

"I just got a letter from your piece of ass!"

"What the fuck? This is crazy. What letter?"

"Don't play innocent with me, you prick! Who's the piece?" Owen tried to gain footing. His mind was racing. The tension was excruciating.

"Read the letter to me, OK?" As Vera read her ire changed to sobs. Stunned, Owen listened, trying to comprehend or make sense of her barrage. 'How could Pat do such a thing? This could ruin everything,' he thought. "Look Vera, I don't know what to say."

"Do you admit the affair, you asshole?"

"My roving has never been a secret."

"How many people know about this affair?"

"No one knows."

"You're a liar. Everyone knows about your dick. How in hell did the bitch get my address anyway?"

"I have no idea."

"It never ceases to amaze me what some women will do to get a piece of your ass, and the prestige that goes with it. I've had it! I want her ass fired!"

"I can't fire the best dancer I've ever hired!"

"That's your problem. Fire her! And if you don't, I'll talk to Vinny Lehrman. I still have some clout. He adores me, always has. Hell, I should have married him when I had the chance. He begged me enough times."

"Listen Vera, I'll take care of this."

"No kidding! You owe me after all the years of humiliation and hurt! I was in love with you, made hits for you, and you betrayed me. I would have done anything for you, you bastard!"

"I'll fix this. In the meantime, sit tight. I'll be in touch, OK?"

"You'd better, Owen. Do you hear me?"

"Yes, Vera, I do." He hung up shaking.

Reaching for a smoke, he lit the cigarette and took a big drag, allowing the smoke to enter his lungs. He was deeply shaken by Pat's actions. He couldn't accept betrayal by a woman he was in love with. It didn't make sense. Something about the thing didn't ring true, and he would get to the bottom of it.

Looking at his schedule for the coming week, Owen booked a flight to Minneapolis. He would confront Pat and stall Vera. He'd have to act fast. Vera was capable of anything in her frame of mind. She had stored up enough bile to work the world over.

Back in Kansas City, Griff took a moment from his paperwork and phoned Mally.

"I've been thinking about you a lot today. How goes it?"

"We're good. Say, where are you planning to stay in Minneapolis?"

"I'm going to stay with my folks. Frank, my step dad, has offered to chauffeur me to and from the burbs. I don't drive."

"Isn't the commute a lot of trouble?"

"Normally, yes, but I haven't seen my folks in ages. They are really looking forward to having me there."

"I understand."

"Oh by the way, Mom is planning a cast party the first weekend of the run. Do you think the company will come?"

"I'm sure they will, Darling."

"Good. Love you, Griff."

"Love you too, Darling."

The phone rang, waking Pat.

"Hi Baby. It's been awhile."

"It's been forever since Miami. Owen, I miss you so much. Thanks for your wire. It meant a lot."

"What have you been up to?" 'A strange question,' she thought.

"We've been snowbound. Ironically, the houses have never been better."

"Good."

"You okay?"

"Why?"

"You sound more tense than usual."

"Well, that's why I'm calling. I miss my girl. I'll be in Minneapolis next week. I'm aiming for Wednesday, staying at the Radisson."

"Are you sure you're ok?"

"I'm fine."

"I love you Owen."

"Yes. Bye." Pat sat back, her stomach tightening. Next week seemed so long from now.

Chapter 50

Heading North

Bravo Business was moving on. The load out went smoothly considering the amount of snow. Griff and his crew flew out Sunday at 7:00 a.m. bound for Minneapolis. He had worked the Orpheum Theatre many times. Originally a vaudeville house, it had been rehabbed recently to accommodate the big set shows. He liked the local techs and the hotel was convenient to the theatre.

Blizzard conditions had passed. Cal Friedkin was at the helm, introducing himself as he dispensed Pullman assignments. The train pulled out of the station promptly at ten a.m. Heavily coated trees dotted the snow-laden Currier and Ives landscape, as the train continued north.

Phillipe was feeling better. The head cold that plagued him for nearly two weeks was gone. He and Jonas decided to socialize. They went to the club car to visit with the company, who dispensed gossip, played poker and consumed coffee and donuts.

Mally felt rested and encouraged Pat to join her for breakfast and a catch-up. Dana and Dick passed by and waved.

"Are you excited about going home, Mal?"

"Yes, I am! I'll be staying with my folks!"

"How will Griff get along without you?"

"Griff will be fine. He loves Minneapolis. We'll spend time together between shows." A waiter appeared. Breakfast was on special and everyone ordered the biggest platefuls available.

Sonja had closed the door to her Pullman. As she started to undress, an abrupt knock caught her off guard. As she peered out she saw Jackie. Reluctantly, she opened the door. Jackie pushed her way in and sat down.

"I sent that letter last Monday and here it is Sunday and nothing is happening!"

"Maybe there was a delay in mail service due to the weather," said Sonja, benignly.

Jackie stood, backing Sonja into the opposite seat. "Remember, keep your mouth shut. You got that?"

"Yes, Jackie, I understand."

"Good. Then I have no further business with you." Without another word Jackie pushed open the door and left. Overcome with nausea, Sonja locked the door and reached the sink just in time to throw up her breakfast.

The train pulled into the Milwaukee Road Depot in downtown Minneapolis around six p.m.

Those standing near the exits felt the frigid cold immediately. The steam rising from the underside of the cars was in an instant freeze. Porters were scurrying around assisting those looking for a quick way into the warmth. The platform, running the length of a full city block was exposed to the fierce wind, blowing from the Mississippi River north of the station.

The gypsies hurried along, hunched over, cringing from the bite of the frigid temperature and ingesting cold air with each breath. On the streets outside, streams of cars waited at traffic lights, their exhaust forming clouds of vapor, covering traffic like a huge gray blanket.

Mally looked around for her folks. As she got her bearings she saw two familiar figures waving.

"Mally, welcome home," said Frank warmly, giving her a big bear hug.

"Muffin, oh, muffin, I'm so happy to see you!" Mally starting tearing up as she hugged Paula. Several cast members arrived all chattering at once. Mally spotted her pals in the crowd.

"Mom and Frank, I'd like you to meet some great friends. This is Patricia Byrne, my best friend and the most fabulous dancer in the company." Pat blushed.

"And this is Jonas Martin, another fabulous dancer in the company." Jonas grinned.

"I'm glad she said that. I felt demoted all of a sudden. And this is my partner, Phillipe Danier."

"I am pleased to meet you both," said Paula.

"Welcome to Minneapolis," added Frank, warmly.

"Anyone who can handle this freeze is tough in my book. You have my utmost respect and sympathy," laughed Jonas.

"Well, thanks, Jonas. We'll do our best to melt the ice," laughed Frank.

"Can we give you all a lift?" Everyone accepted. Piling into the huge station wagon, the five gypsies shared laps as Frank started the car.

"Where are you all staying?" Jonas produced a piece of paper and tried to read it as the car passed under the streetlights dotting Hennepin Avenue.

"It looks like the Hotel Dyckman." The others agreed. Frank turned on to South Sixth Street and pulled up to a medium-sized hotel midway up the block. Everyone got out with their dance bags in tow.

"Thanks so much for the lift," said Pat.

"You're welcome. We'll see you opening night," said Paula.

"Mom, I gave Pat your phone number." Turning to her pals she reiterated, "Guys, check with Pat and call me, ok?"

"Lucky you, home cooked meals! Some girls have all the luck. Bye Mal," yelled Jonas, as Phillipe pulled him into the hotel. As the gypsies disappeared into the lobby, Frank pulled away from the curb. On the way home there was time to catch up. It was decided that the cast party would take place on Sunday, when the show was dark.

Mally was delighted to feel crackling warmth coming from the fireplace as they entered the house. A delightful aroma filled the house from the simmering contents bubbling in a big cast iron kettle on the stove.

Toots, Frank's Bulldog, greeted them as they came through the front door. Enthusiastically he licked all over Mally's face when she kneeled to hug him, filling the house with her laughter.

Kicking off her shoes, she walked down the long hall to her old bedroom. She hadn't been in the house for a year and a half. Everything was as she left it. Her old bed stood begging for its former occupant, the covers drawn back invitingly. Her clock radio, the same one that had jolted her awake for two and half years while she attended university classes, stood on the nightstand, filling the room with music from her favorite station. Later, she joined Frank and Paula to share her touring experiences.

"I have something important to tell you."

"Oh?"

"I'm in love with Griff Edwards, our production stage manager."

"How long has this been going on?"

"Well, it started last October in Wilmington, Delaware. But I knew he was the one the first time I saw him."

"Sounds serious," Frank teased.

"It is serious. You'll see." Yawning, Mally stretched as she gathered her shoes.

"Muffin, it's so good to have you here. We've waited a long time for this. Mally hugged her folks and headed to her old room. "It's good to be home!"

Chapter 51

Minneapolis

The Orpheum Theatre was bustling with activity as the company began the pre-show hustle.

Paula, Frank, and a group of Masonic friends waited for the curtain to go up. The Hermans were popular lodge members, delighted to have their pals along. They were eager to see Mally perform on stage.

In the dressing rooms, face paint transformed faces as curling irons pressed hair into submission. The leads warmed their vocal chords as humidifiers steamed warm, wet air into an atmosphere dried by indoor heating.

The local dressers, in the designated change area, were ready for the five-minute call. Musicians practiced a few measures of the score, while Sandy paced. He always paced. He was a perfectionist.

Griff made the five-minute call, requesting a short meeting of the cast in the green room. The company gathered and chatted and stretched while they waited. Griff came into the room and everyone quieted down.

"Company, for those of you who haven't played the Twin Cities before, the audiences here are very savvy. Be sure to hold for laughs. Mally will be doing the Buccaneer number tonight in Dana's spot, dancers." The group applauded briefly as Griff ordered places. As the group filed out of the green room, Mally stopped to hug Dana.

"Thanks, Dana. I really appreciate your letting me do your spot tonight. My folks are in the audience." Dana returned the hug and added a wink.

"I know how this feels. It's magical! Have fun!"

As the lights went down in the house, Frank took Paula's hand and squeezed it as he whispered, "This night belongs to our Mally." He wasn't surprised to see glistening eyes as Paula fought back tears of pride.

The show was outstanding. The cast's collective energy carried the performance to new heights of excellence. Mally did an extra warm-up to prepare for the Buccaneer number. The four-minute, non-stop dance was a challenge. To swing the number occasionally took more strength than doing it eight shows a week. A dancer built endurance and tolerance by repeatedly performing the demanding choreography. Mally knew it would take every bit of energy she had.

As she kneeled in the treasure chest, her heart was pounding. Pat noticed and took her hand, giving it a squeeze.

"You'll be great, Mal. Just remember to breathe once in a while," she whispered.

The music swelled to a specific moment in the choreography when Chad pulled a gold cloth cover off the top of the box. The girls popped up to the surprise of the audience and held their pose until the men's section was over.

Mally felt the familiar rush as she pranced down to the footlights with the others to begin the combination. The opening section was demanding in its precision. She kept up with the regulars holding her own as she cut through the movements, developing her kicks from her knee as she executed several ball changes in succession.

Mally was a strong performer. Bright, instinctive with impeccable timing and verve, she passed through each section of the choreography with sustained energy. In the final minutes of the number the dancers mixed as they formed couples, partnered in an intense combination involving strenuous legwork and unique bodyline. With the final count of eight, the couples jumped into the final pose landing in frozen motion as chests raised and lowered in hyperventilation.

The Minneapolitans greeted the dancers with thunderous applause. As the lights went to blackout, the group moved off stage carefully. Jonas and Phillipe caught up with Mally, as she headed for the change area.

"You were marvelous," said Phillipe. Jonas added a big wet kiss to her cheek.

"You're dynamite, sweetheart. I'm so proud of you!"

"Thanks, guys. What a ball! I could see my folks in their seats. They were grinning from ear to ear."

The evening ended with a standing ovation. The cast took bow after bow. When at last the curtain finally came down, the cast scrambled to change, unwind and have a few drinks.

Mally and her folks visited a nearby Italian restaurant, Café Di Napoli. Griff came by following his tech wrap-up. Paula and Frank cordially greeted him. The conversation continued until closing. As her folks walked ahead to the ramp, Griff and Mally followed hand in hand.

"Do you think I passed inspection, Darling?"

"Oh my, yes!"

"Good! They can see how in love I am!" Large snowflakes began to fall.

"Do you want a lift?"

"No thanks, Darling. I've been cooped up in that theatre for over fifteen hours. A walk in the fresh air feels good."

"It's great to meet you, Griff," said Frank, shaking hands.

"You, as well," said Griff. He leaned down to kiss Mally. "See you at call."

The packed house and enthusiastic crowd on Wednesday afternoon was motivating to the gypsies, who collectively gave a full-out performance. It was always better for the cast to have a high-energy audience otherwise the afternoon would drag, causing some to mark instead of working to capacity.

Pat changed quickly and went back to the hotel. Cold weather never agreed with her and she was ready for a hot dinner and a power nap between shows. The phone rang.

"Hi Baby, how are you?"

"Owen, where are you?" Pat felt the familiar tightening in her stomach.

"I'm at the Radisson on 7th Street. I just got in. The weather is nasty. We were backed up all the way from Cleveland last night. Lucky I didn't spend the night there."

"When can I see you?"

"Come here after the show. I'm in Suite 800."

"I'll see you later!"

"Later, Baby."

"Owen, I love you." Pat heard the dial tone.

Pat was noticeably quiet. "Are you ok?" Pat didn't blink as she retouched her make-up and slipped into a form-fitting jumpsuit.

"Yes Mal, goodnight." As Pat picked up her bag she noticed Jackie staring at her.

Pat was chilled and decided to take a cab to the Radisson. It was snowing again and large flakes coated her flaming hair creating a veil over her head. When she arrived at the hotel she paid the driver and stepped out under the awning. A pleasant doorman held the door as she scurried into the warmth. As she reached the elevator she was sweating. Her nerves were on edge.

The elevator stopped on eight. Pat hesitated when the door closed. Slowly she walked down to Owen's suite. Knocking, she waited. Moments later Owen appeared. He didn't speak as he took her by the hand, leading her inside and closing the door. He set her dance bag aside.

Loosening her scarf, he unbuttoned her coat. Pat felt the familiar stir of excitement, waiting for his next move. Instead, he forced her to sit. Standing above her he glared down, his hands on hips.

"Well?" He was shaking.

"Well, what? Owen, what is going on?"

"I want to know why?"

"Owen, I honestly don't know what you're talking about!" Owen trembled as he lit a cigarette and took a drag.

"What is wrong with you? What's going on?"

"Why did you write that letter? Explain!"

"What letter, what are you talking about?"

"I got a call last week from Vera. She was hideous, vile. She claimed to have received a letter from you telling her of our affair, and that we were planning to live together. The letter was signed by you."

"Is this some kind of joke?"

"Pat, she read me the letter verbatim. The letter was postmarked from Kansas City."

"This is insane. Why in heaven's name would I do this? I love you!"

"There's more. She wants you fired. She's prepared to go to Vincent Lehrman."

"Owen, I swear to you that I didn't write that letter!"

"Well, someone has it in for you."

"There's only one person I can think of, Jackie Eldridge."

"Shit, it figures."

"What do you mean?"

"Jackie and I had a thing years ago. When we broke up, she didn't take it well."

"And yet she keeps working for you."

"Whatever happened between us has nothing to do with her dancing ability. She's a hard worker and a reliable dancer. So I hire her. Believe me, there's nothing there for me anymore otherwise."

"What do we do now?"

"I need time to figure this out, Baby."

"Oh Owen, I'm so sorry this happened. I love you and would never do anything to jeopardize us."

"I know, Baby, I know. Let's go to bed." Pat nodded, as Owen lead the way.

Chapter 52

A Plan

Owen needed a plan and fast. After much deliberation he sought Griff, finding him in the light booth.

"Owen, this is a surprise."

"Griff, there's a matter that must be solved immediately." He explained the letter, Vera's reaction and threats. Griff listened intently.

"How can I help?"

"I have reason to believe that Jackie Eldridge is behind this whole mess."

"Jackie? Well frankly Owen, I'm not surprised. Jackie has been salt in an open wound since this tour began. What do you need?"

"I need her fired!"

"We'll have to prove she did this."

"Does she have a confidant in the company?"

"I'll ask Mally. I know her to be a model of discretion."

"Good. Find out what you can."

"I will. Frankly, I don't want any trouble in this company." When Owen left, Griff phoned.

"Mally, it's Griff."

"Hi! You caught me napping."

"I have a question. Does Jackie Eldridge have a friend in the company?"

"It's common knowledge that she talks to Sonja Berger."

"That's all I need. Thanks!" After hanging up, Griff dialed Owen.

"Jackie talks to Sonja Berger."

"What's the next move?"

"I'll work on it. By the way, I'm calling the cast at the five minute mark tonight."

"Thanks Griff, I appreciate your support. The matter must be settled soon."

"Oh, it will be."

That evening the company assembled in the green room. Owen walking into the assemblage was a surprise followed by applause. Only Jackie stood apart from the group. "Shit," she mumbled, quietly.

"It's that inevitable time when a touring show needs a clean-up. I'll be holding a rehearsal at 1:00 pm on Friday. It is mandatory that all dancers be there, warmed up and ready to go. Jonas, take notes out front tonight. I'll base the rehearsal on what needs doing." The cast was dismissed to start the show. Sonja was the last to leave the room. As the first strains of the overture were heard, she felt a tap on her shoulder.

"Sonja, I would like to see you in Mr. Edward's office before you leave tonight. We'll just need a couple minutes of your time," stated Owen.

"Ok."

"Not a word of this to anyone." Sonja nodded and made her way to her starting position. Lost in thought, she failed to see Jackie, who abruptly stepped from the darkness and grabbed her wrist.

"Why the fuck is Owen Matthews in town?"

"How should I know?" Jackie tightened her grip.

"You listen to me. If you ever breathe a word you'll regret it."

"You've made yourself clear," said Sonja, trembling.

Later, as cast members left, Sonja dawdled. Jackie had given her the cold shoulder all night, which she found to her benefit. Ever since Jackie's plot and subsequent action, she wanted to break away. She was sick of Jackie's evil ranting, her negativity. It was time to make new friends.

Sonja turned off the dressing room light and hurried down to Griff's office. She looked around to make sure no one was watching as she knocked carefully. The door opened. Griff welcomed her closing the door and drawing the window shade. Without ceremony, Owen began.

"Sonja, we understand that you and Jackie Eldridge are friends. Is that true?"

"Well we were, but I've called it quits."

"Why is that?" Owen moved in closer as he offered her a chair. Griff sat behind his desk observing.

"Well, she's a very disagreeable person. From the beginning of this tour she has tried to poison my thinking and I allowed it. I realize I've been a fool."

"I see. Do you have any knowledge about a certain letter sent recently to my wife, Vera Daniels? We need the truth, now." Sonja began crying as she buried her face in her hands.

"Oh, I'm so sorry. I was aware that Jackie was plotting something against Pat Bryne, whom she despises." Both men looked on, impassively.

"She said she'd 'get that bitch.' Jackie is full of talk, you know? I couldn't believe she'd actually go through with it. When she mailed the letter she bragged about it. I was stunned. She threatened me. I don't know what to do now."

"What you can do is help us set a trap for Miss Eldridge. Will you?"

"What do I have to do?" Griff got up and walked around the table toward Sonja.

"Get Jackie to talk, in short, a confession on tape. You won't be fired. But in the future, Sonja, choose your associates with more discretion. Where are you staying?"

"We're all at Hotel Dyckman."

"Good. Ask Jackie to meet you in the bar off the lobby tomorrow night. Come to my room first, number 810. I'll set you up with a pocket recorder in your handbag. You'll push 'record' before you go into the bar."

"Ok, I'll help."

"Good. Get her to talk about that letter."

"Yes, I'll do my best." They concluded their meeting.

Jonas woke up and decided it was a good day for a brush-up. He liked his role as dance captain, finding it a challenge to keep the show tight as well as perform it. Jonas was re-writing his notes when Phillipe woke up, turned over, and smiled at him.

"Hon, what time is it?"

"It's 10:30, Babe. Do you want me to order room service this morning? You had some workout last night." Phillipe sat up and tossed the sheet aside. One look and Jonas could see that Phillipe was ready to go again.

"Breakfast can wait, but I can't," insisted Phillipe.

Jonas eagerly complied, joining Phillipe, who teased and taunted him as he removed his clothes. Phillipe adored Jonas' firm, taut body, the tight buns, muscular legs, and the generous cock. Jonas loved the control and power of Phillipe's dominance. Jonas writhed and begged until he felt the familiar thrusting, the ache, the build-up and at last, the release.

When he had calmed down he took a turn, pushing Phillipe on his back. Taking him in his mouth he brought Phillipe to a quick climax. Phillipe had had ample time to enjoy his building arousal doing Jonas. Both satisfied, they curled up for a few minutes and chatted as they planned their day.

Owen began the rehearsal promptly at 1:00 PM with Jonas at his side. Griff was there to open the theatre, set the work lights and clear the stage area. Sandy Irwin provided an accompanist, a local he knew from previous tours. The ensemble was warmed up and ready.

Working from Jonas' notes, Owen ran the Buccaneer number. Spacing had become sloppy.

The repetition brought on by eight shows a week had loosened the otherwise tight look of the number. Some of the style had relaxed and needed drilling. After working the number and repeating sections over and over, Owen was satisfied.

Next he reviewed other dance sections in the show and gave notes. Rehearsal ended at 4 o'clock and the dancers headed to the hotel to rest before the evening show. Sonja caught up to Jackie at the stage door.

"Jackie? Can we meet after the show?"

"That depends," said Jackie, tightly.

"I want to clear things up. Buy you a drink?"

"Oh, all right. Where do you want to meet?"

"How about 11:00 in the hotel bar?"

"We've got two shows tomorrow. Don't keep me waiting."

That evening the Orpheum was packed to the rafters. Tempos were brisk, the choreography polished, company energy bountiful. The audience showed their appreciation with a standing ovation. The cast was pleased.

Sonja hurried through her change, her heart accelerating as she thought about the task at hand.

She was afraid, but determined to end Jackie's evil influence.. As she made her way back to the hotel four blocks away, the wind had picked up and the falling snow swirled around her ankles.

Sonja got off the elevator and walked to Griff's room. Pausing for a moment, she gathered her courage, and knocked. Griff opened the door and she stepped quickly inside.

"Here, Sonja," said Griff, handing her a small recorder. "As you can see it is quite compact, easy to conceal. I have already pushed the volume to the max level. All you need to do is push 'record' before you meet Jackie. I suggest you do it in the elevator."

"OK, I'm ready," whispered Sonja. Griff could see the trepidation in her eyes.

"You are doing the right thing, Sonja. I guarantee it," he spoke, reassuringly. And I thank you for your cooperation. This is important for your future as well as Pat Byrne's." Sonja slipped out and headed down to the lobby.

On the descent Sonja reached into her shoulder bag and found the record button. Her heart leapt in her chest as the door opened. It was one minute to eleven. She spotted Jackie in a corner booth.

"Hi."

"Sit," Jackie commanded. Sonja settled into the booth placing her shoulder bag on the seat next to her.

"What are you having?"

"I'm doing Martinis. You notice I said plural. After what I've been through these past twenty-four hours I can use all the booze available. And you?"

"Oh, I'll just have a white wine." Sonja felt a trickle of sweat running down between her shoulder blades. Jackie caught the waiter's eye and ordered for Sonja. Then she settled back, lit a cigarette, and studied Sonja carefully.

"So, you've come to apologize."

"Yes."

"Did you think you could get along without me? Or that anyone else in the company cares about you?"

"I'm sorry for doubting you," said Sonja, playing humble pie.

"Oh, that. Well so far, I've got nothing, zip. Owen didn't so much as bat an eye at Pat during rehearsal. Do you think he's broken up with her or what?"

"I don't know. Say, you never told me the contents of the letter."

"Why should I?" Jackie took a sip of martini, and squashed her cigarette. Then, she smiled.

"Oh, all right." Lighting another, she leaned forward, elbows planted on the table, relishing the moment.

"I wrote such an unconscionable letter that Vera had to have gone ballistic when she read it. What I can't fathom is how Owen took it. He doesn't appear to be upset. He is so strange, that man."

"How come?"

"Well, when he was balling me years ago, he was so elusive, so hard to read. Suddenly, Jackie's face changed into a scowl. "The bastard broke my heart. I want him nailed to the wall. He deserves it. Pat Byrne is merely an innocent, just as dumb as I was. The bitch needs a lesson."

"So what happens now?"

"Damned if I know," Jackie said, shaking her head. I guess I'll have to sit tight. But shit, after what I wrote, I would think Vera lopped off Owen's balls! Boy would that do my old heart good."

Jackie ordered another martini before she finished the current one. It was obvious that she was getting smashed. Sonja sat nursing her wine, trying to keep her wits about her. When she finished her glass she started to rise.

"I haven't dismissed you yet," Jackie slurred, grabbing Sonja's wrist. "Remember what I told you. You'll be done if you ever betray me. I'll tell management you wrote that letter."

"You'd be wasting your time. No one would believe I had the balls to do that." Jackie grinned laconically as she chuckled.

Sonja continued. "You know what, Jackie? I looked up to you, admired you. But, you're nothing more than a used-up, bitter, old bitch!" Sonja picked up her bag, grabbed the check and glanced back.

"Go fuck yourself, Jackie!" As she walked away, her heart was pounding as she headed to the register. After signing the bill, she hurried to the elevator and pressed for floor eight.

Jackie sat in her alcohol-induced stupor and finished her fourth drink. She took one last drag off her cigarette, and squashed it in the ashtray. Attempting to rise she found her feet slowly and wove her way through the deserted lobby. It was time to find a pillow.

Chapter 53

The Firing

It was late, around twelve-thirty a.m. Sonja hurried back to her room and removed the tape recorder from her bag. A sudden ring of the phone startled her. Cautiously, she picked up.

"Sonja, this is Griff. Are you all right?"

"Yes, Griff. I taped the whole thing."

"Good. I would like to stop by in about five minutes, and pick it up if you don't mind."

"OK."

Owen returned to his suite at the Radisson and called Pat. She came immediately. He greeted her with the ardor of a lover returning from war. Taking her in his arms he kissed and held her, afraid of letting go.

"Baby, I'm so glad you're here. I'm so sorry I doubted you. Can you forgive me? This whole letter mess is going away. Griff and I have proof that Jackie wrote and sent it to Vera."

"Owen, I hope so," whispered Pat, as she curled up next to him.

"Pat, I'm getting a divorce. It's time."

Astonished, Pat reached for Owen, her emotion swelling through tears. She was unstoppable. Owen's desire matched hers. They became one, rolling and twisting, groping and breathing with a heavy cadence and intensity that was boundless. Clothes came off as they fell into total consumption of each other. Pat's hair fell loose on Owen covering him as her flesh seized his, burning with total abandon and ingenuity. They were flawless lovers, in perfect syncopation.

When they were finished they lay locked in each other's arms, their bodies glistening. Totally spent, they fell into a deep sleep.

Saturday morning came quickly. Griff ordered coffee and pastry from room service. At ten there was a knock at the door.

"Well let's get this over with," said Owen, moving in quickly. It was more than obvious that he wanted resolution as soon as possible. Griff pressed the playback. Together they listened intently as Jackie spilled her guts, playing into their hands. Griff turned the recorder off.

"Owen, I will take care of this. Let's keep you out of it altogether. I'll give Jackie her two-week salary and pay her insurance through run of the contract. I will arrange her return to New York on Sunday."

"Excellent!"

"The next step is to quickly find a replacement. Know anyone offhand?"

"Not really. We'll need a strong dancer/singer. Jackie has her shortfalls, but performing isn't one of them. She shows up eight shows a week. What you see is what you get."

"I'll check the Lehrman roster. We'll have someone here next week."

"Thanks, Griff."

The gypsies assembled to prepare for the afternoon performance. Griff called half hour.

Jackie arrived, hung over and oblivious. She ignored Sonja, who had moved to another spot in the dressing room. Grudgingly, she began the ritual of putting herself together.

The predictable announcement, "Places, please," came at two sharp. The cast assembled in the wings ready for Sandy's downbeat. The first act went quickly. During intermission, Griff asked Jackie to stop by his office following the matinee.

The rest of the show flew. Griff asked Dick Landry to finish the post-show details. Then he disappeared into his office. He had barely settled before he heard a knock. "Come in." Jackie entered, closed the door and sat down. For a few moments there was awkward silence.

"Well, I assume there's a reason you asked me here?"

"Yes. Jackie, I'm letting you go. You will receive two week's pay and your insurance coverage for the run of your contract. Arrangements have been made for your return to New York tomorrow."

"Shit! Is this some kind of joke?"

"No joke. You're fired, out of this company," Griff said, impassively.

"Damn it, I want to know why. You have to have justifiable cause to dismiss me, Edwards."

"Your recent behavior is justifiable cause, Jackie. Certain actions on your part are unacceptable. I take full responsibility for this action, and my decision is final. Your last performance is tonight. Your trunk will be shipped to your New York address." He handed her a piece of paper.

"Your flight is on Northwest #180 leaving the Twin Cities at noon tomorrow. Pick up your ticket at will-call, Northwest ticket counter, Wold-Chamberlain Airport."

Jackie sat stunned. This was a development she hadn't considered. Without a word she left Griff's office. She had no axe to grind with Griff, personally. On the other hand, a certain someone in the company would pay. That someone would pay dearly.

Griff returned to his suite to shave and rest. He had no appetite tonight. He felt relieved that he had taken care of business, but he felt uneasy. He would be relieved when Jackie was on her way to New York.

Now he was faced with the task of replacing her. Once again he pulled out the Lehrman roster of performers employed over the past five years. Scanning the list, he spotted a familiar name. Kathy Olson. She'd worked a tour with him. But, was she available? He noted her New York number and dialed.

"Kathy Olson, please."

"Who's asking?"

"This is Griffen Edwards, production stage manager of *Bravo Business*. We need a replacement dancer for the national tour. Interested?" There was a long pause.

"When do you need me?"

"Well, we actually need you immediately. We'd like to fly you out on Monday to Minneapolis. You will be rehearsed and placed on Friday, opening in Vancouver the following week."

"This is highly unusual. You mean I don't have to audition?"

"A quick decision is necessary under these circumstances. I remember you from a production of *Over A Rainbow* a few years ago.

"Yes, I remember. Say, my former roommate is in your show, Mally Winthrop."

'How perfect,' he thought, a smile growing.

"Wow, this is an amazing coincidence. It really is," said Kathy, unable to hide her enthusiasm.

"Can you act on such short notice? What is your apartment situation?"

"This is wild. My brother and his wife are staying with me. They can sublet for a while."

"Great. Your ticket will be waiting at La Guardia, Northwest ticket counter. Just bring an I.D. when you arrive at the airport Monday. Your flight will depart at noon. I'll have you in Minneapolis and settled by evening."

"Will I have accommodations when I arrive?"

"Yes, at the Dyckman Hotel with the rest of the cast. You'll begin rehearsing on Tuesday morning. Save all your receipts. Do you have any questions?"

"No. You've certainly covered everything. Thank you, Mr. Edwards."

"Please, call me Griff. We'll look forward to seeing you. Have a good trip." Griff phoned Owen immediately. It barely rang before he picked up.

"Owen, I wanted to update you. Jackie's been served notice and will leave as of noon tomorrow. Her replacement, Kathy Olson, arrives Monday. I've worked with her before. If memory serves, she's a solid performer."

"You amaze me Griff! Nice work."

"Will you be stopping by tonight?"

"No, I'll keep a low profile right now." There was a pause then Owen added, "Thanks for everything."

Saturday nights were usually energetic as cast members anticipated a day off. There would be no road travel the first weekend of the two-week run. In the meantime, Mally posted an invitation to the Herman party on the callboard.

It was unusually quiet, as the gypsies' freshened make-up and hair, askew after the early show. Two acts of performing under hot lights, doing quick changes, and the amount of running usually required a stringent redo. The sound of the audience gearing up for them through the squawk box brought excitement. Saturday night audiences were generally the best.

Later, following the show, spirits were high in the women's dressing room. Mally was busy with details of the party, enthusiastic chatter reigned as the girls undressed and prepared to leave.

Jackie stood. Slowly she made her way to Sonja, who was drying off from the shower.

"Sonja?"

"Yes?" It was sudden, violent. Jackie slapped Sonja so hard she fell back against the radiator. Immediately, blood spread over her face. A piercing scream broke all activity. Heads turned.

Jackie's strength was overpowering. Sonja was pulled from the corner and dragged across the carpet, nude and disabled. Squatting, Jackie held Sonja down, who tried to thrash free, kicking and screaming.

"You little snitch. You're a first-class little asshole!" You did it, didn't you?" Jackie's voice shattered the air as she punched and cursed. Bedlam broke out.

Dana grabbed Jackie, as she attempted to pull her off Sonja. Jackie was strong, too powerful for Dana, shoving her out of the way. She had a clear shot again, and dove for Sonja. Pat, now in the fray, tried to separate Jackie from Sonja, who was sobbing uncontrollably. Mally ran to the door and yelled.

Moments later, Jonas, Phillipe and Chad bound into the room. Immediately, Jonas separated the two women while Phillipe forced Jackie into a chair, pinning her arms behind her back. Chad assisted, holding her down.

"You fucker, let me go," Jackie yelled, as she squirmed, trying to free herself. Her efforts were futile, as Phillipe held firm.

"Mal, get Griff," yelled Jonas. Glancing at Pat, he could see she was trying to cover Sonja with a robe as she attempted to help her up. On first try, Sonja crumpled, unable to support her weight. Dana joined Pat in lifting Sonja and once she stood, helped her to a chair.

"Please, keep her away," whimpered Sonja, barely audible. Griff bounded into the room. He was furious.

"What the hell is going on? I want full disclosure, every detail, and I want it now!" No one moved. Sonja stood and limped to Griff. All eyes on the room followed her.

"I had just showered. Jackie walked over and attacked me," she said, her voice cracking into sobs once again.

"Jonas, please take notes. This must be reported to Equity. Continue, someone," Griff demanded.

"Jackie attacked Sonja out of the blue without provocation! She dragged her across the room, hitting her repeatedly. If we hadn't intervened, Sonja might be unconscious or dead." Jackie tried wrenching herself free, but it was useless.

"Why, Jackie? An explanation, now," ordered Griff.

"This little piece of shit knows why," she screamed, pointing at Sonja. "Tell them," her voice now a croak.

"Shut up," bellowed Griff. "You're through. Let me hear from someone else," insisted Griff, having lost all patience.

"Griff, I saw the whole thing," said Dana, glaring at Jackie. Jackie was pretty savage." Jackie stared coldly at the group during the report. Her face was red and her mouth twitched. Griff turned to her.

"Is this true?"

"Yeah, and she deserved every bit of it, the little bitch."

"Enough! Collect your things and get out of here. A report of your action will be sent to Actor's Equity. You will face suspension, a fine or both. I never want to see you in my theatre again." Phillipe and Chad released Jackie, who slowly stood up, averting her eyes.

"The rest of you may leave now. Thank you." Griff put his arm protectively around Sonja and walked her out of the room. Mally, Pat and Dana followed. The boys filed out.

"Do you wish to press charges, Sonja? You're within your rights. Jackie Eldridge assaulted you. That's more than just cause for legal action."

"No Griff, I figured it might end this way."

"I want you to go to the emergency room," said Griff.

"Dick and I will take her."

"Are you sure? I don't want to be any trouble, Dana," said Sonja, softly.

"What trouble? We're staying at the same hotel. Dick and I will be able to look in on you."

"Sonja, use your insurance card and any additional charges should be sent to me care of the Orpheum. If you need to reach me call me at the Dyckman, room 810," assured Griff.

"Thanks, I'll be okay."

Frank was waiting at the stage door as Griff walked Mally out. "I'll see you tomorrow, Darling. Don't worry about anything, ok?"

"Thanks Griff. I love you. Take care of yourself." Griff watched her get into the car and drive off. He quickly returned to the dressing room. He watched Jackie intently, waiting while she finished collecting her things.

"Leave your dance shoes, tights and all remaining items belonging to the production here. They will be collected Monday," he said firmly. Griff escorted Jackie to the stage door. There was stillness in the theatre as he walked her through the backstage area. And then she left. It was over.

Griff watched Jackie disappear down the street in the falling snow, until she was out of view. He breathed a sigh of relief. 'She's out of my company, thank God,' he thought. Making his way to the hotel, he breathed the icy winter air, a welcome relief from the stuffy confines of the theatre. The past few days had been trying. He looked forward to his day off.

Chapter 54

Home & Hearth

Mally woke to the aroma of freshly brewed coffee. Putting on her old bathrobe, she padded out to the kitchen. When Toots saw her, he sat on his haunches waiting for a treat from the jar on the counter. Once she produced it he snuffed, his jowls waving a spray of drool, as he claimed the morsel. Satisfied, he ambled off to find a warm spot near a sunny window.

Finding her way to the shower was a welcome wake-up of warm water as it cascaded down her tight limbs. Another eight-show week was behind her. As she was drying off she heard voices from the kitchen. Realizing that Paula and Frank had returned from the store, she changed quickly into her favorite jeans, a turtleneck sweater, and a sweatshirt bearing the University of Minnesota colors. 'Had she really been gone from the U of MN almost two years? Incredible,' she thought, walking to the kitchen.

"Muffin, Frank and I thought lasagna and salad with garlic bread would satisfy the cast. What do you think?"

"Great!"

"The liquor cabinet is fully stocked," Paula continued. What do these folks drink?"

"Beer mostly, and pop. Griff likes a martini now and then."

"We've got it all, sweetheart. The house is clean, and we're ready for a party," chirped Frank.

"Are you making your famous sauce for the lasagna?" His was her favorite.

"Of course," he said, merrily.

"Muffin, Curt Wiley and Wayne Davenport can't wait to see you. I've invited them both," said Paula.

"Curt?" Curt Wiley, her drop-dead gorgeous pal, was a business major, who switched to theatre and worked as a model doing print ads and runway work to pay his tuition. Back then, Mally's girlfriends begged her to fix them up with Curt. She was always mystified. Curt was strictly a friend, and not terribly colorful.

Wayne Davenport was her best friend and confidant at the U. How she had missed him! They shared time on production crews, spending time together during late night study breaks, often over cups of Constant Comment tea. Secretly, she had always wanted more, but he never pursued her romantically. He had not come out to her. Being 'out,' was a sensitive issue, even in the theatre community at that time. The department heads never acknowledged or discussed a staff member's sexual orientation openly.

As the day continued, her folks continued to prepare for the gathering. About five p.m., when the streetlights cast the only available light over glistening snow, the first cabs arrived. As introductions were made and coats were deposited in the back bedroom, the gypsies settled in, ready for some Minnesota hospitality. The roaring fire, stereo music, and the aroma of baked lasagna was a feast for the senses.

Griff arrived and greeted Paula and Frank warmly. He immediately made himself at home chatting with Frank about his Masonic work and technical background. Curt showed up with a date, a pretty brunette, who hung on his every word and arm. She clearly was more interested in him than in the gathering.

Some musicians arrived ready to provide music for dancing and set up in the basement. Paula served the lasagna and Frank distributed drinks.

Jonas and Phillipe finally arrived. Mally hugged them both just as Wayne walked in. Spotting her in the throng, he ran over and lifted her up, twirling her around as she screamed with delight. After he put her down, she introduced him to Jonas and Phillipe, who eyed him with interest, recognizing one of their own.

Wayne was eager to hear about life on the road. He was a gifted actor, who chose to spend his life in academia, working as an associate professor of theatre. He enjoyed the predictability and security of a regular paycheck. Unable to take that leap of faith and face the unknown, as every dedicated actor must, he remained in Minnesota.

The boys found him sweet and funny. Though he was obviously gay, he seemed uptight about his sexuality. There were exchanged innuendoes, but no plans were made to pursue more contact. Instead, the boys chatted, passing time drinking and enjoying Frank's lasagna and Paula's immense knowledge of theatre.

Jackie was forgotten. Last night's showdown was never mentioned. Sonja was absent, tending to her needs. The Landrys had chosen to stay behind should she require help.

Pat passed on the party, spending the last hours with Owen before he went back to New York. They had much to talk about. He was prepared for a final showdown with Vera and the sooner the better.

Back at the Herman's, the evening wound down. It was obvious that many had partied too hard.

They would require recovery before the next performance.

Curt hugged Mally on his way out. His date faked a smile as she departed attached to his arm.

Wayne was the next to leave. Tenderly he hugged her and kissed her on the cheek. They paused for a moment. His eyes filled as he made a hasty retreat.

Griff remained by the fire, enjoying some of Frank's cognac. Mally sat down next to him to soak up the ambience of warmth filling the room. Paula approached.

"Griff, would you care to stay the night? It's late and we have a comfortable guest room."

"I have to be at the theatre at noon tomorrow."

"It's two in the morning and cabs are hard to get at this hour. Frank, could you run Griff downtown in the morning?"

"I'd be happy to. What do you say?"

"Yes, I would appreciate that. I must be on the road by ten, ok?" Swallowing the remaining cognac, Frank excused himself to make up the guestroom. Paula began to pick up the remnants of cigarette butts and drink glasses, as Mally followed her from room to room.

216   *Gypsy Nights*

"Muffin, we can finish all this in the morning. Relax! Good night, Griff."

"Goodnight."

Mally sat down next to Griff and, cradled in his arms, watched the fire die. Toots trotted into the room, sniffing Griff to show his welcome. After deciding that Griff passed inspection, he lay at his feet, snorting contentedly.

Griff was shown to a charming bedroom with a brass bed. Mally found a fresh towel, facecloth, and a new toothbrush under the vanity. Leaving him to wash and brush, she slipped into bed and waited. Returning, Griff found Mally poised against the pillows.

"Mally, we can't sleep together in your parent's home. It wouldn't be right."

"I just want to feel you next to me for a few minutes. I have missed you so much," she replied, as she beckoned him into bed. Holding Griff tightly, she kissed him and then rested her head on his shoulder.

"Last night was horrible. How do you feel?"

"Well, it's never easy to fire anyone. In Jackie's case, it was necessary."

"Who's replacing her?"

"A surprise," he said, with a chuckle. "Kathy Olson."

"What? Oh, my God! Griff, you won't be sorry. Kathy's a quick study and a good technician especially in jazz. She'll be a tremendous asset."

"I'm glad it worked out. She arrives tomorrow evening. She'll start in Vancouver."

"Wonderful! Thank you, Griff." They kissed and she slipped out of bed and into her room.

The single bed of her college years seemed strange. She belonged with Griff. As the full moon lit the wall next to her, she contemplated a future with him.

Kathy Olson was thrilled to be working again. She had been out of work for a while and was eager to perform. Taking classes had kept her in shape, but the routine was monotonous with no outlet or venue to apply her technique.

Arriving at the Orpheum Theatre, she looked for the stage door. The wind was blustery and she felt a shiver as she pulled her coat together and buttoned it. Winding her muffler around her neck, she waited as the driver brought her bags to the entrance. After tipping him, she headed inside. The stage doorman was on hand to sign her in.

"Where may I find Mr. Edward's office?"

"Can't miss it," he explained. "You go straight back to the far wall and make a left. Feel free to leave your bags here." Kathy loosened her scarf as the first drop of perspiration ran down her back. She removed her coat placing it over her arm as she walked to Griff's office.

Griff was deep into paperwork. When he saw Kathy he removed his glasses and rose, extending his hand warmly.

"Kathy!"

"Hi Griff, long time no see."

"How was your trip?" He offered her a chair and then reached for the contract.

"It was actually pretty uneventful until we stopped in Chicago. What a mess."

"Ah, yes, O'Hare. Now there is a snarl most of the time," he said matter-of-factly. "Kathy, here is your contract. You know the drill, sign all three copies and keep the pink for yourself." After handing her a pen, he settled back, giving her as much information as she could digest to get her started.

"The Hotel Dyckman is three blocks north of here off Hennepin Avenue to the right, mid-block on Sixth Street. It's quite comfortable. For the time being you will be rooming on your own. Smitty, our doorman, can call you a cab. Do you have bags?"

"Yes. Actually he is watching them for me."

"Good! Then I'll let you get settled and we'll expect you this evening. Come back stage and I'll introduce you. You can watch the show. Jonas Martin will be rehearsing you all week. You'll begin tomorrow at ten sharp."

"Thanks for all your help, Griff. It's great to be here." They stood and shook hands. Kathy left his office, collected her bags and waited while Smitty made the call.

Owen arrived in New York and went straight to his apartment. He had unfinished business. Dropping his bag he walked to the phone, lighting a cigarette en route. He dialed and waited. After two rings he heard the familiar voice. Owen took a deep breath, navigating carefully.

"Vera. Do you have a minute?"

"Yes, of course. Do you want to stop by?"

"Yeah, I'll be right over." He stopped to relieve himself and splash cold water on his face, bleary from the trip. This had to be fast and hopefully, painless.

Grabbing a cab, he headed to Vera's place on Central Park West, a coop they had shared during their marriage. The doorman recognized Owen and nodded. Ascending to the top floor, Owen stepped out of the elevator and knocked. He heard singing from within. 'My God, she's in a contrite mood. So much the better,' he thought. The door opened. Vera stood in a black see-through negligee. She was holding the familiar cigarette and a glass of bourbon, no ice.

"Come in Owen. Would you like to sit in the den?" He followed her to the room he had loved most. The overstuffed furniture was inviting and the fire crackling kept the space cozy. They had made love often here.

She pointed to a well-stocked wet bar. Owen helped himself, pouring a double shot of scotch into a glass. As he added ice, he glanced back at Vera, who was eyeing him from a prone position.

"Come here, Darling," she insisted, patting the pillows. Owen crossed the room and sat across from her. Keeping his distance was difficult.

Vera looked radiant considering the mileage. Today was one of her better days. He had never lost his attraction to her. In spite of the break-up, he had loved her as much as anyone. And, had he loved fucking her! 'She's the best lay, ever,' he thought.

Knowing Vera's pliability when drinking, he thought about his next move. 'God, I could take her right now,' he thought, smugly. 'It's a perfect opportunity.'

Vera rose and walked to the bar, filling her glass again. When she returned she stopped in front of Owen. Loosening the front of her negligee, she playfully revealed her long legs, her thighs, still firm and soft. Her bare-shaven mound showed through the folds of her garment, and her generous breasts stood at attention, waiting for action. Owen was already hard.

"Want to fuck me Owen? Come on, I know you do," she said slyly, egging him on. "Are you still man enough to satisfy me?" He was fighting his arousal, trying to hold back. He lost.

In a sudden move he was on her, forcing her down. Rudely, he pulled open the front of the negligee, running his hands over her breasts. Her genitals felt warm as he pried her open. Vera, already wet, moaned and begged for him to enter, repeatedly moving her pelvis against him. Quickly unzipping his fly, Owen found his way to the familiar fit, thrusting with total abandon. All the while Vera panted and clung to him begging for more, forcing her mouth on his. The taste of booze and cigarettes on her lips was suffocating. He came in a burst of frenzy and then collapsed on her. He waited briefly, then, calmly got up. Tucking himself in, he zipped his fly with great effort. His penis was still partially hard. The release had been terrific.

"What do you think you're doing? You're not through. I haven't come yet." Owen returned to his drink, and lighting a cigarette, took a deep drag.

"I'm through, Vera. Play with yourself. I imagine you can get off pretty good," he said coldly. Vera sat up, rearranged herself and stared in disbelief.

"What do you mean coming here, fucking me, and not finishing the job?"

"That's the point, I'm not your job. I'm not one of those boys you rent by the hour. I came over to tell you I'm filing for divorce."

"What? Do you think some little road tramp will make a difference in your twisted life?" Owen's anger was building. He set the glass down and put out his cigarette.

"Back off, you bitch! That 'tramp,' as you refer to her, didn't write that heinous letter. Someone else did and she's been fired."

"So?"

"Don't you get it? It's time to stop this craziness. I don't love you, Vera. I haven't for years. It is pointless to keep up this facade!"

"I hate you, you fucking bastard! That's what you are!"

"And you're a sad, washed-up piece of shit. You have no one to blame but yourself. I'm tired of all the bullshit you've laid on me for years. You'll hear from my attorney. Good bye, Vera." Owen walked out.

Vera sat motionless. Through her haze she was lucid enough to realize that it was over. She had tried to hold on to Owen. It hadn't worked. He was gone, gone for good.

Chapter 55

An Alliance

Sonja Berger arrived at the theatre and was told to see Griff. Responding to her knock he asked her in and offered her a chair.

"How are you doing? Are you feeling up to performing tonight?" It was a fair question.

Sonja had taken quite a beating.

"Yes. I'm still a little shook up, but I'll get over it. The bruises will heal quicker than my psyche. My x-rays were normal."

"I'm glad to hear it. Management is sorry for any abuse you suffered." He excused himself to begin the half-hour call.

At five minutes of the hour he called the company to the green room. Kathy Olson was introduced. The company welcomed her warmly. When the hubbub died down, she walked over to Mally and gave her a big hug.

"Can you believe this? I am so happy to see you, Kath."

"Good to see you, too!"

"Enjoy the show." Kathy was shown to the back of the house. There was standing room only in the theatre tonight. Ready with notebook in hand, she wanted to observe Owen's definitive style and choreography.

Kathy had never worked for him, but she knew the demands of his work from others. She wanted to be ready.

Following the performance, she stood to the side at the stage door, watching cast members leaving for the night.

"Hey Kathy, glad to have you on board," shouted Chad, as he hurried out the door. Dana approached.

"It's good to see you, Kathy. Which tour did we do together?"

"It was *Give My Regards,* remember? How's Dick?"

"Wonderful! How did you like the show?"

"It's a fabulous production and so fresh," said Kathy, feeling less a stranger as the minutes ticked by. Company members continued to file past.

"Hi." Kathy turned and noticed an attractive blonde.

"I'm Sonja. Welcome to the company." Kathy nodded, perusing the young woman. Sonja was tiny, with a full figure, slender legs and pretty green eyes.

"It's good to be here. Say, I'm wide-awake. Is anyone going for a drink?"

"Gee, I don't know. Are you staying at the Dyckman?"

"Yes, as a matter-of-fact."

"There's a bar in the lobby. I'm game, but maybe just one, OK?"

Sonja and Kathy made their way out of the stage door and down the street. The wind picked up as they scurried along until they had reached the warmth of the lobby. Ahead of them was a small cocktail lounge with the sounds of a piano coming from within.

After getting settled in a corner booth, Sonja removed her hat and opened her coat. Kathy unwound her muffler and slipped out of her winter jacket. A waitress approached.

"What will it be, ladies?"

"I'll have a brandy and seven," ordered Kathy.

"May I have a white wine? What do you have by the glass?"

"We have a house Chardonnay."

"That'll be fine, thanks." The waitress left. For a few awkward moments they sat without talking. Sonja caught Kathy staring at her.

"How do you like touring?" Sonja relaxed as Kathy attempted to make conversation.

"I love it. It's so new for me. I did an off-Broadway review that bombed and a season of stock, so this is pretty thrilling." The drinks arrived.

"Here's to touring and friendship," toasted Kathy. Sonja followed suit, clinking Kathy's glass and taking a sip of the chilled wine. Kathy felt relaxed with Sonja.

"Thanks for coming." The girls sipped in silence. When they had finished, Sonja insisted on paying.

"Well, I guess I'll see you at my placement rehearsal on Friday."

"Yes, good luck this week. I hope it goes well. Owen's choreography is a challenge, but so brilliant, especially being taught by Jonas Martin."

"I've heard about Jonas. I hear he's thorough and very patient." The girls walked through the lobby to the elevator. Pushing buttons for their respective floors, they rode in silence.

"Goodnight, Kathy. It's nice to have you here."

"Thanks, Sonja. See you soon." Sonja got off the elevator and the door slowly closed.

Kathy put the key in the door to her room and entered the darkness. Slipping out of her clothes she stepped into the shower and began to ruminate as the water cascaded over her body, tired and taut from the long day of travel. As she continued to stand under the water spraying against her, she allowed her hands to pursue and explore herself. Bringing herself to orgasm was easy as she had so many times before.

Turning the water off, she reached for a waiting towel. The bed beckoned and she cooperated fully. Slipping under clean sheets, she relaxed. She felt safe here.

As she lay in the darkness, she thought about how it had all come about. It was the summer she attended a dance camp in the Catskills. She received a scholarship during her first year in New York. Her hard work in class was rewarded when she was chosen as one of a select group of promising young dancers to attend.

Arriving at camp, she was shown to quarters. There were three others in the cabin, all young hopefuls from the New York dance scene. The four claimed their spots picking the bunk they preferred.

Kathy was introduced to Fawn Metcalf, an elegant ballerina, tall and lithe; Denise Carter, a strong technical jazz dancer; and Corey

Dugan, a modern dance specialist with flawless timing. Kathy got the top half of the bunk bed while Denise took the lower. They hit it off immediately.

Fawn and Corey stuck together exclusively. When a break was offered at the end of each grueling session, Kathy and Denise got acquainted. Fawn and Corey were in their own world and weren't interest in joining the conversation.

The weekend was filled with required classes during two full days. The girls were required to attend technique, composition and lecture sessions. The staff planned a get-together on Sunday night as a reward for all their hard work. Everyone was expected to attend.

It was a star-filled evening, enticing Kathy to walk down to the river after the catered dinner. She was full and needed to shake down the heavy feeling in her stomach. Normally she didn't eat like this in New York. She felt like a bloated cow.

The river wound snake-like through the campsite as a full moon cast a waving path of light through the dark water. Lanterns were placed along the walkway for the safety of the walkers.

Reaching the shore she heard splashing a few yards away. Startled, she followed the sounds as she walked through the underbrush, glancing carefully ahead of her. There, not more than ten yards from her, she noticed two heads bobbing up and down in the water. She heard the sound of laughter and more splashing, then silence.

As her eyes adjusted to the darkness she noticed two young women playing together in the water. One broke free of the other, giggling as she moved toward the shore through the shallow. The other followed, trying to keep up. The first tripped and fell at the water's edge. The other caught up, joining her. They grappled and teased as they continued their playful ritual, nude and in the throes of something surprising.

Kathy recognized her two cabin mates, Fawn and Corey. They were engaged in obvious foreplay. Rather than turn away, Kathy stayed and watched, growing more excited with each passing moment.

The two young women twined around each other, their long wet tresses winding them more tightly together. The moon highlighted the wetness and sheen of their passion. Each took a turn giving pleasure to the other. The sound of the gentle river lapping against the shore hardly camouflaged the sounds of their lust. Minutes passed. Kathy was wet and aching for the same.

Kathy had dated and had been bedded by few men. She had never been sexually satisfied. Most of the men she encountered were gay while straight men were on the prowl, using and dumping women. They put her off. They certainly hadn't satisfied her.

That night Kathy realized she was gay. Since that night, she waited and watched for the right someone. Sonja was the last thought she had before she fell into sleep. Could Sonja be that person? Would her attraction to Sonja be reciprocated? How could she take a risk like this? And then, she slept.

Kathy was rehearsed all week. On Friday, the rest of the ensemble joined her for a run through.

Jonas not only ran the musical numbers, he drilled the dancers hard. That was the way Owen worked. That was the way Jonas was handling his new role as dance captain.

Load out was going smoothly on Saturday evening after the performance until a storm front came through. In the midst of the strike and loading the show onto semi trucks, it began to snow. At first it fell lightly, but as the night wore on it built in intensity. The Minneapolis area was in the midst of a major blizzard, the largest of the season so far.

The weather conditions made the load out a challenge. The sets, rigging, lighting paraphernalia, drops, cyclorama and wardrobe and prop crates became difficult to handle with visibility so hampered. The blizzard was creating a whiteout.

The locals stood their ground in spite of the tough conditions. Working closely with these Minnesotans Griff knew the job would be done to his satisfaction. They were all pros and worked under similar conditions four months a year. They finished the job with no mishaps.

Griff invited the crew to a round at a bar down the street. The men accepted, trudging through the white piles growing higher along Hennepin Avenue. As the blizzard continued, the group sat swapping stories of backstage life. They shared photos and talked about their families and girlfriends. Having wrapped up a very successful run, the show was ready to leave the City of Lakes.

Griff was anxious to move on. The weather was oppressive, and he missed Mally. He appreciated her need to spend time with family, but his arms ached for her. Moving the show to Vancouver would give them needed time together.

Later, while packing, he thought about his future with her. He wanted to marry her and have children. Settling down where he could still access his work in technical theatre and have a normal life was what he wanted most.

But, was she ready? Mally was just starting her career. She was a very capable dancer-singer and a promising actress. With more training, more breaks and a good agent, there was no telling where she might go in the business.

Another consideration was the fifteen-year age difference. He was ready for a committed relationship, but was she willing to settle down? He was ready to let go of the transience of nights alone, the repeated routes. Pondering these thoughts, he fell into bed exhausted. The alarm was set for an early day. The production was moving again.

Paula and Frank planned to attend the final performance. Griff had held on to Mally's trunk during her stay at home. She brought her travel bag to the theatre earlier. She would stay with Pat that night in order to head out to the Great Northern depot first thing in the morning. The next phase of the tour would take the production to the Pacific Northwest.

As the curtain came down, Mally found her folks waiting at the stage door. It had been a wonderful visit.

"Be sure and write," Frank said, hugging her.

"I will, Frank. Thanks for driving me back and forth." Turning to Paula, she could easily feel her tears welling.

"Bye, Mom."

"Bye, Muffin. Take care of yourself." As they hugged, she felt her mother's tears against her cheek.

"Don't worry Mom. I'll write you. And Griff sends his regards."

"Give him our best and tell him to take good care of our girl, OK?"

"I will, Mom. Turning away, she hurried back to the Dyckman Hotel. Her sleep would be short tonight.

The next morning the company assembled at the Great Northern Depot. There was the usual hustle as the gypsies approached Cal Friedkin. Outside, along the length of covered platform and tracks, the cast was exposed to bitter cold. The temperature dropped overnight. More snow was predicted and the wind was picking up.

The trip would take them through North Dakota, Montana, Idaho, and Washington State and continue north to British Columbia, a trip covering eighteen hundred miles of rail. The show was set to play one week at the Queen Elizabeth Auditorium in Vancouver.

The facility was considered state of the art. Canada's finest theatre boasted the newest technology and advanced equipment, expansive playing and backstage areas; modern, spacious dressing rooms; and a full service green room, including closed circuit TV and snack bar area. The sound booth was situated at the back of the house and the basement had a lounge for crew and orchestra members.

Griff and his group flew out Sunday morning with only a slight delay due to weather. They would arrive sometime Sunday afternoon to check in and begin prepping the theatre for the trucks due on Monday afternoon. Weather conditions could be challenging for over-land freight, but Griff's drivers were the best on the circuit. They had pulled out before one a.m. on Sunday morning.

Mally was drained from the past two weeks and welcomed the long ride to unravel and recharge. Pat found her cocoon agreeable as always. She needed time away. She missed Owen, whom she had not heard from him since his visit. She wanted to think about him with no other distractions. Hopefully he would call her in Vancouver.

Jonas and Phillipe found the club car and decided on Bloody Marys. As they sipped their drinks they spotted Jim Sorenson and Joe Pinto heading their way.

"May we join?" Joe had been scarce for weeks and it was obvious that he and Jim were having some fun. Jonas thought that Joe was bet-ter company when he had a boyfriend of his own.

"So what's new with you two, as if I couldn't guess," teased Jonas, winking at Phillipe.

"Well, how do I put this? We've been hiding the stick a lot," said Joe, grinning. Jim sat impassively. The two ordered black coffee and Danish pastry.

"Have you ever played Vancouver? I've heard they have a groovy night scene," said Jim.

"I have several times. The bars are ok, but the underground scene is better. They have some pretty active baths. There's a large, gay Asian community. They have smooth, hairless bodies and tend to be passive. They'll let you do almost anything sexually," reported Joe with authority.

"Well, I wouldn't know anything about that," said Jonas, with mock seriousness. The others laughed.

Down a few cars, Sonja was relaxing in her Pullman when she heard a knock. Opening the door she saw Kathy smiling at her.

"Hi, what are you doing right now?"

"Not much. I was thinking of having breakfast," said Sonja.

"Want to join me? I'm starved."

"I'd love to. Just a minute, let me get my bag." They proceeded forward as the train lurched and moved slightly side to side, rounding a curve. As Sonja followed her up the aisle Kathy was breathless with excitement. The friendship she wished for was beginning to happen.

By afternoon the scenery had shifted from the flat plains of North Dakota to the hilly views of eastern Montana. The change in scene was a prelude of the Rocky Mountains to come. By late afternoon, as the sun etched a soft pink glow in the sky ahead, the mountains with their spiraling forms, stood tall in the distance. As night fell, most of the company retired and quiet descended over the train.

Chapter 56

Pacific Northwest

Steep, craggy gorges and mountainous vistas came into view. Several of the gypsies went to the dome car to better see the splendor of mountain passes. An Elk ploughed through deep snow on the rise of embankment sending chunks of crusted snow back against the train as it sped along. Heavy snow hung from tall pines. The wind produced swirls of white against a sapphire blue sky. Above, the bright sun reigned, over the entire wondrous, magical postcard.

Later, as the sun was setting, creating a glorious glow over Vancouver, the long train pulled into the station and the cast disembarked. Cal was standing by with the sign-up sheet in case some had forgotten their lodging location for the week. Buses waited to assist the cast to their hotels.

Pat and Mally selected a double, as Pat had grown tired of isolation. The two met at the bus and proceeded to board. Jonas and Phillipe joined them as did as Jim and Joe, Sonja and Marcy, Chad and Jerry. Kathy had signed up too late to stay at the same place as the others. She would stay at the crew's hotel.

Dana and Dick Landry preferred staying wherever the crew was. This helped Dick keep in the loop and he would be readily available to Griff to sub for him on request. The show would open on Tuesday night.

Griff left the theatre and took a cab to his hotel overlooking the harbor. He loved the view, and each time he revisited Vancouver he chose this particular place. Throwing his jacket aside, he slipped out of his shoes and padded to the bed. Lying back, he reached for the phone and dialed Mally's hotel, The Queen's Inn.

"Oh Griff, how are you?"

"I'm missing you. When did you get in?"

"We arrived just a few minutes ago. We saw lots of incredible scenery!"

"The Rockies are amazing. I'm glad you're safe. The weather conditions have been challenging. Our trucks got in eight hours late. It's put a bit of pressure on us, but the Canadian jobbers are excellent." He changed his tone.

"Can we get together after the show?"

"Yes, of course."

As Mally hung up she noticed Pat's absence. Digging in her trunk produced her comfortable bathrobe. She headed for the bathroom. Going through her usual routine, she ran a bath, soaked, and then dried off and dressed.

Pat returned with a large package. Spotting a small table in the corner of the room, she produced several white cartons, depositing them there. Mally could smell something delightful.

"I had a craving, and I thought you might like to join me. Someone told me that some of the best Chinese food is right here under our noses in B.C." Producing plastic forks and two paper plates, Pat announced that dinner was served.

"You are so thoughtful! Gosh, I've missed your company, Pat."

"I admit I haven't been myself for a while. I always let my passion for Owen Matthews get in the way of common sense. I need a reality check, and you're it, Mal!"

"Well, thanks, I think," she laughed. The two devoured the contents that included moo goo gai pan, shrimp in lobster sauce and vegetable fried rice. Pat had included hot jasmine tea that really hit the spot after the food.

"When do you see Griff?"

"We're going to get together after the show."

"Good! I was thinking of asking the boys for a night out. I have to keep up with their shenanigans! Frankly, I've missed the repartee. Gay men are just the best!"

"Go for it!"

Mally picked up the garbage and walked down the hall to find a trashcan. She had stopped in the vending area and noticed Sonja and

Kathy as they stepped off the elevator. As they paused before a door, Kathy kissed Sonja. It wasn't a light, friendly kiss, but a deeply passionate one. After lingering, Sonja produced the key, opened the door, and the two disappeared inside.

Mally, slightly shaken, returned to her room. There was no mistaking what she just witnessed. Her former roommate was involved with another woman, something she never would have imagined. She had roomed with Kathy for over a year and Kathy had never come on to her, or brought other women home or mentioned her preference. If Kathy had a girlfriend, so be it. Besides, she liked Sonja Berger, now that she was free of Jackie. She wondered if Jackie was gay, if she and Sonja had been involved sexually.

Later that evening, sleep became imperative. It had been a long trip to the Pacific Northwest. The week in Vancouver lay ahead. How would the Canadians react to the American material of *Bravo Business*? They would know soon.

Chapter 57

Vancouver

The Canadians wasted no time in welcoming the *Bravo Business* Company. Opening night was a sure success and the rest of the week was sold out, making it an excellent place to start the first phase of the Pacific Northwest.

Pat had arranged to meet Jonas, Phillipe, Joe and Jim for drinks at a gay watering hole down the street. Marcy White joined the party. As they walked to a bar called 'Last Stop,' Marcy thought about the night in Atlanta when she met and danced with Phillipe. She felt that keeping company with gay men was somewhat liberating. They posed no sexual threat, were always up for a good time, and made nurturing companions. Straight men were becoming bores.

A chilly drizzle started earlier that evening. Comfort was first, so Mally put on slacks and a turtleneck sweater and headed down to the stage door.

Griff was waiting outside, catching some fresh air. He took her hand, leading her to a waiting cab. Both were starved and ready for dinner and a night together. As they drove off, rain pelted the roof, making their embrace more cozy as they held each other.

On Wednesday, Pat received a large floral box revealing two-dozen long stem yellow roses. She needn't have read the card. It was clear that Blaine was in town. His intention was obvious enough. He wanted to see her. He was staying at his condo in Vancouver for a few days. He insisted on inviting her to dinner following the show that night.

Pat weakened once more. She was horny and in need of male attention. Following the performance she hurried through the post-show ritual, not bothering to explain her plans. She left quickly and headed to her hotel where she would meet Blaine.

Pat was proud of her body. She knew it was sensational, so she chose one of her most provocative dresses, destined to arouse Blaine.

Her generous breasts and flawless skin were her hallmark. The black sheen of the sheath made her pale skin provocative against the dark fabric. A row of buttons ran the entire length of the skirt. Stepping back she scrutinized herself in the mirror. 'Very good, Irish,' she thought. 'He'll have easy access, just the way I like it.'

The phone rang, announcing Blaine's arrival. He was waiting in the lobby and beamed at the sight of her.

"Oh Pat, you're sensational!"

"Thanks, Blaine. It's great to see you." As they hugged, Blaine brushed Pat's lips with his. Escorting her to his limo, he helped her settle in the backseat. The driver pulled away.

"Where are we going?"

"It's a surprise."

"I like your surprises," she said, smiling provocatively. After a few minutes, the driver pulled up to a gated property. As Pat got out, she looked up at the tall building. Without hesitation, Blaine led her into the lobby to an elevator. When they arrived at the top floor, an open door revealed a vast penthouse.

"Oh my God, where are we?"

"Welcome to my new condo. Oh, Franklin, this is Miss Byrne, my guest for the evening."

"May I take your coat?" The formally attired gentleman went about the business of seeing to Blaine's every need. Pat was impressed with his attention to detail and his precision.

"Would you like a view of Vancouver?"

"Oh yes."

Blaine led Pat across the vast living area to a terrace set behind a length of glass sliders. Before them, the city of Vancouver blinked seductively, etched into a background of dark mountains to the north and east. To the west, a vast body of water hugged the shore reflecting the lights of the buildings standing by.

Blaine stepped closer and kissed Pat softly, tracing her face with his fingertips. "I've missed you, Patricia. I've thought about you so often these past weeks." As he was about to kiss her again, Franklin's voice broke the mood.

"Dinner is served, sir. I've set up in the den."

"Very good, Franklin, we'll be right in." Delaying long enough to kiss Pat again, he took her by the hand and led her to the den complete with a crackling fire and soft light provided by candles placed in elaborate candelabras.

Dinner was exquisite and brilliantly presented. Franklin brought a cart laden with caviar, steamed artichokes with drawn butter, Caesar salad and filet mignon served with white asparagus and Brussels sprouts on the side. Bananas Foster followed the main course, created at the table. There was coffee and cognac.

Following the meal, Franklin was excused. Blaine led Pat to a sofa in front of the fire. As they sat together, Blaine moved in closer.

"I want to make love to you. We're quite alone." Before Pat could respond, he began.

Blaine removed Pat's clothing slowly and deliberately. As each piece came off, she became more aroused. She returned her longing by undressing him. As the clothing ritual ended, Blaine gently laid Pat on a soft sheepskin in front of the fire.

Taking her hands in his, he pinned them to the floor over her head. Slowly, he ran his tongue down her body, pausing at her breasts to lick and tease. His mouth continued to explore her as he traced a wet trail over her abdomen stopping between her legs. There he remained.

Pat shook as his tongue brought her pleasure. When her desire built to an excruciating level she purposely changed the choreography reaching for him, insisting he straddle her. As Blaine kneeled over Pat, she returned pleasure with her mouth, accelerating over his shaft with such force and intensity that Blaine was consumed completely, audibly expressing his lust.

He entered her with passionate fervency. His thrusts grew as she let loose her pent-up longing, moaning her delight. They rolled and twisted and clung to each other as the firelight cast a glow over them. Later, an exhausted Blaine carried Pat to his bed. There he held her as they fell asleep, oblivious to dawn moving over the buildings of Vancouver and the mountains beyond.

Returning from Griff's hotel the next morning, Mally noted Pat's absence with curiosity. She began her daily regimen, first, indulging in a lengthy shower. After towel-drying her hair she put on her underwear and began her morning stretch on the floor. The phone rang.

"Hi, it's Owen."

"Oh, Owen, I'm afraid Pat's out. May I take a message?"

"I'm coming to Seattle next week. "I've got business to attend to and while I'm at it, I'll stop in at the theatre."

"See you then. Have a safe trip." Mally hung up the phone and continued her stretch just as the door opened. Pat entered, looking disheveled and exhausted.

"Good grief, what happened?"

"I partied a little too hard. Jonas and Phillipe let me flop there last night," she lied.

"Do you want breakfast? Personally, I'm starved."

"I want to clean up first." Silently, Pat undressed and removed her make-up. Then stepping into a shower, she reluctantly removed traces of last night's love play. As the warm water ran over her, she quietly relived all of Blaine's moves as her hands found their way to her mound. As her orgasm ruptured under the torrent of water, she stifled her moans so that Mally wouldn't hear her. Instead, she let the ripples of her self-made pleasure subside. Quickly stepping out of the tub she reached for a towel.

The time grew closer for the company's departure to Seattle. Blaine called Pat every day and every night she slipped quietly to him, consumed in endless pleasure. She couldn't get enough of his intense lovemaking. And she returned it, sustaining hours of raw sex. It was as though Pat had been deprived so long she was insatiable and Blaine matched her need.

Blaine was about to embark on a three-month business trip to Europe and the Far East. He would have to do without Pat. It was obvious that Blaine was in love with her. On the other hand, she had no intention of allowing her feelings to deepen. In spite of his pluses, he was no match for Owen, pure and simple. Blaine was merely an escape, a means of sexual relief, a companion to ease her loneliness.

When she returned that last night to her hotel, she and Mally prepared their trunks for pick-up. Once more the gypsies were on the move. Soon they would encounter mist, rain and mild weather in Seattle.

Chapter 58

Seattle

Mally and Pat sat with Jonas and Philippe as the train slipped out of the station. The mood was light as they shared conversation and a continental breakfast. The boys talked about the Seattle clubs they would visit, while the girls discussed their stay at the Belmont, an apartment hotel. For three weeks, they planned to save money by cooking in and enjoying apartment living, a rarity on tour. Their hotel was a short walk to the Moore Theatre.

The girls found the Belmont old, but clean and cozy. Their corner apartment was on the third floor with a view of downtown that stretched for blocks. There was ample space with a day bed in the living room and a small bedroom off to the side. A classic 1940's kitchen as well as an old-fashioned claw-foot bathtub in the bathroom completely leant a Bette Davis movie ambience. The arrival of their trunks brought comfort, knowing their personal possessions were with them. While they were unpacking, the phone rang.

"Griff! How's it going?"

"Well, the Moore is an old movie house, with some problems to sort out, but we'll handle it. We're on break right now."

"Griff, we love the Belmont. It's spotless."

"Ah yes, the Belmont. I stayed there in the early days. It's tidy and the owner is a peach.

Enjoy your evening and we'll catch up tomorrow night."

"Bye."

The company was psyched. A new town brought renewed energy and surge of enthusiasm from cast and audience alike. Seattle audiences were known for their generosity. The three-week run was already sold out.

On Wednesday afternoon, Dana and Phillipe were dancing stage left. Suddenly, Dana dropped to one knee, having tangled feet with Phillipe. Trying to recover, she failed. It was obvious she was hurt and unable to put weight on her foot. As Dana limped off stage and into a stagehand's waiting arms, Mally was out and in position, grabbing Phillipe's hand. When he turned around he was stunned to see her grinning back at him. Never missing a beat, they finished the number as partners. Dana prognosis was a severe sprain, requiring rest for at least two weeks. Mally would swing Dana's spot until she could return.

The rest of the week continued without incident. Griff and Mally toured the old World's Fair site and enjoyed drinks high above the city in the famous Space Needle. They took a boat trip along Puget Sound and spent some cozy nights at Griff's hotel.

Their first Sunday off, they ordered in and watched *The Ed Sullivan Show*. Ed Sullivan made his customary announcement. The curtains parted revealing four young lads with mop haircuts skin-tight pants, and short coats. The Beatles were unique, stylish and new. The roar of the studio audience following their set was proof they had caught on.

Seattle was awash with continuous rain so intense that the company arrived at the theatre soaked, and returned to their hotels in the same condition following the show.

Following Wednesday's matinee, Griff called Jonas to his office. Without delay Jonas hurried downstairs and found Griff seated, his glasses perched on his nose.

"Jonas, Owen is coming in tomorrow. He wants you to step out of the weekend shows. Chad will cover."

"What's up?"

"He'd like you to join us for a meeting on Friday."

"OK, I'll be there. Thanks." Jonas left and Griff resumed his paperwork.

At the five-minute call on Thursday evening the cast was summoned to the green room. They mingled and chatted softly.

"Ladies and Gentleman, we like to give you a surprise on occasion. Owen?" Pat stared in disbelief as Owen sauntered through the group.

"Hi Guys. I had some business in Seattle this weekend so I thought I'd stop by. I'll be checking the show, so I expect to see your best work."

"OK company, places please," commanded Griff. The cast filed out of the room.

"Pat?" She felt a hand on her back.

"Baby, you look fabulous."

"I can't believe you're here."

"You'll believe it later. Have a great show, ok?" He walked to the nearest exit and disappeared into the house.

Pat immediately thought of her recent week with Blaine. 'This is too close for comfort. Damn, Irish, you've got to be more careful from now on,' she thought, shivering. 'What if Owen finds out? He's the key to my future, not Blaine.' Mally stopped her.

"Pat, are you all right?"

"I had no idea that Owen would be here," Pat said, with an edge.

"Well, he called the other morning while you were out."

"Where was I?"

"You were with Jonas and Phillipe. You crashed with them, remember?" Heaving a sigh, Pat felt sheepish as she walked into the stage light. Later, as she hurried to Owen's hotel, she tried to put her nagging guilt aside. Knocking softly, she melted when she saw him. Slowly, he led her into the room and over to the fire.

"Baby, get out of those wet clothes. There's a robe in the bathroom." Pat excused herself and took a quick shower. Wrapping herself in the fluffy white warmth, she walked into the sitting room.

"Come here, Baby. Let me hold you." To her surprise, Owen didn't pounce, but instead, held her, gently. "I missed you," he said, staring at the fire.

"Seattle is a long way to come."

"I have some business here. I'm hiring Jonas to assist me on the new show."

"Wow! He'll be thrilled."

"I'm hiring Griff as my permanent production stage manager." He paused than grew serious.

"Pat, there's one more thing."

"Oh, what's that?"

"I'm heading to Las Vegas."

"What's in Las Vegas?"

"How does a divorce sound?"

"Owen, you're serious, aren't you?"

"I couldn't be more! Vera has finally agreed to a finish. The joint assets are being divided, including the penthouse. I don't want the dog." Together they laughed, cried and made love, sweetly, and in no particular hurry.

Owen met with Jonas and Griff the next morning. They grabbed coffee and bagels, and settled back. "In the fall I'm bringing a new concept to Broadway, an all-dance revue, using the best dance ensemble New York audiences have yet to see. Jonas, I want you to come on board as my assistant. You'll replace my long time associate, Manny Johnson. He's going into producing. I am offering you a permanent place in my organization. Well?"

"Yes, of course!"

"Good!" Owen turned to Griff.

"Griff, it's time to get off the road! I want you to head the production."

"I'd be honored, Owen."

"Great! We'll continue these discussions as the project moves along. Oh, by the way, I have pre-cast Patricia Byrne. She'll go through a token audition for my backers, but she's my definite choice for the lead. This is not for public knowledge, right?" They nodded.

After the meeting, Owen headed back to the hotel, Jonas floated back to his apartment, and Griff continued his day with tech matters. The rain continued.

Chapter 59

News

Owen left for Vegas. The quick embrace and kiss before his departure always left Pat uneasy. Outside the rain had let up. Inside, Pat gathered the few personal items she brought during her stay with Owen. She missed him already.

There would be a divorce. She was beyond ecstatic, and yet, fearful. Would it really happen? Was Owen really on the level? Only his arms holding her and his reassuring words could ease her insecurity. As she hurried back to her hotel she spotted Phillipe and Jonas.

Jonas could read Pat's moods immediately.

"How are we today?"

"The Irish madwoman has another page for her diary!" They laughed as they walked to the front desk. The concierge handed Jonas a note. When he'd read it he looked up, barely breathing.

"It's from my father. I'm to call immediately." Jonas hurried to the house phone. Requesting an outside line, he dialed his old home number. Jonas recognized the formal voice of his father, Charles Martin.

"Jonas. Thank you for calling. I'm sorry to have to tell you your mother died last night. She was gravely ill for the last two months. I had to hire a detective to locate you. The funeral is Saturday at 10:00 a.m. at John the Baptist in Santa Barbara. Will you attend?"

"Yes, of course."

"Would you care to stay at the house? Your sister Roxanne will be here with her husband and children."

"Thanks, Father. I'll get there as quickly as I can." Jonas's hands trembled as he put down the phone. No longer holding back, he sobbed uncontrollably. Phillipe took hold of him and, assisted by Pat, got him upstairs to the apartment.

"Oh God," Jonas wailed. Phillipe helped Jonas onto the bed where Pat removed his coat and shoes.

"Cheri, I'm here," Phillipe said, softly. Pat slipped out of the room as Phillipe covered Jonas with a comforter. In minutes he was asleep. Later, Jonas found Griff at the theatre just as half hour was being called.

"Griff I need a couple of days off. My mother died last night."

"I'm so sorry, Jonas. We'll cover you. May I assist in finding you a reasonable airfare?"

"Thanks, Griff. I appreciate your help."

"Anything else I can do?"

"Thank you, but no." As he left Griff's office, tears consumed him. He stopped at the men's room to compose himself. In the background he could hear Griff calling half hour.

On Friday, Jonas left for California, leaving all pertinent information with Phillipe. They kissed furtively in the elevator.

"I love you, Cheri," whispered Phillipe, taking Jonas' hand.

"And I love you," returned Jonas, hugging Phillipe quickly before getting into the blue and white taxi. When Jonas pulled away, Phillipe felt a tug in his stomach. Already, he felt the longing for Jonas building. It would be an interminable three days.

He and Jonas's dalliance in Atlanta had grown into an intense partnership. For the first time, Phillipe was not the opportunist, as he had been with his former older, wealthy lovers. He had fallen in love with Jonas, and loved him for who he was.

Jonas found his soul mate in Phillipe. Phillipe had made an honest man of him. He no longer needed the elusive one-night stands to fill his life. Their growing relationship was based on mutual respect, trust and an intense desire to satisfy each other's emotional and sexual needs. Being unfaithful never crossed either's mind. The commitment was intense and in place.

Chapter 60

The Return

The jet descended over LAX. Below, the view was murky. Smog obliterated the skyline of downtown L.A. with a thick, gray veneer. In a matter of minutes, the plane landed.

As he walked the concourse, Jonas noticed a stocky, gray-haired woman waving as she approached. Jonas hardly recognized her. It was Roxy, his older sister.

"Jonas! Oh my God, you've changed," her voice breaking. She held him tight. Jonas awkwardly returned the embrace.

"How's Father?"

"Dad's been through a lot. He took care of Mom the last months. He refused to leave her side. I honestly think he fought the cancer more than she did."

"I wish I had known. Somehow, I should have known," said Jonas, trembling, as tears came.

"Don't blame yourself, Jonas. How could you have known?" The two arrived at baggage claim and waited for the carousel to move. Jonas spotted his bag and lifted it off the conveyer belt. Roxanne led him to her car.

The drive to Santa Barbara seemed long. En route, they sat quietly, occasionally glancing at each other. When at last they arrived at the Martin home, Roxanne pulled up the long driveway and parked at the front door. As Jonas reached in the trunk to retrieve his bag, he noticed a tall, robust man walking toward him with his hand extended.

"I'm Roger Fairchild, Roxanne's husband."

"Hi," said Jonas, casually, carefully returning a strong handshake. He wondered if Roger was homophobic.

Jonas had a lot to process. He would ease his way along. When he entered the house he was introduced to his young nephews, Chandler and Wesley. They were distant, but polite, excusing themselves to play before dinner.

Roxanne led Jonas up the winding staircase to the second floor and down a long corridor to a beautifully appointed room complete with a canopied four-poster bed. A fire was crackling in the immense stone fireplace. Rich drapes of tapestry curtained the large bay window allowing a view of an enormous pool and cabana, a regulation sized tennis court and a green house. Cypress and olive trees cordoned the entire area.

"I thought you would be more comfortable back here, Jonas. It's quiet and out of the main traffic of the house. Your old room over the garage is now used for storage."

"Thanks. Where's Father?"

"Dad has been out making final arrangements for tomorrow. He'll be back for dinner. We'll eat at 7:00." Roxanne politely made her exit.

Jonas unzipped his garment bag and unpacked the one suit he owned, a black gabardine. He found a place to hang it on the back of the closet door. The room seemed to close in on him as he continued unpacking his toiletries and the few clothes he brought.

Noticing a phone, he decided to make a call. He dialed and waited. An operator connected him. The familiar French-tinged voice answered.

"Hello?" Phillipe's voice brought tears.

"It's me," whispered Jonas, his voice cracking.

"Cheri, are you all right?"

"So far, yes. I haven't seen my father yet. That's coming."

"It'll be fine. Remember, he's hurting too."

"I needed to hear that. I'm nervous. I haven't been in this house in over twelve years."

"It must be difficult to take all at once, but remember, this is your family. At least you have one."

"I miss you already. I love you so much," Jonas murmured, softly.

"I love you too, Cheri. By the way, where is the service taking place?"

"It's going to be at John the Baptist Church in Santa Barbara. Why?"

"I was just curious."

"I dread tomorrow."

"Don't project, Cheri. It will go better than you think. And Jonas, I miss you more than I thought possible. Hurry back."

"I will." The call ended.

At seven, Jonas made his way to the formal dining room, trying to calm himself as he noted the family already gathered. Jonas immediately recognized his father—twelve years older and somewhat withered.

His father's outstretched arms beckoned Jonas. As the two embraced Charles attempted to maintain his usual decorum. Jonas trembled as he returned the embrace, trying to stay calm. He was startled by the obvious change in his father.

Once everyone was seated, James, the family butler, was summoned to pour the wine. Passing Jonas, he smiled warmly. Charles raised his glass in a toast, his hand shaking. "Welcome, Jonas. And thank you all for being here."

As the family sipped, two maids assisted James. Conversation amongst the group remained general and pleasant. Following the meal, Charles retired to the library, inviting his children and Roger for coffee and cognac.

The library was warm and inviting. The large, overstuffed leather furniture seemed to swallow them. James served coffee. Courvoisier and cigars were offered. Charles chose one of the finest and gently rolled it in his hand. He sat, quietly allowing the cognac to fill his senses. A sip of brandy following a satisfying dinner was pleasant distraction as he attempted a smile. Then, his expression shifted into a drawn and tired frown. He turned his attention to Roger and Jonas.

"I would like you both to act as pallbearers tomorrow. I have asked my brother Harry and his three sons to assist. Do you remember your cousins, Jonas?"

"Yes, they're close to my age as I remember."

"Yes. They all live in the area. Craig's a lawyer, Garry's in real estate, and Peter teaches. All married, all with children." There was silence. Roger broke the awkward moment.

"Tell me about your job, Jonas. I understand you're a professional dancer. Is that right?" Jonas tightened.

"Yes. I have been dancing professionally for the last ten years," said Jonas, hoping the inquiry would end there.

"That's pretty impressive. What sort of dancing?"

"I've been doing musical theatre, touring companies, a couple of Broadway shows."

"Is that right? Does it pay well?" Jonas swallowed, the brandy burning a path down his throat.

He tried a sip of coffee.

"It does if you stick to it long enough. I'm dance captain, and do feature work."

"And he sings and acts too, right Jonas?" Roxanne sensed Jonas' discomfort at being grilled.

"That's right. The more versatile you are, the longer the career," Jonas tossed off.

"What happens after that?"

Roxanne rolled her eyes as she turned her attention on Roger. "Jonas is going to choreograph and direct, right?" Jonas smiled.

"Yes. In the fall I will assist Owen Matthews on a new Broadway show," he said confidently.

"Who is Owen Matthews?" Roger was getting tight. Roxanne jumped in.

"Roger, there's more to life than investment counseling and golf. Owen Matthews is probably the greatest living director in the musical theatre. He creates hits!"

"Well, who gives a rat's ass," Roger slurred.

Roxanne stood and took Roger's glass. "Darling, you've had enough. Come on, it's a going to be a long day tomorrow," she coaxed.

"Yes, I agree," said Charles, who put out the remainder of his cigar and took a last sip before helping his son-in-law to his feet.

"You're tight. It's a difficult time. Get some sleep."

He turned to Jonas. "Do you have everything you need, son? Is the room satisfactory?" Jonas felt suddenly relieved.

"It's fine. Thanks."

"Then we'll see you all in the morning. Join us for breakfast at eight. We'll leave for the church at nine. Goodnight."

"Goodnight, Dad. Love you," murmured Roxanne. Roger waved as he teetered away. Jonas took his time. As he reached the staircase he passed James, who stopped.

"Sir, may I speak with you?" Jonas nodded.

"Sir, I was here the night Mrs. Martin passed. Before she slipped into a coma, she was quite lucid. She talked about you with great pride. You know, she was never quite the same after you left home. Oh, she tried to keep up appearances for Mr. Martin. The truth is, she lost her will."

"My mother was my heart. She understood who I was. Do you understand?"

"I do indeed. You had a life to live as you saw fit. Every man must do this. You never disappointed Mrs. Martin. She was proud of you."

"Thank you. I appreciate this more than you know," he said, touching James' sleeve.

"You're welcome. Mrs. Martin was a great lady. I was in her employ for twenty-five years. Well, good night, Sir."

Returning to his room, Jonas undressed, washed, and brushed his teeth. The fire was now a faint glow, as the room seemed to close in. Jonas slipped under the covers. As he lay there, he felt totally lost. Warm tears wet his cheeks. Grabbing his pillow, he buried his face in the softness, stifling the sobs. How long he wept, he didn't remember. He fell into a deep sleep, dreaming of being held in his mother's arms.

Jonas' travel alarm blasted soon enough. As he rolled over to turn off the annoying sound, he paused for a moment to get his bearings. 'Oh yes, this is the day,' he thought wearily.

Showering and shaving, then putting on his one suit, he paused in front of the mirror. The figure before him was framed in formality, not the spontaneous, campy, chorus boy he knew so well.

One final check and he was on his way to the dining room. Stillness engulfed him as he descended the large staircase.

They all were there, seated and somber. Only the sound of his nephews speaking in curious whispers brought a sense of lightness, the undeniable truth that life goes on. Charles sat at his familial post, the head of the table, absorbed in silence as he finished his coffee.

When breakfast was complete, they all dispersed, meeting at the portico to begin what was to be Elizabeth's final journey.

Chapter 61

Coming Out

Jonas was filled with dread the moment he walked into the chapel. It was impossible not to notice the sea of flowers tidily arranged around the casket. Stepping up to the open cover, he looked down at his mother. He was stunned by the funeral director's obvious—and failed —attempt to mask the struggle she had.

Jonas kissed Elizabeth the way she had kissed him goodbye as he left for school every morning. In his mind he could hear her laughter at his silly antics, her cheers at soccer matches, and he pictured the torment on her face when he was hurt. Warm tears meandered down his face leaving a faint taste of salt on his lips.

A touch on his shoulder brought him around. Charles had come to claim him. Together they walked into the sanctuary. The funeral director followed, wheeling the casket. Jonas was impressed by the size of the throng. As the service unfolded, countless speakers eulogized his mother. A choir of voices sang so sweetly, their music pulled tears from him once again.

Charles wept quietly throughout the service. Jonas watched until he could not longer hold back. As he moved closer and embraced his father, Charles collapsed, sobbing. When the sobs subsided, Jonas offered his handkerchief. A long hour passed before the service finally came to a close.

Jonas joined his uncle, cousins, and brother-in-law, lifting the casket and together, they filed out of the church. The sun disappeared behind a bank of clouds as they placed Elizabeth in the hearse. Cars pulled out one by one, and drove to the cemetery a short distance away. The crowd dispersed following the benediction.

Jonas stood alone. The rain had picked up as he stared at the ivory casket, topped with lilies and roses. Carefully, he plucked a pink rose from the cluster and placed it in his coat pocket. He hurried to catch up to the family.

Later, following the reception at the Martin home, Charles and Jonas walked through the house looking at the many floral arrangements brought back from the church. Stopping before one of the loveliest, a spray of Casablanca lilies, champagne-colored roses and purple tulips, Charles reached for his glasses. "To Jonas Martin: Heartfelt sympathy to you and yours with love, Phillipe." Jonas read it and put the card in his pocket.

"Who is this Phillipe, Jonas? It's not a name I recognize," said Charles.

"Father, I need to speak to you in private." They headed to the library and Charles closed the door.

"Would you care for a drink?"

Yes, please." Charles went to the bar. Reaching for the cognac, he poured into two snifters. Jonas gratefully took a sip of the warm liquid. Charles sat down across from his son. He held his favorite cigar in his free hand.

"Well?" Jonas took a deep breath.

"Ever since I was a little kid I knew I was different, someone I imagined not acceptable to you. I tried to fit in, but I couldn't. So, I studied dancing in L.A. Mother encouraged me, paid for the lessons, and watched me develop my talent, all without your knowledge. She knew you would never approve."

"So you left home because you couldn't live up to what you thought my expectations were of you?"

"That's partly it. A dancer's life isn't exactly stable, or one a parent wants for his child. It's rough. No guarantees. I've done rather well, and I'm grateful for that."

"That's good, Jonas. However, I feel there is something else." Jonas took a swig and put his snifter down.

"I've been afraid to come clean."

"Why? Come now, what is it?"

"I'm gay." Charles put down his cigar.

"Yes, I know." Tears sprang to Jonas' eyes.

"You know? My God, how do you know?" Charles stood and walked behind Jonas' chair, placing his hands on his shoulders.

"It's something I figured out. At first I blamed myself, but then, I had to look at the bigger picture. I realized you were special. I didn't have all the answers, certainly not for you. Jami was killed, you left home, and your dear mother developed cancer and lost the fight. Through all of that, I learned what's important."

"I've always wanted to tell you," cried Jonas, hugging Charles. Moments passed.

"Who is Phillipe?" Charles returned to his cognac and cigar.

"Phillipe is my partner. He's my soul mate. I met him on tour in Atlanta. There was an opportunity for him to join the show, and he took it."

"Is this relationship serious?"

"Yes, it is."

"Son, you have my blessing. I will look forward to meeting him."

"Thank you, Father!" Silence was etched in a long pause, before Jonas spoke again.

"What will you do now?"

"This house holds too many memories. I'm thinking of putting it on the market and getting myself a nice condo. What do you think? I'll be retiring in another year and it's time to down size. I'll travel a bit. Who knows, I might come to New York to see you and Phillipe."

"That would be great! Thanks, Father. Thank you for everything." The emotions ran strong as they embraced once again.

In the morning, Roxanne drove Jonas to LAX where he boarded a plane for Seattle. It was an unexpected departure of light and peace. Somehow he knew that his mother had brought it about.

Chapter 62

The Girls

In the midst of the Seattle strike, a deluge descended, challenging the men working and Griff's patience. However, he and his staff managed to catch a commuter flight on Sunday. Every minute counted in order to have the show ready Monday evening.

The train carrying the cast and orchestra left Seattle later through a thick haze of gray drizzle. Mally and Pat made their way to the club car as the train lurched and picked up speed. They ran into Jonas and Phillipe, who were already seated.

"How are you doing, Jonas?"

"As a matter of fact, couldn't be better," he enthused. "Everything went well. I never expected my father to be so open and accepting."

"What do you mean?"

"I came out to my father, and now he wants to meet this good-looking fellow next to me. Can you beat that?"

"Oh, Jonas, this is great news! I am so happy for you," Mally exclaimed.

"This calls for a celebration," added Pat, enthusiastically. "Is it too early for a beer?"

"I think not," said Phillipe, gesturing a waiter over. "We'll have four beers, please."

Jonas glanced around and noticed Kathy and Sonja at the far end of the car. He was surprised to see them kissing. Quietly he brought the others' attention to them.

"Do we have a romance here?" Phillipe glanced casually in their direction. They were barely visible as they hunkered down in their seats.

"It sure looks that way," said Pat.

"Lesbians on board! Talk about coming out in front of the world. I give them a lot of credit," said Jonas. "She's your old roommate isn't she, Mal?"

"Yes. I've known her for a couple of years, but I never knew she was gay."

"How long have they been together do you suppose?"

"I think it started soon after Kathy joined the company. I spotted them kissing in the corridor in Vancouver. It's really their business, right?"

"You're right, Mal. We all have our own private sex lives," said Jonas, quietly. The beers arrived.

They pulled into Portland at 4 p.m. The incessant rain had turned to a soft mist as the gypsies got off the train. Once again, the girls decided to go their separate ways. Mally would stay at the Stewart with Griff while Pat planned to flop at the Manchester, where most of the gypsies would stay. The rates were reasonable and it was convenient to the theatre. Check-in was always hectic as the company descended on the front desk staff. It took a while to sort through the reservations.

Kathy and Sonja checked into the Manchester as well. By now they were inseparable. Sonja had blossomed and Kathy was content. Their newfound relationship brought each to new physical and emotional heights. Sonja had developed responsibility, self-assurance, and stronger communication skills. Kathy was at peace with her sexuality for the first time in her life. Sonja made Kathy feel attractive. Kathy was nurturing, kind, and respectful. Sonja's dancing improved. They had developed a strong alliance.

On opening night, the humor and innuendo of the script's satire caught on immediately. The comic-book proportions of the characters and the ingenious staging won raves. The cast and audience were completely simpatico by show's end.

Mally and Griff dined after the performance. Pat joined Jonas and Phillipe for a night out, dragging Marcy along for laughs. There were a few gay bars in the downtown area and the group decided to check out the scene.

Joe Pinto and Jim Sorenson were on hand to check out the locals. They were now casual lovers with the understanding that they could trick any time or place, together or solo. Joe was the more aggressive of the two, always looking for action, relentless in his pursuit. Jim was the more passive, inclined to cooperate with Joe's whims, joining in the fun or retiring to his room.

After the show, Sonja and Kathy craved pizza. They hurried through the rain in search of a joint and spotting one through the down pour, entered the cozy, dry place. The combined aromas of sausage, onion and garlic hit them immediately. Shaking out and hanging up their outerwear, they found a back booth. Ordering beer and a large pepperoni pizza, they settled back, holding hands and chatting.

"Glad you came?" Kathy smiled and squeezed Sonja's hand.

"The best part of this tour is meeting you," said Kathy, softly.

"Oh, Kathy, the feeling is mutual." The pizza arrived and the girls ordered two more beers. Their appetites were in high gear, as usual, following a performance. Digging into the pizza was pure pleasure.

When the second round of beer was finished, the girls ordered a third. The beer began taking hold and the girls were getting tipsy. Finishing the last of the pizza, they washed it down with the remainder of beer. Dividing the bill, they grabbed their coats and headed out. The rain was coming down with such force that they huddled together and ran under awnings all the way back to the Manchester. They were high and loose as they stepped into the elevator.

When the door shut, Kathy backed Sonja up into the corner and kissed her with such force the two fell, laughing, on the floor. Sonja was delightfully surprised and turned on. Reaching for Kathy, Sonja groped her breasts as she kissed Kathy passionately. Struggling to get up off the floor, they exited the elevator and headed for their room.

Shutting the door and bolting it they began to peel out of their soggy clothes. First, Kathy undressed Sonja. When the last piece fell to the floor, she backed her to the bed and pushed her down. Kathy held Sonja's arms down while she kissed her breasts, moved to her abdomen, and traced her way to her mound. All the while Sonja begged for more, pushing her pelvis toward Kathy's tongue as she felt her orgasm building. Her insistence was a turn on for Kathy.

Sonja felt the pressure in her genitals as her mounting orgasm exploded. As Sonja writhed and rocked through her orgasm, Kathy felt excruciating pleasure. She ached to be done.

Once Sonja had experienced the rush, she reached for Kathy. Sonja now removed the remainder of Kathy's clothes, throwing them aside as she kissed her on the lips, breasts and finally, between her legs. She continued sucking Kathy, reaching up to play with her nipples. She felt powerful as she brought Kathy to another peak, running her tongue in and out of her. There was no stopping Sonja's desire to bring satisfaction.

All through the ensuing dance of sorts, they took turns. In spite of their drunkenness, each had experienced new heights of pleasure and release. When they were done, the air was generous with female fragrance.

Showering, they repeatedly played with each other, as the running water softened their cries of pleasure. After towel drying each other, they climbed into bed and entwined themselves in each other's arms until the morning light invaded the room.

All week, lines of potential patrons wound around the block, as many tried to get tickets no longer available. The Lehrman organization was pleased with their constantly full coffers. *Bravo Business* had continuously proved to be one of the most popular musicals running, both in New York and on the road. However, the advance word was that the Salt Lake audiences weren't as generous in attendance, or appreciation of new material.

Those who had played there on previous tours mentioned the conservative influence of the Morman church. Others reported difficulty dealing with the altitude and the raked stage at the Capitol Theatre, a stage that had a slight pitch to the floor. Potentially, it could throw off a dancer's balance.

Mally wasn't concerned. She was psyched. She had never been to that part of the country. She marveled at her good fortune. *Bravo Business* was an awakening mile after mile.

Chapter 63

Salt Lake City

Mally joined Pat at the Farraday, a small hotel in downtown Salt Lake, minutes from the theatre. The girls found their trunks at the door. An hour passed before a jangling phone broke the silence. It was Griff.

"How was the trip?"

"Long, but I slept through most of it. The constant rain tired me out!"

"Low pressure systems. How do you feel now?"

"Hungry!"

"We've been at the Capitol all day, but we're finished. How about being my dinner date?"

"I'd love to. When are you available?"

"Well, unless you want me sweaty and dirty, how about seven-thirty? I'm at the Davenport, about ten minutes away. I'll phone when I arrive."

"See you soon!"

It became obvious during Tuesday's opening that the reported raked stage wasn't a rumor. The physically sloped area was uneven and difficult, making footing uncertain in the glare of the footlights. Owen's staging, so familiar after months of repetition, felt awkward on the rake. Even the veterans were extra cautious.

During the second act, the dancers felt the effects more profoundly as the angle put strain on lower backs during the Buccaneer number. By mid-week the complaints to the management were frequent, especially following two shows on Wednesday. Griff reassured the company that the Capitol's rake was the only one they would encounter the rest of the tour.

On Thursday, an arrangement of yellow roses arrived for Pat. She took a deep breath as she opened the card. 'Put some shine on these mountains. Love, Blaine.' Pat quickly tucked the card away as she continued making up. Staring at the handsome bouquet, Mally asked, "Are they from Owen?"

"Blaine." It was obvious that Pat was preoccupied. Her mind was filled with conflict. Blaine was the distraction she needed, but she would have to be careful. She couldn't and wouldn't lose Owen. During the overture Pat cornered Mally.

"Mal, this Blaine thing is no big deal."

"Why is he sending you flowers?"

"It's fun. He's thinks I'm hot stuff, and he's definitely a distraction I need," said Pat, with a defensive edge. "Look. It's easy for you to judge. You've got your lover here. You can get laid whenever you want to. It's lonely, Mal. I need affection. Why can't you understand?"

"I understand you want it both ways. What's happened to you anyway? When did you become such a taker?"

"What?"

"You've changed, Pat. You've turned into this opportunist, this completely selfish person!"

"Oh fuck you, Mal!"

"Oh that's great, Pat!" Mally's adrenalin was in high gear watching Pat walk away in a huff. Her heart was beating wildly as she considered what just took place. She had to hurry to her opening position.

The next night, as cast members filed out of the stage door, many took notice of the handsome man standing near a limo. Jonas did a double take.

"It's that rich guy, who digs Pat. He's hot, no doubt about it." Phillipe glanced back at Blaine.

"He's attractive, but I've got the hottest, Cheri!" Jonas smiled at the obvious compliment. The two headed back to the hotel to explore the notion.

Blaine was more than pleased to see Pat. He kissed her and offered his arm, as he led her to the car.

"I've missed you so much, Patricia."

"I thought you were in Europe."

"There's a deal brewing, a possible merger with another company stateside, so I'm back. Would you care to join us for a drink?" Pat tightened. "Us?"

"Remember Rod and Johnny? I believe you met them in Jacksonville. We're here to ski. We leave in the morning."

Pat, clearly disappointed, stood her ground. "You were unexpected Blaine, and frankly, I'm beat. Have a nice holiday." She relished the disappointment on his face.

"May I drop you at your hotel?"

"Yes. I'm at the Farraday." As the car pulled away, Blaine suggested a drive. Pat was more amenable now that she was alone with him. They had driven a short distance when he pulled her close.

Kissing her gently at first, his ardor began building until he aggressively explored her with his tongue. Moving deftly down her neck, Pat did little to resist, feeling the familiar stir. She was wet as she pulled at Blaine's belt, hastily unzipping his fly. He was already hard. Blaine slowly eased her down on her back.

Without further delay, he expertly unbuttoned her jeans, and began pulling them down. Pat cooperated fully as she raised her rump allowing Blaine to slide them off. Undoing her blouse and loosening her bra, she gave him complete access, moaning with each caress. As her lust built, she began squeezing his erection through his shorts.

"Oh Blaine, give me all you've got," she begged, all the while her body quivering.

Foreplay turned into raw play, as Blaine forced Pat's legs apart. Mounting her he entered applying all his strength, dominating her completely.

Pat gasped. Blaine had never been so aggressive. Being taken forcefully was exciting, a complete turn on. Pat begged and squirmed, her lust overpowering her as Blaine continued, going deeper with each thrust.

"Oh, Blaine. Do me good!"

Blaine turned Pat over on her stomach, grabbing her hands, pinning them behind her. He entered her again thrusting with all his strength. He could no longer hold back. Pat screamed as her orgasm erupted with Blaine's climax. They let go in a unified explosion. Together they lay exhausted, sweat mingling, breathing syncopated.

Moments passed before Blaine lifted off Pat, releasing her hands. He leaned back against the seat and began dressing. Pat sat up slowly.

Groping around, she found her clothing on the floor in front of the seat. As she put on her panties, she winced, painfully aware of the soreness between her legs. Blaine watched, savoring her reaction.

"You are incredibly hot," said Blaine, in a hoarse whisper. Pat was in a trance as she finished putting herself together. "That's the best sex yet," she said, breathlessly.

"You think so? Well, you can have as much as you want, as often as you want it."

"I don't understand."

"I want you with me always," he said, forcefully taking her hands and holding them tightly. Pat's heart sank. Her mind was racing.

"I hadn't considered this a permanent arrangement," she said, weakly. He pulled her to him and took her face in his hands.

"I have. The fact is I'm in love with you, Patricia." Pat was quiet as she calmly removed his hands.

"Blaine, I can't. I'm not in love with you."

"Patricia, please. You've got me so crazy in love with you I can't think straight. I have never felt this way before. I want to marry you!"

Pat stiffened. "Marry me? You can't mean it! Occasional sex is one thing, but marriage? I couldn't possibly."

Blaine sat back, trying to process Pat's reaction. "What have I done wrong? I know you weren't faking during our lovemaking. You're on a pedestal, Patricia, a Goddamn pedestal. I would give you the world!"

"I don't want the world, or you," she said sadly, looking away.

Stunned and hurt, Blaine picked up the car phone. "Darren, please stop at the Hotel Farraday."

Putting the phone back he looked at Pat. "Pat, I thought we had a future together."

"You thought wrong, Blaine. I'm sorry, there is no future." The car came to a stop. Blaine reached for the door and pushed it open. Climbing out, Pat turned to him. "I've had a wonderful time. Thank you for everything."

Without another word, Blaine looked away. She trembled as she pushed through the revolving door, only looking back when she reached the lobby. The limo was gone.

Pat was carefully quiet as she entered the room. Quietly she slipped out of her jeans and winced, remembering the rough play. Deciding on a warm bath she filled the tub and removed her make-up, looking intently in the mirror.

'Well, Irish, you've come to your senses.' Turning off the water, she slipped into the warmth of the bath. She thought about sex with Blaine Courtman. She felt cheap. "How could I? Oh, Owen," she cried, emptying all her emotion until she shook the regret away. Later, she retreated to bed, covering herself as she lay tucked on her side. Mally was awake, having heard the sobbing.

"Pat, are you all right?"

"Mal, I've been such a bitch! What you said earlier is true. I've been such a taker. Please forgive me," she cried. "It's over with Blaine. I called it quits," she announced, as she reached for a tissue. Mally got out of bed and reached for Pat, hugging her.

"Well, welcome back!" In minutes they were asleep, and the week in Salt Lake City, over. This was one booking they could have done without.

Chapter 64

Symptoms

The trip to Omaha cut a long swath through Colorado and Nebraska. In the evening, several cast members got together in the dining car. The talk was light and good-humored.

Pat, Mally, Phillipe and Jonas sat at one table, while Sonja, Kathy, and Marcy sat at another. Joe and Jim, Chad and Dick took over the third. Dana was conspicuously absent from the group. After placing dinner orders, the gypsies settled into a round of drinks. Pat turned her attention to Dick as he worked on a beer.

"Where's Dana?"

"She's nauseous. She's been nauseous every morning. It's hard to convince her to eat."

"That's so unlike her, said Pat. She's always hungry!"

"I know. But lately she's put off by food, especially the smell of it," sighed Dick.

"Is she tired and moody?"

"Yeah, come to think of it, Kathy. Why do you ask?"

"My sister Jean and her husband came to visit me for a few weeks. Jean, who's always Miss Pep Rally, complained of nausea, fatigue and cried at the drop of a hat. Guess what? She's due in July! I'm going to be an aunt," said Kathy, gleefully.

"Oh, my God, that's it," said Dick. "We've been trying to get pregnant for months."

"Well, be sure and see a doctor in Omaha," said Kathy.

"This calls for a smart toast," announced Jonas, raising his beer. The others joined in the gesture.

"To the parents to be!" Applause and whistles filled the car as dinner arrived.

By morning, the mountains of Utah and western Colorado had given way to flat land as far as the eye could see. Bravo Business was in the heart of cattle country and Omaha was a short distance.

The hotel in Omaha was pedestrian at best. The girls chose The Riley, a smaller hotel two blocks from the Music Hall. The weather in late March was still cold on the plains, so they opted for the shortest possible walk to work.

The dreary gray and chill of early spring did little to improve the ambience of Omaha. The downtown area was more that of a small town than cities like Houston or Seattle. The Music Hall was a barn at best. Theatres of that size were generally cold and impersonal. It would take a large number of ticket-holders to fill that house and empty seats have a subduing effect on audiences.

Griff observed a house half-empty on Tuesday night. He had worked the Music Hall countless times and wasn't partial to it. Normally, he and his crew relished additional space for sets, but the distance to cover created a timing problem for his staff as well as the cast.

The audience response was lukewarm at best. Everyone felt as though they were pulling teeth for a smattering of reaction. When the last note was sung, the company withdrew to change and go about their business.

The Landrys made an appointment to see an obstetrician. Dana was irritable, nauseous and tired, so much so that Dick was concerned about how her condition was affecting her work.

In a downtown medical building, they waited quietly for other passengers to enter the elevator. Dick held Dana's hand all the way to the doctor's office. He remained in the waiting room during Dana's examination, observing other women at different stages of pregnancy. He tried to imagine Dana with a huge belly protruding out in front of her, hiding the feet that worked so diligently.

He remembered the first time he saw her. It had been love at first sight. And, he remembered the first time they made love.

Chapter 65

The Landrys

It was an unusually muggy night in Manhattan, the kind of oppressive heat that convinced Dick to ask Dana out for a drink after their show. Restaurants air conditioning was most welcome.

As the Broadway houses spilled patrons into the streets, the combined crowds pushed and shoved throughout the theatre district. The nightly crush of people moving through Times Square was a testament to the allure of The Great White Way. Theatre patrons swarmed restaurants, bars, parking lots and memorabilia shops dotting Broadway, 7th and 8th Avenues.

Dick and Dana walked north on Eighth Avenue to 56th Street and ducked into a little Italian joint. After beer and pizza, they talked until closing time.

Stepping into the heavy night Dick felt the first sprinkles of rain. As the shower intensified, he took Dana's hand as they ran through the downpour, ducking under awnings whenever one beckoned. In a matter of minutes, they were soaked with no cabs in sight. Laughing and splashing through puddles they sprinted off curbs, leaping over gutters overflowing with soggy debris. "We must look like Gene Kelly times two," laughed Dana.

Shiny and wet from the deluge, the streets reflected headlights from passing vehicles. Heavy rain muted the red, yellow and green colors of traffic lights. Only the brashly bright neon from bars on every corner burned through the downpour.

"You're soaked, kid. We're only a block from my place. Want to come up and dry off?"

"Yes," shouted Dana as they turned the corner and ran west.

Dick made a sharp right and, with Dana close behind, ascended stairs to an old brownstone. Unlocking the door and turning on a light, Dick made his way to the kitchen and returned with towels.

"Here, take a shower if you like," he suggested. "Would you like some tea?"

"Yes, thanks." Spotting the bathroom she headed there. Dick shouted after her as he filled the teakettle, placing it on the stove. "There's a bathrobe on the back of the door. Feel free to take your wet things and put them on the towel rack."

Dick went into his room to change. He wriggled out of his wet clothing, choosing a pair of jeans and a tee shirt to replace the soggy pile now on the floor. He returned to the living area. Moments later, Dana joined him.

"I've hung my wet clothes over the shower rung. I'm afraid I squeezed out as much water as will squeeze."

"OK. The tea is ready now. Would you care for some cognac with it?"

"Gosh, I don't know. I've never had cognac." Dick got up and went to the cupboard to fetch the brandy and two shot glasses. Pouring the amber liquid, he handed Dana a glass, taking one for himself.

"Here's to a great evening," he toasted. "This sure is fun." He took a sip and set his glass down. Dana looked gorgeous even with her wet hair pulled close to her head. Though she was camouflaged under Dick's large robe, he could see her slender ankles peeking out, her crimson toes wiggling.

"You're incredibly lovely," Dick said softly, moving closer. She smiled and took another sip, the warmth of the drink invading her senses, relaxing her.

"Are you warm enough now?" I can find you a pair of socks," suggested Dick. Dana giggled imagining Dick's socks. He was easily a size twelve.

"No, I'm fine. But, I'm wondering how I'm going to get home? I live up near Columbia University and my clothes are soaked."

"No problem. You happen to be sitting on a comfortable convertible couch. Won't you stay? If the sofa isn't to your liking you can have my bed. I'll sleep out here. Your clothes will be dry in the morning."

"Gee, Dick, I don't know," said Dana. "I'd hate to impose."

"My dear Dana, you couldn't possibly impose. And as an added inducement, I'll fix my special cheese eggs and freshly squeezed orange juice in the morning."

"All right, I'll stay. My roommate is on tour, so she won't miss me."

"Good, then it's settled. You will permit me to spoil you a little, ok?" Taking the glass away and setting it down, he kissed her gently.

"I have wanted to kiss you for months." Without hesitation, Dana kissed him back, lingering for a moment enjoying the warmth of his lips.

"Actually, I was just waiting for you to make the first move," she murmured, snuggling closer to Dick.

"I've wanted to make love to you since the first day we met. Now is as good a time as any," he whispered. Slowly he stood and picked Dana up and carrying her down the narrow hallway to his bedroom. Gently placing her on the bed he untied the robe and let it fall to the floor. His breath shortened as he saw her nude for the first time.

Dana was intoxicating. Tall and willowy, she had a long torso and equally long legs that seemed to start at her shoulders. Her small breasts were firm and her soft belly beckoned him further.

Eagerly, she allowed Dick to trace her body with his fingers, taking his hand and leading him on an expedition, arriving at her pelvis and below. There she stopped and placed his hand on her mound. Dick took Dana's hand, allowing her to unzip his fly, exposing his erection. Sliding his jeans off and removing his tee shirt came easily.

As he continued to touch her she became wet and opened her legs for him. He knelt before her and began stroking her with his tongue. She moaned all the while he tasted her. As he changed his rhythm, his tongue moving deliberately, her sounds became more intense. Spreading her legs with his hands, he continued to ply her with pleasure until her moans were urgent.

"Oh, Dick, please come inside, now."

Straddling her he entered into what he imagined paradise to be, the warmth of her capturing him and holding him tight. He felt himself coming and held off, waiting for her. When they climaxed together, the intensity of their passion brought them to a swoon. Their combined sweat seemed to fasten them together as Dick kissed Dana repeatedly.

"Oh, Dana, you are quite incredible."

Dana had never experienced an orgasm until now. Her sexual experience was pedestrian at best. Dick had rocked her foundation. She had new feelings and sensations. Perhaps it was the difference in their ages. He was ten years older and far more experienced. He was patient, daring and above all, loving.

"Oh, Dick, I love you," she cried, weeping waves of emotion until they came to a gentle stop. Dick held her close as he felt his own tears surface and sting his eyes.

"I love you too, Dana. I really do."

Dick sat smiling as he remembered that night. How perfect it had been. Ever since their first time their commitment was total. Through his reverie, he heard a familiar voice. Opening his eyes he saw Dana coming toward him.

"Hi, Honey," he said, cheerfully, holding out his arms to her. "Are you?"

"We'll know in about a week. The doctor's nurse will notify us while we're in Des Moines. I gave her the hotel number. Until then, we'll just have to keep guessing, and I'll keep throwing up!"

"Yikes. I'm dying to know, Honey," muttered Dick.

"I know, but it takes time to get the results. So let's hunker down and eat pickles or something," she laughed. They returned to the hotel. Dana needed a nap before the show and Dick had paperwork to complete for Griff.

The rest of the week dragged. Dana continued to find food unappetizing and picked at her meals. She passed on a steak dinner between shows on Saturday. Omaha was known for outstanding beef, but the very thought of chewing a filet mignon made her nausea worse. She stayed at the hotel, ordering scrambled eggs, toast, and tea, attending to their packing.

At last, Omaha was over. The cast was only too happy to move on. The winter blahs had descended on the gypsies, but Easter was coming to Des Moines the following weekend.

Joe Pinto was looking forward to playing his hometown. He hadn't been back in ten years.

Leaving Des Moines for the lure of New York had changed his perspective on life. His devotion to his career and his lifestyle had left little room for a return visit, but now he would be back.

Chapter 66

A Surprise

Bravo Business arrived in Des Moines. Gathering luggage, the company dispersed to the Lorraine Hotel, a short walk from the KRNT complex which housed a TV station and the theatre, covering two square blocks. Though it was the first week in April, the anticipated spring weather eluded the company. Instead, they were greeted with rain, sleet and heavy wind.

Griff and his crew encountered these conditions driving in the pre-dawn hours from Omaha to Des Moines. It had been a long night, but it was not uncommon for the tech staff to skip meals and sleep in order to get the show in on schedule and technically up to par.

On tour, a set-up error could be costly, putting the cast at risk and the show in jeopardy. If losing precious time led to a performance cancellation, revenue could be lost. The Lehrman organization was not in the business of canceling performances or losing money.

The Monday night show was sold out. The company hurried to prepare for the performance with high energy and spirits even higher. The chorus dressing rooms echoed with the sounds of the enthusiastic ensemble. Mally sat next to Pat, and Dana, next to Mally. The others lined the three-mirrored walls forming a rectangle of women immersed in make-up and pre-show chatter.

Dana was quiet, trying to save her energy for the show. She was tired. Her legs felt like iron and her feet hurt. Bloated and moody, she lacked her usual energy and verve.

"When will you know?"

"By the end of this week, I hope. The doctor's office in Omaha is supposed to call. Dick's going crazy waiting. Mal, I've been such a moody bitch lately," she admitted, fighting tears.

"Dana, for heaven's sake, your hormones are working overtime. Don't be so hard on yourself, OK?"

"Thanks, Mal. I love you guys."

"And we love you, too," shouted the others. Pat stood and began an impromptu routine.

"You must have been a beautiful baby, 'cause baby, look at you now," sang the women, forming a half circle around Dana. Only Griff's fifteen minute warning broke their serenade.

At intermission, Griff handed Joe Pinto a note, which he opened immediately. 'I would love to stop by after your performance. Cheers, Jordan Hendrix.' Closing the note he headed to the dressing room. Surprised, he wondered how Jordan had found him.

The rest of the show went fast. Joe rushed through post-show details, grabbing a shower and dressing quickly. Hurrying to the stage door he noticed a group standing to the side. The doorman gestured.

"These people are here for you, Joe," he said, adding a nod in the direction of a couple with two young children. The attractive man stepped toward him. Joe stopped dead in his tracks.

"Jordan?" The man smiled and extended his hand.

"Good to see you. May I present my wife, Diane, and our children Andrew and Lily? Diane heard the show was great, so we decided to check it out. I was pleased to find your name in the program."

Joe was stunned. Jordan's family was picture perfect. His wife was gorgeous, fashion model material. Tall, slender, impeccable features and blonde, she was a knockout. Andrew was the image of his father with snappy black eyes and ringlets of dark curls. Lily was blonde, blue-eyed and slim like her mother. She did her share of staring at Joe as she held her father's hand.

"It's been a long time," mustered Joe, feeling awkward.

"Could the kids have your autograph? They loved the show, right kids?" Lily nodded eagerly. Andrew looked bored, shifting from foot to foot as he tugged on his mother. Handing Joe the program, Jordan stood with his arm around his wife.

"How long will you be in town?"

"We play until Sunday. We leave for Indianapolis," Joe replied. He was still processing Jordan's façade. 'What an act! The guy wants some action.'

"Where are you staying? I hope your accommodations are satisfactory," said Jordan.

"We're at The Lorraine. It's fine. Well, if you'll excuse me, it was nice to meet you and your children, Diane. Good seeing you Jordan," Joe said, extending his hand.

The next morning a jangling phone woke Joe. He opened one eye, trying to shut out window light as he reached for the receiver. Jim lay sleeping soundly.

"Joe, Jordan. How are you?"

"I'm trying to wake up. It's kind of early for a call," he remarked tightly.

"I've been awake for hours. What does your day look like?" Joe was fully awake now.

"Loose, why?"

"Want to meet for lunch? My company has a standing suite at the Hotel Des Moines."

"Yeah, what time?"

"I'm free about noon. I'll meet you in the lobby." Joe hung up just as Jim stirred.

"Who was that?"

"A guy I came out to my senior year of high school. Man, what a turn-on! We did each other all summer until he went off to college and I left for New York."

"It sounds like he wants some more," said Jim, relishing the notion.

Joe arrived at noon. As he scanned the lobby, he felt a tap on his shoulder.

"Hello."

"Hi. Where are we going?"

"Fifteenth floor," said Jordan, pointing to the elevator. Joe followed nonchalantly. When they arrived, Jordan produced a key, opening the double door to 1500.

The suite was beautifully appointed with a formal sitting room complete with a well-stocked bar. The plush ambience lent an odd tone of formality to the casual nature of the occasion.

"My company hosts a lot of out-of-town clients here," said Jordan, as he picked up the phone.

"Are you hungry? The special is the house steak sandwich with fries. How do you like yours?"

"Rare."

"Would you like a drink?"

"A beer's good, whatever you have there," said Joe.

Jordan removed his coat and loosened his tie as he walked to the bar. Joe watched with passive interest.

"Tell me about your life," said Jordan, handing Joe a beer.

"Not much to tell. I dance eight shows a week. It's a good gig," replied Joe, casually. "Tell me about your life."

"I met Diane in college. When we married, I joined her dad's company. We've done pretty well. My kids are great. She's an excellent mother." Suddenly a loud knock interrupted.

"Must be lunch," said Jordan walking to the door. A stout, older bellman walked into the room, pushing a food cart.

"That will be all, thanks," said Jordan, refusing the pen offered. "I won't be signing today," he added, producing cash.

"Have a pleasant afternoon."

Joe and Jordan made small talk as they ate. When they had finished Jordan rose and nodded toward the bedroom. 'Man, he's anxious to get it,' Joe thought, as he followed. Before the king-sized bed, they removed their clothes. As the last article dropped to the floor, Joe nudged Jordan down on the bed. Taunting and tonguing him was easy. Jordan was only too willing and eager to be taken, begging Joe to accelerate his action. In no time Jordan was ready. Turned on by Jordan's insistence, Joe entered him with ease.

"Oh, yes, yes," cried Jordan, writhing with anticipation. Joe grew more fervent as he applied his strength, thrusting in and out, until he felt his climax building. No longer able to hold back, they came, their bodies joined as one: the familiar rush, the after shock, the glistening of sweat.

Moments later, Joe got off the bed and began to dress. Jordan lay breathing rapidly, consumed by his release. After a few moments he sat up slowly and reached for Joe, kissing him passionately.

"Man, you're hot. What's this straight act?"

"I love my wife and kids," muttered Jordan, defensively.

"Oh, the married bit. But, you love this, too, right?"

"You don't understand. I can't be queer in this town."

"Hey, I understand."

"You have no idea how rough it is. I've been adept at pretending. Then, out of the blue, you show up. I'm half crazed wanting you. You know, I haven't had another man for a long time, since Diane's last pregnancy. I'm not proud of it, but I couldn't stop."

"So, what's next?"

"Please, Joe. Same time tomorrow?"

"Ok," said Joe, casually. "I gotta go." Jordan, still nude, stopped him. Placing Joe's hand on his penis, he tongued Joe aggressively. Joe, fighting his growing arousal, broke free and winked, playfully. "See you tomorrow, hot stuff." He left, closing the door.

Jordan waited for the sound of the elevator outside. Returning to the bathroom he turned on the shower. Allowing the rush of warm water to wet his skin and rinse off any evidence, he thought about Joe and sex. As he stood under the steady stream, he wept. His weeping turned to sobs as his hands fondled his genitals. His longing was cutting a hole in his psyche. The pain of his deception was stabbing his soul. How could he face Diane and the kids? He dared not dwell on it.

Joe and Jordan kept at it every noon in suite 1500. For Joe, having sex with Jordan was convenient and surprisingly hot. He enjoyed dominating Jordan, who played the submissive, allowing Joe total control of him. He found Jordan to be insatiable and he, in turn, was ferocious. Each encounter brought amazing pleasure and release.

Joe wasn't kidding himself. He knew as soon as the show moved on, so would he. He never fell in love, never allowed permanence with partners. For him, tricking was the name of the game, the only way he could operate.

Jordan relished his time with Joe, and for the few hours they were together, he was at peace. However, returning home was painfully difficult. He felt like the biggest fraud to Diane and the kids. Joe was his drug of choice and he had to have him.

On Friday, the phone rang in the Landry's room. Dick handed the phone to Dana, who trembled as she guessed the nature of the call.

"Mrs. Landry? This is Doctor Mason's office calling. Your test came back positive. Congratulations!"

"Oh my God," cried Dana, shaking. "When am I due?"

"As near as we can calculate, late December."

"Thank you, oh my God, thank you so much," Dana managed, as tears ran down her cheeks. Dick took the phone from her.

"You're going to be a daddy, Honey," whispered Dana, holding tightly to Dick.

"Oh my darling, Dana, you're going to be the most wonderful mother! I have to find cigars!"

Later, Dick and Dana broke the news to management. It was an official cause for celebration. Griff ordered champagne for the whole cast, crew and orchestra. As the group gathered on stage, following the performance, Griff was the first to make a toast.

"Congratulations to you and your future gypsy. We love you!" Everyone clapped and cheered the happy parents-to-be.

Jordan hadn't slept well. His mind tried to stop the clock, hoping that Sunday would never come. Joe was leaving. That agonizing thought was just one of many racing in his mind as he headed to the hotel.

He lied to Diane again. This time the boss had called him for a Saturday evening client confab and he would be late. He kissed his children goodbye and told Diane to expect him after supper sometime.

Joe arrived still sweaty from the matinee and decided to shower, inviting Jordan to join him. As they stood under the rush of water, Joe kneeled and serviced Jordan bringing him to climax. Then Jordan returned the favor. In bed they gave each other pleasure repeatedly until it was time for Joe to return to the theatre. Without a word they showered and dressed. Jordan tried to prolong the minutes, dreading the end. When Joe was ready to leave Jordan stopped him.

"I will never forget this," he said, choking back the tears. "You've made me feel so wanted, so accepted." Joe gently put his hand on Jordan's mouth.

"I enjoyed it too. You're hot, kid. Don't ever forget it." Then, Joe did something uncharacteristic. He wrapped Jordan in his arms. He could feel Jordan's heart beating quickly and felt warm tears on his face.

"Take care of yourself, OK?" He slipped out the door, not looking back.

For a few minutes, Jordan stood silently. A rush of loneliness engulfed him. Pouring a glass of scotch, he steadied himself, allowing the warm, amber liquid to anesthetize his senses as he swallowed, savoring what took place.

All he cared to remember was the smell, taste and feel of Joe Pinto. He thought through all the details of their lovemaking. How good it all was! Downing the last of his drink, he stood up, set the glass in the sink and picked up his coat.

As Jordan left the hotel the night had turned cold. Finding his car in the ramp nearby, he got in and started it. Pulling out into traffic he passed the theatre, a few blocks away. The gypsies were arriving for their final performance in Des Moines. Joe Pinto was among them. It was Saturday night and Jordan Hendrix was going home.

Chapter 67

Indy

The weather was bleak and dark. Unrelenting rain fell. Once again the cast wore heavy clothes to ward off the chill during the nine-hour ride to Indianapolis.

Joe was unusually quiet as he worked the *Des Moines Register* Sunday crossword puzzle. Jim noticed.

"You're quiet. Was it tough to say goodbye?"

Joe smiled. "Jordan's a decent man, and one of the hottest. I feel for him. He's totally gay and playing it straight. Shit, I couldn't handle that." For the rest of the ride he kept to himself.

The production was slated for the Murat Shrine Temple Auditorium. Indianapolis audiences were fine-tuned theatre buffs, who filled the house to capacity night after night. Acclaimed touring shows sold out months in advance. The Murat housed two full-size theatres. Soundproof, and acoustically one of the best theatres on the circuit, it was regarded as a top venue to play.

Monday evening, the cast slipped into the theatre and found their assigned dressing rooms. The chorus usually occupied the top floors, moving to the basement change area during the performance to expedite fast changes.

The leads occupied dressing rooms on the first and second floors or as near the stage as possible for easy access. Principals were assigned personal dressers during the run of the show. There was a definite pecking order in the cast and most of the principals had agents and managers negotiating details in their contracts.

Opening night, the local Shriners hosted a cocktail party after the performance. Everyone was required to attend. As the gathering got into full swing, the gypsies mingled with their hosts. It was easy to spot the Shriners wearing their signature fezzes. The rest of the crowd was comprised of reporters and invited guests.

A jazz trio performed at one end of the room. The female vocalist was exceptionally good. Several bars were set up for the convenience of the large crowd mingling in the lobby. A loud wave of talk rolled over the room as cigarette smoke thickened in the air.

Some dancers drank and conversed among themselves while the principals were introduced to public officials and other distinguished guests. The mood was pleasant and the hosts and their wives, definitely cordial.

Jonas and Phillipe found themselves engaged by several women, who fawned and flirted with them. This was nothing new. Gay male dancers were attractive, socially adept and fine physical specimens, perfect objects for women's fantasies. Wealthy women—often bored— were particularly vulnerable to the latest trendy pastimes or even an affair. Some would attempt to take gay men to their beds with disastrous results. Some straight male guests sought the chorus women, who were more striking and interesting than their wives and girlfriends. Two men approached Pat.

"Hey, I really liked the show," said one, trying to get her attention. His breath reeked of garlic as he sucked a stub of a cigar, the smoke still curling over his double chin. Showing a five o'clock stubble, he was much too paunchy and pasty for his years. In spite of Pat's disgust she rose to the occasion, using her best acting.

"What did you like most?"

"Gig loves legs. You sure have great stems," he slurred. "Right, Gig?"

"She sure does!" Hey, I'm Nick. What's your name, Honey?" Pat steadied herself.

"I'm Patricia," she said, with forced formality.

"Pat, huh? Are you available?"

"What do you mean, available?" Pat began to feel her Irish rising. By some miracle, Chad noticed and moved in.

"Pat! I've been looking all over for you. Let's go back to the hotel. I'm horny as hell," he said with a wink. The two locals gaped.

"I'm Chad, Pat's boy," he deadpanned, as he extended his hand. "You'll have to excuse us. We've got some serious balling to do." With a flourish like the great Fred Astaire himself, Chad twirled Pat to him. As they danced away, he waved back at the stunned locals. At a distance Pat let go.

"Thanks Chad, you were great! I really appreciate the rescue." She gave him a quick peck on the cheek.

"Well, on the level, I'd enjoy being your boy," he said, slyly. Pat tightened.

"Chad, don't spoil it," she snapped. He nodded and left.

It had been well over six weeks since Owen called. She'd heard nothing about his proposed Vegas divorce. Insecurity was rearing its ugly head. As she lay in bed contemplating, the phone rang. She eagerly picked up.

"Pat."

"Owen! Oh my God, how are you?"

"I'm missing you like hell, Baby. I'm sorry I haven't been in touch. I stayed on in Vegas for a few weeks. A friend of mine, who produces shows at the Sands, lost his choreographer over a wage dispute and needed help. He asked me to stay and finish the rest of the show, starring Mamie Van Doren."

"How was it?"

"Good."

"No, I don't mean the show at the Sands."

"Oh that show," said Owen, with a smile in his voice. "Vera and I are history. I haven't felt this great in years."

"I miss you," murmured Pat.

"I might come to Pittsburgh. It's an easy jump from New York."

"That would be great." Her mind was in overdrive as she fought back tears.

"Baby, what's wrong?"

"Nothing," she lied.

"Pat, don't start with that shit. Lighten up! I'll call you in a couple of weeks."

"I love you Owen," Pat said, to a click. Trembling, she put down the phone. Why was she so afraid? What was going on? Why the insecurity over Owen? Perhaps sleep would dispel her doubt, at least temporarily.

Griff and Mally wandered through the party throng conversing with their hosts. He adored escorting her in public, his pride visibly showing. Griff had made up his mind to ask her to marry him. Finding the ring in Seattle was accidental. He had dropped by an old friend's jewelry store one afternoon and saw the exquisite ruby, her birthstone. The setting was delicate, including a tiny circle of diamonds mounted around the stone. Griff, still lost in remembering, heard his name. He turned to see his ex-wife smiling in his direction.

"Elise!"

"My God, you look fabulous. How long has it been?" Griff immediately began to freeze up.

"Excuse me, Elise, this is Mally Winthrop. Mally, this is Elise Mitchell."

Mally was ignored. "You have no idea how many times I've thought about you, Griff. How I've missed you."

Griff shifted uncomfortably. "What are you doing here?"

"I'm doing a gig with my trio. We've been traveling the country for the past two years, mostly one-week stands, but the pay is good, thanks to my fabulous manager. And you?"

"I'm here with Bravo Business. We've been out on tour since last October," he replied, tightly.

"Still at it, I see. Where can I get in touch? We'll be here through the weekend. I'm flexible."

"You'll have to excuse us, Elise," said Griff.

"I'll be in touch, Honey. We have a lot to catch up on."

Griff pulled away holding Mally's hand, and walked briskly to the exit. He hailed a cab.

"That was my ex-wife," remarked Griff, casually. He was shaken, but remained as steady as he could in front of Mally.

She broke your heart, right?"

"That's right. This is the first time I've seen or talked to her since the night I left."

"Griff, it appears you two have some unresolved business."

"We have no business. This was a chance encounter, that's all. I am shocked to see her."

"Well, she's obviously pleased to see you."

"Darling, please don't be upset. I never wanted to see Elise again."

"Griff, please explain to me what happened."

"What happened never happened," he said, tersely.

"All right, forget it." The cab pulled up in front of the hotel. Griff paid the driver. They walked through the deserted lobby to the elevator and rode silently. The suite was a welcome closure to the world.

The bed had been turned down. A single long-stem rose and a miniature box of fine chocolates rested on the pillow. On a cart next to the bed a silver stand held a chilling bottle of champagne accompanied by a silver bowl containing large, plump strawberries. A note was propped nearby: 'Welcome Mr. Edwards. It's our pleasure to serve you.' Griff took Mally in his arms and kissed her. He held on as if his whole life depended on it.

"Mally, I'm so sorry."

"I know, Griff. I'm sorry too. I over-reacted and I apologize. I just didn't like that woman."

"You have reason to dislike her. She's a taker. Something you know nothing about," he said reassuringly. "Come on, let's relax and forget the whole thing, OK?"

"OK." Griff broke open the champagne and they toasted. Suddenly, a ringing phone jarred them.

"Griff Edwards."

"Hi, Honey. Guess who?" Griff froze.

"What do you want? It's late," said Griff, stiffly.

"I asked one of your fag dancers where you're staying. Want to get together tomorrow night for a drink, following the show?"

"Elise, we're over. Don't you get it?" His voice was rising.

"I get that I want you. Imagine, after all this time!"

"Elise, don't call me again. Do you understand?" He hung up abruptly. He waited a few seconds and then called the concierge.

"This is Mr. Edwards in Suite 1200. I want all my calls held until further notice. Is that clear?"

"Certainly, Mr. Edwards, will that be all?"

"Yes, for now. Thank you."

"It's going to be ok, Griff," Mally whispered, kissing him gently. Slowly, tenderly, they made love, and then, they slept.

Chapter 68

The Proposal

The Indy crowds clearly understood the satiric nature of the show and roared their approval over the footlights each performance. It was gratifying to the cast having such consistent response.

Griff invited Mally to dinner between shows. He said it was important and her curiosity was aroused. As she finished her make-up she noticed Pat, staring straight ahead, as if in a trance.

"Are you all right? What's going on?" Pat's eyes welled as she undid her chignon.

"Owen got divorced five weeks ago. He waited so long to call!"

"Pat, stop worrying so much! He loves you!"

"Thanks, Mal. I get so anxious every time he calls. I don't know what's wrong with me."

Mally put her arms around Pat and gave her a squeeze. "Try to let go a little, OK?"

"I'll try," said Pat, reaching for tissue.

Griff was waiting at the stage door, debonair in a navy sports coat and gray slacks. He nuzzled her neck playfully followed by a kiss that was both tender and promising.

On arrival by cab, Griff escorted Mally to Sakura, one of the finest restaurants in Indianapolis. He chose the Sakura for its view and special ambience. Bamboo screens enclosed the dozen or so tables on site. Exotic plants were everywhere and Japanese music filled the air. When they were seated a waitress brought menus.

"May we have some green tea?" The waitress nodded.

When the tea arrived, Griff poured cups for them. Turning his attention to the waitress, he ordered sukiyaki for two. The server left.

"My love, what are your plans following the tour?"

"Why?"

He made his way to her side, dropping to one knee. Reaching in his pocket, he produced a velveteen box and opened it. Gently he took the ring and placed it on Mally's finger.

"Mally, would you do me the honor of becoming my wife for the rest of our lives?" Tears surfaced and gently ran down her cheeks. Overwhelmed, Griff felt his own tears welling up.

"Oh, Griff, of course I will!" For a few moments they held each other until the waitress returned to start their dinner.

When the sukiyaki was ready, they relished each bite of the tender beef, bean curd and vegetables served over rice. When they had finished the waitress cleared the table. Griff leaned in.

"Now that it's official, when would you like to be married?"

"Let's wait until the new show is up and running!" Griff smiled. 'My darling Mally knows me well,' he thought to himself.

As Mally walked into the dressing room she was glowing. Heads turned as she walked to her place, the ring glistening in the light.

"It's happened," screamed Pat, hugging Mally enthusiastically. "Congratulations, Mal!" The girls lined up, each taking a turn, hugging and checking out the ring.

"Mal, Griff's getting the best girl in the world," Dana gushed. The merriment brought the men in to see what the fuss was. Jonas was half dressed as he pushed his way into the crowd. Phillipe, Joe, Jim, Chad and Dick followed close behind.

"Mally and Griff are engaged," yelled Pat.

"No shit? This is the best," declared Jonas. "Anybody got champagne?"

"We'll celebrate in Louisville," announced Pat. "Agreed?"

"Yes!" The boys hugged and kissed their girl until Griff announced, "Fifteen minutes!"

The performance was high off the ground that night. Psyched by the news of their engagement everyone was spurred to brilliance. When at last it wound down to last notes of the score, the crew began striking the show as they prepared to load out.

Much later, Griff returned to his hotel, bone-weary from the strike. He stopped at the front desk for messages. Ascending to his floor, he reached for his room key as the door started to open. Preoccupied, he didn't see her.

Elise Mitchell was waiting. With speed and intention, she shoved him through the open elevator door. As it closed, she pressed the button for the top floor. Backing Griff into the corner, she tongued him as she reached his fly. 'It's happening,' he thought, struggling.

She was strong, determined. He felt his zipper slide down, her hands on his shaft, the warm breath as he felt the familiar excitement of her handiwork. He was hard already, succumbing to her, losing with every passing second. Then, he suddenly remembered. 'Mally!' Abruptly, he pushed Elise away.

"Back off!" He tried putting himself together. Elise, determined, reached for him again. Griff shoved her with such force she fell to the floor. Enraged, he knelt down, grabbed her shoulders, fixing her with a stare as his fury mounted.

"You bitch, we're through! Don't you get it?"

"How come you're hard? You want it! You always wanted it from me," she hissed. Griff was boiling. Abruptly, he pulled her to her feet, pinning her to the elevator wall. Elise tried pulling him closer, her pelvis in overdrive.

"Yeah, you remember, I like it rough. Come on, do me!" She was panting now, out of control. Griff released his grip quickly, backing away. She looked at him with a cold stare.

"What's the matter? Am I too much woman for you?" But Griff wasn't listening, only remembering.

"Do you know how much I loved you? You betrayed me. You screwed every guy in sight! You fucked me over! Now get the hell out of my life, and stay out," he shouted, pushing the button to start the elevator. Slowly they returned to the lobby. Elise stepped out, a wicked smile spreading on her face. She faced him squarely.

"You know, you're right. I did screw other men when we were together. I wanted to. You weren't man enough to satisfy me. And now, you get another chance and you blow it, Griffen!" Nonchalantly she gave a little wave, and walked away.

For a moment Griff stood without moving, his breath shallow, hands shaking. As he rode the elevator he began to calm down. Putting the key in the door, he thought about the minutes before. Shaken to the core, he began to cry, feeling the first salty tears touch his lips. How could he have come that close? Compromising his relationship? Unthinkable! Slowly he undressed and slipped into bed. The trip to Louisville was only hours away. Thank God! He'd try to forget this encounter. He'd have to.

Chapter 69

Louisville

The famed Kentucky Derby town was framed by a vast blue sky. It was just noon on a Sunday and springtime was everywhere.

The company was destined for the Brown, a well-appointed hotel. Part of a larger complex, it included shops, small businesses and the Brown Theatre, their venue for the week. From the hotel, the company could walk through the lobby and down a concourse to the stage door. How convenient it would be after the many weeks of heavy rain and intense snows.

Griff and his crew arrived at dawn on Sunday and began setting up. The Brown was one of the more cooperative theatres technically. Griff favored it. The men started at noon on Sunday and that evening the show was up and ready to run.

The house was buzzing with excitement Monday night, while backstage the cast prepared to wow the audience. Enthusiastic applause greeted the cast as the curtain rose. Bravo Business was off to a great start. At intermission, Dick Landry's voice could be heard from the squawk box.

"Ladies and gentleman, there will be a party following the show in the lobby of the theatre. Come and celebrate a special event!"

The mood was jovial after the performance. Management had provided champagne. Mally and Griff looked radiant as they accepted the company's toast. Cheers rang out as they kissed. When the champagne was gone the group dispersed, leaving only a handful of gypsies to chat. Griff and Mally held court, exchanging pleasantries with their pals. The lobby was deserted when they left for the night. Returning to their room, they undressed and slid under the sheets.

Griff was in the mood to talk.

"Do you remember when I told you months ago that I couldn't talk about my former wife?"

"Yes."

"There was still a lot of pain then. I feel reborn with you!"

"Oh, Griff, I love you!"

"I know that. And I love you, more than anything." They fell into a deep slumber, tucked in each other's arms.

Chapter 70

Reunion

The week was marked by glorious temperatures, as the spring-like weather continued. Some of the cast tried trail riding, exploring the woodsy countryside around Louisville. Others enjoyed local history and culture by sightseeing, hunting antiques and touring stately mansions.

Jonas and Phillipe were entranced by the ambience of old Louisville, exploring the entire area, absorbing the town's history. As they returned to the Brown one afternoon, Phillipe spotted a large poster in the main lobby.

"Oh my God, it's André!" Jonas stepped closer and read the text.

'This weekend only, André Glessier, international fashion designer to show his fall collection, at the Brown Hotel, main ballroom one to five pm." Turning to Phillipe he could see how shaken he was. "Holy shit, it's him!"

"Cheri, I don't know what to say."

"Well, do you want to see him?"

"I don't know. I haven't had contact since we separated. When we parted I moved on. So did André, who moved to Paris."

"It's never over 'til the fat lady sings,' to quote an old adage," said Jonas, trying to act as casual as possible. "Maybe you should find out if you're still in love with him."

"Cheri, I'm in love with you. Why make waves, n'est-ce pas?" They continued through the lobby and up to their room. Just as they arrived the phone rang. Jonas picked up.

"Phillipe Danier, please. This is André Glessier." Jonas handed Phillipe the receiver. Then, motioning to the door, he stepped out. His hands shaking, Phillipe tried to calm down.

"André. What a surprise!"

"How are you, Mon Cher?"

"I'm good, very good. Happy."

"I'm here until Sunday, have you time for a drink?"

"Well, André, I don't know." There was long pause.

"Not to worry. I'm here with my lover. How about Friday night, following your performance? We could meet in the lounge here at the hotel."

"See you then." Phillipe hung up the phone and sat down on the bed, his mind racing. The door opened and Jonas returned.

"Well?"

"I agreed to meet for a drink Friday night after the show."

"I think you have to," said Jonas, knowingly. Though he was apprehensive, he had to accept the fact that Phillipe and André had a past.

"Cheri, you are kind and wise. I do need to do this."

"Well, yeah. Come on, let's take a nap before the show and have a quick bite of dinner."

On Friday night, Phillipe prepared to meet André. He purposely dressed conservatively, wearing relaxed jeans, a turtleneck sweater and sneakers. In the past, he would have chosen a pair of skin-tight Levis to enhance his equipment, a tight-fitting shirt to reveal his well-toned chest, tucked in and unbuttoned to the navel, and one of his exotic fragrances. As usual, he ran a wet comb through his waves, catching them back in a fold at the nape of his neck. When he was ready he modeled for Jonas, who was pleased with Phillipe's understated look. Leaving the theatre together they walked briskly down the concourse toward the hotel.

"Don't worry, Cheri. I'll be back soon." Giving Jonas a furtive hug he turned and headed toward the lounge. Looking around he spotted André.

"Come here, Phillipe." He found André sitting in a booth and sat down opposite him. André ordered champagne.

"You look splendid. This gypsy life agrees with you."

"Thank you. You look marvelous as well," intoned Phillipe.

"I am very happy. My life agrees with me. Pierre and I are deeply in love. And you?"

"I've found my soul mate."

"Jonas. That's his name, yes?"

"Yes. It's difficult to explain how free I feel. Do you realize this is the first relationship I haven't been with an older, wealthier man, who calls the shots?"

"And it feels right, yes?"

"It is right! Look André, being with Jonas has changed my life. I'm using all of my talent and contributing something for a change. I'm no longer the taker you knew."

"Mon Cher, this is wonderful. I can see you are genuinely happy."

"And you?"

"Pierre demands only the best from me. A reverse of roles, yes?" They both chuckled and drank the remainder of champagne.

"Thank you, André. I needed a second look, you know?"

"Yes, I understand." Before André could retrieve the check, Phillipe had it in hand. Pulling out his wallet, he winked. André smiled.

Chapter 71

Pittsburgh

The Nixon Theatre was home for the next three weeks. Beyond this engagement, the production would do an open run in Boston.

Mally and Griff were now sharing quarters in an attempt to save money and make future plans. Pat was solo. It was a situation she welcomed. Her mercurial moods required isolation and down time.

Lately, she had plunged further into her self-induced funk due to lack of contact from Owen. The old fear of abandonment was a constant tenant in her mind and she was lonely.

Jonas, on the other hand, had a marvelous mindset. He was making good money now. He received hazard pay for the "*Fix*" number, requiring him to walk to the orchestra pit and jump as part of the choreography. He was making extra money as dance captain, and was extremely savvy with his money. His former partner, Gary Hanson, had taught him to budget for that inevitable rainy day in the theatre. As a result, Jonas never spent beyond his means.

Phillipe, on the other hand, had never had a bank account of his own until he joined *Bravo Business*. In exchange for his sexual servitude in the past, his well-heeled patrons had financed him. Making road minimum was an eye opener. Suddenly he had to make do with what he had. Even as a stripper he earned more money than he was now making on tour.

Jonas taught him to cut back, to keep his desire for luxury items like jewelry and high-priced clothing in check. Phillipe also enjoyed exceptional wines and fine dining and, while Jonas appreciated the finer things, he had learned to do without.

A typical gypsy's life included sub-let apartments, vintage clothing stores and shopping anywhere for groceries except Zabar's, D'Agostino's or Gristedes, high-test grocery stores, catering to the well-heeled. Chorus people shared everything from trade papers to sheet music and dance wear. They weren't proud.

Those who did well had nice apartments, bank accounts and were vested in Equity League. Some married while others kept partnerships, but very few raised families in the theatre. The lack of steady income forced one partner in a marriage to have a regular job while the other tried to make a living in the business. There was little left over to support a growing family of dependents, when the monetary demands of New York living was considered.

One made more money touring than working chorus in New York. As a result, Dana and Dick Landry had chosen the road as a means of putting money away for the day they would leave the stage for a normal life in New Jersey, raising kids and buying a washer and dryer.

As a result of Dana's pregnancy, they were getting closer to their goal. Dick had enough experience as assistant stage manager, knowing that it was a matter of time before he could work the management side. Dana had danced for as many years as she cared to. She had no designs on becoming a star attraction, never had. She was content being Mrs. Landry and soon, a mother.

Pat lay in bed absorbed in a new paperback. The phone rang.

"Hi, Baby!"

"Owen!"

"I had a break in meetings. Thought I'd call. We're getting closer to putting a show together," he said excitedly. Pat marveled how Owen could still be enthused after all his hits and awards.

"How would you like a warm body next to yours?" Pat's pulse picked up. "I'm coming to that pit of a town this coming weekend to do business and see my favorite girl."

"I'm your favorite?"

"Come on, Pat, don't start with that shit, OK?"

"OK. It's just that I miss you so much I'm out of sorts."

"Baby, you won't be out of sorts for long. Come to the Pitt-Sheraton. I'm horny as hell. Bye."

'Owen is amazing,' thought Pat, as she put down the phone. The obvious wetness between her legs proved it. For now, she decided on a warm bath. Running the water she added a bubble mixture she had stashed away. Disrobing she slid into the foamy drink and felt the warmth of the water envelop her. She was horny with anticipation, and Owen would soon be there.

On Friday the cast gathered in the green room at five minutes at Griff's request. Owen arrived. A general cheer went up as the company welcomed him. This time Pat was prepared for his appearance and blended with the others as they clustered around him.

"Hi, gang. Good to see we still have enthusiasm in this troupe. I will be out front checking my staging, so dance well. I expect only excellence. Have a great show!" Griff called 'places.'

Following the show Griff and Mally headed to the hotel. Griff ordered from the room menu and while they waited, they undressed, showered and curled up on the sofa.

"Darling, I'm starved!"

"So, what else is new? I never knew a dancer who wasn't hungry following a show."

A knock at the door got their attention. A bellman with a rolling cart was visible on the other side of the door. Griff let him in and signed the tab.

"Thank you sir, and have a nice evening," said the young man.

"And you as well." After closing the door and double locking it, he wheeled the cart into the bedroom.

"Now, I can have an intake of fuel," said Griff with a wink. The two ate with enthusiasm.

Chapter 72

Old Feelings

Pat felt the familiar nervous energy as she headed over to the Pitt-Sheraton. She felt happy. Owen looked fabulous at the theatre. The man never aged! His boyish features and fit body belied his actual age of 39. He was perfection!

Stopping before the door she drew a deep breath and knocked. Within seconds the door opened. Owen stood shirtless in a pair of tight jeans. He was barefoot, his cropped hair was wet from the shower. Reaching toward Pat he gently drew her in.

"Oh, Baby, I've waited too long for this." Slowly, as though admiring a piece of exquisite sculpture, he made a detailed inspection of Pat, his eyes covering her from head to toe.

"You are more beautiful than ever. God, you turn me into a horny bastard. I could come in my pants!" Pat blushed. Owen's attention was overpowering. As much as she craved him, she was still intimidated after all this time.

"Come on in, I was just unpacking."

"Nice suite. Have you stayed here before?" She sat on the edge of the bed as Owen continued to put his things away.

"Not lately. I haven't had one of my shows on this circuit for a while. Nice old town though, very hip. How about a drink? I've chilled some champagne."

"That sounds great," said Pat. Drinking always relaxed her.

As Owen worked the cork, he envisioned Pat in bed. He loved finding new ways to please her. Her unquenchable sexual needs aroused him. The cork popped. Pouring the contents into two glasses, he handed Pat the first, then raised his own.

"To us," he said, chugging the contents.

Pat sipped slowly, allowing a buzz to gradually take over. She liked feeling slightly tipsy when Owen got to work. Owen kept pouring and drinking. Pat kept up. When the bottle was empty, he began his magic.

He was already sporting an immense erection as he slipped out of his jeans. Slowly, deliberately, he made every move camera perfect. Stroking himself, he kept his eyes fixed on Pat's face. Feigning arousal, he swayed his hips as he approached her face. Then, true to his choreographic style, he placed himself in her mouth. Placing her hands on his buttocks, he moved his pelvis as she gave him pleasure. Deeply aroused, Pat knew that Owen had to have it his way if she was to have full benefit. How could she deny him the pleasure of taking her as he planned? He had carefully set the stage.

Knowing Owen expected creativity in return, Pat began peeling out of her clothing. When she had stripped down to her panties, she reached under the soft, elasticized crotch of lace and fingered herself. Owen joined in, fingering and sucking with increased intensity.

"God, more, Owen," she moaned, as he continued, enjoying her reaction. When Owen had Pat ready, he turned her face down. Holding her hands behind her back he entered her carefully, sliding in and out.

At first he moved slowly, deliberately, but soon, he changed the choreography, moving with quicksilver speed. Then he stopped and pulled out. Turning her over, he stroked her lightly, his fingers doing a little dance. Occasionally he would stop and remove his fingers to tease and build her want, then return, plunging to find her g-spot.

"Come inside now," she begged. At that moment, Owen entered and together they climaxed with a force that moved the bed. Fueled by their mutual need to get off, they released what was pent-up for weeks. It was a total climax, one of their best. Owen sat up and reached for a cigarette. Exhilarated, he lit it, taking a deep drag.

"My God, Pat, you're absolutely incredible. I love you. I honestly love you." Pat pulled herself up and reached for the cigarette, sucking deeply and letting the smoke out slowly.

"So where do we go from here?"

"What do you mean?" Lighting another cigarette he let the question hang in the air.

"Well, I mean after the tour." Owen shifted a little and took another drag.

"You're starring in the new show."

"I mean us. What about us?"

"Here we go. You want something concrete, is that it?"

"When two people are in love, a future is important."

"The future holds us. Please, Pat, I just got divorced. I love you and want you. That has to be enough," he said, conclusively. Pat let out a long breath.

Owen's reaction was predictable. He wouldn't have it any other way now or ever. The evening ended as Owen nose-dived into slumber. Pat lay by his side, insecure as ever.

In the morning she awakened first. As she watched Owen sleeping she made a decision to put aside her neediness. Stepping into the shower she washed last night's activity away. She was groggy and the rush of water was refreshing as it hit her face. When she finished, she stepped out and dried herself.

Determined to stick to her guns, she returned to the darkened room and sat in a chair opposite the bed. Carefully, she towel-dried her hair now hanging in wet cascades. Reaching in her bag she pulled out a thick-pronged brush. Meticulously working the knots and tangles out, she finished and sat up, tossing her hair back. Owen was watching.

"Baby, you're up early," he said, through his smoke screen. She rose from the chair and walked nonchalantly to him.

"I have a few things to do today," she said, with forced nonchalance.

"Oh? You were going to leave? Just like that," he snapped.

"Owen, I know you're here on business and short of time. I thought I'd get out of your hair." He relaxed and reached for her.

"You're never in my hair, but, if you have something on your mind, let's have it."

"Nothing, Owen."

"It isn't always going to be like this, you know. In a few weeks you'll be back in town, in the new show, and with me. By the way, I have something." Owen opened his wallet and handed a small object to Pat.

"It's a key," she said, turning it over.

"It's your copy of a key to my new place. With the sale of our old coop on Central Park West, I had a few bucks to throw around. I purchased a new pad. Why don't you come some weekend during the Boston run? I want you to get your mind back on New York."

"Oh, Owen, I'd love that," she said throwing her arms around his neck.

"I'm across from ABC TV on West 67th, near where the new Lincoln Center is going up," he said, writing the address and phone number on a pad. But, Pat wasn't listening. She was already there.

"Here," he said, handing her the piece of paper along with a kiss. Pat stayed.

Owen held a brush-up rehearsal on Friday. Pleased that the cast and the repetitive nature of touring hadn't compromised the integrity of his work, he relaxed with his newly formed team on Saturday between shows.

Owen, Griff and Jonas toasted the future. Griff and Jonas were dazzling new additions to Owen's organization. He reveled in his decision to hire two individuals at the top of their game. The trio would bring a sure winner to Broadway.

The final week sold out. Each new audience brought energy to the cast and they in turn, gave it back. A perfect marriage! It was a great way to wrap up Pittsburgh. Excitement over the anticipated Boston open-end run was contagious. Bean-town was waiting for them!

Chapter 73

Bean Town

The Colonial Theatre was a perfect venue, a fitting finale for *Bravo Business*. The seating capacity, design of the house and lobby, orchestra pit and backstage area was like a typical Broadway theatre.

Since the show was slated for an open-end engagement, Griff chose a downtown hotel until they could find an apartment to sublet. Some principals rented sublets, hoping to add a touch of home to the long engagement. Many apartments became available as students from Boston University cleared out for the summer. Many of the women in the cast insisted on roommates. The unsolved case of the Boston Strangler was still very much in the news and women living alone were considered an easy mark.

The Tremont Hotel was the hotel of choice. Rates were reasonable and the proximity to the Colonial was convenient. The Massachusetts Transit Authority had a station conveniently located a few feet from the Colonial's lobby. MTA trains provided a cheap and easy means of traveling around the city.

Working in Boston had its advantages. The ambience and history of the city, the sophisticated public, and the recreational opportunities were all pluses. The proximity to New York was also helpful. A company member could, with special permission from management, venture to Manhattan after a Saturday night performance. A gypsy could arrive in the city about six a.m. on Sunday by catching a bus at midnight. Some preferred the train, a trip that was an hour and a half shorter, though bus fare was $5.00 less.

Pat was lonely. Owen's departure only intensified her feelings. Mally was the only girlfriend she had in the company. Spending time with her over the nine months had been wonderful, like having a sister. But now, she was engaged and preoccupied with her coming wedding. Other female cast members were pleasant, but she didn't feel nearly as comfortable with them. She had learned that being too trusting was dangerous. The gay boys were good pals for outings and gossip, but there was a limit as to how far the friendship could go.

Jonas and Phillipe were content. Their growing relationship was solid and they were deliciously in love. As soon as they arrived at the Tremont, Jonas found a city guide with a list of attractions. He had played Boston in the past, but Phillipe had never been to the east coast. Jonas decided to plan several day trips. Phillipe was amenable and ready to explore. They intended to check out the bar scene together. Dana Landry was feeling better. The daunting first weeks of pregnancy had passed and she was ready to grow fat and lazy. Her costumes were growing tight around the waist and she was sprouting generous breasts, something she had never had nor desired until now. She couldn't wait for the tour to end so that she could park her dancing shoes and settle in their New York flat, planning a layette and preparing a nursery for baby Landry.

She and Dick wanted the security of knowing that the baby was healthy. Dana had increased her vitamin intake and had located an obstetrician in the city to guide her through the Boston run. When she wasn't performing the show, she was taking daily walks around the Boston Common, writing letters home to Atlanta to her sisters and talking weekly to her mother, filling her in on her progress.

Dick and Dana's passion for each other hadn't waned. If anything their desire had increased. They couldn't keep their hands off each other. Dana was horny all the time. Dick had little trouble keeping her satisfied because the more visibly pregnant she became the more beautiful and sexy she was to him. Dana brought attention to herself one night in the dressing room, as she laughed uproariously.

"What's so funny Dana?"

"Well it's either my hormones racing or I'm a sex maniac! Ever since Dick and I got pregnant, I can't get enough."

"Is the sex really that good?" Pat was ready for details.

"Well, I'm on Dick constantly, horny all the time. I even get aroused when I'm performing. That's how intense it is," she said, quietly.

"Wow, for me, pregnancy would be redundant," laughed Pat.

"I don't know. I'd hate getting fat," Mally confessed.

"Well, I'm getting fat, but so are my tits!" The women broke up. Only the fifteen-minute call quieted them down.

Chapter 74

Revenge

Owen met with his producers. The financing was coming together. He was satisfied that his needs were understood, what it would take to bring his show to Broadway.

The concept was simple. He would conceive and execute an all-dance show, adding nuances that would electrify an audience. Multiple composers, a minimal set, and a cast of extraordinary dancers would be thrown into the creative mix. He wanted youth, vigor, talented and committed gypsies, who would dazzle and beguile the public.

He looked forward to using Pat in the lead. Her phenomenal technique, gorgeous body and presence would carry the ensemble. His male lead would come from the growing ranks of hopefuls on the Broadway scene.

Chad Chapman was one dancer he would consider. Chad was a mainstay in the current tour. His technique was flawless and his youthful good looks and masculine presence would attract both men and women in the audience.

Phillipe Danier was another possibility. Though *Bravo Business* was his first legitimate job in theatre he was a quick study, a forceful performer and had the kind of sensuality Owen liked aesthetically. He would ask him to audition at the end of the tour.

Joe Pinto would be a shoe-in. Of all the men in the current company touring, he was second only to Jonas Martin in experience. He would offer Joe a spot. Joe's audition would be a mere formality. Like Pat, he had the charisma to be one of a select few needed for the show. Owen was considering using eight and eight with two swings for each gender.

Jonas Martin would assist, replacing Manny Johnson, who had worked with Owen for eight years. No one was more capable than Jonas. He was exceptional when it came to teaching and executing Owen's style, better than any dancer he had worked with in the last decade.

Following meetings, Owen decided to stop for a drink. Andy Klein, a regular bartender at the Taft Hotel bar, waited on him. Andy had been a top notch dancer, but was forced to retire after sustaining severe injury to both knees. He worked at the Taft to keep in touch while making a few bucks.

Owen sipped his scotch, enjoying the smoke from his cigarette as it curled around him. Lost in thought, he hadn't noticed her. As he glanced to the right, his breath shortened! The blonde seated next to him was gorgeous, young, and definitely hot. Pouting lips, deep brown eyes, and a stunning body were irresistible. Her generous breasts peeked and flirted from the soft drape of her décolletage. He was sporting a hard on just looking at her. Casually, she returned a glance.

"I'm Meredith, Meredith Smith."

"Owen."

"Yes, I know. Everybody knows."

"Oh?"

"Buy me a drink?" Without hesitation Owen signaled Andy. "What would the lady like?"

"I'd love a vodka martini, straight up with a twist, please."

"Would you care to sit at a table in back?" She nodded.

Owen ordered a second scotch for himself. 'This babe is a complete turn-on, someone I'd fuck in a minute,' he thought. Then he reasoned. In spite of the heat she was giving out, he had to be cautious.

"How old are you?"

"You shouldn't ask that," she said demurely. "But, since you insist, I'm twenty-one, de-clawed, and housebroken."

"I like that," he replied, his cool never wavering.

When the drinks arrived he motioned Meredith to follow. After they sat, Owen took out a cigarette, lit it, and took a deep drag. Exhaling, he studied her carefully.

"Tell me, Meredith, do you dance?"

"What do you care?"

"I'm always looking for good dancers."

"Yes, I've heard that. So, are you good?" Meredith reached over and took a drag of his cigarette. Owen was losing the fight to his supreme horniness with every passing second. He wanted to nail her right on the spot, unfortunately not acceptable behavior at the Taft. He tried the business approach.

"I'm casting a show in September. Interested?" He felt Meredith's hand on his thigh.

"I'm more interested in how you fuck." He let his breath out slowly.

"Do you want to find out?" She nodded. Owen rubbed out his cigarette and walked to the bar.

"Check, Andy?" Andy disappeared down the bar. Owen turned.

"Let's go to my place. It's just down the street from here," said Meredith, confidently. Owen paid the tab. They exited the bar and walked up the block. He was ready to dive into carnal oblivion as they hurried to the apartment. A man needed his playtime.

Following the first week of the run, Griff found a one-bedroom furnished flat in the Back Bay on Beacon Street. The sublet was available for two months. They decided to take it.

On Sunday they checked out of the hotel and took a cab to their new home. Griff arranged for their trunks to be delivered.

When they arrived they found the flat spotless. After unpacking, they shopped for groceries at a small grocery around the corner and that evening they cooked their first meal together. Following, they made love, showered, and got into their new bed, lumpy, but cozy. As they spooned each other, a gentle breeze came through the open window ushering a gentle rain.

Pat waited for Owen to call. She thought he would be in touch more often with the show closer to New York.

It was possible that the new show was occupying him totally. Still, Pat felt uneasy. Reassuring herself was useless. Would she always feel this clingy and insecure? From the beginning of their relationship she felt the nagging insecurity of not knowing where she stood. Long silences would bug her. Expressing any insecurity would irritate him. She did her best to keep her fears to herself.

Back in Manhattan, the new show was keeping Owen engaged, as was Meredith. What began as a one-night pick-up quickly became his fixation. The fact that she wasn't a dancer was superfluous. Meredith was consuming him. He never gave Pat a thought.

For Owen sex was like oxygen. He had never fought his rampant sex drive. Meredith was as hot as any woman he had encountered. She got him off with a strange twist. She completely dominated, plying him with kinkier sex. Soon, he preferred it.

When he didn't see her for a day or two he'd call, insisting on seeing her. Sometimes she'd agree, but at other times she'd hold out on him, bending him into total submission. When at last she'd relent he would be so malleable that she could do whatever pleased her. Owen's game had backfired and she was setting the rules.

Meredith was creative. One of her specialties was to tie Owen's hands behind his back and tie his ankles, leaving him unable to move. As she tasted and teased him, it was obvious she preferred fellatio to intercourse. She gloated over his arousal as she played, stopped, and played once more, continuing her game as he begged and pleaded to get off. She had no intention of cooperating until she was good and ready. When at last he was allowed to come, he was wild, his body bucking. Meredith appeared to enjoy her handiwork more than the pleasure of sex with him. Owen became obsessed. He wanted, needed, and had to have Meredith beyond all reason. His addiction to her was complete. He could think of nothing else. What started as a casual pick-up had evolved into a necessary fix and as often as possible. There were no consequences with her. He liked that.

Then one day she stopped, refusing to have anything to do with him. He'd call or stop by, but to no avail. She didn't answer his calls or the door. She had disappeared. His lack of her was driving him crazy. She had turned him on and then cut him off.

294   *Gypsy Nights*

Spring had turned to instant summer. It was a sultry, trying day in Manhattan. Owen finished his meetings and needed a drink. The Taft was packed with patrons, all escaping the heat, as they enjoyed air conditioning and an assortment of libations.

Choosing an available stool he caught Andy's attention. Owen ordered a double scotch on the rocks and lit a cigarette. He was tired and unfortunately, horny as hell. He hadn't seen Meredith in over a week. His craving was making him irritable. Andy put the glass down on a napkin. Owen took a generous sip allowing the liquid to relieve his senses.

"How've you been, Owen?"

"Frustrated, and you?"

"The same," agreed Andy, always happy to chat.

"Say do you remember the blonde I met here a couple of weeks ago? It was late and she and I started at the bar and ended up at that table over there?"

"Who could forget? Man, what a piece," ventured Andy, lighting a cigarette and resting his elbows on the bar.

"Ever see her in here again?"

"No man, that was the only time in here. I did see her one other time."

"What do you mean? You saw her before somewhere?"

"Yeah, I would say about three months ago. I went to a party one night up in the west 70's. There was a lot of weed being passed around. I got pretty wasted, but not enough to miss her. Boy, I could have nailed her in a heartbeat. What a hot bitch! She was new in town, apparently staying with her cousin, who was throwing the party. Do you know her? She used to be a gypsy. I think her name is Jackie, yeah Jackie Eldridge."

Owen caught the burn of his scotch as it went down. His cigarette landed on the counter as his jaw slackened. He began to cough uncontrollably as he gulped for air. His mind whirled as he tried to process what he just heard. When he regained control he moved closer to Andy.

"Did you say Jackie Eldridge? Is she about thirty-five, dark curly hair, big tits?"

"That's her. She's a coarse bitch, really outspoken. I found her unappealing as hell."

Owen's mind began to whirl. 'So Meredith was in league with Jackie all along. Got me into bed and played me like a tune.' He'd been set up, fucked, and abandoned by a piece he couldn't do without. By now Owen was swearing as he pulled out his money to pay the tab. He excused himself and left the bar. Thoughts kept colliding as he hailed a cab on Eighth Avenue.

For the first time in Owen's life, the tables were turned. Jackie was determined to get back at him. She had succeeded.

Back in Boston, the show was in its third week. The weather was summer-like. In the evenings following the show, Griff and Mally would walk arm and arm past the Common, into the Back Bay where they would partake of cappuccinos at one of the many sidewalk cafes that stayed open late on weekends. Catering to the after-theatre crowd, the cafes were packed with patrons still high on the production. Mally and Griff enjoyed overhearing comments about the show as they sipped their coffee and talked about the future. The warm evenings brought fragrance from the full-flowering trees. Summer was taking hold in all its glory.

Chapter 75

The Visit

Pat considered calling Owen. He hadn't bothered to contact her so she thought she'd take the initiative. She had enough of the waiting game. Between shows on Wednesday, she made her move.

"Hello?" Owen's voice was distant, tight.

"It's Pat."

"I'll be damned. How did you get my number?"

"What do you mean? You gave it to me in Pittsburgh, remember?"

"I'm just a little distracted. I've got a lot going on."

"I see. Well, I'm taking your suggestion. I want to come to New York this weekend. I miss you!" There was silence.

"Gee, Baby, I don't know. It's been a rough week." Pat's heart sank, but in moments, she regained her grit.

"Owen, do you want to see me or not?" Owen sighed.

"All right, why not? How soon can you get in on Sunday?"

"There's a train at midnight. I can be in the city and at your place about five am.

"OK, Baby, but promise me you'll take cabs. I don't want you wandering around at that hour on your own in Boston or Manhattan." Pat relaxed. He did want to see her after all.

"Pat, please let Griff Edwards know where you'll be. It's OK. He knows we're involved. Legally you should not be leaving the show under any circumstances except for an emergency. Keep our business to yourself. No one else with the show should know your whereabouts."

"I'll be there Sunday. I love you."

"Have a good trip." There was a click.

Saturday's two shows seemed interminable to Pat. She was counting the hours until she was with Owen. She was slightly distracted during the two performances and when the show came down, she hurried to change. While removing make-up and putting on her street clothes, she skipped the pleasantries, focusing only on her trip. At the hotel she grabbed the small bag she had packed, and had the concierge call a cab.

It took only minutes to get to the station. Running to the ticket window, Pat purchased one round-trip ticket and climbed aboard the train bound for New York City. The train pulled out at midnight.

Pat settled back and closed her eyes. The movement of the train was like a sedative and in minutes she was fast asleep. As she fell deeper into a dream-like state she saw Owen and an exquisite blonde, nude, in the throes of heavy sex. A doorbell sounded. Owen walked to the door with the blonde in tow and flung it open, revealing Pat. When Owen saw her he showed no embarrassment. Instead, he and the woman laughed raucously, jeering her. As Pat fled the entire floor shifted and suddenly, she was upright in her seat, covered in sweat. 'It was a dream,' she thought, relieved to have it over. 'How could I dream that?' She shuddered.

At 4:30 am the train pulled into Pennsylvania Station. Pat grabbed her bag from the overhead and hurried from the car, heading up the concourse to the main level. Once on the street she looked for the nearest cab and got in, giving the driver Owen's address. Pat sat back and watched the familiar images of Manhattan pass by as the taxi lurched in and out of moderate traffic. She was tired and anxious.

The cab pulled up in front of 51 West 67th Street and Pat paid the driver. As she got out she took a look at Owen's new home, a modern apartment building with an awning over the front entrance complete with a uniformed doorman.

"I'm looking for Owen Matthew's apartment. I'm Patricia Byrne, his guest."

"Certainly, Miss. Mr. Matthews is in 1210. Shall I ring him?"

"No, that won't be necessary."

"Very good Miss. Goodnight."

Pat found the elevator around the corner of a mirrored lobby. As she rode to Owen's floor she fumbled in her bag for the key, finding it just as she got to his door.

She was suddenly scared. She had never been on Owen's private turf. Up until now they met in hotels. 'This is kind of a debut,' she mused. Without further hesitation, she slipped the key into the lock and turned the handle.

Behind the door was another world. The walls in the front hall were covered with red silk fabric holding a dozen or so theatrical posters, reminders of Owen's many Broadway successes. Rounding a corner she noticed a den with a soft glowing fireplace and books everywhere. She glanced at framed prints on the walls representing abstract expressionists and impressionists, an interesting dichotomy.

At the end of the hall she came to the master bedroom. There, Owen lay asleep in a giant brass bed. The TV was still on, a nebulous pattern of blurred images running across the screen.

Pat found a chair and undressed, placing her clothing over the back. She stepped into the adjoining bathroom and washed her face, brushed her teeth and hair and slipped out of her underwear. Turning out the light, she made her way to bed, reaching for the top sheet, slipping beneath it.

Owen looked like an angel, so peaceful, so still. Gently she reached over and touched his hair. He stirred, but didn't awaken. Then taking a deep breath she slowly relaxed and allowed sleep to come.

In the morning the aroma of fresh coffee brewing greeted her nose. Sunshine filled the room making it hard to stay put. As she stretched out her limbs, the thought of getting up was short-lived.

"Don't move, Baby." Owen was standing in the doorway nude, the ever-present cigarette dangling from his lip. To study Owen was to partake of a feast. He was taut and slim. How she loved his muscular legs, delectable buns and generous cock. Quickly, he squashed out his smoke and climbed into bed. He wasted no time.

Covering her mouth with his, he fervently caressed her breasts. Pat was her usual putty cooperating fully, letting Owen touch and taste whatever he wanted. With each movement she became more aroused.

Owen's hot breath came to rest between her legs. As he licked and teased she grew more sensitized and ready. Switching places Pat wasted no time in bringing him pleasure. Her mouth found his shaft. Owen moaned his satisfaction and grabbed her hair guiding her head, forcing her to accelerate her action.

"Harder baby, give it to me as hard as you got," he pleaded. He writhed as though he couldn't get enough. Owen was always the aggressor, calling the shots. It was surprising how he now insisted she take the lead.

When at last he was ready he pulled her on his belly and slipped inside her. Grabbing her hands, he forced her to hold him down. As Pat moved up and down on him her own pleasure was reaching new heights. Then Owen stopped.

"Baby, see that bathrobe over there? Take the belt off and tie me up." He was covered with sweat, breathing heavily.

"Why Owen?"

"Just do it," he demanded. Pat lifted off of him. Her legs were weak with longing as she tried to walk. Gingerly she pulled the belt tie through the loops and returned to him.

"Now tie my hands behind me. Make it tight so I can't get loose." He was panting as he instructed her. Pat complied. As she tied his hands she felt an odd sensation between her legs. She liked what she was doing. Turned on and aching with excitement, she pushed Owen down on his back.

"Good girl. Now get to work!" Pat cooperated fully, applying her mouth once more. The more Owen vocalized, the more determined she was to please him, applying everything she had. The result was delicious to watch. Owen lost control.

When he came he moved in waves, as he lay tied. Pat enjoyed watching Owen writhe with the pleasure she had brought him. She felt dizzy with power.

"Good girl, man you're the best. Ok, untie me." Pat quickly freed his hands. In seconds Owen turned the tables, tying Pat's hands in the same way, before he began his handiwork. Pat was cooperative. She wanted her orgasm. His play became ferocious, insatiable. At the height his action, he bent close to her ear.

"You like this, Baby?"

"Oh yes! Oh, please don't stop," she pleaded.

"Oh, I think I will," he said, mocking her as he sat upright. Pat lay on the bed puzzled, wet with anticipation. Owen walked to the bureau, shook out a cigarette, lighted it, and returned to sit on the edge of the bed. He took his time enjoying his smoke, gloating as he watched Pat intently. Taking another drag, he crushed the cigarette, and returned to action. She was completely his now. Soon he was pumping every nuance of his lust into her. When she was ready she let go, screaming. Owen fell forward on top of her. The only sound was their combined heavy breath. After a few minutes, he lifted off of her. Pat smiled weakly as Owen slowly untied her wrists. He was spent and happy, as she was dazed.

"Did you like that, Baby?"

"Oh yes. You never tied me before."

"I've been saving this for a special occasion. This seemed as good a time as any. Would you like some champagne? I think we should toast, don't you?" Pat nodded and rolled over. Reaching for one of Owen's cigarettes she lighted it and then plumped up two pillows on the bed. Owen excused himself and went out to the kitchen.

Pat took a drag, letting the smoke curl around her face as she pondered this newest turn on. Owen returned with two glasses and a large bottle of champagne in a silver bucket, nicely chilled. Letting the cork pop he immediately filled their glasses and handed Pat one.

"Welcome to my new home." They took a sip and then Pat curled up with Owen.

"Do you like the place?"

"Yes. It's beautiful."

"It's got a great view. I'll show you later, OK?"

"OK," she murmured. They sipped quietly.

"Do you want something to eat? I have bagels, cream cheese and some fruit. I started the coffee not knowing when you'd wake up."

"I'd love a bite. I haven't eaten since between shows last night."

"OK. You stay comfortable, relax," he offered. Pat agreed and Owen left the room. Sliding down on the bed Pat felt fabulous. Stretching she reached over her head to get the kinks out. As her hands touched the area between the mattress and the headboard, she felt something soft, stuffed next to the wall. Twisting, she reached further down and brought it up for closer inspection.

She held a pair of black see-through bikinis. Startled, she sat up, making a closer inspection. So whose panties were they? She felt her stomach tighten and tears spring to her eyes. Owen returned with a tray and set it down on the nightstand. Coming closer he noticed her distraught change of face, and an object in her hand.

"What's that, Baby?" Pat put out her cigarette and threw the panties at him.

"What the hell? Where did these come from?"

"You tell me, Owen."

"I have no idea."

"I found them wedged between the headboard and your mattress. Whose are they?"

"Christ, Baby. I don't know."

"Don't lie to me!"

"Baby, I swear I have no idea where they came from. No, wait a minute! Wait a minute! A friend asked to stay here a couple of weeks ago. As a matter of fact, it was while I was in Pittsburgh. He needed a place to crash for a couple of nights. He has a girlfriend. They're probably hers."

"You bastard, do you expect me to buy that?" Pat made a lunge for Owen, attempting to slap him. Owen ducked, catching Pat by the wrists and forcing her down.

"What the fuck's wrong with you?" I told you I don't know anything about them." He was boiling now. "I invite you to come here, I make love to you and you question me? You're the only one! When are you going to get that?"

"All evidence to the contrary."

"Pat, get this. You're going to have to trust me. If not, get the fuck out," he yelled, indicating the door. Without ceremony he released her and stormed out.

For a moment Pat lay in a daze. She didn't know how to feel or react anymore. At her core she was in love with Owen. Maybe he was innocent, maybe not, but she had to trust him. He gave her no choice but to play by his rules or not at all. Slowly she rose from the bed and walked down the hall. Rounding a corner she saw Owen, sitting on the terrace. She knelt before him.

"Oh Owen, I'm so sorry. I had no right to accuse you," she said, fighting back the tears. He was quiet for a moment as he studied her face.

"Please forgive me," she begged. Gently, Owen took Pat in his arms and stroked her face and hair.

"It was a misunderstanding. I forgive you, Baby. Let's forget it and enjoy our visit, OK?"

The rest of Sunday was carefree. Owen and Pat made love, ordered in to fuel their sexual exploits, and relaxed in a hot tub. Toward late afternoon, they ventured out for some fresh air in Central Park, and capped off the remainder of their time consumed in carnal exercise.

Pat left for Boston on Monday morning. She was reluctant to leave Owen, but she had to go back to finish the run. Her deep desire to return to him, and the prospect of the lead in his new show was first and foremost in her mind.

Chapter 76

On Notice

Vinny Lehrman decided to pull the plug. On Monday of the sixth week the cast was given a two-week notice. The sudden news came as a shock to the gypsies, who had set their sights on working through the summer. All the new shows would not be cast until the fall.

Griff called a meeting of the company the next evening. As they gathered in the greenroom, somber faces greeted him. It was clear the group was disappointed.

"Company, it is with deep regret that the Lehrman organization is serving you a two-week notice. The show will close a week from this Saturday night. Arrangements will be made to transport you back to New York at our expense. Unfortunately we can't give you a bonus as much as management would like. You have been an incredible cast and I'm proud to have worked with this company."

"I don't get this. The show has sold out and audiences love it," said Joe Pinto.

"True. The closing has nothing to do with the quality of this production or failure on anyone's part. It's a matter of dollars and cents. There are new projects in the works. The producer is grateful to all of you for making this production one of the most successful national tours of all time. With that in mind let's go out and give these last two weeks all we've got."

There was a rush of mixed feelings as the cast of Bravo Business worked the remaining two weeks of the tour. Having survived the rigors of nine months on the road together, the company had become a unified group. They had worked together, traveled together and had come to know each other, some intimately, some casually, but they had succeeded in making the show successful. Starting with the early rehearsals, the blocking, the music, and the staging had all become second nature to the gypsies.

The repetition, night after night, month after month had forced them to fight to retain the freshness that Owen had worked so diligently for. They hadn't let him down. The show was a dazzling, colorful whirl, a mixture of numbers and scenes that brought the audiences to their feet time and time again. Boston audiences were no exception, and that made it harder for the company to let it go.

Soon they would disperse, to begin a new chapter in their lives again. The task of auditioning among the numbers of out-of-work performers seeking employment was always staggering—a galling necessity.

Working steady for nine months gave the gypsies ample time to stockpile money to live on while they looked for other jobs. A stash had to include enough money to support continual training and maintenance of one's instrument between auditions whether one was a singer, dancer or actor.

The cost of day-to-day living in Manhattan rose higher every year. Often it was weeks before one received unemployment insurance from the state of New York. To qualify, a performer would have to work the required number of weeks in succession. Applicants then waited for an assigned reporting date at the unemployment office. There they had to convince the clerk, often a hostile and humorless individual, that they were actively seeking work. It meant going to every chorus audition that was listed in the trades, *Show Business*, *Backstage* and *Variety*. Principal performers with an agent called every day to remind him or her of their existence.

Auditioning at a cattle call was no guarantee of employment. However, your chances were better the more one showed up and tried. Statistically, the average income in 1963 for a performer in the theatre, spread over the entire membership of Actor's Equity, was $98.00 a year. Being gainfully employed was comforting and essential.

Autumn, the busiest time in the business, would bring many new projects to Broadway. All the shows threw out a large net to fill with hopefuls. Stringent auditioning was required in order to narrow the field to the best and most suitable talent. Producers looked for new faces, while some of the more established director-choreographers would rely on a stable of known performers, ones with whom they had worked before. Occasionally an outstanding individual would turn up at one of the non-union cattle calls.

Those who experienced rejection trying to nail chorus jobs had to look for other means of employment. The work hours had to be flexible in order for the gypsies to attend union and open-call auditions, held during daytime hours.

There was a wide range of jobs sought by the unemployed. Some gypsies waited tables, trained as bartenders, or clerked in retail stores, preferably after six pm. Some provided cleaning services, pet care and house sitting or drove cabs. Serving as nannies was steady and provided housing and food, but involved consistent commitment and less flexibility of time.

Those who had connections with talent agencies could arrange hourly or project-to-project work as an assistant or go-for. Sometimes advertising agencies would hire food tasters to provide feedback for test-marketing new products. Occasionally there were opportunities in sales such as Fuller Brush or Avon.

With the notice in, Pat felt the need to call her family. Old insecurities came swimming up. She was feeling isolated and vulnerable in spite of her recent visit with Owen. Between shows she phoned home.

"Patricia! How are you?"

"The show is on two-week notice here in Boston. I'll be home soon."

"We weren't expecting you until later this summer."

"I know, but the producer decided to close the show. It's about dollars and cents."

"Are you OK with that?"

"Mom, I'm ready for a change. I've missed you, and besides, there's another show starting up in the fall that I have a good chance for."

"Not another long tour, I hope!"

"This one's going to Broadway. I'll be home."

"Well, that's great. Dad and the boys will be happy too."

"Great. I'll see you soon, OK?"

Pat thought about the change coming. She'd be in the city again, but how much would she see Owen? She pushed the thought away as she prepared for the evening show. A rush of anxiety mixed with excitement filled her as she looked ahead to the coming audition.

Mally and Griff decided to hold off on the wedding until after the new show was mounted, tried out and brought back to Broadway. They felt there would be too great a rush between the closing in Boston and Griff's impending new project with Owen.

They would live in Griff's apartment when they returned to New York and slowly develop plans for the wedding. It seemed like the most feasible course of action. There was no need for Griff to feel any additional pressure. They had made a commitment and they were both comfortable with the delay for practicality's sake. Mally was eager to get back to class, start her voice and acting lessons again, and possibly slip in a trip to Minnesota to visit Paula and Frank before auditions began.

Jonas was ready for the closing. He was psyched about Owen's new show and his new position. He was confident that Phillipe would be cast, that he had proven himself a viable performer in management's eyes. Together they planned to set up housekeeping when they returned. They would live in Jonas' rent-controlled apartment, share expenses and continue their relationship. Both men had matured on tour. Falling in love and settling down had proven satisfactory to both. They were ready for a new creative adventure side by side.

Joe Pinto and Jim Sorenson would go their separate ways, but continue to stay in touch. Theirs was a casual relationship, one built on mutual sexual needs and the lure of the chase. Each understood the other, and knew there was no permanence in their way of life, at least not now.

Kathy and Sonja were committed partners. Kathy would continue to find work in the business and Sonja would try to work and go back to college. She wanted to finish her education degree, as it was incomplete when she headed for the lure of New York theatre. They would look for a new apartment and start fresh together. Kathy's brother, wife, and new baby would take over Kathy's old lease.

Dick and Dana continued to make plans for their coming arrival.

Baby Landry would be Dana's main focus, while Dick would wean himself from performing and continue to build his future with stage management his ultimate goal.

Chad was going home to Detroit for a few weeks to try and convince his girl back home to move to New York. He wanted to marry her and continue a career in the musical theatre. He had his sights set on Owen's new show. He knew he stood a better than average chance of acing the audition.

Owen continued developing the new show. He had his backers and budget, a pretty good idea who he would cast from the audition calls, plus a few surprises thrown in to make his project the best yet to come to Broadway. His concept was solid and he looked forward to having Pat back. He would have her at all times, at his beck and call, at his whim. He had to have her. He needed her both in his bed and on stage. He would build the show around her immeasurable talent. How could he lose?

The divorce from Owen Matthews had been devastating to Vera. Financially, it was amicable, each taking half of their joint assets. In addition, she had insisted on the penthouse, furnishings, and their Poodle, Beatrice. Years before, Owen had left with personal items including clothes, books, some art work and his personal awards. He had little use for objects that reminded him of her.

Vera was no longer Owen's estranged wife. She could no longer indulge in the pretense of thinking she owned or controlled him. What once had been the most successful team in Broadway history was now finished. It had been over for years, but Vera had never accepted it. Now the future was unimaginable. The fantasy of Owen's return to her was just that, a fantasy.

Gary Hanson had recovered. The fateful accident ending his dance career forced him to return to New York. Through slow, steady rehabilitation he had time to think about his future. 'What can I do? What would I be good at?' The answer came with a call from a writer pal at *Backstage*, one of the Broadway trade papers. Leonard Maggli, associate of Joseph Kaplan, the producer of the new Owen Matthews show *Centipede*, was seeking a new assistant. Gary interviewed and was hired on the spot. He looked forward to a new direction in a familiar field.

Jackie Eldridge was washed up. Returning to New York, all she could think of was the embarrassment of being fired, yet another injury and humiliation suffered at Owen Matthews' hands. How she hated him! Thoughts kept whirling in her mind. 'I gave myself to him totally and all he cared about was a hit show and a piece of ass!' She continued ruminating. Jackie had orchestrated the set up for Meredith Smith to use Owen, feeding his sexual obsession and then dropping him. 'Oh no, my friend, it's not over yet, not by a long shot,' she mused.

Blaine Courtman was hurt to the core. His plan for Patricia Byrne was not shared. He was insanely in love with her, and would have done anything to have her permanently. Thinking a marriage proposal would hold her, he had failed and now she was gone. How could anyone compare? For him, having money wasn't everything.

Back in Des Moines, Iowa, Jordan Hendrix threw himself deep into his career. He couldn't bear his falsehood toward his wife Diane and children, Andrew and Lily. They meant the world to him and yet, they weren't enough to fill the ache in his soul. 'I'm a fucking gay man, in love with Joe Pinto, and I want to tell the world,' he thought through tears. 'How long can I hold on?' Only time would enable him to break free.

Closing night came soon enough. The air crackled with the tension of the show's fate. The production that took the company through nine-months and the twenty-one stops was about to close.

Up in the dressing rooms of the Colonial Theatre, the ensembles were buzzing with a mixture of pre-show gossip, the usual shoptalk and the exchange of phone numbers. Some sat quietly, doing the make-up that had brightened faces every night, while others stretched silently or vocalized in the restrooms. At the half hour mark, the familiar voice of Griff Edwards came through the intercom once more.

"Ladies and gentleman, please report to the greenroom at five minutes. Thank you!" Through the soft undercurrent of voices, the cast slowly prepared for one last go at the material that had come to fit in their collective bodies, voices and minds.

"Five minutes!" Griff's voice cut through the air once more as last minute actions were taken. Then, as the greenroom filled, it was obvious that the cast shared mixed feelings as the last night ticked away. Griff waited for them to quiet down.

"Company, I just want to say to all of you how very pleased I am with your performances these past nine months. Your consistency, attention to detail and constant effort to keep the show fresh is remarkable. It has been my privilege to work with all of you. I wish you all well. Please turn in all your costumes, shoes and accessories to Dorcas at the end of tonight's show. For those of you with wigs or hairpieces, make sure that Norry gets them. Remember, there will be prop boxes set off stage right and left, so when you are finished with a prop, please deposit in those receptacles. Be sure and check the dressing rooms thoroughly to see that all personal items are removed and taken with you. The call for tomorrow's return and other details are posted on the board outside. Check the time of departure and have your trunks ready and out at 2:00 am, tagged with your New York addresses plainly written on them." The room was silent. Then Jonas spoke up.

"Griff, the company has asked me to speak. We just wanted you to know how much we appreciate working with you. Your professionalism and personal concern for each of us is amazing, and we will always be grateful. We got together and got you both something." He gave Griff an envelope.

"Should I open this now?" A collective yes rose from the group. Carefully opening the envelope, he read the card, saw the gift certificate and beckoned Mally to him. Then he turned to the group, his voice catching.

"I don't know what to say."

"We wanted you and Mal to have a special night at the Waldorf following your wedding, so we all chipped in. We knew that a honeymoon was out of the question time-wise, so it's the next best thing," said Jonas, tears welling up.

"Thank you all. This is so special." A collective cheer went up.

"And now, places, please." The cast filed out while Mally walked Griff to his desk stage right.

"Have a great show, Darling. I love you!"

"I love you too!"

In moments the house lights dimmed, the spot caught Sandy on his way to the podium, and the overture began once more. Bravo Business would soon be a memory, and so, too, all those gypsy nights.

Glossary of
Show Business Terminology

Advance Man—Responsible for scheduling and booking productions in advance of tour at various theatre venues.

AEA —Actor's Equity Association – the union for stage performers.

Ape—To mimic or follow.

Circuit—Collective theatre venues frequented by national companies.

Belt range—A singer's chest register.

'Break a leg!'—A superstitious phrase used instead of 'Good Luck!'

Bus and Truck—Refers to method of transport contingent on routes and costs.

Cattle Call—A mass audition open to all performers who show up.

Company Manager—Oversees the details concerning the company needs.

Cyclorama—Fabric backdrop designed to hold colors of light changes.

Dance Captain—Individual in the ensemble responsible for keeping numbers clean, teaching and rehearsing replacements.

Equity League—Actor's Equity department of pension and welfare benefits.

Green Room —A designated lounge for performers within a theatre.

Gypsy—A performer, who goes from show to show.

Hazard Pay—Additional pay to individual assigned to dangerous feats.

House—Where the audience sits.

House Seats—The best seats are set aside and available upon request for dignitaries.

Load Out—Striking a show and loading it up for transport to next venue.

Marking—Running through choreography with minimal movement.

'Merde!'—Another phrase used on openings instead of 'Good Luck!'

National Company—A remake of an original Broadway show to tour the United States.

Producer—Finances, staffs, initiates and supervises the production.

Proscenium—A stage arch that separates the playing area from the audience.

Pullman—Individual compartments on trains assigned to performers.

Ronde de jambe—Another ballet movement term.

Route Sheet—List of locations, dates and theatres of the touring show.

Scrim—A backdrop, weighted down, to provide passage and masking.

Stage Manager—Responsible for the entire production and running the show.

Strike—Dismantling the production to prepare for the next move.

Swing Dancer—Understudy/stand in/cover for regular assigned dancers in a number who may become ill, injured or on vacation.

Teaser—A vertical hanging piece that is used for masking off stage.

Tour jete'—A ballet movement term.

Trades—Newspapers specifically published for show business.

Coming Soon

Christine Fournier's second novel

GYPSY CITY

The gypsies have just returned from a nine-month, twenty-one city national tour. There was no time to be lax for a new Broadway show was about to hold auditions. There would be scores of dancers looking for work. Those lucky enough to ace the competition were indeed lucky. The bar was raised, the stakes were high, and passing muster was critical for the privilege of being cast in a new show headed for Broadway!

Please turn the page for the first two chapters.

Chapter 1

The Audition

"Hey, watch it, lady!" The yellow cab narrowly missed Mally, as she hurried across the intersection of Broadway and Forty-Sixth Street, the driver giving her the bird as he honked and sulked his way through morning rush hour.

The yellow haze hung over midtown, like a heavy comforter, unwanted at this time of year. What little air there was proved annoying, its consistency, hot and thick.

A line of women moved slowly toward the beckoning stage door on Forty-Sixth Street. It was a relief to step out of the sun and into the shade of the theatre this September morning.

Entering through the stage door, Mally stopped long enough to present her Equity card and was promptly handed an audition form, bearing the number 77. It was standard procedure to fill the card with the usual information, notably, age, height, weight, color of eyes and hair and a spare listing of one's credits. Protocol demanded the impersonal and yet necessary form to be turned into the management holding the audition. Mally smiled, noting that any combination of '7' was lucky for her. 'We will see,' she thought to herself as she headed for the designated changing area in the basement of the theatre.

Passing several women moving toward the stage area, she descended the basement stairs, finding a spot to squeeze into as she worked her way into the clump of animated chorines in the throes of undressing. Tension filled the air and murmurs from the hopeful gypsies punctuated the tight changing space, adding ambience: a mixture of anticipation, dread and necessity.

Auditions were a necessary evil in a craft that demanded every ounce of one's being. There was also the need to feed, clothe and shelter one's self in order to remain in New York to study, work, and grow in the highly competitive world of the New York theatre.

Mally was just one of hundreds of female dancers who would be auditioning for the new Owen Matthews show, *Centipede,* bound for Broadway the first of the year. The production, an all-dance-review would feature cream-of-the-crop dancers, hand-picked for type, ability, and experience. Those emulating Owen's demanding and unique style had the best chance of working in one of his ensembles.

Recently returning from a national tour of *Bravo Business,* one of Owen Matthew's biggest hits, Mally felt confident, fresh and ready for a new challenge and a more substantial credit. One of an original Broadway show. She was excited at the prospect of using her skill and challenged by the fact that there would be others vying for a spot in Owen's universe.

As she removed her street clothes, first kicking off her loafers and sliding out of her jeans, she noted a few pounds missing in recent weeks, as evidenced by the baggy fit of her pants. She took off her jacket and blouse, revealing the lavender blue leotard underneath, chosen that morning, because the color buoyed her confidence. It was by far the most flattering for her. Reaching into her dance bag, she pulled out her jazz shoes and finding a spot to sit, put them on.

"Hey lady, don't I know you?" Mally spotted Patricia Byrne coming toward her. Smiling, she stood and wrapped her arms around Pat. "God, I'm glad you're here."

"You know I wouldn't miss it." Pat and Mally had met at the Equity audition for the national tour of *Bravo Business.* Traveling together and being roommates for nine months had developed a deep friendship.

"How many women do you think are auditioning?"

"My guess is three hundred or so at this call. Another two hundred at the open call," recited Pat, who was no stranger to this nerve-wracking ritual.

"The numbers seemed to have doubled in a year. Oh well. You ready?"

"Ready, kiddo," said Pat, grabbing her dance bag and nodding to

Mally, as more women arrived to take the space they had just occupied. "Come easy, go hard, I always say," muttered Pat with a wry air.

The two hopefuls ascended the staircase, found their way to the wings and waited to the side as the first groups were being taught the steps, some of Owen's most demanding. Looking through the throng, they spotted Jonas Martin, their pal from the tour and Owen's new assistant, demonstrating the combination they would be required to execute in order to pass muster.

As their numbers were called they took their places in a group of eight women, nervously attempting to wait out the lull before Jonas started shouting counts.

"I hate this part," whispered Pat, nervously, stretching in place, her heart thumping wildly in her chest. Mally leaned in. "Relax, you'll be absolutely sensational." From then on, it was a blur.

"Step cross touch front, step cross touch back. Kick ball-change, kick ball-change, step relevé turn and deep plié adding two outside pirouettes, then to the left and another kick ball-change, hold. Repeat to the other side, ladies," Jonas chanted, dancing the steps to perfection. Mally and Pat's group observed and followed, each finding her own niche, through her own body. There were four sets of eight as the combination became more complex, punctuated by an increase in the tempo. Then Jonas stopped the group.

"Pat, Mally, down here, please," shouted Jonas pointing to spots in the front line dividing center. "Other ladies, this is how the combination should look. Again."

The pit pianist banged out the music following Jonas' "5,6,7,8!" Again, shouting out steps, Jonas led Pat and Mally as they ran the combination adding performance to the technical elements. At the conclusion, they moved back to their former positions and waited. Jonas ran the combination twice more and at the conclusion, called a halt. Turning he shouted out to rows of seats, "Anything to add, Owen?"

From the darkened house a commanding voice was heard. "Jonas, I'm coming up." Shifting from foot to foot, the group of women, sweating and panting, watched Owen Matthews, the best director and choreographer in New York, move down the aisle with typical cat-like grace. Taking the stairs two at a time, he crossed along the edge of the orchestra pit and came to center. After consulting with Jonas, he turned to the group.

Slim and fit, in a dark shirt, tight jeans, and desert boots, he was every bit the icon of a young dancer's dream. His short, cropped hair, dimpled cheeks and mustache only accented his sensual allure. As he spoke, a stub of cigarette clung precariously to the corner of his mouth. And around his neck hung a whistle, known to stop his charges on a dime.

"Ladies, Jonas knows my style inside and out. Pay attention and watch. I don't want to see mechanics. I want subtext, performance. Pull out all the emotion and energy you have and dance as though this is the last time you ever will. You are all giving me about 75% and I want to see double that. Watch the style nuances. For instance, on the step cross touch, your shoulders should dip with the movement, your head held high, the feet very staccato, crisp, clean, punctuated. I don't want to see overcooked spaghetti. I want pointed toes. Exaggerate and accent it." He turned to Pat and smiled.

"Miss Byrne, give me more." Then, he winked and walked back to the stairs. "Jonas, run them again and let's keep this going. We have a lot of dancers to see today."

Jonas ran the combination full out again twice and then eliminated everyone in the group except Mally and Pat, who were excused and told to come back the next day at ten am. Another horde of women, waiting anxiously to the side, were next to be put through the grueling pace of Owen's demands and Jonas' instruction.

The audition continued well into the late afternoon. Dancers came and left. Hearts were broken, confidence, too. The elimination process was never easy, and never fair. Who knew what was in the mind of the power folks making decisions that would change one's life drastically, or keep one status quo? Only Owen Matthews knew for sure, and he wasn't telling, at least not now.

Deep sighs, pulled muscles, sweaty tights, and lost smiles punctuated the run off of dancers as more and more were eliminated. Being good enough to dance on Broadway, or being good enough to catch the eye of the director, was a feat not meant for the faint of heart, nor easily attained. Grit was the ingredient needed most, followed by talent, tenacity, and thick skin to even walk into a stage door, onto a stage filled with hundreds of others to begin the ritual of the audition process of gain and loss. Sweat, fear, loathing, and hope were the by-products. In time, some would emerge triumphant, on their way to being part of an integral whole. To dance in a Broadway show! Heaven help them!

Chapter 2

Flashbacks

Mally was primed. She felt rested and ready. The women she would meet today were those narrowed down from a larger field of hopefuls from the previous day's audition. Now, she would be competing with the crème de la crème of New York's dancers. Owen Matthews had an eye for talent and would pick only the best. Undaunted, she arose with the first annoying sound of her alarm.

Hurrying through the ritual of shower and make-up and under dressing dance clothes, she slipped into a favorite royal blue leotard. She added jeans, a short-sleeved top, socks, and tennis shoes, finally adding dance shoes and sheet music to her dance tote.

The weather was muggy and comfort was key on the trip to and from the theatre. Walking to the subway took no time at all. She hurried down the stairs to the token booth below. As she placed a coin in the turnstile she heard the familiar sound of a train closing in on the station from the long, winding tunnel at the far end of the platform. With a screech and a gust of wind, the long, silver snake came to a gradual stop. Doors opened with a suck of air, expelling passengers as new ones entered with perfunctory efficiency.

Mally boarded, and taking a seat, opened a copy of *Backstage*, the trade paper most-read by gypsies. She felt a pull as the train began to move, picking up speed as it entered the black abyss and sped on to the next station stop.

Looking up from a page for a moment, she glanced around the car, spotting Kathy Olson and Marcy White holding on to a pole a short distance down the aisle. The girls, former cast mates from the national tour of *Bravo Business*, caught sight of her and waved enthusiastically as they headed her way.

"Mal," how great to see you," said Kathy, hugging her enthusiastically. She had been Mally's roommate prior to the first tour and was hired as a replacement when the show hit Minneapolis.

"You look terrific! Being in love and engaged certainly agrees with you," added Marcy.

"How is Griff, anyway?"

"Griff is wonderful, couldn't be better. He's running auditions for Owen's new show."

"Well, that's a plus. We're on our way to finals," said Kathy, excitedly.

"You are? That's great! Me, too. Pat Byrne's also called back."

"Now why doesn't that surprise me?" Kathy knew Pat's work from their previous association and knew she would be a shoe-in for the lead, given Owen's fierce regard for her talent and their intense relationship off stage.

"Well, I'm sure she'll be cast," Mally said with assurance. "There isn't a better female dancer in New York."

"Hey, here's our stop," said Marcy, moving toward the door, followed by the others. As the train stopped, the doors opened, and the girls moved quickly across the gap. Their girl's conversation was lively as they walked down Broadway, each bringing the others up to speed as to their activities since the tour's closing.

"How's Sonja?" Kathy and Sonja had found each other on tour. Their budding friendship had turned into a committed relationship and both had blossomed.

"Sonja is great! She's enrolling this fall at NYU. She wants to teach on the college level, preferably after she completes her master's."

"That's wonderful. Good for her! Please send my love," said Mally, spotting a line of women already at the stage door up the street.

"Oh, oh, here we go," said Kathy, feeling the pressure rise.

At the theatre, a smaller crowd from the previous day gathered, the top contenders for a position in *Centipede*. Clumps of attractive and fit women stood waiting to be called forward. Mally spotted Pat amongst the hopefuls and inched her way through the throng.

"Hi, Pat!"

"God, I'm glad you're here, Mal. There sure are a lot of new faces! Oh, I see Kathy Olson and Marcy White. That's a plus," noted Pat, waving to them across the stage.

"Have you talked to Owen?" Mally knew that he was Pat's ticket to her future and she, his muse, on the coming show.

"He said he'd call after auditions. You know Owen. Always elusive until he's ready to move on his time," said Pat. Mally nodded, knowingly.

She had been in on Pat and Owen's affair from the beginning. Owen had made his move opening night in Norfolk, VA, seducing Pat, whom he greatly admired as a dancer, and lusted for off stage. He had won her completely on both counts. He was the flame to her moth. Their affair was intense through the entire tour and beyond.

Pat fell head over heels for her mentor. He, in turn, made it clear that in order to be with him she would have to accept the limits he placed on their relationship. He was based in New York and she was committed to a nine-month tour at the time.

Owen was still legally married, though separated from Vera Daniels, his former wife and muse. Together they had shared many Broadway triumphs. He had made her a mega star and she helped make his reputation as the Great White Way's most acclaimed director and choreographer. His rampant and repeated infidelities and her alcoholism had driven them apart. Vera refused to give Owen a divorce, fiercely hanging on as punishment for his indiscretions. Her anger overrode her reason.

When Owen showed up on the road, it was non-stop love making with Pat until he departed for New York. Pat would fall into a deep funk that only his calls or occasional visits would abate.

Without admitting his need for her, Owen sometimes went for weeks without calling. Then, when he did turn up, the intensity of his unquenchable horniness and her emotional need would fan the flames of their mutual passion. Pat longed for his brief visits. He became her whole world.

Then the unimaginable happened! Owen began to need Pat, falling in love with her. Never had he invested such emotion in one woman. Pat had won him, and now she had a spot in his new show headed to Broadway. The audition was merely a formality. He already knew her abilities beyond the bedroom. He would make her a star.

On stage, Jonas Martin was demonstrating the audition step from the previous day. He had added four more sections of eight counts. His grace and attention to detail was inspiring. He knew Owen's style inside and out, and would place demands on these finalists never experienced before at an audition.

Mally and Pat were called to the first group of four. Running through the steps felt good and eased the tension as they repeated exactly what Jonas asked of them. When they were ready, the accompanist pounded out the introduction mingling with Jonas' "5,6,7,8!"

Pat's dancing was inspired. Her limber body met the demands of the combination with ease as she twirled and leaped, kicked and stomped. She was easily the best in her group. Mally's bright personality showed through her technique, as she danced Jonas' instruction to perfection. When both women had finished, they were asked to wait.

Several more groups of young women repeated Owen's steps. Kathy and Marcy held up well as they out-danced the others in their group. When it was over, they were asked to remain. Then, the inevitable!

Placing those who had auditioned in a line-up, Jonas awaited orders from Owen, who mounted the stairs to the stage with his usual fluidity. He was every bit the legend as he appeared to glide to center stage.

"Ladies, you are all excellent, but I only need eight. When I call your name please stay. The rest, thank you very much." He began going through the dance cards as Jonas stood by his side. As numbers were announced, Mally spotted Griff out of the corner of her eye. He was standing at the orchestra rail holding a clipboard going through papers with marked efficiency. The same efficiency that had attracted her the first time she laid eyes on him.

"Mally Winthrop, Patricia Byrne, Marcy White, Kathy Olson, Cynthia Charles, Fran Fairchild, Liz Gunther, and Nora Blake please stay." There was a shout of jubilation from the chosen few. The other women dejectedly walked away in search of their dance bags and other belongings scattered around the perimeter of the stage.

"Congratulations ladies, and welcome to *Centipede*! As Owen walked the line, he shook hands with each of the glistening winners, noting the attractive ensemble he just put together. "This is Jonas Martin, my assistant. You will be working with him throughout the process and his word is mine."

Jonas smiled at the introduction. He had waited for this day a long time. He was no longer just another gypsy in a mass of contenders. He was an integral part of Owen's creative infrastructure, a position hard earned.

"Griff, please come forward and meet our ladies." Owen waited as Griff ascended the stairs to the stage, coming toward him as he walked the line of smiling young women. "Ladies, Griff Edwards is your production stage manager. There is no finer in the business. I leave you in the best hands." Owen turned and left the stage with Jonas at his heels.

"Ladies, you will be called in the next two weeks to sign your contracts at the offices of Joseph Kaplan and Leonard Maggli. Rehearsals will begin October first. Be prepared to sign a standard chorus contract with possible upgrades. The details will be discussed with you at the time of your signing. Thank you."

Mally watched Griff walk away. Her fiancé delighted her with his professional demeanor and dignity. She could hardly wait to get him alone. They were now sharing an apartment.

"When are the guys auditioning?" Kathy was excited as she hugged Mally, Marcy and Pat.

"I think their call back is this afternoon at two."

"Well, I'm sure glad this torture is over. I hate auditions," said Pat, noticeably relieved.

"Did you ever doubt you'd be cast?" Kathy knew that Pat was chosen months ago.

"What do you mean by that?"

"Well, I think Owen knows your capabilities by now. I'm sure there was no question in his mind. That's all I meant," said Kathy, now carefully steering away from the subject. She knew how touchy Pat could be regarding Owen.

"Hey, we should all celebrate," suggested Marcy, changing the subject. How does lunch sound at Jack Dempsey's?" A group affirmative went up as the girls slipped on their street clothes over their dance wear and headed out. *Centipede* was now a reality, their first Broadway credit. An adventure was just beginning.